# Blood Upon the Sands

A Novel By
Sheldon Charles

This is a work of fiction. Names, characters, businesses, places, and incidents either are products of the author's imagination or are used fictitiously. Any resemblance to actual events or locales or persons, living or dead, is entirely coincidental.

Blood Upon the Sands by Sheldon Charles, Published by Valkyrie Spirit Publishing, PO Box 4357, Battle Creek, MI 49016-4357. http://www.valkyriespirit.com



ISBN 9781733958806 (Paperback)
ISBN 9781733958837 (ePub)


Available in ePub, Paperback & Hardback

Printed in the United States of America

# Dedication

For my father, who taught me everyone has a story worth hearing. Take time to listen.

"To hold a pen is to be at war."
Voltaire

# Table of Contents

# Preface

Having lived in Kuwait, I was able to get to know several Kuwaitis and enjoy their culture. Kuwait is a beautiful country with a rich and vibrant history. The people are friendly and dedicated to their family, faith, and friends. Overall, I consider my time there to have been a very positive experience.

Except for the rare mention in the news, the topic of the *Bedoon* population was largely hidden. It was not until I departed the region, I discovered their situation. Because of that discovery, they became an integral part of this story.

Even though this book speaks about a controversial issue, my admiration and respect for the Kuwaiti people remain, along with the hope they will be able to resolve the citizenship issue fairly for everyone involved.

Michigan, 2019.

# Acknowledgments

With a few exceptions, it is a myth that an author spends 24 hours a day sitting alone in a writer's garret spewing out words waiting for the right ones to come out in the correct order to be worthy of being put on a page and read by others. Yes, a lot of time is spent tucked away like that, but then there are instances when an author needs to reach out for information or opinions from another voice or another human versus the internet or a reference book. There are also so many different elements that go into publishing a book that no single person could possibly have within themselves.

These folks were there when I reached out and made this book better because they took the time to lend a hand when needed. I thank them wholeheartedly, and I am glad I have people like these in my life. *For some, last names omitted to protect their privacy.*

Brandy, Corey, Eden, Harry, Katherine, & Steve

These folks lent their talent in one way, shape, or form to contribute to what you are reading today. I am grateful to them.

Akira007, Dr. Joe, & Fern Cottllesworth

Many thanks to my puppy MacBeth for being there when I needed to find my own *Satori*

Finally, thank you, Constance, for your love, support, words of encouragement, advice, and putting up with me during this journey.

# Chapter 1



The staccato sound of the horse's hooves pounding against the hard sand-filled Hamad's consciousness as he and his stallion *Eadala* headed deep into the desert darkness. Hamad leaned forward; his arms wrapped around the horse's neck until his face was close to the animal's ear. He whispered words of appreciation for the animal's loyalty and speed; Arabic words *Eadala* seemed to understand and appreciate. Showing his gratitude, the horse lengthened his stride and increased his speed as he devoured the terrain in front of them.

The sky above the pair was clear, and the heat of the desert was slowly fading with the sun, helped by cooling breezes off the waters of the Gulf to the west. As he rode deeper into the desert, the man-made lights faded. More twinkling stars appeared in the skies above, turning from hundreds to thousands to millions. He was riding on a centuries-old trade route; the path beneath the horse's hooves was packed tight. The rising moon alone provided light for their way ahead.

Hamad rose upright in the saddle and glanced around at the reflection of the growing moonlight against the sand, as he gently slowed *Eadala's* pace. Even with the breeze, the temperature was extremely warm, and Hamad did not want to exhaust his mount unnecessarily. He looked down at the horn of his saddle, his thumb caressing the star carved into the leather. It was the maker's mark, from the craftsman in Texas who made this saddle. It was created entirely by hand and built expressly for Hamad.

Of all the things from America Hamad owned, this saddle was his favorite. He wanted something more than a saddle created by a local shop and opted to contact a company in the United States to have the saddle designed for him. Texas, by his logic, was the best choice since the state seemed to maintain its Wild West legacy. Several months later the saddle was delivered by Armac Delivery, the modern Pony Express. Ever since, it was the only saddle he used. As the years passed, his body shaped it, as the leather darkened from its constant use.

As *Eadala* crested the top of the ridge, Hamad pulled back on the reins and brought him to a halt. He changed his position in the saddle, looping his leg around the horn and leaning back to look at the stars above him. Reaching into his pocket, he removed his *tasbih*, prayer beads, and began to absentmindedly move each bead between his fingers. Even though this was a ritual, the sight of millions of stars twinkling above the desert never ceased to cause his heart to soar and fee the spirituality of the moment.

"Allah has been most generous." He said aloud, even though the only audience was *Eadala*. He relaxed, closing his eyes for a moment to let a memory of his son Khaled play on his mind.

"But *Baba*, why do I need to learn to ride a horse at all? We have automobiles and roads now," the 10-year-old pleaded, trying to interject his youthful logic into the conversation.

"This is your heritage; our family has been horsemen for centuries. It is your connection to the past, and this is a talent that runs deep within you – it is in your very blood. Someday, you will teach my grandchildren how to ride," Hamad answered with patience, and in a softer tone, reserved only for his son.

"Alright *Baba*, I will do as you say," as he said this, he wondered what grandchildren his father was talking about; when the meaning of the man's words became clear to him years later it caused him to smile.

Khaled mounted the horse, a gelding, which had only a blanket upon its back. His father insisted he learned to ride bareback first, as it would give him a deeper connection to the animal. It also allowed the boy to gain greater control and essential balance skills needed to tame the beast. It was not unlike learning to drive a car with a stick shift first; even when you moved on to a car without one. It was a skill you would never forget and have available should the need for it ever arise. As soon as the boy was securely on the horse, Hamad slapped the rear flank of the animal causing it to take off at high speed.

The boy leaned forward and clutched the horse's mane in one hand and the reins with the other, as he tightened his legs around the horse so he would not fall off. *Instinct*, Hamad thought, *It's always in the blood.*

Hamad prodded his horse and was soon in pursuit of the boy. *He's becoming a horseman, soon he will be ready for a stallion.*

The sound of the phone roused him from his daydream, and Hamad reached into his robes, found the device in a cleverly hidden pocket, took it out, and held it to his ear. He did not speak, but the voice on the other end immediately began talking. The voice was apologetic as it explained he was needed.

Hamad disconnected the call and returned the phone to his pocket without speaking as he reluctantly returned to a sitting position in the saddle. After tucking his *tasbih* into a pocket, he took a deep breath and absorbed the desert vista around him, before turning *Eadala* toward his encampment to the east. The horse took off at top speed, sensing his master's desire. Within moments Hamad was riding across the desert night with the memory and spirit of his son riding beside him.

Maksim Fillyp Bondreovich sat in the fast-food restaurant drinking a cup of coffee, studying his assigned target. He grimaced while slowly stirring the flavorless swill in his cup with a plastic spoon. *Kuwait is a land with excellent Arabian Coffee, how could any establishment be allowed to serve this vile dishwater and call it coffee?*

He observed the population here was so anxious to turn this place into an Arab America, they abandoned their roots in favor of whatever the entertainment establishment from the US was selling. Maksim hated Americans almost as much as he hated Arabs. In fact, he concluded *I hate people; which makes me ideally suited for my profession.*

Maksim developed and honed his unique mix of lethal skills under a program known as Siberian Rime. The Foreign Intelligence Service of the Russian Federation (SVR) managed the program, and it was one of the few that made the transition from the KGB after the Soviet breakup.

Siberian Rime was an experiment to create ultra-effective solo assassins, who were on the razor's edge of being uncontrolled sociopaths. Aside from typical spycraft, they were trained in hundreds of killing methods as well as basic human anatomy and morbidity for times when they needed to be inventive. The participant's existing footprint was entirely obliterated, leaving no traceable history, and all methods of identification other than DNA rendered useless. Candidates with unremarkable features, average size, and build were ideal because they could slip in and out of crowds and situations unnoticed.

The SVR formally abandoned the program in early 1998, only two years after going operational. It was quickly realized it was difficult to control those given individual autonomy coupled with permission to kill. By late 1998 they launched Zaslon, the resurrection of Siberian Rime with some variations. The most significant change was Zaslon agents worked as a team and therefore under the constant watchful eye of someone else in the unit rather than operating independently.

The decision to terminate the program made deactivation of existing assets necessary. Trails of dead bodies were used to find and exterminate most of Siberian Rime's graduates. Maksim was an exception the new government required until an alternative solution was fielded. He enjoyed killing to the point it became intently gratifying, and he took great pride in completing assigned missions cleanly and efficiently. Since Maksim derived extreme sadistic sexual pleasure from his violent actions, he was most anxious to move from one assignment to the next. For the time being, the agency found him useful enough to ignore the occasional collateral damage; the body of an overly curious prostitute whose removal he deemed necessary.

Maksim was intelligent enough to realize that even though he was given free rein in the past; it was coming to an end as the last of the old projects were discovered and terminated. With no desire to become part of a mass unmarked grave, he began to explore possibilities that might exist as a freelance asset. Freelance missions paid better and gave him more control over assignments.

The pursuit of those opportunities led him to a vast underworld of rich people needing services he could provide with no questions asked other than details about payment transfers. He would enjoy this more. No paperwork and no investigations if things happened to get bloodier than intended. Maksim would also be able to work when he felt like it and take only the most exciting jobs.

If this assignment worked out, he could orchestrate his exit from the SVR in such a way to prevent the need to ever bother searching for him. *Those plans are for later. First, let's succeed with this job.*

From behind mirrored sunglasses, Maksim stared out the window at the massive 15-story hotel in the distance, the Hotel Sultana. He was not admiring the architecture of the building but instead of trying to find an opening – a vulnerability he could exploit.

His disguise was perfect, allowing him to blend with the local populace. Maksim was wearing a traditional *dishdasha* and *gutra* headdress; his green eyes were now brown thanks to contact lenses, and his hereditarily darker skin let him blend in with the Kuwaiti population well enough that no one took note of him or his actions. His command of the Arabic language was almost flawless, with only the occasional colloquialism missing from his vocabulary.

The Sultana consisted of a large, flat center structure with the traditional square towers on either end. The towers rose above the rest of the structure and had large openings near the top. Historically, this feature was a functional method of keeping building interiors cool before the advent of air conditioning.

The openings, which existed on all four sides, would allow breezes to be captured regardless of which direction from which they originated then funnel the cooler air into the structure. When there was no breeze, the hot air would naturally rise out of the top openings while cooler air was being sucked in from vents located on the bottom. With air-conditioning now ensconced in Arabian culture, the openings at the bottom of the tower were omitted, but the basic structure of the top remained, as a homage to this older form of architecture.

If the building had not been graced by the blue glass on the front of the building, it might have looked similar to a large marquee, rather than the stylish structure which now existed. One side of the entire center portion of the hotel was covered, from the ground to the 15<sup>th</sup> floor, with what appeared to be a single piece of blue glass. Students of architecture often traveled to Kuwait to see this remarkable feature. The unique outward appearance of the glass' one-piece design was achieved with multiple lines of clear carbon filament which held several hundred large pieces of interlocking glass together. Additionally, the panes were polarized; if you stood in the lobby looking through this wall of glass the effect was almost magical, as the glare of the desert was suppressed, giving the exterior a deeper 3-D feel. Before the hotel opened a contest was held to name the large sheet of glass that defined the appearance of the hotel. The name selected was *Kuat Zurqa'* – the Blue Oculus.

The lower four levels of the hotel were mostly used for public areas. This included the guest reception area, a restaurant, and a jumble of meeting rooms occupying two floors. From the fifth floor up were the guestrooms, which started at opulent and went to palatial as you rose to the top. Western oilmen favored the luxury Hotel Sultana because of its five-star rating and its proximity to both the outer edge of Kuwait City and the national oil refinery. It was the custom of the hotel to put oilmen on the side of the hotel giving them an unobstructed view of the refinery. Most appreciated it and found it welcoming.

The Sultana complex connected to an upscale mall with restaurants and designer stores. All of this sat in an older section of town known as Fahaheel. Just across the street from the hotel was a traditional *souk*, with stalls of independent merchants selling their wares. The surrounding neighborhood featured large apartment buildings where hundreds of Indian expatriates lived, and various grocery stores and eateries. The Hotel Sultana and mall were like an island sitting amongst it all.

When Maksim was initially contacted about this mission, the person paying for his services said she wanted the entire building leveled. But, once he arrived on site and saw the scale of the job and the inside access which would be required to ensure complete destruction, she balked at the cost. However, once he was on site and realized her true ultimate goal was to cause massive chaos rather than destruction, he provided her with an alternative: use explosives to turn the 15 stories of glass into nothing but broken shards.

Those shards would serve as shrapnel on the lower public floors with the razor-sharp glass sailing through those open and public spaces at the speed of sound shredding any and all human flesh in its way. The result would be grisly enough to guarantee that even if the building were left structurally sound, it would probably be voluntarily demolished due to the permanent visual impact of the afterimages of bloodstained broken glass. His new employer quickly agreed to the alternative Maksim had come up with and at a more reasonable price he now a quoted.

Maksim had spent a week in this area watching for the unusual at the hotel. The Sultana's security procedure required inspection of all cars coming close to the building before they were allowed to proceed. The examination included a mirror inspection of the undercarriage and visual check of both the trunk and under the hood.

Sitting at the hotel checkpoint was a silver Nissan sedan and even though the driver released the hood latch the guard doing the inspection was having a hard time getting the hood to unlatch and open. Rather than causing further delay, the security guard pressed the hood down to latch it without examination and waved the car into the driveway ellipse leading to the hotel's main entrance. Maksim felt a rush – he recalled a similar incident that occurred in the preceding days. Something about that model car made the hood challenging to open, and led to the guard allowing it to proceed without being properly cleared.

Maksim found the vulnerability he needed. His discovery was a way to deliver death to the hotel's main entrance. He allowed his vision to adjust taking in all 15 floors of the Sultana as his breath quickened at the thought of how his handiwork would lead to its destruction and the shattering the *Kuat Zurqa'*, the building's trademark blue-tinted plate glass window. Maksim smiled and prepared to leave.

As he stepped through the door, Maksim realized his selection of timing was unfortunate as the call for prayer echoed out of the loudspeakers on the street, and the pedestrians shifted directions to head towards the mosque. To keep his native identity secure, Maksim walked with them to the mosque and upon removing his sandals he entered and took his place among the congregates. As he knelt and began his memorized prayers, his mind was racing ahead to what he would need to do to claim his latest paycheck. Once Maksim's head was down, and as his forehead and nose touched the carpet, he allowed himself a private smile at the number of deaths he would cause this time; in his mind, he could already smell the blood.

*Western Michigan*

Evan stared down at the open suitcase on the bed; *what am I forgetting?* No. A better question: *Why the hell am I doing this at all?* Less than a year after his return from Afghanistan he was preparing to return to the Middle East for a writing assignment not within his usual realm. Again. He picked up his Go-bag from the floor beside the bed as he spun around and sat down with the backpack resting on his knees.

Evan took a moment to examine the black Swiss computer bag, which became a vital part of his life when he was an embed. The contents inside the bag were honed while he was there, and its many zippered pockets filled with useful and comforting items – chargers, aspirin, computer cables, fingernail clippers, wet wipes, a spare toothbrush, and more. The goal was to have a single bag with enough essentials to handle most situations. It now did. He unzipped one of the more extended pockets on the side and withdrew a ten-inch Buck knife. He considered it for a moment before tossing it on the bed – *TSA would never let me get on the plane with it, besides I'm not going to a war zone, just a boring hot, sandy place.*

The bag he held was not the exact bag he carried in Afghanistan; the original was stained with Sergeant First Class Feliciano "Brian" Vazquez's blood during the last field operation while there. Vazquez survived, but the Go-bag was permanently stained and looked a bit too *field* for the World. The bag he held was the same model. Therefore the placement of all items was able to duplicate the original exactly. The Go-bag remained ready at the top of Evan's closet for his next call to duty. All he needed to do was to unzip the back compartment and drop in his laptop.

Holding it now, made his upcoming assignment immediately tangible. The whole thing happened so quickly, just 72 hours ago Arlen called him about the job.

"I don't know why he is doing this, Evan. They told me he wants you to produce an article a week for some local paper about any subject you want to cover, as long as it shows the achievements, compassion and human side of Kuwaiti society," Arlen, his literary agent, was pacing back and forth in his office as he spoke.

"I'm a novelist Arlen; I don't do human interest stories for newspapers."

"Sure, that is what you said before you became a war correspondent," Arlen exhaled and shifted his tone. *Stoke his ego.* "Look, you're a great novelist, Evan. Your last book was eaten up by the critics and the public. What did that one guy say? Oh yeah… 'made the unlikely not only believable but embraceable as the way it should be.'" *Now for the switch to logic,* "but in the end, you are a professional writer – it means you write for money. When you write for money, you write what your employer wants you to write. Look, this guy read all your pieces from your time as an embed, and liked them. He wants you to spend six months there writing about the local people. You can do this easily, and the pay includes housing, meals and a paycheck of 50K - tax-free," Arlen was on a roll, he knew Evan was about to capitulate.

"50K? US dollars or funny money?"

"Actually, the 50K is in Kuwaiti Dinar; hang on a sec," Arlen said as he leaned forward and entered a few keystrokes on his computer, "Damn! It's almost $175K US."

"I'm in," Evan agreed.

"Super, I will send you a bio on your employer. Interesting guy, he's a philanthropist who raises Arabian horses but dabbles in diplomacy on the side – not your average Arab. Get this, the locals have a special nickname for him *Al Hakim*. It means The Wise One; so, he can't be all bad. A bonus? This time you won't be getting shot at or blown up," Arlen said happily before disconnecting the call.

The details were worked, but Evan insisted on being flown over to meet with his employer in person before the contract was signed; he wanted an escape route if this turned out to be too out of line. The day after the call, he received a package from Arlen's secretary with the First-Class ticket from Detroit to Kuwait City, along with the promised biography of Hamad Jaber Al-Bourisli.

The secretary included briefing books and other printouts about the region and its history – *I'll read through it all on the plane.* Evan slid the pages into his backpack. He took a deep breath and exhaled slowly, a technique he used to handle stressful situations allowing him to control his anxiety before it could grow.

Life after his return from Afghanistan was less normal than what he hoped. He and Marci were together for about three months before their similarities started to drive them both nuts. When she came in one day and told him she was leaving, Evan was more relieved than surprised. They both knew it wasn't working; each had built the other into something they were not while they were away from each other. Unfortunately, it was not the person either found in their arms when reality happened. After a month or so of the intense and burning passion for fantasy, things settled into the norm, and both realized their error.

Evan also suffered from minor post-traumatic stress during this period, feeling ill at ease in some situations and having nightmares of the worst parts of his time as an embed. Because he was a civilian journalist, he did not have access to the military's support system for PTSD. Some counseling helped him, but he found a higher level of relief by conversing via the internet with others who were experiencing the same issues.

Thanks to those groups, he learned techniques such as guided imagery, which help him better cope with the stress and make it manageable. When his anxiety began to rise, he would imagine scenes and places which were peaceful, with an emotional connection. Over several weeks he was able to find a dozen visualizations that helped him combat stress-triggered anxiety. Evan could now sleep undisturbed, but in some ways, tense situations could cause an almost unnatural state of awareness within him. At the suggestion of several within the group, he was in the process of acquiring a support animal for further relief.

He took a final look at the contents in the suitcase lying open on the bed in front of them. *If it isn't in there, I don't need it.* He closed the suitcase, then taking it and the Go-bag he walked into the foyer just as the cab driver rang the doorbell.

Handing the suitcase to the driver, he slung the backpack over his shoulder as he turned to take a last look around his house before walking out.

A sense of foreboding always accompanied Evan's departures, even if he was just going away for the weekend. Mentally, he brushed it away - *this was going to be a good thing.*

*Premier Office Tower 2, Kuwait City*

Sheikha Al-Shammari watched the whirlpool form above the drain as she poured the dirty mop water into the service sink. She found it somehow magical such a thing appeared because of nature instead of anything manmade, but she was busy with no time to give it more than a passing dalliance. Sheikha dutifully rinsed the bucket out before sitting it on the floor under the sink. Today's cleaning was done, and it was time to go home

Sheikha hated working nights, but by doing so she was at home to send her son off to school every morning. After sleeping the day away, she would also be there when he came home in the afternoon. She chose not to send him to a *madrasa*, or local state school, but instead sent the boy to one the English schools in Kuwait favored by foreign diplomats for their children. Sheikha was relying on a unique scholarship program a benefactor set up at the school for the *Bedoon* tribes of Kuwait.

The term *Bedoon* means "without," and it was used to describe those people who lived in Kuwait but who did not have citizenship in Kuwait or anywhere else. The creation of this class of person was the fault of Kuwait's 1959 Nationality Law, which defined nationals as persons who settled in Kuwait before 1920 and maintained residence until the date of the law. At the time, about a third of the population was recognized as founding families, the law naturalized another third, and the remainder were classified as *bidun jinsiya*, without nationality.

These people were now inherently stateless and as such prevented from obtaining social services or other benefits for which Kuwaiti citizens were eligible. This designation applied to people like Sheikha, even though her family had been in Kuwait for three generations when she was born. Now her son was the fourth generation of the family to be trapped in this situation.

Being stateless left them with no documentation to leave Kuwait. They were left teetering on the fringe of society and civilization with no power or sway within the politics of Kuwait. They waited for a leader within their ranks to rise up to free them, as Moses freed the Israelites.

Sheikha did not have time for such dreams; her priority was a 12-year-old with interests in science and math. She hoped he would be the first of their family to leave Kuwait to make a prosperous life for himself in the West. Today, however, was his field trip to the Science Center in Kuwait Center, and as she fixed Meteb breakfast, he excitedly told her about it. She nodded and smiled as he described to her about each of the exhibits he was going to see. Sheikha swelled with pride and wondered what the boy's father would have thought of Meteb if he had not left her upon discovering she was pregnant. The last night she ever saw him was still a vivid memory.

"Sheikha, everything will be fine," he insisted, taking her by the shoulders holding her close.

For the first time in her life, Sheikha ignored her faith and family to first secretly meet and later make love to this young man who held her. Now, she was cursed for her arrogance – *How could he claim all would be well?* As he held her, his hand moved her *hajib* to the side and as he gently stroked her hair to comfort her. It was not working.

"After they meet you, they will love you as I do. Then, I can take my father aside and explain what has happened. He is very wise and will know how best to fix this." He said softly.

"No," she said pushing him away and turning from him, "He will tell you I was a foolish woman who did this to trap you or I am somehow unfit to be your wife then forbid us marrying."

As he stepped behind Sheikha, he wrapped his arms around her and whispered into her ear, "I will love you forever. Nothing will ever change that."

But it did change. She had met his mother, and even though it seemed to go well, he had gone strangely silent after their meeting. A few days later, she was handed a letter by a courier. The message said he discovered the child she carried was another man's. Therefore, there was no obligation to her. A further bit of devastation: He was now betrothed to another. She was never to contact him again.

Her heart shattered, she did not allow herself to love any man since. But she saw him in her son's eyes, which looked at her daily – a constant reminder of the only man she ever loved.

"Good-bye Momma," cried out Meteb as he dashed through the door, schoolbag in hand.

*Meeting Tent in Al Jahra*


"We can't continue this way," the young man argued, "the only way we will be victorious is by pushing them by any and all means available." The men around him grumbled, some in agreement, some not. One of the older men at the front of the room slowly rose to his feet and holding out his hands motioned for silence from those gathered.

"My young friend, we are on the cusp of getting both what we need today and desire for our future. The world is watching now, and soon we will be counted as citizens of the State. Not because we pushed them but because they'll realize welcoming us will bring them further acceptance on the world stage and make Kuwait stronger in the end," Talal Al-Enezi spoke in a calm voice but there was extreme emotion under them, and the men in the room seemed to understand this.

"But the Kinship is..." Nassar interrupted

"Not in any way connected to our struggle," Talal said raising his voice and taking control of the conversation, "The Caliph Kinship has different goals and ultimate desired outcomes than we do. Our lot is cast with the Emir and with the State, not with outside agitators."

Nassar rose, shaking his head, then glowered at the old man for a moment before turning and storming out of the tent.

Talal stepped toward him and called his name, but Nassar was gone. *How could I have raised such a disrespectful son?* He then realized each man must ultimately find his way in the world. Sometimes it meant a father and son would come upon a fork in the road. Tonight, his son Nassar took a different path from his father upon reaching the fork. He hoped Allah would keep the young man safe and eventually their roads would again cross and bring them back together.

Talal's cell phone rang; he glanced at its screen before raising his hand causing the room to fall silent quickly in obedience before he answered.

After listening for a moment, he said, "Absolutely, Sir. I will handle it," he ended the connection and turned to face the room of bewildered men.

Making his excuses to the men, Talal quickly left the tent and drove home. Once there, he changed from the casual clothes he was wearing into a tailored suit and silk tie that was more appropriate for his alter ego. With the change of clothes came a change of personality, leaving the *Bedoon* activist Talal Al-Enezi behind and becoming the Indian ex-patriot executive assistant Roshan Patel.

Like many *Bedoon*, Talal served as part of the Kuwaiti resistance during the occupation following the Iraqi invasion. Like many, he saw such service during the Gulf War as a way of proving his loyalty to Kuwait and hoped it would result in citizenship after the war. During that service, Talal found it necessary to assume a new identity that would allow him to move freely in the controlled country. His facial features, unlike some, were not those thought about as being distinctively Arab. In fact, without additional factors like language or his clothes, it was impossible to discern Talal's nationality. That factor, along with his fluency in Hindi, made it easy for him to slide from Talal Al-Enezi, *Bedoon* liberation fighter, to Roshan Patel, a third-country national (TCN).

Within days he was provided with all appropriate documentation required for the identity by the resistance and found himself able to move within the country freely since the Iraqi occupiers felt no threat from TCNs. This level of freedom exceeded anything he knew as a *Bedoon*. He was not seen as an equal, but he was not seen as worthless either. It was a feeling he quickly embraced and appreciated.

During the closing days of the Gulf War, Talal was coordinating resistance actions with the *Al-Meseila* Group against the Republican Guard occupiers. He arrived at *Al-Qurain* to pass on intelligence just as the Group was assaulted by the Iraqis. In the confusion of the *Al-Meseila* Group's last stand and the beginning of the liberation invasion, it was mistakenly reported Talal Al-Enezi perished in the fighting.

In the upheaval after the country's liberation, Talal allowed the report to stand while he patiently waited for a level of normalcy to return. When it became evident the *Bedoon* were further ostracized rather than rewarded, he decided to continue in his identity as Roshan Patel.

It was in that persona he was introduced to Hamad, who initially hired him to work as a translator handling reconstruction contracts. Roshan's role quickly expanded, and within a matter of weeks, he became Hamad's personal assistant. Now, over a decade later, he was

Hamad's most trusted advisor and facilitator, handling details and all manner of confidential matters for his employer. Even though they worked closely for many years, Hamad was still unaware of Roshan's true identity.

Until recently, no one other than his wife was aware of Roshan's true identity. But with the advent of his son's 17th birthday, Roshan felt a sense of responsibility to his fellow *Bedoon* to use his current position to help them achieve full citizenship in Kuwait. The decision led him to be part of a group that was looking for ways of negotiating their way into society through peaceful means. Even though he felt comfortable using his real name within the group, he maintained a low visibility background role so he could continue his employment with Hamad.

From the beginning, Talal admired Hamad, and the man's efforts at creating a just and fair way of settling differences between people. Early on, he even considered revealing his identity to his employer, but the opportunity to do so never seemed quite right, and eventually, he felt it was too late for such a confession to be seen as anything less than betrayal. Talal knew someday the truth was going to come out and it would cost him the trust and friendship of a man he came to love and admire.

Duality became part of his life as he slipped between one name and wardrobe to the other as needed. His unique status allowed him to be in the room when critical political matters were discussed while at the same time developing the strategy which would allow his people to overcome decades of prejudice, based on that knowledge.

# Chapter 2



*Aboard an Etihad Boeing 777*

Evan's journey to Kuwait paused once for an airline change at Washington-Dulles Airport. As he entered the cabin of the Etihad aircraft, he was guided to his seat by a flight attendant. Evan was surprised by the luxury of the space awaiting him. He flew First Class a few times, but never on a transatlantic flight, and never in Etihad's Diamond First Class.

The seats were like personal cocoons with individualized entertainment, and touches which included a fresh rose on the tray table. As the plane took off from Dulles, Evan relaxed into the large recliner style seat and stared out the window as the lights of America's east coast passed by. Soon it was time for a dinner of steak and vegetables before he settled in and opened the package of material Arlen's secretary sent with the tickets.

There were several fact sheets on Kuwait and its history, a paperback entitled *Speaking Kuwaiti,* and a smattering of newspaper and magazine clippings pasted into a binder along with a fact sheet about his prospective employer, Hamad Jaber Al-Bourisli, who was called *Al Hakim* by those who respected him.

Hamad was assumed to be at least a multi-millionaire, assumed because like most men of wealth in the Middle East he kept his wealth both fluid and geographically diversified with holdings in the United States, Switzerland, the Cayman Islands, and banks around the Middle East. He spent a majority of his time and energy in Kuwait breeding and raising world-class, high demand, Arabian horses; rumor was Hamad tested every stallion personally before allowing it to leave his ranch. A fact not widely known was Hamad's generous donations of his family's wealth to charitable causes within Kuwait.

These charities were not the type providing give away assistance, but those investing in the future using the money for scholarships, loans, grants for new businesses, and bringing diversified industries to Kuwait. Hamad was brilliant in his choices of causes to support and was smart enough to keep information about his participation private. *How did Arlen's secretary find this out if it was secret?*

Hamad's father invested early in the fledgling oil industry in Kuwait then moved his capital into other ventures before oil nationalization. *Insider knowledge?* Using the wealth as a starting point, he built the family holdings with transport and logistics companies, as well as investments in the American stock market. Hamad's father also obtained land and returned to the family's historical roots by establishing one of the first formal equine ranches in the country.

Hamad's branch of the Al-Bourisli was *Hathar*, which meant they were Arabs who worked skills and trades that led them to live within the city walls, historically. The family's history in equine husbandry was explained in a well-known bit of family lore.

A long distant male Al-Bourisli relative, due to a bit of peacemaking, was half of an arranged marriage to a bride who was not *Hathar* but *Bedouin* – an Arab who primarily lives in the desert and works as a herder. At the wedding, the couple received a breeding pair of Arabian horses as part of the dowry. Typically, a *Hathar* would have considered them an asset to be bartered away quickly, rather than an asset to be kept. However, the man was cunning in his thinking and realized this breeding pair could produce foals that would bring in more money in the long run than the pair, since this stock was among the most desired in the region.

This decision forevermore changed the family and left them in a profession askew from the norm. However, with their mind for business, this bit of trade was the basis for the family fortune. Over the years the family moved on to other enterprises, but Hamad's father reestablished this piece of family history as a going concern. On Kuwait's eastern coastline, he established *Shamal Mazraea*, a ranch named for a northwesterly wind which blows across the Persian Gulf. The ranch's singular goal was to breed and raise champion Arabian stallions.

Being the oldest son of eight children, Hamad was being groomed from birth to take over the vast family holdings, and so he was sent to the United States to attend college at the University of Maryland. He was doing well in his studies, devouring not only courses in business but also classes in philosophy and rhetoric, even joining the debate team. As he was getting ready to start his third year, he received a telegram announcing the unexpected sudden death of his father. Hamad immediately returned to Kuwait to handle the arrangements. Even though his mother tried to convince him to return to the university, Hamad's fierce sense of responsibility for the family forced him to give up his education to ensure their future.

Evan read on and discovered after Hamad fully assumed control of the family business, his mother arranged for him to meet and court Huda Al-Khaled. Huda was a tall, beautiful young woman from a family who pushed her education rather than marital prospects. This background led her to become a woman who was intelligent and knew of the world beyond the kitchen and bedroom. As a result, she was an ideal match for Hamad, who was accustomed to and appreciative of opinionated, strong women, from his brief time in the US. Hamad had found a partner, and Huda found a man who accepted the woman she was.

Hamad's ability to see multiple sides in an argument, along with his desire for a simple private life, led him to become a favored mediator in disputes and negotiations for the royal family with foreign governments. He worked diligently behind the scenes to settle deeply emotional tribal feuds, and became the uncredited diplomat who among other things negotiated for the West's assistance after the August 1990 invasion by Iraq.

The West was immediately on board, but it was Hamad who worked out many of the details for a status of forces agreement once peace eventually came. He worked with Saudi Arabia as well, and in the end arranged for US bases to have an enduring presence in the region under terms favorable to both. Hamad considered this to be among his most significant achievements, though unknown to most in Kuwait.

At this point Evan found himself thumbing back and forth through the report but saw no information regarding children, grown or otherwise. He guessed Hamad and Huda had a few, but information about them was not in the report.

After the war, Hamad felt a yearning to return to his ancestral desert roots. When approached by the royal family wanting to reward him for his wartime efforts, he asked for a section of the uninhabited desert so he could establish a tent compound. They obliged, and Hamad created a traditional encampment he called *Rihlat Alsahra'*, the Desert Journey. Hamad spent a few weeks of every month there.

Many Kuwaitis performed a desert pilgrimage a few months out of the year, choosing, of course, the cooler months. Over time, creature comforts were added, and tents were outfitted with air conditioning and large screen TVs. Hamad on the other hand, kept his compound traditional and primitive, using oil lamps for light and having all food prepared over open fires. Hamad now divided his time between riding and training championship horses, handling his family's investments, and acting as a shadow diplomat and settler of disagreements.

"Sir, care for another pillow or blanket?" the flight attendant asked.

"Um, no not at the moment, but can I get bourbon and Coke please – and if you have any more of the nuts from earlier that would be great," Evan said as he slipped the papers back into their folder.

"Gentleman Jack or Maker's 46?" she asked.

Evan thought for a moment, then decisively said, "How about one of each, that way I can perform an in-flight taste test," *Better do it now, neither will be available where I'm headed.*

She nodded before she disappeared. Moments later she brought the requested drinks, a small bowl of assorted warm nuts, and an unrequested glass of ice she thought might be needed. Evan reclined his chair and let his attention turn to the flat screen in his compartment. He selected an unfamiliar Bollywood film. Evan decided the movie would not be exciting enough to keep him awake, but light enough to help him relax. He was right, and within 45 minutes the whiskey was gone, and

Evan slept as his plane covered the remaining miles to Kuwait.

Najila wrapped her hands around the coffee mug as she lowered herself into the chair. She looked out across the Persian Gulf, and thought again about why she returned. In the end, the best her jet-lagged mind could come up with was that the strength of family bonds brought her back.

Najila was gone for almost six years and near the point where she could not see herself returning to Kuwait for longer than a week or two; then her Uncle Hamad called and asked her a favor of her. She could not deny him the request, not only was he her favorite uncle but he was such a smooth talker. By the end of the conversation, he almost convinced her that she asked him for the favor. Najila had been here for three days and was starting to feel normal. She closed her eyes and remembered Uncle Hamad's call.

'Najila, you're the only one I trust with this request – not only because you are my niece but because you are ideally suited to it. You were educated in America, but you are and always will be Kuwaiti and Al-Bourisli – you know our people, our country, and our culture. You'll be able to explain things to this American writer, and you will be able to guide him as he discovers the beauty of our land and people," Hamad explained patiently.

"I understand Uncle, but you realize over the past few years, as I have grown and matured, I have made several changes and adopted a more Western-style for myself," Najila explained, preparing to shock him, "Uncle, I no longer wear the hijab."

She paused and listened to the silence on the phone line, waiting for the reaction.

"You're a grown woman, you can make your own choices, and I must be ready to accept even those I disagree with as I must accept you are no longer the little girl who used to ride with me on my horse through the desert pleading 'Faster! Faster!','' Hamad said, in an accepting tone. He needed her, and she was indeed the only one he could think of to trust with this part of his plan.

She could not help herself, she remembered those times fondly, then she said, "Yes dear Uncle, I have grown up, but you will always be my favorite Uncle because you listened, and rode faster."

Najila calmed as her big concern was discussed, and he did not hang up or disown her. Deep down she knew Hamad was a far different man than others in her family, and short of conversion to Christianity he would always accept anything she did.

"How long will I need to be there?" she asked.

"It depends, I will need you here to meet with the writer when he arrives. If he chooses to stay, you'll be here for six months; if he doesn't stay, you can leave on the plane with him. So, you will come to see my grown-up niece?"

"As long as you take me riding when there is a chance, then yes I will do it."

"Fantastic! I will look forward to riding with you again." The joy in his voice was such Najila began looking forward to the trip as soon as they hung up.

Now, not so much. The flight was uneventful, but Najila had forgotten the dust and crowded feel of the city. Since she was not wearing a hijab, she felt more liberated than when last here, but there were times when she felt more stifled than in America. There she felt a certain freedom that came with being far from home and her family's watchful eye and judgment.

Najila's biography to this point was anything but ordinary. When she was nine, she lost both of her parents in the opening salvo of the Iraq invasion of Kuwait. A stray artillery shell hit their home killing them both. Luckily, she was at a friend's house when it happened.

A week later she was told her older brother, who was an Army Reservist, was killed while he was hiding with his unit waiting for resupply and an opportunity to strike back at the invaders. Reports would later tell the tale of the men being shot wholesale by sadistic Iranian Republican Guard who rather than accepting their surrender chose to use them for target practice as the Kuwaiti's tried to flee in fear.

Najila's world changed as she went from an ordinary, happy Kuwaiti girl with a close family, to a homeless war orphan who lost almost everyone she loved. During the occupation, she was passed among family members until she wound up at her Uncle Hamad's compound, where she stayed until Kuwait was liberated by the American-led forces. She remembered the country's joy that day, but hers was a muted by insecurity.

During the occupation, while Hamad was busy negotiating, Najila spent a good deal of time with her Aunt Huda. Huda was friendly enough but was not a good surrogate for the loving and warm home she enjoyed up until now. As a result, when her Uncle was available, Najila would cling tightly to him, and they developed a deep relationship. Her uncle would gladly have allowed her to stay and grow up with him and his wife, but Huda convinced him the girl would be better off with other relatives who had children of her age so Najila would have pseudo-siblings. In the end, Hamad agreed and made arrangements, which included financially contributing to the family to help offset the added expense to the family. So, Najila was to live with Muhammad, Zurafa, and their three daughters.

The next ten years of her life were lonely, and angst-filled. It is hard being a teenager, and it is worse when your world has been destroyed. Najila did well in school but had no social life, preferring the seclusion of books. Zurafa, her foster mother, did little to discourage this since it gave her more time for her natural children and it seemed to make the girl happy.

As Najila came of age, she showed little interest in boys. Zurafa was busy trying to get her natural daughters matched up and did little to showcase Najila for prospective mothers-in-law. Soon, the three sisters were married off, and Najila, a beautiful woman of 19 years, was alone and at a crossroads. Her Uncle would again come to her rescue.

Hamad kept watch over Najila; even though she was not in his home any longer, she had burrowed herself into his heart during her short stay. He would take her riding in the desert with him from time to time and spoke with her on the phone sending her presents on her birthday and other days of importance. Hamad hoped his niece would marry and return to normalcy, but he realized this might take longer than the usual.

He arranged for her to have a position in one of his ventures, so she would not spend her days isolated at home, and might meet a suitable young man. With nothing more than a High School education she became the Office Manager and the youngest employee in the company; since she was the boss' niece, not a word was spoken against her elevation to the position. She also moved into a small two-room villa at *Shamal Mazraea*.

Najila attacked the job with tenacity, not wanting anyone to feel she held the position solely based on her family connections, or *wasta*. She took the time to learn the functions of the office and became a valuable and respected member of the enterprise. During her time there, she occasionally dated, but seldom allowed herself to feel anything more than friendship for the men she went out with; it was just too painful to allow her heart to open to let them in. After seven years, she decided if she was going to have a career instead of raising a family, she needed a proper formal education.

Najila applied to, and received a full scholarship from, the University of Texas, to study international economics. Hamad felt a deep sense of pride in his niece and augmented her scholarship with extra money so her life there would be comfortable. After five years she graduated with dual degrees in International Economics and Business. Then, for the past year, Najila taught at the University while toying with the graduate degree program, without being formally enrolled.

During her years in Texas, Najila changed in many ways. Since she was no longer being guided and monitored by family, she could explore her own thoughts and meanings of faith, life, and morals. She stopped wearing the hijab when she concluded this was cultural versus a religious requirement. Doing this also led to more men being bold about their interest in her since her long thick dark hair accented her pretty dark eyes and smile, and made her seem more open and available.

Najila also started to date men outside of her faith and even dated an atheist for a short time. She found those men to be less concerned with her ability to be a good wife and mother than her ability to be a life partner and have a successful career, which made her happy. Nothing changed in her ability allow these men any closer to her heart, even though she gave freely of her physical affections to keep the men interested. Then came the call from her Uncle.

As she sat looking out at the Gulf and warming her hands on the coffee mug, she wondered what this writer would be like, and how spending six months back in her homeland would affect her. She was happy to see her Uncle Hamad again and even welcomed some time with her Aunt Huda, but being under the microscope of her family, tribe, and society would be difficult.

*Rihlat Alsahra'*

As Hamad came closer to *Rihlat Alsahra'*, he could see the figure of a man smoking a cigarette while pacing in front of the entrance to his *diwaniya*, a reception room where he met guests and discussed business. He realized it was serious when he got close enough to see it was a uniformed police officer.

"*As-salamu alaykum*," the officer, Jefzar, said, as Hamad dismounted his horse and handed the reins to a waiting stableman.

"*Wa `alaykum as-salâm*," Hamad responded as he took his younger sibling by the shoulders and leaned forward to kiss both his cheeks, in a traditional greeting.

"Take his saddle off and feed him, but I'll be out later to brush and groom him myself," Hamad called after the stableman, who turned and bowed acknowledging he understood.

"So, my brother, why are you standing out here rather than

enjoying the hospitality of my tent?" Hamad asked Jefzar as he put his arm around his shoulders and guided him towards the tent's opening.

"Because, *Al Hakim*, if I have to be in the same room with either of these two young men, I fear what I might do. Besides, out here I can smoke a cigarette while I wait. How was your ride?" Jefzar said, stopping their forward advance so they could speak before entering.

Hamad nodded, realizing he was again being called upon to settle a disagreement. It was a role he enjoyed and for which he was uniquely talented. His uncanny ability to look at all sides of a conflict gained him a special place within the legal system. If the people who were disagreeing both agreed to allow him to act as arbitrator, they could forgo the slow court system and get an almost immediate settlement of the matter. Likewise, he was allowed to settle minor crimes by handing out sentences of appropriate community service versus jail time and an arrest record. Sometimes, it was both. Tonight, sounded like it might be one of those instances.

"My ride was relaxing and a reminder of the beauty found in the night desert," Hamad responded, "but, what is the issue troubling you tonight?"

"Young men are such fools. They waste the beauty and strength of youth." Jefzar started "These two say they are friends, but as you'll see they treated each other like the worst of enemies and were picked up on Gulf Road in the midst of a public fistfight."

Hamad nodded taking his *tasbih* out of his pocket and twirling it around his fingers, "I take it none of their associates who witnessed the brawl saw fit to stop it or to remain once the police arrived?"

"True. The two were surprised to find themselves quite alone when my officers broke them apart. Normally, public brawling could have resulted in my putting them in jail, at least overnight. However, one of them is Al-Bourisli and told his friend of your unique *wasta* for issues such as this."

"Silly business this, but I'll settle it. Both young men have the fee?"

As was custom, for his part as an arbitrator, Hamad could collect whatever honorarium he chose to charge for his time. For a civil matter, he would adjust the fees based on the party's ability to pay; this sometimes led to the fees charged being higher than the monetary value of the matter decided. In cases like this one where the activity was illegal, the cost was a flat 100KD. He would work out payment over time for the less fortunate, however. Not needing the money personally, he turned it over to his wife Huda, who had the responsibility for getting it to a rotating list of deserving charities.

Jefzar held out the bills he took from the young men towards Hamad, who placed them in his pocket without counting.

"Let's get on with this. Afterward, you and I can enjoy a *sheesha*, and you can explain to me again how you chose to become a police officer instead of joining me as a horse breeder, my brother," Hamad said this as he opened the flap, and both men ducked down to enter the *diwaniya*.

Hamad's eyes quickly adjusted to the lantern light filling the *diwaniya*. The area was large, and a patchwork of Arabian carpets covered the floor. A diverse landscape of pillows formed a circular meeting area in the middle of the room. Tables off to one side held a teapot and other refreshments Hamad directed be available when he was conducting business.

The two young men were on their knees in the center of the tent; each with a muscular police officer standing behind them, so neither Ibrahim or Amr said a word or moved. Hamad could see the effects of the fight by the darkening facial bruises on one and the swollen lips of the other. Neither walked away unscathed.

Hamad sat down on a large pillow, folding his left leg under him and raising his right knee as a resting place for his arm. He looked at both young men briefly, before gesturing to Amr as a signal for him to speak.

The young man launched into a lengthy description of the evening's events included dinner with several friends.

"So, because you ate dinner together, your friend attacked you?" Hamad finally said interrupting him.

"No, no. It was the dog which caused the fight," Amr said.

"A dog caused two men to engage in fisticuffs? Explain please," as he prepared to listen, he began to slowly count his way through the three sections of eleven beads each that made up his *tasbih*, taking each between his thumb and index finger and rubbing it before proceeding to the next.

"*Al Hakim*, when we were leaving, a stray dog came towards me and attempted to bite me, so I pushed the dog away repeatedly. Then suddenly Ibrahim attacked me for no reason. I think the dog's aggressive spirit may have affected him," Ibrahim said trying to make sense of this to Hamad.

"I see," Hamad said while stroking his beard, "Your side?" he said looking at Ibrahim.

"The evening went just as he said until we got to the parking lot. However, *Al Hakim*, the dog did not approach him, Amr called the dog over whistling and calling to it. When the dog came close, Amr attempted to grab the dog who was not wearing a collar."

"I did not!" Amr insisted, but as he began to rise, he felt the presence of the officer behind him and remained seated.

Hamad looked at the officer for a moment then at Amr, "You've already told your side of this, I want to hear his. Go on."

Ibrahim swallowed hard while looking directly at Hamad, he continued "When at last he captured the dog, Amr looped his arm around the dog's neck while he was digging in his pockets with his free hand. I saw a flash of light reflected on his knife as he withdrew it from his pocket and opened it. When he placed the knife against the base of the dog's ear, I realized he was going to injure the animal, so I pushed him down and hit him to prevent the animal from being maimed."

Hamad heard of such things too often. Youths using the idiotic notion that dogs were evil to justify their cruelty to a helpless animal. Often the poor dog was left without ears or a tail as a result of abiding by its nature and coming over to a man calling it. Ultimately the animal would end up dying in pain unless saved by one of several animal rescue organizations in Kuwait.

Hamad was usually a calm and patient man who reflected in both his behavior and attitude. Because of this, when he was angry the change in his demeanor was so dramatic anyone on the receiving end had no doubt the rational man they had been dealing with was gone, replaced with one of anger and drastic action. So, when Hamad suddenly stopped playing with the beads of his *tasbih*, stood, and stepped toward Amr the assembled group went suddenly quiet.

"Is that true?" As he said, this Hamad pointed an accusing finger directly at Amr who violently shook his head. Hamad then looked toward Jefzar and asked, "Did you find an injured animal?"

"No, *Al Hakim*, we saw no animal – only these two fighting," Jefzar answered.

Looking towards Ibrahim, Hamad took a deep breath to calm himself before he said, "Do you have any proof? Witnesses? Evidence?"

"No," Ibrahim said softly without raising his head.

Jefzar stepped forward and handed Hamad a chrome pocket knife, "We took this from Amr when we searched him."

"We know you had a knife, but so do many people," Hamad said calmly.

After thinking a moment, Ibrahim dared to speak saying, "Open it, *Al Hakim*."

Hamad looked at him a moment, then realized what he was saying. Looking down at the knife, he opened it revealing a sharp blade with blood and several strands of course light brown hair on it. Any calm or resilience which remained within Hamad vanished in an instant.

"Amr, one of the rules regarding this process is the parties involved must be truthful. You've not been honest," Hamas said slowly in an angry tone.

"Please do not cast me out!" Amr pleaded, realizing what was about to happen, "I did only as my faith has taught me – I was attacking evil."

"Do not attempt to claim faith as a reason! The *Qur'an* speaks of a man who risked himself by descending into a well and bringing a drink of water to a thirsty dog, using his shoe as a vessel. In the end, Allah blessed the man for his actions. No animal created by Allah could ever be inherently evil. Any man who would be purposely cruel to any animal is the evil one. On that basis, I should cut off your ears and release you to wander the depths of the desert as a deaf man." As he said, this Hamad took a step toward Amr holding the knife in his hand.

The young man's hands shot up and covered his ears "NO!" he screamed.

Hamad looked up to see Jefzar smiling at him from behind the two. Jefzar knew it was not in his brother's nature to act on such threats, but the reaction showed the desired effect on the young man.

"Ibrahim," Hamad said as he motioned for him to stand, "I find nothing wrong with your actions. You acted to save one of Allah's creatures from cruelty and only acted against a much lower form of life," as he said this he sneered at Amr while he took the bills from his pocket and returned the fee to Ibrahim.

Placing his hand on Ibrahim's shoulder, Hamad looked him in the eye and said, "I want you to return to where you fought and locate the injured animal. I'll send a few of my men with you to assist. When you find the animal, please take it to K's Path, my people will provide you with the information,"

Ibrahim nodded.

"Kindness is always repaid, if not immediately then within one's life," Hamad said taking the boy by the shoulders and kissing his cheeks.

"*Al Hakim*, please do not be too hard on my friend," Ibrahim said softly, "He is not evil, just misguided at times."

"Each act has its own resolution," Hamad said smiling, then he winked at Ibrahim and guided him to the tent flap.

"Jefzar, your officers can go now – I am sure they are needed elsewhere," Hamad said as he sat back down in his place and once again began fidgeting with his *tasbih*.

The police officers departed, leaving only Hamad, Jefzar and Amr in the *diwaniya*. Jefzar sat down behind Amr, in a position allowing him to see around the young man and watch his brother. Hamad took his prayer beads from his pocket and twirled them between his fingers as he spoke.

"You cruelly injured a poor defenseless animal, you fought in public with your friend when he came to the animal's defense, then you lied to me about your involvement. Three rather grave offenses," Hamad summarized

"At least three years or so of incarceration for the fight and lie alone," Jefzar said, knowing there were no Kuwaiti laws regarding animal cruelty.

"True. True," said Hamad nodding, "Alas, I cannot give jail sentences. I believe we'll settle your transgressions this way. I have arranged for the dog to be turned over to K's Path for treatment and handling; you will pay for three years boarding there to allow the animal time to be adopted. I believe the cost is 4KD a day-- this will amount to 4300KD or so. We'll round this to 4500KD to make it easy. Agreed?"

"Yes, *Al Hakim*," Amr said, grateful he would keep his own ears.

"As for the fight, you will pay Ibrahim 500KD for his injuries, and apologize to him. Also, you will donate a like amount to the Grand Mosque's fund for the poor as an *inaba* – an act of penitence. Agreed?"

"Yes, *Al Hakim*," Amr agreed. *Why shouldn't I – it's only money.*

"Finally, the lie was an offense against me and my authority; it will cost you 500 hours of your time to be used as I see fit – all within the next six months. This means you will report here on Friday after services and all day on Saturday as well as evenings during the week to perform duties I deem appropriate. Agreed?" Hamad said.

"Uh—" Amr stalled trying to think, but realized there was no choice "Agreed, *Al Hakim*," he finally said.

"Fine. I will have my scribe draw this up for your signature; you can make arrangements for immediate payment. Once done, you will find the head stableman and tell him you are there to clean the stables for him."

Jefzar arose and led the young man from the tent, while Hamad called out for tea to be served and a *sheesha* prepared. Shortly, a servant entered and placed a tray with two glasses of tea just as Jefzar walked back in and sat down. The men took their drinks, as a smoking *sheesha* was situated in the center of the room, and they were each handed a mouthpiece.

"So, almost 6000KD and 500 hours of service, all for a dog's ear. Very expensive," said Jefzar placing the end of the mouthpiece into his mouth and drawing in the smoke.

"There is so much more at play here than just an animal," Hamad said taking a sip of his tea, "It is about instilling a level of humanity in our young, before their cruelty extends from animals to other people."

The two men then began to share stories of their youth. Two brothers who grew up together but whose life experiences led them down different paths. As time passed, they found themselves back on a single road serving in diverse ways for the same purpose – a just and civil society.

Several hours later, when Jefzar gathered up a dirty Amr and left, Hamad went to the stables and groomed the mount he rode earlier. As he combed *Eadala*, he thanked the animal for the power of his ride out loud in a low voice. Later, when Hamad walked into the residence tent, he found his wife Huda reading a book by the glow of the lamp. She always waited up for him, interested in the details of negotiations just concluded. Hamad told her all about the two young men and the dog. She listened intently before she took the money from him. She had been helping him with this part for over 20 years and enjoyed being part of his duty to the people.

*Maksim's Apartment in Al Funnayhil*

The KGB perfected the science of fingerprint transference before the start of Siberian Rime. This allowed all of their agents to change fingerprints to match those of dead people on a regular basis. With the advent of widespread DNA testing, hair became an enigma for the program. The hirsute nature of most Russian men led them to experiment with various methods of permanent body hair removal as well as insisting on shaved heads and faces.

As Maksim stood in front of the bathroom mirror naked, he carefully examined his face as he prepared to shave. This assignment led to a departure from his routine of shaving both his face and head. He let his facial hair grow into a neatly trimmed goatee, and the hair on his head become just long enough to show its color, which he dyed black, but not long enough to part.

He stared into the mirror while using the razor on his face and considered his current assignment. He did not know who his employer was; not unusual for contracts such as this one. What was strange, was the amount of freedom he was given in both targets and methodology. His employer was not as much interested in the end result as in the level of disturbance and mayhem each of the incidents would bring to the general public. The contract allowed for him to bring in any additional talent he deemed necessary with his sponsor paying a flat rate for each of these personnel – double payment if they were killed during the operation.

One might expect, this double payment would somehow work its way back to the killed employee's family; but Maksim already decided this fee was his for having to find another employee to take the first one's place. He was also provided with an amply monetized account to be used to purchase supplies and equipment he deemed necessary. Most of this was being done through direct cash transfers to offshore numbered accounts, since the majority of what he required was not within the realm of legally obtained merchandise.

After wiping his face off, Maksim walked back into the bedroom of the apartment where he was staying. Asleep on the bed, face down, was an Asian prostitute he picked up after completing his prayers at the mosque. She was bold enough to walk up to him and hand him a card with her number on it.

"And suppose I want your services now?" Maksim said to her in accented English.

"I go with you," the woman said matter-of-factly.

That decided, she followed behind him as he led her down the sidewalk and through a labyrinth of small alleys and side streets until they reached the building where he was staying.

The sex was routine, nothing unique or unusual about it. When Maksim finished, he instructed the prostitute to wait while he showered, in case the mood struck again afterward. She remained in the bed, naked, and fell asleep while waiting for him to return.

As he observed her lying there, Maksim found himself becoming aroused again when his phone rang. He glanced at the screen and saw the caller blocked their number. He switched the phone on and pressed it to his ear without saying a word.

"Are you ready to move forward?' The voice said in Arabic. The gravelliness of the voice was distinctive.

"Things are going well, I have found the opening I was looking for, but I want to perform a test first, and I will need some time to prepare things to exploit what I have found," Maksim changed to speaking Arabic once he knew his caller's identity.

"Very good. As you prepare, begin the other operations we discussed and keep me apprised. It is vital each incident be clearly signed and attributable," the voice said, still speaking in English.

"But of course," he said hanging up the phone.

Maksim walked over to the bed and looking down at the sleeping woman realizing there was a detail to take care of; it really was of no matter as he truly enjoyed this side of his work. It is possible she was asleep and did not to hear him or that she spoke no Arabic. Either way, he could not take the risk.

He threw the sheet back exposing her naked body, and from the floor, he stretched his leg out over her and took a position straddling her at her waist. Her eyes flickered open because of the bed's jostling and after a puzzled moment smiled at him revealing nicotine-stained teeth. He leaned forward and placed his lips on hers, kissing her gently while he felt her hand slide across his body and finally grip his manhood.

Breaking the kiss, she pointed to her open mouth as she squeezed him in her other hand. Maksim nodded, letting her know he understood this bit of universal body language.

As he repositioned himself, moving up her body, she took the pillow from over her head and moved it to the vacant bed space beside her. She did not notice he grasped the pillow as soon as she released it. When his body was straddling her chest, Maksim raised himself up and allowed his body to drop like dead weight full force onto her chest.

All the air was forced out of her lungs, and when he was sure the wind was knocked out of her entirely, Maksim prevented her from being able to inhale by covering her face with the pillow he was holding. Her body went rigid, she was confused and instantly in pain as her diaphragm was temporarily paralyzed. Her hands were trapped on either side of her, under his legs so she could only suffocate, but Maksim was not contented yet.

As soon as she stopped struggling against him and the will to live was overcome by the lack of air; he slid down her body again and returned to his place straddling her waist. He lifted the pillow from her face and threw it on the floor. He performed a few chest compressions to get the oxygen back into her lungs and waited for her to open her eyes.

When her eyes fluttered trying to focus on him, he placed his hand around her throat and started to squeeze. He watched the confusion in her eyes become alarmed as he tightened his grip on her neck. Through the web of his hand between his thumb and forefinger, he could feel her pulse as he tightened his grasp slowly cutting off blood and oxygen to her brain.

At this point, no fight was left in her. She took in enough air to regain consciousness but not enough to fuel muscle movement or a thought process to realize she needed to mount a resistance. The only thing she was capable of was pure animal fear; the fear was what Maksim wanted to see. Her terror led to deep arousal in him, and his body started to react as he saw the life slowly drain from her eyes, and he felt her pulse gradually weaken, slow, then stop. After several moments, he released his hand from her throat and stared down at her lifeless body.

Maksim allowed his eyes to caress her naked body slowly. He was now aroused mentally and physically. The arousal was not because she was attractive but because taking life fed his sexual compulsions. It was why he brought her back with him from the mosque. The thought of killing all those people in the Hotel Sultana aroused him, and she presented an opportunity to release the arousal.

Now, however, things were a bit lonely because by killing her, he no longer possessed an active participant to help him release the sexual arousal brought on by the act of killing. Maksim reflected on this for a moment before deciding: *If I don't take advantage of her now her body will soon grow cold.* That settled, he shifted his position lying down on top of her using his legs to spread hers to gain entrance. He was in such a state of arousal he quickly found orgasm atop her lifeless body.

As Maksim stepped out of the shower, for the second time in the last hour, he knew he needed to change his residence to avoid any connection between him and the prostitute. Just as he killed her to prevent complications, he would need to relocate to avoid any peering eyes. Maksim quickly packed his things into a medium-size suitcase before he folded the naked prostitute's body at the waist, like so much baggage, and stuffed her body into a duffel bag. Because she was not heavy, he was able to carry both bags down in one trip and put them into the trunk of his rental SUV. Later tonight, he would drive deep into the desert and leave her body for the elements to dissolve. If she were scovered before the body rotted, the police would write her off as a victim of human trafficking with little fanfare or concern.

*The Souk*

"But you don't understand," Sheikha pleaded, "I've had this phone for a year and have always paid the bill on time, why is it no longer functioning?"

The shopkeeper shook his head, "Please Miss, you are not behind on your bill; the SIM card has just expired. Show me your Civil ID, and I will give you a new card for free, and you will even be able to keep your same phone number."

"I forgot to bring it with me," She lied.

As a *Bedoon* she did not have a Civil ID, the shopkeeper knew this before she ever lied to him about forgetting it. He dealt with these types all day long.

"Can nothing be done?" Sheikha said this while sliding a 50KD bill across the glass under her hand and slowly tilted it to reveal the bill to the shopkeeper.

The merchant looked around and slowly placed his hand next to hers and waited for her to slide the bill under his as he withdrew his hand and the bill.

"Ah yes, we should be able to work something out, but you'll have to change your phone number," he said as he turned to a row of drawers

She sighed and said, "I understand."

The shopkeeper took a form from the drawer containing the records of expatriate customers which either left or quit their phone service. A quick phone call and a few keystrokes later and American Melvin Seymore, who left for South Carolina a few months ago, now possessed a brand-new cell phone account in Kuwait. The merchant wrote the phone number down and handed it to Sheikha.

"It will be 75KD for activation and the first month," he said

Sheikha started to object but knew there was no chance of getting a phone without paying this blackmail, so she took the bills out of her purse and handed them and her phone to the shopkeeper. If she possessed a Civil ID, she would have gotten a new SIM card for free, even if she were opening a new account it would have cost her at most the government mandated price of 35KD. Based on the math, she calculated her *Bedoon* surcharge at 90KD – over twice the standard rate for this transaction.

It was outrageous, and one of the ways discrimination against the *Bedoon* was not only constant but at such an economic cost it became a contributing factor to their poverty and limited potential for rising above their circumstances. Sheikha's employer required her to have a phone, in case he needed to call her in early or to tell her not to come in at all. She could only pay what was required, almost a week's salary.

Concluding her business, she headed out of the *souk* and into the crush of pedestrians busily about their own shopping. There were many things she was prevented from doing or participating in because of her status. None of it mattered to Sheikha, all that mattered to her was her son and giving him a future far from here where he would be treated as a person, not a lesser caste.

# Chapter 3



*360 Mall, Zahra*

Maksim dressed as an expatriate in jeans and a golf shirt when he moved on to the next step in the process. To test the Hotel Sultana's vulnerability, he would need to borrow a car for a short period. Maksim could have rented a car more easily but doing so would produce a paper trail. Borrowing a vehicle for a short period might still leave a trail, but one which would lead to some innocent bystander and away from him.

He drove around for an hour or so before locating a large parking lot near a shopping center. Maksim pulled into the lot and parked. He then began the tedious and time-consuming task of waiting for someone to pull in with the correct model of car and the appearance they might be shopping for an hour or so.

Maksim waited almost two hours before he gave up, deciding to look for in another location. As he got back onto the Ring 6 highway, he spotted a family in the model Nissan he needed and followed. Maksim allowed another car to pull between him and the Nissan he was stalking so he would not be noticeable. He was not sure where the journey might end, but he hoped it would lead to a situation he could exploit. After going a bit further down the highway, they took an exit. Their destination was the 360 Mall, a luxury mall with high-end shops, eateries, and a theater.

All three cars entered the underground parking area with his Nissan target pulling into the first available slot. Maksim slowly rolled past them so he could observe. They were apparently out for the day, and he rolled down his window just in time to hear them talk about going to see a movie. *Perfect. That would give me at least two hours to use the car and return.*

He proceeded to the end of the row and turned around coming back a row or so over from the parked Nissan before parking. Maksim gave them enough time after entering for a return trip, in case they forgot something, then he got out of his car and walked over to theirs. With a bit of skill, Maksim quickly entered the car and started it. After backing the car out, he went back to his own car and moved it into the parking spot he just vacated. This way, he could return the Nissan to the correct parking spot. Using his own parking ticket, he paid and exited the mall heading towards the Hotel Sultana.

Maksim found out long ago, when he arrived for any job in the Middle East, it was most efficient for him to hire several young third-country nationals, TCNs, to perform minor tasks as needed. These TCNs were usually reliable, and only interested in the money. Of course, he would apply his skills of influence to enhance their loyalty. Maksim would pay them well and provide them with a cell phone, as he wanted them always available. At the end of the operation, he would take care of them as a minor detail the same way he took care of the prostitute. The transient and undocumented nature of the TCN populace would prevent most curiosity regarding their disappearance.

While en route, he called one of his TCNs and told them to meet him in a parking lot two blocks from the Hotel.

"Rajeesh, drive this car to the Hotel Sultana, enter the traffic ellipse like you're going to pick someone up, wait there for a few minutes before returning here." Maksim was using an American accent and speaking in English even though he was also fluent in the young man's native language, Hindi.

Rajeesh nodded vigorously, eagerly taking the keys from Maksim and getting into the car. *So much money, for such easy tasks.*

Once Rajeesh left, Maksim waited until he was beyond the TCN's line of sight then he ran to get to a vantage point to watch what happened. Maksim stopped near a dumpster which provided him with some cover while he observed the security operation at the hotel. Rajeesh arrived a few moments later and pulled in to the security checkpoint.

He stopped, and the security guard walked to the rear of the car, knocking on the trunk as a signal for the driver to open it. Once Rajeesh complied, the guard looked inside the trunk, closing it as he proceeded to the front of the Nissan. There the guard signaled for Rajeesh to trip the release for the hood before he attempted to lift it. The guard could not get the hood open. Although Maksim could not see it, he imagined the guard was sliding his fingers into the opening between the hood and the grill of the car looking for the manual release. After several moments, the guard put his hands on the hood and pressed down locking it back into place. The undercarriage of the car was next examined with mirrors, completing the process.

Maksim watched this with delight. At this point, his man made it through the checkpoint without having the engine compartment examined. He saw the guard inspecting the car's undercarriage when a limousine pulled up behind the Nissan. The guard immediately stood and waved not only the Nissan through but also the limousine. This caused Maksim to smile as he realized the constant traffic at the hotel would play against its own security procedures. *Perhaps, I should consider getting a limousine instead?* He then shook his head realizing even though the limousine could carry more explosives, it was also much riskier.

Maksim walked back to his starting point and waited for Rajeesh to return.

"Anything more?" Rajeesh said upon exiting the car, anxious to keep his wealthy American boss happy.

"Not today – No. But keep the phone on for the next time I need you, Rajeesh" Maksim said climbing into the vehicle and handing his minion a 5KD note. He could've afforded to tip the young man much more, but it would arouse attention and perhaps suspicion.

After Maksim returned the car to its place in the mall, he pulled out onto the highway in his own vehicle and headed out of the city to dispose of the detail in his trunk. He smiled to himself, his test was successful, and things were now ready for the next step. This not only meant money in his pocket but it also meant soon there would be blood upon the sand.

"Mr. Davis, I am Roshan," the thin man in front of him said as extended his hand outward. Standing next to Roshan was a man in uniform with a clipboard who remained motionless.

Evan walked off the plane after fourteen hours and was slightly unsteady as he took Roshan's hand and shook it while continuing to look around at the strange new world in which he landed, "Please, call me Evan."

"Absolutely" Roshan replied.

Evan had never seen so much marble and glass used in an airport. He would find out later most Kuwaitis considered the airport to be somewhat a disgrace compared to others in the region. *Apparently, they never passed through the airport in Newark.*

"Sir, Mr. Al-Bourisli has taken care of everything for you, if I may have your passport please," Roshan said again with a slight smile and extending his hand, this time waiting for Evan's passport to be placed in it.

Evan took his passport from one of the pockets in his Go-bag and handed it to Roshan, who in turn gave it to the Immigration Officer standing next to him. The Officer opened the passport and without looking inside of it, placed it on the clipboard and stamped it. The Officer closed the passport handing it back to Evan without saying a word. The man gave a slight bow, then turned and left.

"Welcome to Kuwait, Mr. Davis," Roshan said motioning in the direction in which he wanted Evan to walk, "This way, please."

Evan corrected Roshan again, telling him to use his first name. Which prompted another "Absolutely" from Roshan. They walked through an unmarked door, and Evan was guided through several non-descript hallways to another unmarked door Roshan opened. When he walked through the door, Evan realized he was now in the Arrivals Area having skipped the lines for both Immigration and Customs.

"My bags?" Evan asked.

"Already in the car, Mr. Davis. I am here to make sure such details are handled," Roshan said, smiling again and adding a small bow.

Evan was about to correct Roshan again but thought better of it. *Absolutely*

The two walked through the Arrivals Area then out of the terminal and on to a wide covered sidewalk outside the building. A blast of hot, dry air hit Evan immediately as they walked through the door, it reminded him of what it felt like when he opened the pizza oven at the place he worked when he was a teen. The air was so dry it made his skin sting as his pores closed up immediately trying to prevent the loss of moisture.

Roshan raised his hand to signal a limousine, which pulled up immediately. As soon as it stopped, Roshan opened the back door and motioned for Evan to get in; upon closing the door, Roshan walked to the other side of the car to get in. Inside the limo, Evan found himself in the rearmost seat, facing forward, with Roshan sitting in the seat opposite him but on the other side of the car. As soon as Roshan was in and closed the door, the vehicle took off. Roshan looked over his shoulder and said something in Arabic, and the driver immediately raised the privacy divider.

Evan observed that Roshan was a very exact individual. Dressed in a grey suit, he possessed a well-trimmed mustache, dark hair parted on the side and a non-committal but pleasant expression on his face, except when he smiled. Roshan was one of those men who did not reveal what he was thinking. *Poker face.* Roshan's suit was neatly pressed, and he wore a silk tie, *how could he wear a suit and tie in this heat?* Evan also noticed he a recent manicure; *not one who does a lot of manual labor.*

"Forgive me for asking, but are you Kuwaiti? Your accent is like none I've heard, but your appearance would seem to indicate you are from here," said Evan.

"No offense taken. My grandparents were originally from the

Punjab province in India," Roshan paused for a moment before continuing. Evan had no way of knowing the rest of what the man said was a lie, carefully crafted and orchestrated over the years. "I came to Kuwait as a child when my father migrated for employment." The truth was Roshan was born in Kuwait almost a decade before it existed as a country. His son was also born here.

"Ah, that explains the accent - so you are Kuwaiti now?" Evan asked.

Roshan was surprised at Evan's interest in such things. In his position as manservant to Hamad, he was used to be being ignored.

"Well, no, there is no naturalization process in Kuwait. Being born in Kuwait, even as a second or third generation, does not make you Kuwaiti. That is a different matter entirely. I am still considered an expatriate," Roshan explained. *Which is a better story and life than my true lineage would have allowed.*

"Really? How does that work?" said Evan, genuinely wanting to know more.

Roshan then started to explain the convoluted history of how the rules of citizenship were first established in Kuwait. "Some who have been here, working here for generations, are not considered Kuwaiti, and therefore not eligible for the benefits of citizenship." Roshan wondered *How much should I tell this American and will this come back to harm me later? Although, he does seem different – this American writer.* As he watched Evan's reaction to his words and attentiveness, he felt more comfortable with the man and the kind of person he was. *Perhaps the man could become an ally – a useful one. Would he be empathetic to the stateless Bedoon?*

As Evan listened to Roshan's fascinating tale of how Kuwaiti citizenship worked, he was surprised the man seemed at once proud of this country and yet Evan could sense an underlying suppressed anger about the way things like citizenship worked. Evan knew the various paths of citizenship in the United States; the most effortless was just being born there, regardless of the parent's nationality. *Here it worked in such an abzocky way.*

As he talked, Roshan would pause from time to time to point out landmarks as they drove past them. Evan was surprised by the look of the modern skyscrapers, which were scattered among the older boxish buildings. There was not as much green as he expected, having read about the extensive planting and gardening projects on his flight over.

As Evan took in his new surroundings, the thought remained ever-present in the back of his mind - *Can I spend six months here and not feel threatened or imprisoned?* He had not even heard what was going to be expected of him, but it did not trouble him as much as that question.

"We will be going to the Hotel Sultana first, so you can get a shower and relax for a bit. Later, we will go out to meet Al-Bourisli at his desert compound, *Rihlat Alsahra'*," Roshan explained, "The Sultana is only a five-star hotel, but I hope you will find it acceptable."

"I'm sure I will," wondering where on the star scale his normal road residence the Hilton or Marriott would have landed. "Should I dress formally for this meeting with Mr. Al-Bourisli? Will he expect me in a suit?"

"Not at all. Mr. Al-Bourisli expects you to be comfortable and relaxed, so you can discuss your business without pretexts or barriers." Roshan was repeating word for word what *Al-Hakim* told him as they were preparing for today's meeting, "He is a very unusual man for someone of his position. I think you will be both surprised and delighted."

Evan nodded and looked out the window as the streets of Kuwait rolled past.

As they pulled off the road and into the driveway for the Sultana, the driver lowered the privacy divider and spoke in Arabic to Roshan.

"A security checkpoint, this will take but a moment," Roshan translated.

Evan looked through the windshield of the car and could see a silver Nissan sedan in front of them being inspected with undercarriage mirrors by a security guard. Having gone through many checkpoints in Afghanistan, this did not strike him as unusual. The guard then waved the sedan through and allowed the limo to follow the car with no inspections at all.

The sedan stopped directly in front of the main entrance to the hotel, and the limousine pulled up just behind it. When it appeared, the Nissan was not going to proceed, the limo driver honked the horn for it to move forward, which it did. This allowed the limo to pull ahead far enough so when Roshan opened Evan's door, he stepped out directly on to a red carpet, which led into the hotel.

*Kuat Zurqa',* the wall of blue-tinted glass that made up the front of the hotel, was so overwhelming Evan took a minute to look up at it. As Roshan and Evan entered the Sultana, Evan looked up and was surprised to find the lobby of the building was open all the way to the roof. Its UV blocking properties made it possible to view the surrounding area without the direct glare from the sun. Because the glass went from the ground to the top of the building, the view was totally uninterrupted.

The two men were immediately greeted by the hotel's General Manager, who spent several minutes welcoming Evan to Kuwait and the hotel, before guiding him to a bank of elevators. Evan would be staying in the penthouse, and it possessed a private elevator, which took a special key to access. "Your key," the manager explained. Once inside the elevator, it immediately took off without the need to press any buttons; when it stopped the doors opened to a large sitting room with a couch and several large chairs arranged around a huge flat-screen TV. There was a long conference table off to one side, and a pair of overstuffed chairs facing a large wall of windows overlooking the national oil refinery. Even though Evan had no idea what all of the machinery in front of him was, the view was still impressive.

The manager provided a quick tour of the room. Evan was surprised to see his suitcases already in the larger of the suite's two bedrooms. He showed Evan the mini bar, and the location of the refrigerator hidden inside a cabinet. It was the first mini-bar Evan ever saw which contained nothing bar-like - no booze at all - he read Kuwait was a dry country. The General Manager then presented Evan with his business card, stating his personal cell phone number was on the back before he departed.

"I will be back to pick you up in two hours," Roshan told Evan, then he handed Evan a cell phone, "This phone will allow you to call me if you need anything before then, or if you decide you need more time to relax and freshen up."

"Thank you," Evan said taking the phone.

"Absolutely. Well, I will be off. See you shortly Mr. Davis," Roshan, said turning and heading for the elevator.

"Roshan, please at least when it is just the two of us, call me Evan."

"As you wish, sir, absolutely," as Roshan said this he turned and entered the elevator, its doors closing after him.

Evan went to the mini-bar and selected a chilled bottle of sparkling water. Walking back over to the picture window, he decided upon one of the overstuffed chairs before he plopped down in it with a heavy sigh. As he sipped the water directly from the liter bottle, he let his eyes wander over the refinery with its skeletal structures and tall gas flares which looked like giant candles.

"Why do I do things like this?" he asked out loud. "Oh yeah, to pay the bills!" he smiled at his answer. At least he was truthful to himself.

With that, he got up and headed to the bathroom for a welcome long, hot shower. Then, he lay down on the bed naked and went to sleep.

*Najila's Villa on Shamal Mazraea*

"Uncle Hamad!" Najila shrieked as she turned and saw him standing in the doorway.

"My favorite Niece!" Hamad responded opening his arms wide to take her into them and give her a warm welcome.

"I did not expect to see you today, I thought you wanted me at *Rihlat Alsahra'* later this evening. Have you perhaps come to take me riding with you?" Najila said playfully teasing him.

"Alas, no," he said noting her smile turned to a slight pout, "perhaps this weekend – but first let us catch up on a bit of family news."

"Yes, so how are Huda and my cousins?" Najila asked.

It was Kuwaiti custom to start meetings with discussions of family and news before you ever broached the true subject of your being together. As Hamad spoke to Najila, he also took the time to observe how his niece changed over the past few years.

Of course, as one of the male members of her family, he saw her dressed casually, but now he realized the way she was dressed now was the way she would dress in public. He could accept it, and it made her ideally suited to the job he had for her, which was to act as a cultural liaison to the writer. Even though she looked like many women from the West, her heart and history were Kuwaiti. He was relying on it, and he knew if any member of his family could walk that fine line, it was Najila.

After Hamad spent some time catching her up with news of the family, Najila began telling him tales of what she was doing in the United States. Hamad knew she would do well, and she did not disappoint him. At some point, one of the house caretakers brought some biscuits and tea for them, which they enjoyed together while laughing and getting reacquainted.

Hamad then set about discussing his plan with Najila. Up to this point, he discussed it with no one, preferring to keep his own counsel, but he knew if anyone in the family would understand his goal it might be Najila even though she might not agree with it. His goal was significant, but the way he wanted to go about it was relatively simple. Hamad hoped to raise the world's perception of Kuwait and Kuwaitis, through the use of this American writer.

Too often, Kuwaitis found themselves lumped together with bad actors in the region, and were victims of their own excesses. The press much preferred a story regarding a misbehaving Kuwaiti playboy at Cannes or in London, then discussing the scientific, literary, or artistic triumphs of his countrymen. Hamad wanted to change the perception. He wanted it to be the one gift he could give the Kuwaiti people which would positively affect them for generations.

Hamad spent a great deal of time reading international news. In the previous year, he was introduced to Evan Davis through the stories he wrote while an embedded reporter in Afghanistan. He was so impressed with the few he read that Hamad had one of his assistants dig up all of his prior stories, and ensure he saw all subsequent articles the writer produced. Hamad, being a very open-minded man, allowed Evan's words to influence his feelings towards what was going on in Afghanistan.

Through Evan's words, Hamad got to know each of the soldiers and found himself caring about them even though he knew nothing more than the words on the page. Hamad knew he was not the only one who could be influenced by the way this man wrote. He, therefore, started devising a plan to bring Evan to Kuwait to help improve the world's perception of his homeland.

"Your thoughts?" Hamad asked after he felt he provided Najila with enough information about his plan.

"Uncle, I think you're right about the world needing to know more of the good things that Kuwait contributes. I met many at school who possessed the wrong idea of who and what we are. At the same time, I think your idea of having the story told to the West by an American is ingenious. The words will be written by an American heart and is a voice that cannot be imitated. How do you know what he writes will only be positive?"

"I don't. In fact, I'm sure one of the things I will have to promise is the writer will have full control to write what he sees fit." As he spoke Hamad removed the *tasbih* from his pocket and began to subconsciously count its beads, "His agent hinted he is a very strong-willed individual so I would expect nothing less. However, perhaps it will be a good thing. I think if all the stories were good, they wouldn't be believable. As long as a majority of them are telling the truth of our people and our State, then there will be a benefit. If all else fails, and the stories turn decidedly negative I can always just pay off his contract and send him home," Hamad said, revealing to Najila he thought about that possibility as well.

"Now your role in all of this will be to serve as his guide and de facto cultural liaison. There'll be many things he will not understand, and you're to serve as a bridge to ensure he not only understands the reasons for something but also the significance. Since he is an American, he will accept this guidance more easily from a woman, especially one with a gentle persona and a lovely smile," Hamad silently congratulated himself for choosing her for this function. *She's perfect.*

"I will do my best for you my Uncle, but you should be aware I intend to go back to the United States when I am done with this assignment for you." Najila gave up any pretext of being anything but totally honest with her uncle, even if she was speaking of things he did not want to hear.

"I understand." *I'll work on that one myself.*

Hamad and his niece stood up, and he gave her another hug, kissing her cheeks and saying he loved her.

"I will send a car for you later," Hamad said on his way to the door.

"Good, how is Roshan?" Najila said walking with him.

"Both he and his family are well. Since you left, he has become my right-hand man. Currently, he is busy with Mr. Davis so you'll have to make do with one of my other drivers."

As she closed the door behind her uncle, she turned her back to the door and leaned against it. *So, I'm to be the caretaker of the famous American writer who captured the eye of my uncle due to his unique writing style. I wonder if he's handsome. If nothing else, I hope he'll at least be tolerable.*

*Rihlat Alsahra'*

Huda watched her husband leave that morning to take care of various family businesses, before meeting with their niece Najila in town, before seeing some American in the evening. It was her function to ensure everything was prepared for this evening's meeting, as Hamad wanted it to be both traditional and relaxing. Huda would take the

58

responsibility seriously, even though she disagreed with her husband's methods in this particular instance. She felt it was unnecessary to worry about Kuwait's image on the world stage until specific lingering issues were firmly handled at home.

Huda's staff of both Indian and Filipino domestics were there to assist her in the daily routine and upkeep of the house. Of course, *Rihlat Alsahra'* customarily required significantly less personnel than their formal home at *Shamal Mazraea*, but for a more extensive event like this, she would have staff brought from one place to the other to give her the resources she needed. Even though her position allowed her to sit idly watching the preparation take place, her personality would not let it happen. Therefore, she would select some part of the evening to be prepared personally by herself, so there was a reason for her to stay in the kitchen and observe all of the other preparations. In this way, she allowed herself an acceptable level of involvement and maintained control.

Before she got started, a personal errand required her attention. She sat at the vanity in her bedroom looking down at the piles of Kuwaiti dinar sitting in front of her. The collection represented all of the mediation fees collected by her husband over the last two weeks. He settled several substantial civil arguments and just last night, one situation which could have resulted in criminal charges. She added the 100KD he gave her last night to the pile in front of her and set about counting the bills to prepare them for donation.

Years ago, Hamad left this part of the process entirely to her. He trusted her to select deserving charities in the State, and based on a discussion at the time, knew she would rotate which of the charities received the funds on a weekly basis. Once every few weeks Huda would take all of the cash Hamad gave her and count up the proceeds. Using the list she kept in her vanity drawer, she would decide which charity would be the recipient. This week she received almost 5000KD in fees, which would go to a charity which helped the blind.

With the *who* decided, she placed the money in an envelope then without sealing it she dropped the envelope into her purse. After looking over herself in the mirror and ensuring she was presentable; she grabbed her bag and headed out the door of the tent into a waiting car, which took her directly to the closest branch of the Bank of the Gulf.

Inside the bank, she was greeted by one of the vice presidents, Mohammed, who immediately walked her to the vault with little fanfare. This vault was one of two inside the bank and was used exclusively for safety deposit boxes. The interior of the vault was covered with hundreds of small doors, each with two keyholes. In the center of the vault was a small table with two chairs.

Mohammed first inserted his key into one of the larger doors in the bottom row then after taking the key Huda offered him, inserted it in the second keyhole. After turning both, he opened the door, and with some physical effort, he pulled the box out of its assigned slot and lifted it onto the table. As he did this, a groan escaped his lips owing to the weight of the box. After sitting the long metal box on the table for her; the banker left without saying a word, closing a privacy curtain as he stepped out of the vault.

Once she was sure she was alone, Huda walked over to the table and opened the box, after using the dial to enter the combination only she possessed. Looking into the box, she removed a manila folder that sat on top of stacks of wrapped Kuwaiti dinar and set it aside. Removing the envelope full of Kuwaiti bills from her purse, Huda quickly counted out 4500KD and placed it inside the security box. She then put the manila folder back into the box, closing it once again before spinning the dial of the combination lock. With this bit of business done, she sealed the envelope with the remaining fee money and placed it back in her purse.

Huda looked over at the vacant spot in the vault wall from which this box came and quickly counted the seven rows of doors to the left of the open slot. She knew each of those doors also held a safety deposit box and each belonged to her. Huda did not feel she was disobeying her husband's wishes, to her all of the money in each of those boxes would be used to improve Kuwait. *After all, he left that bit of methodology up to me.*

Huda opened the privacy curtain and waved to Mohammed who

was standing nearby. He immediately reacted by entering the vault, placing the safety deposit box in the open slot, then closing and locking the door. Immediately upon removing her key from the door, Mohammed turned and handed it back to Huda, who he escorted from the vault toward the main entrance to the bank. On her way out, Huda gave the envelope holding the remaining Kuwaiti dinar to Mohammed telling him to ensure it found its way into the account of this week's deserving charity.

After watching her depart the banker returned to his desk and opened the envelope Huda had given him. Mohammed removed two bills before writing some information on the front of the envelope so he could pass the chore of making the deposit on to one of his minions. Placing the two bills in his pocket and straightening his tie, *Lunch today will be on her.*

The sweat slowly rolled from the side of his face and down his nose to the tip before dropping off into the sand. Usually, Maksim would not do something like this during the light of day; but because it was also the heat of the day, he was sure no one would see him and time was of the essence. As he dug the hole, the sand played against him refilling the just cleared space almost more quickly than he could empty his shovel. No matter, he did not need to dig the hole too deep, just deep enough so he could cover the body. He wanted scavenger animals to find this tasty snack quickly. As part of his process, he planned on dumping a liter or so of hungry carnivorous beetles onto the body so they could aid with its decomposition.

He looked down at his work and noticed the hole was now about half a meter deep, *sufficient for my needs.* Maksim went to the trunk of the car and removed the duffel bag, dumping the prostitute's dead body unceremoniously into the hole. He unfolded the body before using his knife to cut long slits into the flesh of her arms, legs, and torso to make the body's decay speedier and therefore more accessible for the insects. He was careful not to cut so deep he left marks on the bones. Finally, he poured the beetles onto her body and watched as they scrambled across it, with many going directly into the slits he cut. Maksim took the shovel and gently scattered a light coating of sand across the body, which served to cover the body and protect the insects from the heat of the day, making them more eager to consume the flesh of their new host.

Maksim looked down at her expressionless face as he poured the sand from the shovel onto it until it vanished. He let his mind go back to the scene in the hotel when he first strangled her before bringing her back to life only to kill her. This, of course, led to him being physically excited again. He smirked at the thought of how he defiled her corpse after killing her, then turned, picked up the empty duffel bag, and walked back to his car.

As he drove across the desert road heading back to the paved highway; Maksim found himself thinking again about the smell of blood which would permeate the air once he destroyed the Hotel Sultana. *Alas, before you have a magnificent conclusion, you must first build step-by-step to the climax.*

Once he started his mission, it would be unnecessary to dispose of the bodies. In fact, their discovery was much more desirable. Of course, those bodies would be of humans which mattered, not some random prostitute. Those bodies were meant to bring about fear and panic.

*It is time for mayhem to be unleashed.*

*Rihlat Alsahra'*

Hamad went from visiting with Najila, directly back to his desert compound to prepare for his meeting with Evan Davis. He was feeling quite pleased with himself and decided he might take a ride before the writer arrived. He parked his older model pickup truck in an open expanse of dirt behind his tent. Hamad was not one to replace something that worked. This truck was an example of his ethos. A dent here and there did not harm its function, and he enjoyed driving it even if the event were far too rare. If it were up to him, he would keep his life simple and perform even the most mundane of chores himself. But due to his success in life, he lost some of the pleasure of manual labor due to the value of his time. *But today, I get to drive myself.*

Hamad walked directly from his truck to the stable tents. Upon entering, he saw motion a distant corner and walked over to investigate. There he found Amr doing a rather poor job of raking up the soiled straw. Hamad tried to keep his movements stealthy so the young man would not notice him. Amr was muttering to himself unintelligibly as he raked the horse manure and straw into a pile. After observing a few moments of this, Hamad spoke,

"*As-salamu alaykum.*"

Amr was startled at first, then quickly brought himself to some semblance of attention before he responded to the older man.

"*Wa `alaykum as-salâm,*" Amr managed to say.

"I see you are hard at work again today. I like seeing that you are anxious to settle this debt as quickly as possible. It is an excellent thing indeed," Hamad said.

The young man was stunned to receive a compliment from Hamad but was grateful the man noticed he was anxious to work off this debt as quickly as possible.

Since the evening he first met Hamad, the young man heard many stories concerning *Al Hakim.* Most were of his benevolence, but there were several rather graphic examples of his sternness in dealing with what he considered to be crimes against helpless victims. Amr's vivid imagination raised his anxiety level since his offense was against a defenseless animal.

"Thank you for your kind words, *Al Hakim.* I hope to settle this quickly and, in a manner which will leave you thinking much better of me than you did on the night we met," Amr said, gaining some confidence in himself.

"Well, we will have to see as time passes and your efforts are evident. However, you are off to an excellent start, and you've pleased me by showing your sense of responsibility," Hamad said to Amr, then patting him on the shoulder and turned to leave.

"Thank you again for this opportunity at redemption," Amr said.

His words were unexpected and caused Hamad to turn and smile again at the youth before he walked to the other end of the stables. As he walked, he realized he missed the cooler part of the day entirely, and now the air was much too hot to take a ride. Still, Hamad could take a bit of time for his noble animals. Entering the stall of a stallion which was almost ready for sale, he picked up a grooming brush and starting at the animal's neck began to brush it as he let his mind wander, as it usually did at times like this, to memories of Khaled.

"*Baba*, we have many workmen here. Why do I have to groom the horse?" Khaled asked as he brushed the animal.

"Life is about the connections you make, not those which are taken care of on your behalf. You took this horse for a ride earlier today, didn't you? As you traveled across the desert, it reacted to your every instruction, even though she might've had other ideas, she was obedient and responsive, yes?" Hamad explained as the boy nodded.

"Now," the father continued, "it was you who received the benefit of the horse's efforts and not some stable hand. Surely you understand she will know the difference between the person to whom she gave his great effort and someone else who is doing the grooming for some obligation other than having received the horse's loyalty? You must connect yourself to those things which serve you in life. You must personally thank and give to those who have given to you. Do you understand?"

"I think so. I was the rider, so I should be the one to groom. She will know I am the one grooming her so next time I ride she'll obey me again because she knows we are connected," even though Khaled was unsure of his explanation he did not falter as he spoke.

Hamad felt a sense of pride in his son grow within him. He

walked towards the boy and took him in his arms and held him close, "Yes my son, you understand."

Hamad possessed many friends and often listened to them speak of their own children and some of the difficulties they were having raising them as children of privilege. Even at a very young age, these children were becoming belligerent and ungrateful of the situation in which they were lucky enough to find themselves. Khaled's understanding showed him how he was raising his son, connecting him not only to the world which surrounded him but also making Khaled work for those things he wanted, rather than just having them given or done for him. Deep in his heart, Hamad wanted his son to be a human being connected directly to the world around him, rather than one who was set apart and above it.

When his son finished grooming the horse, the boy walked towards the animal's head and raising his hands placed them around the horse's neck, which caused the animal to lower his face towards the boy. Khaled put the side of his face directly against the animal's raising himself up on his toes as he spoke softly into the horse's ear. He then released the animal and gathering the grooming tools exited the stall walking past his father.

"So, what secrets did you tell the horse?" his father asked, amused by what he witnessed.

"It was a promise. I told her I would brush her every day because I knew she would be my loyal mount and allow me to ride through the desert on her back. I think she understood."

"Well done my son. I'm sure she did," Hamad said smiling broadly.

"*Al Hakim?*" Amr said.

Hamad turned from the animal towards the stall opening and saw Amr standing there with a pitchfork and shovel in hand ready to clean out the stall. Hamad nodded knowingly and bent to pick up the grooming tools which sat at the animal's feet. Without saying a word, Hamad exited the stall, returned the implements to the tack room, and walked toward his tent from the stable.

# Chapter 4



There was a time in Evan's life when he would wake up in an unfamiliar place and peacefully accept whatever strange environment he found himself in. Waking up and not knowing where he was or who he was with was part of a lifestyle from his past. Now, after his tour in Afghanistan, waking up in a strange place would cause immediate anxiety, until Evan could assemble his thoughts and recollect where he was and how he got there. After getting out of the bed, he noticed this particular awakening was accompanied by an unusual visual as he found his naked form staring back at him from the mirrored closet doors. As he was observing his reflection, he noticed the orange-yellow light he was bathed in was continually wavering and moving.

He walked into the sitting room and glanced out the picture window revealing the source of the flickering light filling the room. Below, the oil refinery stretched out across the desert horizon as the light from a dozen or so oilfield flares illuminated the skeletons of its equipment. This strange and new visual was further accented by strings of individual lights running up and down each of the stairways throughout the refinery. Evan realized as he slept Kuwait experienced its sunset. *Damn, I'm late.*

He ran back to the bedroom looking for his pants so he could retrieve the phone Roshan gave him earlier from its pockets, but in the dark could not find them. After flipping on the light, he discovered the clothing he remembered leaving strewn across the floor were missing. *What the hell?* As he was visually searching the room for his pants, he realized his suitcase was also gone. From where he stood, he could see his Go-bag was still sitting on the floor next to the chair in the main room. An unfamiliar string of musical notes sounded from the bedside table, *the phone.* Upon retrieving it, he glanced at the screen before connecting the call. It was Roshan.

"Hello Mr. Davis, it is Roshan. I hope I didn't disturb you, but when I didn't hear from you, I thought you might have overslept. On Mr. Al-Bourisli's instruction, I allowed for an extra hour before calling. Should I expect you shortly, or did you need more of a rest?"

"Uh, yes you woke me but I need to be up to get used to this time zone. What time is it? And where my bags?"

"It is currently 1900, I mean 7 PM. As for your bags, it is quite possible the staff assigned to your room unpacked for you. Your clothing is probably already hanging in the closet and in the dresser."

As he listened to Roshan speak, he walked over to the closet and opened the door revealing his clothes hanging there.

"Um, okay. Give me about a half-hour to get dressed, and I will be right down. Could you arrange to have some coffee sent up?"

"Absolutely, see you shortly."

Taking a shirt from the closet, he noticed his clothing was freshly pressed as well as being hung up. *How the hell did I sleep through all that? Must be elves*, he thought with a smirk.

After his shower, Evan discovered a fresh pot of coffee sitting on the conference table in the sitting room. He drank a cup quickly as he dressed before he exited the room taking only his Go-bag with him. As soon as he stepped into the elevator, the doors behind them closed and reopened to reveal a smiling Roshan waiting for him in the lobby.

"I trust you were able to get some sleep," Roshan said as he offered his hand to Evan.

"More or less," Evan said as he took Roshan's hand and shook it, "I don't mean to be rude, but I really don't like people coming into my room while I'm sleeping or in the shower. Can you do something about it?"

Roshan didn't say a word but left Evan standing by the elevator as he walked over to the hotel's main desk and spoke briskly to the woman who was standing there.

As Roshan walked back toward him, he said "It's all taken care of. You see when we arranged for the penthouse, the general manager was made aware you were a guest of Mr. Al-Bourisli. As such, the hotel wanted to provide you with superior service and a private staff was assigned to handle you. You see, it is not unusual for the oil company executives who usually occupy the floor to expect what might be called attentive valet level service."

"Understood. Well, I really would prefer the staff not do it if possible. I don't want to seem rude I'm just not used to people roaming around in the room while I'm asleep or in the shower."

As Roshan listened to Evan speak, he glanced to the side and noticed the black SUV which would take them to *Rihlat Alsahra'* had arrived. He motioned for Evan to walk toward the car, then followed him through the doors of the hotel and into the backseat of the waiting vehicle.

This time the two men were sitting side-by-side, but it did not stop Roshan from pointing out various sites as they traveled out of the city and past the oil refinery.

"*Rihlat Alsahra'* means Desert Journey?" Evan asked. Since taking on the role of a journalist, his methodology now included the technique of asking a question with a known answer. It often revealed the truthfulness of the person being questioned and sometimes allowed for an answer more expansive than the information already possessed.

"Absolutely; the land was originally given to Mr. Al- Bourisli by the Amir as a reward for his negotiation and mediation efforts after the Gulf War. Mr. Al-Bourisli established a desert compound on the land to maintain his connection to the desert and his family's history as part of it. Consequent to the establishment of the compound, he found himself being called upon to mediate disagreements between *Bedouins*."

"Wait, it was my understanding the *Bedouins* were somewhat isolated from the rest of Kuwaiti society. How did they find out what he did during the Gulf War?"

The question caused Roshan to smile, *Americans never seemed to fully grasp how a grapevine could exist across the sand the same way it thrived in their office buildings at home.* Roshan took a few moments to explain how information was passed from person to person within the country.

"The *Bedouins* are not antisocial by any means, and many trade and barter regularly with the people who live in the city. Almost all Arab business dealings begin with a joint discussion of family and current events. It is highly likely the Bedouins found out about Mr. Al Bourisli as a result of those discussions. After satisfactorily completing a few, the *Bedouins* began to refer to him as *Al Hakim* - The Wise One. As the frequency he was called upon to arbitrate disputes grew, the government made a decision to officially recognize him as an arbiter of sorts for minor disagreements which might otherwise clog the court system."

"We have mediators in the States providing the same kind of service, can't say I've ever heard of one being called The Wise One." He winced saying this, recalling the arbitrator who handled his divorce.

With the lights of the city fading behind them, the SUV picked up speed heading down the highway into the darkness.

"How far out is this place?" Evan asked.

"We will turn off the highway into the desert in a mile or so. From there about 40 minutes."

The SUV slowed and pulled to the side of the road, at which point the driver got out. Roshan explained the driver was releasing some air from each of the tires so the vehicle would handle better on the sand. Moments later, the driver re-entered the vehicle, and the three of them took off into the blackness of the night.

Evan squinted as he looked out of the side windows but could see nothing around them. As they moved further into the desert, he began to see more stars, and the lack of man-made light started to make the outlines of the distant dunes more visible. With nothing, in particular, to point out, Roshan decided to learn a bit more about this man.

"Were you in the military before you went with those troops to Afghanistan."

"Yes, I was in the Air Force. As a matter of fact, I was in uniform during the Gulf War. Somehow, I was one of the few from my unit who was not sent into Kuwait. I moved forward to Europe and coordinated moving cargo into the war zone."

"Lucky for you then; a war zone is never a good place to be."

"Oh, I agree. I was lucky. At the same time, I didn't realize how such a life experience would change me until afterward. As it was, the time I spent in Europe changed the way I viewed the world from that point forward."

"Living within a different culture sometimes has a way of doing that."

The driver of the SUV turned his head back and said something in Arabic to Roshan nodding toward the windshield.

Evan looked through the windshield and could see lights in the distance.

"The compound?" Evan asked.

"Yes, we are almost there."

The SUV pulled into what appeared to be a gathering of large tents forming a semicircle. They had arrived at *Rihlat Alsahra'*. The vehicle proceeded to a large tent at the center of the encampment, and stopped with the passenger door almost directly in front of the entrance to the tent. Roshan eagerly exited the vehicle and opened the door for Evan, who stepped out in time to come face-to-face with Hamad as he exited the tent.

Placing his right hand upon his heart, Hamad bowed his head briefly saying, "*As-salamu alaykum.*"

Recalling his cultural training from before his deployment to Afghanistan, Evan copied Hamad's bow and responded, "*Wa `alaykum as-salâm.*"

Roshan, who remained speechless during this initial exchange, immediately performed a formal introduction.

"Mr. Davis, may I present Hamad Jaber Al-Bourisli, also known as *Al Hakim. Al Hakim,* may I present the American writer, Evan Davis."

The man standing in front of Evan was slightly taller and dressed in a *dishdasha* and *gutra*. His smile was broad, which accented the lines around his eyes and mouth, Evan would've guessed his age closer to 70, but he had read Hamad was only 61. *Leathery skin due to a life in the desert.*

Hamad offered his hand, which Evan took as each continued to size the other man up by looking directly into the other man's eyes.

"Mr. Davis, *ahlan wa sahlan!* Welcome to *Rihlat Alsahra'*, my desert home," Hamad said as he continued to look into Evan's eyes searching to find the writer of words who could change men's minds.

"Thank you Mr. Al-Bourisli, it is a pleasure to meet you."

While still holding Evan's hand, Hamad raised the opposite one and clasped the man on his shoulder, "Please, no need to be so formal-- call me Hamad."

"Thank you, and please call me Evan."

Behind him, Evan heard the SUV's engine as it moved away from the tent. Roshan also disappeared, leaving him alone with Hamad who motioned for Evan to follow him inside the tent.

Evan's first glance around upon entering made him recall the village elder's tent he had seen in Afghanistan. However, this was a formal *diwaniya* belonging to a man of means. It was much more elegant and well-appointed. The air was filled with a pleasant smell he would later discover was burning frankincense. He followed his host's example and after removing his shoes he took a seat upon one of the large pillows in the center of the room. As his eyes adjusted to the dim light, he noticed on the low table in the center of the room, was a large platter of prepared fruit which made him wonder: *How long is it been since I've eaten?* A teacup was in front of the space Hamad now occupied.

"Would you care for something to drink? Tea, juice, or water perhaps?"

"Water would be great, my body is trying to adjust to not having humidity."

"Yes, the climate here is indeed dry compared with your home, even more so here in the desert than on the coast."

Hamad nodded to a servant who was standing behind Evan. The servant immediately produced a glass with ice and after sitting it on the table poured from a bottle of Evian filling the glass before retreating from the *diwaniya*.

Now that they were alone, Hamad's attitude became more purposeful. He cleared his throat and began to speak in an almost calming voice, "Evan, most of what I know about you is from your writing during your time in Afghanistan. I would like to know more about you as a person if you would care to share."

With Hamad's prompt, Evan launched into a brief description of his family, his sons, and the most recent book he was writing. Hamad took the *tasbih* from his pocket and began playing with each bead between his fingers as he listened intently. Listening carefully to what was being said was in his nature, he was looking to find those commonalities he could match with the man who sat in front of him even though their lives were on differing paths. Finding commonalities was what made him a skilled mediator.

When Evan was done, he shifted positions and leaned forward to take his glass of water and at the same time picked up one of the ripe dates from the tray sitting next to it. Hamad watched as Evan put the fruit into his mouth and bit into it. The sweetness of the date caused Evan to close his eyes for a moment in enjoyment.

*So, the American writer allows himself to indulge and enjoy life's simpler pleasures.*

Hamad shifted positions as well then leaned forward a bit as he began to speak.

"I'm sure your agent, Mr. Maxfield, provided you with some background information on me. I'm sure you probably have additional questions, so please feel free to ask. I think it is important we know as much about each other as possible before we begin."

"As a matter of fact, Arlen did send over a packet of information but, most of it was a basic biography I could have been obtained almost anywhere. I guess what I'd like to know is what exactly you want me to do and why."

"Ah yes, I will get to that in a moment but first let me tell you a little about my family." Hamad was surprised Evan was not more interested in his personal information but instead wanted to jump directly into the business at hand. *Before we get to that, I want you to know more about my family and me. Once you know that, many of your questions should be answered without asking.* Hamad launched into a brief description of his family's history in Kuwait. He told Evan about his wife, brother, sisters and his extended family. Hamad only briefly mentioned Najila in passing and entirely omitted any mention of Khaled. When he finished, he briefly paused to take a grape from the tray and pop it into his mouth. After chewing for a moment, Hamad decided it was time to address Evan's question.

"It was only by chance I came across one of your stories from your time in Afghanistan. Your words were written with such heart they moved me. I felt as if I got to know each one of the people there with you and I began to feel an emotional attachment to each of them as your adventure went on. You have a unique way with words and your talent impressed me greatly."

Evan was not an egotistical man, but no writer has ever been born who did not want to hear those words. The highest compliment a writer can ever hear is he touched someone emotionally with his writing. In spite of the praise, *it doesn't explain why you want me here.*

"I'm tremendously flattered, and I'm glad you enjoyed my work. However, you really haven't told me what you have in mind now."

"In my heart, I feel a man must give back to the country and people which gives to him. Some may call this patriotism or even a sense of nationalism. To me, there is much more, and it is part of the flow of give-and-take every person must reconcile on his own."

Hamad shifted positions again, leaning back against one of the pillows while tucking one leg under him and raising the other, placing his hand on it with the *tasbih* remaining in his right hand. Evan was beginning to see why the locals referred to him as the Wise One, *only the truly wise realize you need to be concerned as much with what you give is what you get.*

"I know my countrymen are thought of as being self-absorbed. Especially with their own personal wealth and position. To some, Kuwaitis are not seen as being generous enough or concerned with the future. Tell me, you have heard from time to time of the country giving a large amount of money to a particular cause?" he paused long enough for Evan to nod before he continued, "However, there is so much more going on here than what is known outside of these borders."

Hamad stopped for a moment to take a sip of his tea then looking into his cup he swirled it for a moment before downing the remaining contents. Hamad held the empty container in the air, and a servant appeared to take the cup. Moments later the same servant placed a new steaming cup of tea directly in front of Hamad. During this transaction, Hamad remained silent but in control of the conversation and the room. It was as if he paused everything long enough for this bit of business to take place before he allowed it to resume.

"You may think my country might need to hire a publicist, or perhaps an advertising firm in hopes of getting this good news out," he paused and nodded towards Evan, giving him a moment to again nod in agreement. Hamad was trying to quell any argument the man might have before it was raised.

"Indeed, I was almost to the point of doing precisely that when I discovered your stories – they provided a different path. Suppose I could find someone who could simply tell the story of what is going on here rather than trying to promote it? Words both warm and human. A story coming from the heart rather than the head. Most of all, a story told from someone outside who, because of a lack of allegiance, would be seen as speaking truths and not merely protecting his own home?" Hamad paused, at this point, he knew he needed more of a buy-in than a simple nod. He was waiting to hear Evan understood his goal. *Would the man take the hint and tell me back the words of agreement I need to hear from him?*

Evan realized Hamad was waiting for him to say something at this point, but he was not really convinced the man's plan would work as effortlessly as Hamad thought it would. He reached forward and took another date which he placed whole into his mouth and began to chew. *Well, I can't speak with my mouth full, that would be rude.* While this provided a momentary excuse, he realized some point he would need to talk. As he chewed the fruit, he noticed the worry beads in Hamad's hand were different than others he had seen. Each bead appeared to be a different color and material, *is there a special meaning?* Once the date was wholly masticated, Evan took a rather large drink of water before changing position, crossing his legs and using both of his hands to accentuate his words.

"I think your plan is an ingenious one," at this Hamad raised his eyebrows and gave a slight nod in appreciation, "but I'm not sure I'd be the right man to act as your voice to the outside world. True, I spent some time in Afghanistan, and while I'm somewhat familiar with Islam, I know nothing at all about Kuwait other than what I've read. Much of what I might see would be wasted because I simply wouldn't fully understand what was taking place in front of me. Your research on me probably revealed I speak only a few phrases of Arabic. How can I even begin to gather information from the local people?" Evan accented this question by raising both palms upward and shrugging his shoulders.

"My dear friend, and I feel we will become good friends, you might be surprised to learn most educated Kuwaitis speak at least a conversational level of English. Also, my country is a welcoming one, and while I am sure you might be able to muddle through this assignment on your own it was never my intent you travel this path alone."

Evan dropped his hands at this point and shifted his position again trying to find one which would allow him some level of comfort as he was still stiff from his long flight.

"If you recall, I spoke of my niece, Najila, who has been studying in America for the past few years." As he spoke, he twirled his *tasbih* around his fingers and back. "During her time there, she has become quite fluent in English and familiar with American culture. I plan to have her act as your guide and, when necessary, translator during the period you are here. Speaking of that, did Mr. Maxfield tell you I was looking for this assignment to last six months?" Hamad was beginning to feel he was close enough to Evan's acceptance and to attempt to gain his full buy-in by adding details about the plan.

Evan nodded but did not speak. His mind already wandered into a world with Najila guiding him around, "So, Najila would be my minder?" *Fine, I'm risking insulting him, but I want to know how this is going to work before I agree to let it work.*

"Definitely not," Hamad's voice for the first time took a sterner tone, and the *tasbih* was now held firm inside his closed hand. It revealed not only his seriousness but the slight insult he felt at being suspected of doing something less than honorable. The look in Evan's eyes told him the point was made, so his voice calmed as he continued "It would defeat the entire purpose of this for you to be guided from bragging point to bragging point. The path goes in the direction your feet decide to take. She will not guide you towards or away from anything. Najila will not prevent you from exploring any subject which might interest you." Evan felt oddly reassured by Hamad's words and for the first time began to accept this might be an earnest effort on his part to display Kuwait's culture to the world.

"Now, in addition to your payment which, through Mr. Maxfield, I was told was agreeable to you, all of your living expenses will be paid. Also…" Hamad went on to speak about how various logistical challenges would be handled during this assignment. In short, if it was acceptable he would continue to reside at the penthouse in the Hotel Sultana and would be given an unlimited credit card to manage any expenses he might have during his stay.

"Your stories will be released through the local press and the international wire services, just as any freelance journalist would release articles." Hamad said bridging from what Evan could expect to receive to what Evan was expected to produce, "Mr. Maxfield has assured me he is more than capable of taking care of the details, my only request is I be provided anything you write before it is sent to him."

"So you can kill stories you do not agree with?" Evan tried to prevent his voice from having an accusatory tone but failed.

"Mr. Davis, as I have repeatedly told you, you have the utmost journalistic freedom in this assignment. No, I won't kill any story you produce, but as your benefactor, I feel I am owed at least the courtesy of a days warning in case something you write proves to be inflammatory so I can prepare as necessary. Understood?" Hamad expected this to be an issue in dealing with an American and was prepared to counter the argument.

"Also, I cannot terminate you because of anything you write. The contract is quite explicit – as long as you provide the articles required, you will be paid for the full length of the contract."

"During the term…" As Hamad began to speak, he was interrupted by the call to prayer from somewhere outside the tent's walls.

As Hamad stood up, he said, "Forgive me, Evan, it is *Salat al-'isha…*"

Evan also rose interrupting his host, "No, please I understand. Your late evening prayers."

Hamad smiled before he began to walk towards the flap of the tent as one of his servants followed carrying a rolled prayer rug. Evan noticed the servant was actually holding a carpet under each arm. Hamad turned before exiting and saw the question on Evan's face, "In case you choose to join me."

As Hamad spoke, Evan saw in his expression an unspoken invitation in addition to the words. Evan chose to ignore it but did need to provide a response.

"Oh, sure. Got it. You want me just to wait here?"

"Indeed, most acceptable," Hamad then turned and exited the tent followed by his servant.

As Evan stood alone in the *diwaniya*, he pondered the conversation he just completed with this man who was so spiritual he would interrupt a business meeting to perform his prayer obligation. It added sincerity and gravitas to the conversation they just completed.

Evan could hear Arabic voices outside of the tent, so he walked over to the tent's flap and peeled it back opening a small slit just wide enough for him to see outside. When his eyes adjusted to the darkness, he could see several figures in prayer prostate in the clearing in front of the tent, among them was Hamad. He watched for a moment as Hamad rose and fell with the rhythm of the prayer. *I'm not sure how this assignment will turn out, but I am sure of the man's faith in it. Six months in the desert… Damn.*

Evan walked back to where he had been sitting and opened up his Go-bag taking out the copy of the contract which Arlen's secretary sent him. Flipping to the back page, he signed and dated the agreement. Closing the folder, he set it next to Hamad's teacup on the table.

Once Hamad finished his prayers, he returned to the *diwaniya* and immediately noticed the folder. While still standing, he picked it up, flipped through its pages and saw Evan had signed the contract. Smiling, Hamad said something in Arabic, which resulted in one of the servants showing up and handing him a pen. He sat down in his place and immediately signed the contract then set it back on the table.

Even though the contract was signed, the two men resumed their conversation until the framework of the agreement had been entirely discussed, explained, and agreed to. Hamad wanted to be sure Evan understood everything, and it was to his liking. It was well after midnight when both men stood to stretch their legs. Roshan reappeared, and Hamad informed him Evan was going to accept his offer, and he would be staying for a while.

Turning his attention back to Evan, Hamad said "Mr. Maxfield has provided account information for us to perform the initial fund transfer. I'm so glad we were able to come to an agreement." He then shook Evan's hand and took him into his arms hugging him as if they were brothers.

Evan did nothing to resist the hug but was not sure how he felt about business deals being sealed this way. Hamad bid him farewell, and he and Roshan made their way back to the hotel in the SUV.

Once Evan and Roshan departed, Hamad went to his residence tent and climbed into bed where Huda was sleeping. As he settled in and began to relax, he was not surprised to hear her speak knowing she would be anxious to hear about the outcome of his meeting with Evan.

"Well, no words on how it went?" Huda said without turning towards her husband.

"He's agreed. It would seem my plan is going to move forward. I hope shortly to see what good fruits it may bear."

Huda was glad he could not see the agitation on her face as she had hoped the American writer would not be agreeable.

"*Insha'Allah*, if it is God's will" Hamad added after a moment.

Agitation turned to anger within Huda. *God's will? No. 'iinaha 'iiradat alshaytan – it's Satan's will.*

After disposing of the body, Maksim took a long nap choosing to sleep away the hottest part of the day like many native Kuwaitis. While preparations were beginning for the finale, the opening salvos that led to it were yet to be fired. That part of the plan could be executed rather quickly and would require more of a physical than mental effort.

No mission of terrorism starts with a rain of fire but with individual sparks. Each spark designed to elicit some level of emotional response within the populace. As sparks gradually grow from petty nuisances into glowing embers that cannot be extinguished, the level of fear would also increase progressively. It is fear which feeds groupthink and public outcry, based upon emotion rather than logic or critical thinking. *It's the steadily increasing heat of the fire that makes things seem so much larger than they are in reality.*

Kuwait possessed its own unique and informal caste system, which governed the amount of access and *wasta* an individual maintained and controlled. Kuwaitis sat at the top of this, naturally, followed by non-tribal citizens. Next came other Arabs from friendly countries and associated tribes. Western and Russian expatriates fell in behind the Arabs and were followed by third-country nationals (TCNs). *Bedoons* held no access or *wasta*, therefore they were not considered in this hierarchy. Lower even than criminals, they just did not matter.

The time had come for Maksim to begin sparking before turning up the heat of terror. He also ignored the *Bedoon. I could probably kill hundreds or thousands, and no one would care or even notice.* Even though he might have personally enjoyed killing such a large number of people, it was not worth the effort, and it was not what he was there to do. *If I succeed, everyone else will destroy them.*

Inside a freshly stolen automobile, Maksim slowly drove through the haunts of professional TCNs. While a majority of TCNs performed only low-level manual labor, there was a select group of well-educated and skilled TCNs who worked at the oil refineries performing engineering and petrochemical jobs. These TCN's were well paid, but also generally ignored by society. However, the disappearance of a vital technician would be noticed even if only peripherally. These would provide a perfect initial spark.

Ejaz Baqri came to Kuwait after finishing graduate school with a degree in chemistry. His job with the Kuwait National Petroleum Company was not an ideal lifetime situation, but it was providing a good and steady income he was able to send back to his family in Pakistan. Ejaz shared an apartment with three other bachelor Pakistanis to save money, with the hope he would save enough money to build his own house at home.

This evening found Ejaz walking back from Shrimpy's with the bag of fried shrimp and French fries he was planning on eating for dinner. Still wearing his work clothes, dress slacks and white shirt with tie, he had just completed his last shift of the week. Because the neighborhood was relatively new, it possessed a network of sidewalks providing him a paved walkway for almost the entire route home. Only one brief half-block segment of pavement was lacking. It was on that segment Maksim's car came up behind him.

Because of the ambient sound of traffic, Ejaz took no mind of the sound of the vehicle approaching from behind him until it was too late. He spun around in time to be blinded by the headlights moments before the speeding car hit him. His body bounced onto the hood before falling off the side of the vehicle and onto the street.

Maksim briefly saw the expression on Ejaz' face after the initial impact, *such wide-eyed fear, perfect.* The impact was of sufficient speed to break both of Ejaz's legs at the knees and guaranteed even if the man did survive, he would never walk again.

Ejaz was fading to and from consciousness as he looked up from where he lay in the street and saw the face of Maksim looking down at him. He attempted to speak but no sound would come out, and the only sound he could hear was a ringing in his ears. As he examined the face of the man looking down at him, Ejaz was surprised, *how can the man's expression be so cold and devoid of emotion?* Satisfied with the result of the accident, Maksim leaned forward and tucked a small slip of paper into the front pocket of the Ejaz's pants before withdrawing and going back to the car.

Confusion and fear flooded Ejaz' mind as Maksim disappeared from his view. *This man isn't even going to try to help me?* Ejaz turned his head to the side to try and follow the man but could only see the scattered and crushed contents of the bag he had been carrying: shrimp, French fries, the desert breeze blowing away wrappers marked with Shrimpy's logo. Suddenly and too late to react, the ringing in his ears cleared long enough for him to hear the sound of an approaching vehicle. Then the world ended for Ejaz Baqri.

After hitting Ejaz a second time, this time crushing his upper chest and throat directly with the car's tires guaranteeing death, Maksim sped away from the area. He would have the car washed before dumping it in a *Bedoon* area some 40 minutes out of the city.

It was almost two hours before the police arrived at the site of Ejaz's body. Any likelihood of witnesses long faded. The call to which the two junior patrolmen were responding was not for a human injury accident, but merely an object blocking the road. No mention the object was a human body. When the patrolman found the body, they summoned an ambulance, but the injuries were too severe for any human to have survived.

By the time the ambulance arrived, Ejaz was dead. The two patrolmen remained at the scene for about half an hour to take measurements and photographs. Because the person who was killed was just a TCN, there would be no formal investigation and the books would be closed based on a determination made by the two police at the scene.

In the report, the officers speculated the vehicle that struck the individual did so accidentally because the pedestrian was not visible at night. It was determined the TCN was at fault because he was on the road and there was no crosswalk nearby. The report did not mention the new visible tread marks going both off and on the road near the body. Aside from adding Ejaz Baqri's name to the final report as the victim, the entire matter was marked as complete and passed on for final review. Chief Jefzar Al-Bourisli signed the cover sheet of the report without reading it.

As the ambulance carried Ejaz's body from the accident site to the morgue, the paramedic in the back began the distasteful duty of going through the man's pockets to see if there was any identification. The paramedic slid a gloved hand into each of the man's pockets and dropped the contents into a small plastic tub on the floor beside him. Aside from a wallet, which contained his immigrant worker pass, the paramedic found a small folded scrap of paper with the single Arabic word written upon it. *Curious* he thought as he dropped it and the wallet into a plastic bag to hand off to the staff at the morgue.

*Beach North of Kuwait City*

Like many *Bedoon* of his generation, Nassar did not have a legitimate full-time job that kept him occupied. Instead, living on the fringes of society as a nonperson, he was forced to take piecemeal opportunities when they arose. While not an ideal situation, it was one which provided him with a variety of skills, due to the differing tasks he took on. Because he did not have regular working hours, he was left with much time to ponder his situation. The frustration and anger at its hopelessness ate away at him.

Taking the final drag off a filter-less cigarette, he flicked the remaining amber into the surf in front of him. The orange glow sailed for a moment vanishing when it hit the water. The ember's arced trajectory was a perfect analogy for the events of his life since completing school. He graduated full of hope, only to have it drowned in a tide set against him. Since the liberation of the country, after the Iraq invasion in the 90s, life for his population spiraled downward.

Even though the naturalization and citizenship decrees issued shortly after Kuwait became a country did not include the *Bedoon*, they were still allowed to be a minor part of society, and have some measure of rights. *Bedoons* served in the military and also worked in government jobs, which allowed them to earn a decent living. But as the country return to normal after liberation, the *Bedoon* found themselves being cast out, as they were told their citizenship identity cards were no longer valid.

Without valid civil IDs, *Bedoons* could no longer work at legal jobs. They were no longer allowed to receive government benefits, to include medical care and subsidies that helped bridge the gap between wages and the cost of living. The entire population also lost any voice in governance, as their input was no longer accepted. Worse yet, even if a person possessed the means to escape, they no longer had a status that would let them exit from Kuwait, or to enter another country wanting identity documents.

Nassar was part of the generation that grew up after these changes, and was being spiritually shredded by the lack of hope for any sort of future. The public education was seen as being charitable, and only contributed to the churn being experienced. *Bedoon* children were made aware of the wondrous world, just to have it snatched away upon graduation as they entered the world where they did not exist.

Nassar wanted to bring about change but had no concrete ideas on how to make it happen. His father, Talal, talked about patiently calling for change from the fringes, hoping attention might be paid. Nassar and many others wanted change now. The entry of the Caliph Kinship into the political fray helped fuel the impatience for change.

The organization possessed many ideas Nassar found distasteful, but they did speak about the need to correct the *Bedoon* issue once and for all. That plank in their platform led many *Bedoon* to side with them even though they might disagree with the strict fundamentalist creed of the Kinship.

For now, Nassar found himself sitting on the beach watching the waves slowly come towards him then fade back into the darkness. He allowed himself to become immersed in what he saw, wishing to be part of one of the waves rushing in to flood the land. He sighed realizing reality was just like the wave – almost as soon as it came ashore, it retreated without making an impact. Nassar was determined to make an impact, but for now, needed to find a way to pay for life's necessities.

Taking out his cell phone, he quickly searched through the messages he received using *WhatsApp*. One of his friends, Rajeesh, mentioned a man who was looking for help and promised to pay well for quietly accomplishing simple tasks. Even though the man was explicitly looking for TCNs, Rajeesh knew most off-the-book employers would not examine Nassar close enough to realize he was a *Bedoon* and not a TCN. Nassar memorized the number Rajeesh sent and created a new message.

```
> Friend sez ur looking for help?
```

Nassar laid back on the beach and had fallen asleep when his phone notified him of a new message.

```
< Yes Contact tomm for mtg
```

Nassar nodded at the screen for a moment and smiled at the thought of having a new job, hoping it would last for a while and provide him with much-needed income. Standing up to brush himself off, he turned back toward shore and walked off the beach.

Maksim closed his phone after replying to the text from the unknown number. Apparently, one of his employees provided his telephone number to a friend and in doing so created two issues

There was the negative issue of having an employee who shared Maksim's phone information with someone else after being told everything needed to be closely held. It would have to be dealt with. At the same time, there was a positive as he was given a lead on an employee who could probably be trusted because he was recommended by someone off the grid.

*Therefore, if I take care of the talker by silencing him, his last act was to provide me with a ready replacement. At least things balance out.*

# Chapter 5



*Penthouse, Hotel Sultana*

Evan stood in front of the mirror and looked into his eyes shaking a finger at his reflection. "Why did you agree to this? You know better." He took a deep breath then exhaled trying to wash away some of the angst he was feeling about the situation, even after his positive meeting with Hamad the night before. It was in his nature to over-think things after making a decision this climactic. Somewhere deep inside himself, he felt a small spark of optimism. All he need do was bring it to the forefront.

As he looked at the countertop beside the sink, he found all of his implements for his morning ritual neatly laid out on a white towel in two rows. The upper row included all the items he might use daily, such as a razor, toothbrush, comb, etcetera. The second row seemed to be items used less often -- a moisturizer, dental floss, and so forth. This arrangement was not his own but was decided by what he has begun to refer to as the *valet elves.*

Last night, when preparing for the meeting with Hamad he discovered his toiletry items laid out in this fashion after getting up from his nap. He used the things he needed, laying them helter-skelter on the counter afterward. When he returned, he found everything once again organized as they were previously. *Dammit.* It occurred to him when he came in last night, he used his toothbrush and left it lying on the counter. Now it was back in its original position. *They were in here while I was sleeping. Again.*

Making a mental note, *I'll have to say something more forceful to Roshan or maybe the hotel management to get this to stop,* Evan began his daily routine. He was preparing to meet his *minder* Najila for lunch. Almost as soon as the thought hit his brain, Evan knew he was unfair. If Hamad was to be believed, she was only to act as a guide taking him where he wanted to go and assisting him on his way. Still, he was not used to being partnered with someone this way, let alone someone he never even met.

Evan dressed in tan colored tactical pants and short sleeve shirt. When he was deployed, Evan found he liked having numerous extra pockets available and upon returning home found he missed having them. His search led him to the pants he was now wearing, which many contractors recommended for use in the Middle East since they came with all the extra pockets "anyone could possibly need." *At home, these were plenty of pockets. But how will they work out here?*

He grabbed his Go-bag and headed downstairs to the hotel's restaurant. Hamad not only provided him with a credit card for expenses but also arranged for the hotel to provide him with any meal service he might desire within the premises, and use of their vehicle fleet. Taking his seat, a waiter immediately appeared, after opening and placing a linen napkin upon Evan's lap, the waiter poured him a cup of coffee. *Not used to this.*

Looking around, Evan noted most of the people around him were dressed in suits and appeared to be Western. Occasionally, there was a table of mixed clientele— Westerners in suits and Arabs in *dishdashas* and *gutras*. One side of the restaurant opened to the window gracing the front of the hotel, whereas the other looked down on a large green and lush courtyard which included a waterfall. As a result, sound seemed to bounce everywhere, and it amplified the murmur of the voices but not the clarity.

Najila entered the restaurant from the public entrance instead of the hotel guest entrance and as a result, came up behind Evan as he sat sipping his coffee. She asked the restaurant manager where he was seated and the manager promptly pointed him out. Since she was behind rather than in front of him, she paused for a moment to observe from a distance before actually meeting him. It was strange to her he carried a backpack which was sitting next to him. She was not quite sure what she expected a writer to carry, *perhaps a notebook, or nothing at all?* Najila could find nothing more to learn or criticize about the man from this vantage point, so it was time to move forward.

Walking to where he was sitting, while still remaining behind him she spoke. "Mr. Davis?"

Evan was startled and immediately stood and spun around towards the sound of the female voice behind him. He knew instantly this was Najila Al Bourisli, even without a formal introduction. She was dressed in a navy-blue pantsuit and appeared to be a little on the tall side. He was not entirely sure if it was her actual height since she, like most women he observed here, probably wore extremely high heels. Her dark hair was thick and long and styled simply, hanging down past her shoulders. The way the light coming through the wall of glass at the front of the hotel accented the hair's shimmer and gave it a slightly bluish tint, *quite pleasing*. But it was her eyes that immediately captured and enthralled him.

Evan was unaccustomed to eyes this dark projecting such sensuality and mystery at the same time. It was not sexual, but they reached out and touched something inside of him, which heightened his curiosity. Like most women in the Middle East, Najila was skillful in the way she applied her eye makeup, to the point it could be called artistic. Aside from using eye makeup so effectively, she matched her features in such a way it was as if her eyes were only meant to be seen the way she prepared them today. It was perfection.

*Is this rude American going to continue to stare at me at me this way, or is he going to ask me to sit down?* After her time in the States, Najila realized some American men were taken aback by her appearance, often referring to her as *exotic.* She knew she was not an ugly woman, but also knew her appearance brought out *Sand Fever* in some Western men. She purposely avoided those men, because she did not want to be objectified for her Arab appearance with olive skin, hair and dark eyes. Now she realized she might be forced to spend six months with one of those *Sand* chasers.

"Oh, you must be Najila," Evan said, at last, extending his hand toward her, "Please, have a seat, and call me Evan." *I'm tripping over myself.*

She walked to the opposite side of the table and stood for a moment next to her chair. When she glanced over at Evan and noticed he sat down without pulling out her chair for her, she took her seat as well. *So, he's not a gentleman either.*

Evan summoned for the waiter, and Najila ordered a cup of tea. Once it arrived, the two engaged in small talk. Weather, how long it takes to get over jet lag traveling from the US to here, and how they mutually felt her uncle Hamad was something of a calm spoken force of nature.

"He does seem to be very impressed with your writing, which says a lot coming from him."

"I'm always a bit surprised when I hear about people outside the United States who read my stories from that period. At the time, I was unaware of any followers outside of the US."

"Ah, I see." *As if we're just a bunch of stupid isolated camel jockeys?*

"Of course, I didn't mean people outside of the US weren't well-informed, just surprised they would be reading the words of an embedded reporter with an American unit."

*Nice save, but I'm unconvinced.*

"Anyway, your uncle told me what he has in mind for you: helping me with cultural understanding, finding my way around, and performing translations."

*Duh. Based on what I've seen, you would get lost in the desert the first day and thrown out of the country for cultural insensitivity on the second.* "As you say, it is pretty much how he explained it to me as well. Did you have anything in mind as to how you want to start on this adventure?"

"Not really. To be honest, I don't really know much about Kuwait other than what news makes it back to the States. This means everything I look at will be seen with new eyes. Realistically it could help me write better because my newcomer enthusiasm should flow through."

*So, we are to bounce between stupidity and the obvious. At least it isn't all stupidity. A plus, I guess.* "If I may be so bold as to suggest, why don't we start with a brief history lesson, we can proceed from there based on what seems the most interesting to you."

"Sounds like a plan, by the way, have you eaten?"

"No, my uncle told me we would be having lunch together. Is this not correct?" *Please tell me you didn't eat, I'm starving.*

"No. I mean yes, I didn't eat. As we discussed, I'm still battling jet lag, so I haven't been up too long. Is here okay?"

"Yes, they have a great menu – a mix of Western, Indian, and Middle Eastern dishes."

"If you don't mind, I would like to gradually ease my way into Kuwaiti cuisine until I get my legs under me."

"Perfectly understandable," *I bet he'll order a hamburger.* Najila nodded towards the waiter to let him know they were ready to order.

After ordering, Evan gave her a bit of his personal history while they waited for their food to arrive. Soon, the waiter reappeared with his hamburger and French fries and her chicken curry. The conversation during the meal turned to their favorite foods and restaurants in the United States.

*Inside SUV, Kuwaiti Desert*

Hamad stared out the window of the SUV flipping his *tasbih* around his fingers, as he and Roshan rode from *Rihlat Alsahra'* to *Shamal Mazraea*. After three weeks in the desert, it was time for him to return to the main horse stables, and tending the family business. Both men were silent; as Roshan worked on his Android notepad, Hamad read the day's newspapers. The movement of a pair of feral Saluki hounds in the distance caught Hamad's eye, and he watched them out the window as they ran through the desert in the same direction as the SUV.

He was amazed at the blur of their legs, moving so fast you could not define their exact shape as they clawed their way through the sand. *Allah has produced no finer hound for this land.* Without warning, the dogs suddenly changed direction and disappeared up and over a dune. The momentary joy of the experience was gone. It caused Hamad to reflect back to the day of his son's graduation from high school, when Khaled's direction suddenly changed from the path he was on, into something completely different.

"*Baba*, can you help me with this?" Khaled said as he walked towards his father fumbling with the silk tie looped around his neck.

Hamad looked toward his son and realized immediately what the boy was talking about. He walked over to him and began to untangle the knot Khaled created.

"You know, I'm still not sure why a high school in this nation would insist its students dress as Westerners to commemorate their graduation," Hamad said as he completed the task of loosening and finally untying the Gordian knot from around his son's neck.

"I told you, we voted on it at school. We were given a choice between dressing in a *dishdasha* – or adopting the Western tradition of a cap and gown. When we decided upon the cap and gown, it forced us to wear Western clothes underneath. Can you imagine trying to deal with a gown wearing a *dishdasha* underneath?"

While his son spoke, Hamad worked on creating a perfect double Windsor knot. When it was decided Hamad would attend school in the West, his own father saw the necessity of sending him to a finishing school in England beforehand. This way he would arrive at school knowing Western-style manners and dress. As he worked on the knot, Hamad wondered if his son would not benefit from the same type of experience.

"There, it is done." He laid both of his hands on his son's shoulders taking a step back to look at him at arm's length. Hamad felt great pride for the young man he and Huda produced. The young man standing in front of him did well in school and was now actively searching for colleges to take him down his own path into the distant future. As he looked at Khaled, he noticed the young man's expression suddenly changed.

"*Baba*, I know you are expecting me to enter college or some other school at the end of summer. But I've decided, I don't want to do that. At least no straight away."

"Oh no?" As Hamad said this, he dropped his hands from his son's shoulder and quietly remained standing in front of him.

"No. I think I would like to take a year and work in the family business, with the horses."

His son possessed considerable skill as a horseman, and his persona would suit him well in dealing with buyers and clients. *Perhaps this is not such a bad idea for him to spend a year growing outside of academia before returning to his studies.* "You know, I've been thinking of hiring another manager to give me more time recruiting new clientele."

"No, not as a manager, just as a horse handler. I don't want to be seen as taking a position I don't deserve just because I'm your son. I want to earn it on my own."

Whenever his son came up with something like this, it would amaze Hamad even though he knew the kind of man he raised. *Of course, he didn't want to start at the top; he knew he needed to earn his position.*

"It is obvious you've given this some consideration," as he said this, he raised a single finger in the air letting Khaled know he was about to say something important, "Convincing *Umma* on the other hand…" Before he could finish his thought, Khaled leaned forward and hugged his father.

"Thank you for understanding *Baba*."

Hamad wrapped his arms around his son and held him close. Even though his son turned from the path he was traveling onto an unknown spur that would take him off into a different direction, Hamad knew it would be all right. The young man he held in his arms now was ready to go successfully down any path encountered. He and Huda prepared him well, and Hamad knew the boy would be fine.

Hamad was brought back to the present when he heard Roshan say under his breath "*Ya lahwi!*"

"Something wrong Roshan?"

Turning electronic notepad over and resting on his lap, Roshan turned to face Hamad and responded, "Uh, no – just surprised at some changes in the world markets."

"Hmm" was Hamad's only response as he went back to staring out the window.

Once his boss's attention was elsewhere, Roshan flipped the Android device over again and reread the news article that caused him to react in the first place. The source was *Liljamie, For All,* an underground electronic newspaper, which provided unofficial news to TCNs in Kuwait.

Ejaz Baqri, a chemical engineer with the Kuwait National Petroleum Company, was killed overnight in a pedestrian accident. Mr. Baqri was found to be at fault.

Such a matter-of-fact and unquestioned ending but Roshan came to accept such incidents as normal even though they were tragic. *How exactly can a pedestrian be at fault for being killed by a vehicle? It wasn't as if he decided to lash out and strike the car.* A moment's consideration led him to the only logical conclusion for the world he lived in: *The man possessed no waste and therefore just didn't matter in the eyes of society.*

As Sheikha sat at the table in the dark, she stared across the top of the teacup she held in her hand. She allowed her eyes to blur the objects in the distance in favor of watching the swirls of steam as they rose from the hot liquid. Moments like these were too few, she arrived home early from work, and it was not time for the Meteb to rise and prepare for school. It gave her a moment to relax and remember.

On the day she first saw *him,* Sheikha was sitting in an ocean view café just south of Kuwait City. Almost a decade passed since the Iraqi invasion and the fear of another faded with teenagers returning to their social norms. She was there with a few friends, and even though there was no legal requirement to maintain sexual segregation, the men were sitting to one side of the café with the women on the other. As the high school girls sat, they made note of all the young men as they walked into the sitting area. Teasing each other and giggling, as they made comments about each of the men's attractiveness and suitability for a relationship.

The first time she saw him, she was immediately enamored. It was not his physical attractiveness, which seemed to reach out to her first, but his aura of confidence and warmth. He arrived with a group of friends, and they took up residence at a table just across from hers. While deciding upon chairs, he glanced over and saw Sheikha before he selected the chair that would allow him to face her directly.

As he sat, Sheikha began to carefully inventory his features. The young man was just over two meters tall, *he's so tall, taller even than my father.* Once he was sitting, she noticed his *gutra* was a white on white pattern, and he wore it with the sides flung back behind his shoulders rather than hanging down the front. *Wearing it that way, his shoulders appear so broad. They're probably muscular. He either works for a living or has time to spend in the gym.* His *dishdasha* was white, *but it is a bright white, I've never seen anything so white. I can't help but stare at this man. He compels it.* She felt her face flush at the thoughts she was having but could not find herself able to look away from him every time she looked his direction.

The rest of the evening was typical of interactions between Kuwaiti youth in these cafés. Glances from across the room, perhaps a cloaked greeting or mouthed words, any means of communicating without directly being seen interacting with the opposite sex. Some of the youth were technologically advanced enough they were texting to one another, painstakingly using standard phone keypads to enter words one letter at a time with multiple pushes on the keys.

Once, when Sheikha looked over at the young man, he slowly raised his mobile phone and gently rocked it back and forth in his hand as he stared at her. This was a sign he wanted to text with her. Being a *Bedoon* and lacking the money or capability to have a phone, she turned her hand empty palm up to let him know she possessed nothing. A small nod let her know he understood.

For the rest of the evening, the two stole glances at each other as they interacted with the people at their own table. A small spark between them gently glowed, but they had no way to communicate other than stolen glances, at least not yet.

A week later, Sheikha again went with her friends to the same café. Upon entering, they took the same table as before, and she was delightfully surprised to see the young man again sitting across from her. Later, when Sheikha went to the counter to order another cup of coffee, she realized the young man followed and was now standing behind her in line. Once both ordered, they moved to the side and joined a small knot of people waiting for their orders to be prepared. *I know he's right behind me*, she found herself inhaling deeply to enjoy the smell of his cologne. *I want to be surrounded by his scent.*

When the barista slid her order toward her, the young man reached from behind her and placed his hand palm down on the counter next to the cup. Sheikha did not turn to look at him, but when the barista turned her back, he removed his hand revealing a small mobile phone. Sheikha nervously reached forward and took her cup with one hand and the phone with the other. As she returned to her seat, she stealthily slipped the phone into a pocket of her *abaya*

Time slowed for the rest of the evening. Sheikha wanted to remove the mobile from her pocket and examine it; she had never held one before, let alone possessed one. But she could not afford to attract the attention of her friends and knew she would not be able to examine it until she got home later. So she sat, hoping her excitement was not visibly apparent, while stealing additional glances of the young man across the way.

Sheikha came to a conclusion, *the fates are torturing me purposely.* Any time she looked up from her friends or around the café, she could see him staring back at her with *such beautiful eyes.* She tried to depart several times during the evening, only to be prevented from doing so by her friends who insisted she stay. There was always some excuse – the evening was still young, or some friend who had not yet arrived was expected at any moment. Sheikha attempted to use going to the restroom as a subterfuge so she could examine the device only to have a friend insist on joining her. It was not the custom of her family for the women to wear a veil, but for the first time in her life, she found herself wishing she wore one to hide her blush, which must have been incredibly visible. *My cheeks are so hot.*

At last, the evening ended. Sheikha and her friends walked from the café and down the street toward their homes. The object of her evening's attention was still sitting with his friends when she left but, in her pocket, she now, at last, possessed the means to communicate with him.

When Sheikha arrived home, she was greeted by her mother, who was standing in the kitchen doing dishes. Sheikha wanted to immediately run to her bedroom and withdraw the mobile from her pocket, but her mother insisted she come and assist. While washing the dishes, her mother wanted a complete accounting of the evening's events. Sheikha was trying not to see her mother's curiosity is being an intrusion, but she was of an age where being asked about her actions was an incursion. *There is no way I could tell her about my mystery man.*

While standing at the sink next to her mother, she felt a strange sensation on the side of her thigh accompanied by a dull buzz. Having never used a mobile phone before, she didn't realize what she was feeling was the notification vibration caused by an arriving text message. *Ya lahwi! Can she hear it?* Sheikha made an abrupt excuse to her mother about needing to go to the bathroom and quickly ran toward the toilet. Closing and locking the door, she, at last, withdrew the phone from her pocket and examined it. The buzzing and vibration stopped, *have I broken it?* It took only a moment to figure out how to open the phone and when she did the small square screen inside lit up displaying a message in English:

> 1 Text Message Received

She gulped a breath of air and held it. Looking at the keypad, she saw a button larger than most in the center with OK printed on it. Pressing the button with her thumb caused the screen to go blank for a moment, next a series of numbers appear to the top with a one-word message below them.

> Hello

Sheikha exhaled, taking a new gulp of air, which she also held. Examining the screen closely she saw two options listed at the bottom, Reply, or Delete. Choosing the button beneath Reply, resulted in the screen going blank with only a flashing cursor being displayed. Though one unfamiliar with the technology, Sheikha watched other people and knew she could use the keypad to enter letters to compose a response. She quickly typed in the five letters of her response and hit the Send button.

< Hello

The pounding on the bathroom door caused her to exhale in panic, quickly closing the phone and hiding it again in her pocket. She flushed the toilet before running the water in the sink as if she was washing her hands. Upon exiting the bathroom, she was greeted by the cold stare of her younger brother who apparently needed the facility. *At least I was able to respond to him.*

"Momma?"

Sheikha was abruptly shaken out of her trance-like state and looked down to find Meteb standing next to her, his hair askew and still dressed in his sleeping gown. *Enough of daydreams, time to attend to reality.*

*Rihlat Alsahra'*

*Of course Mr. Baqri was at fault. He shouldn't have been here — it's not his country,* Huda thought as she read the news from the *Liljamie* website. Around her, a flurry of servants was packing and securing items at the desert compound, as activity moved back to *Shamal Mazraea.* Her husband and Roshan left early, and it was her duty to take care of such details before she departed for the other residence.

Using the touchpad on her laptop, she clicked the link for the *Kuwait Times* to read the latest legitimate news. *Nothing will be in this paper for a while, but soon the mayhem will rise to a level where it cannot be ignored.* The deviousness of her plan caused her to visibly smile, which resulted in looks being exchanged between the servants as they worked. It was unusual for Huda to smile or be friendly without Hamad being present. He may have thought she was an excellent wife, but the much-maligned staff knew better.

When she was sure the kitchen and residence areas were adequately cleaned and secured, Huda directed the staff to proceed to *Shamal Mazraea*. One staff member would be left behind to take care of things as needed, and of course, the stables would remain fully staffed. Once the staff departed, Huda climbed into her Mercedes sedan and went to the Bank of the Gulf to complete a small detail before continuing on to *Shamal Mazraea.*

The safe deposit box procedure at the bank was a familiar one, and as soon as she was left alone inside the vault, she spun the dial which on the box's top and heard the lock release. This time however after removing the manila folder, she proceeded to scoop out handfuls of Kuwaiti bills. Huda then began to count out the bills placing them in piles of 5000KD each. Based on her review of the exchange rates in the *Kuwaiti Times* this morning, she knew she would need almost 28,000KD to equal the €75,000 she required.

When she finished counting the bills, she picked up the manila folder and pondered it for a moment before putting it back in the box. It had been years since she opened the folder and looked at its contents. She purposely placed it atop the contents of the safe-deposit box she was currently using so she would be forced to see and consider it every time she came here.

She slowly opened the folder, revealing the contents: a single hand-written page. Huda looked at the page, not reading the words but allowing her eyes to glide over the curvature of the letters. She allowed herself the realization that what she was looking at was handwritten by her son Khaled. She caressed the page with her fingertips feeling some sort of spiritual connection to her long-gone son. *This was the last thing he ever created before he was gone* – the thought stabbed at her deeply with pain only a mother could know. Slapping the folder shut she dropped it back into the box and slammed the lid down and spun the dial as if to trap inside of the box the pain she was feeling.

"Mohammed," she called out knowing full well the banker was standing just outside the privacy curtain waiting for her to complete her activity so he could return the box to its slot.

"Yes, Mrs. Al Bourisli?"

"I'm done here. Please secure the safety deposit box and arrange for this money to be wired, in Euros, to this account." As she said this, she handed him a small slip of paper with a 36-digit account number on it, "the account is with the First Caribbean International Bank."

"Ah yes, I am aware of Mr. Al Bourisli's accounts in the Caymans."

"No," almost as soon as she said it, she realized the tone was a little too forceful, especially since she didn't want this transaction to be memorable, "Uh, this is the account of an associate, we're buying more breeding stock."

"I understand completely, I will have it taken care of immediately," as he said this, he pressed the call button inside the vault to summon a bank clerk to handle the cash while he returned the box to its vacant spot in the wall. The bank clerk made quick work of counting the money before taking the account number from Mohammed arranged the immediate transfer of the funds.

Huda was impatiently standing in the lobby having turned down a cup of tea from Mohammed while she waited for verification of the fund's transfer. As soon as he confirmed the transfer and provided her with the receipt, she turned and left.

Even if everything flowed without consequence, Mohammed would still remember the file transfer. After all, this was the first time in the decade he was with the bank that Mrs. Al Bourisli removed cash from one of her safety deposit boxes rather than depositing it.

During their tense lunch, Najila asked Evan if he could ride a horse and he nodded without providing any further details. In keeping with the promise, she made to her uncle, she wanted to begin their alliance with a history lesson about Kuwait and the region. She felt there was no better way to accentuate the country's history than on horseback in the desert. The two of them traveled in her SUV to *Rihlat Alsahra'*. The conversation on the way there was light, as Evan asked questions about the various flora he saw growing alongside the road, and she asked more questions about his home in western Michigan.

Upon arriving, they were met by the chief caretaker and were told Hamad and Huda just departed. This was of no consequence to Najila, as long as the horses remained. After speaking with Naveed, the lead horse trainer, she told him to select two mounts and prepare them for desert riding.

Evan watched as the horses were bridled and saddled, then several large canteens of water were tied onto them, an absolute must for a desert ride. While this was going on, Najila vanished and returned wearing jeans and a casual shirt along with Western-style riding boots. Her hair was pulled back, and for the first time, due to the tightness of these clothes, Evan could see she possessed the curvy body shape of a woman. *Unexpected.*

*This man is staring at me again, is it a good idea to ride alone with him in the desert?* Overcome by her own arrogance she suppressed her concern. *Of course. I'm a Kuwaiti in Kuwait – he is the interloper.*

Evan did not consider it lying when he told Najila he could ride. He spent several summers riding horses at various Boy Scout camps he attended and was on average horseman by the end of it all. But his past experience in no way prepared him to take on a high-spirited Arabian mount. He put his Go-bag on his back before he stepped to the side of the horse to mount it. No sooner than he was seated on the saddle, his claim of skill fell apart as the mare immediately reared back and threw him to the ground.

Najila watched, at first with concern but when she saw he was unhurt, she could only find humor in what happened. She was polite enough to stifle her laughter but only with much difficulty.

"Well, they say you have to get right back on the horse once you've been knocked off," Evan said as he rose from the ground and brushed the dirt off. One of the stablemen returned the horse, and after obtaining a quick nod from Najila handed Evan the reins once again. Placing his left foot in the stirrup, he was preparing to step up and throw his leg over the horse, when the animal quickly stepped to the side throwing him to the ground once again.

Najila was not sure how many times Evan planned on attempting to mount the horse. She knew from her experience at college, Western men, like their Middle Eastern counterparts, would sooner kill themselves trying, than be defeated, especially by an animal or a woman. To prevent having to explain to her uncle why she allowed the writer to be killed on his first day, she dismounted and walked over to where Evan just regained his footing.

"Perhaps we should try this another time," the temperature was rising, and it provided her with a graceful way out, "it is probably too late in the day for the horses with the heat intensifying. We'll take my SUV instead."

"Agreed, my horsemanship is apparently a bit too long past."

"As you say."

Before he climbed into the passenger side of the SUV, Evan placed his Go-bag on the seat, so it was between Najila and himself. *It isn't the first time I've used my bag as a line of defense.*

"You know, you shouldn't be embarrassed by your performance. After all, these are purebred Arabians, known for their high spiritedness. Only the best of riders can control them, and even then, it is more like shared control rather than the human being in charge." *Which is true for many Arabian creatures.*

"I can tell, but I think the horse and I would've come to some sort of understanding. I'm just not sure how many more times I would've wound up on the ground before it happened," *let's change the subject*, "Where exactly are we going?"

"That way," she nodded at the windshield and beyond it to the horizon in the East.

She slowly sped up as *Rihlat Alsahra'* faded behind them. Even though the sand appeared to be completely smooth, the SUV rocked back and forth as its wheels glided into the desert. They rode this way silently for almost an hour before she slowed the vehicle down. Evan looked through the windows on all four sides and saw nothing but sand. *Why stop here?*

"What do you know of Kuwait's history?"

*I didn't know I was going to be faced with a history quiz.* "Well, in about 1600 the village of Kuwait was established on the coast and served as a base for a lot of fishermen."

"As you say, the village eventually became Kuwait City."

"The city entered into commerce with several of the countries within the Middle East and became a major trading route, which caused it to grow. Kuwaitis also began designing and building boats. While other parts of the region dealt with internal strife, Kuwait remained stable and was able to prosper as a result."

"All correct. If you would like, at some point I can show you a *dhow*; the basic design of the boat has remained the same for centuries. Were you aware Kuwaitis are known as the best sailors in the Persian Gulf?"

"No, I've not heard that," *What else would a Kuwaiti say?*

Without being prompted, Evan continued on his history recitation, "At some point, the Sheikhdom of Kuwait became a British colony."

"As you say, it remained a protectorate from 1899 until 1961."

"Historically, Kuwait has held a rather unique place in the world because it traded with almost everyone in the region as well as with the West. But because of the connection, it suffered during the Great Depression, because of the West's economic woes."

"Having your economy connected to so many allows for both good and bad possibilities." Without taking her eyes from the road, Najila took a drink from a bottle of water that was sitting in one of the center cup holders. After returning it, she picked up a still sealed bottle and offered it, Evan.

Taking it, Evan continued reciting his knowledge of the country, "Things went on until the discovery of oil, which led to Kuwait massively expanding. At one point, the country was the most modern in all of the Middle East."

Najila nodded at what he said. *Well, it would seem he knows a little bit about us and our country.* Pointing eastward through the windshield she said, "Somewhere just over the horizon is the border with Saudi Arabia. Do you know anything about it?" She was challenging him.

"Well, I know the way Saudi Arabia exists now came about in 1930 or so when – um - *somebody* bin Saud managed to take over the country and unite a bunch of tribes together under his leadership."

"*Abdul-Aziz* bin Saud. At the time he was exiled to Kuwait. In 1902, he started to reclaim his destiny by first capturing Riyadh, and then the rest of the country. Abdul-Aziz remained king of Saudi Arabia until the 1950s." *Perhaps this American is not as stupid about the world as I first assumed.*

Off in the distance, Najila could make out the silhouettes of a caravan of *Bedouins*. She turned the vehicle so its path would intersect with them. They were almost upon the travelers when Najila suddenly slammed on the brakes. *I had nearly forgotten. It's been too long.*

Evan braced himself with a hand on the dashboard, and turned towards Najila, "What the hell was that about!" calming himself, he continued, "I thought we were going to go meet some desert people."

Now she needed to figure a way to cover her own cultural insensitivity, "It was my intent for you to meet these *Bedouin*. However, I'm not sure of the customs of their particular tribe, and I don't want to risk insulting them."

"Since you're dressed Western and not wearing a *burqa?*"

"It is but a small part," *Why do Westerners think everything is about the burqa?* "Also, I'm a woman driving a vehicle, I'm traveling with someone who is not my husband or of my family, and so many other things which might be seen as *haram,* or an insult."

Looking through the windshield, Evan watched as 15 meters in front of them the caravan traveled past without slowing or paying them any mind.

"Ah yes, that which is forbidden: *haram," I almost forgot about the all-encompassing concept which allowed an Imam to immediately control the behavior of his people, and not always by the teachings of the Quran.*

The two sat motionless as the parade of camels, horses, goats, and people went by.

"You know, the *Bedouins* are so adapted to living in the desert they carry everything they need to survive with them as they move from place to place. Of course, once they get to their next destination, they will have to locate a source of water, but aside from that they're pretty much self-contained."

"Amazing," *and I mean it, I have no idea how anyone would survive out here. You have to admire the Bedouin's tenacity if nothing else.*

Once a small herd of goats being prodded along by shepherd boys passed them, Najila put the SUV back in gear and resumed her journey East.

"Where are we going again?" *I wonder how far away from civilization we are now?*

"Almost there," *Why is he so impatient? He needs to calm down and realize what I'm doing will help him.*

Najila made several turns both right and left, eventually going north. Unknown to Evan, they were passing many small settlements of people and towns along the way. She had selected a route that avoided even seeing them, to purposely make the entire journey seem more remote and desolate.

"You have reached your destination," said the app on Najila's phone, the robotic female voice speaking for the first time during their journey.

She abruptly spun the steering wheel while stopping the vehicle causing it to slide dramatically like a car in a TV commercial.

"We're here."

Evan was befuddled, he looked through each of the windows of the SUV and saw nothing other than more nothing. He slowly nodded his head although he was not sure what he agreed to.

"Do you know where we're at?"

"Um, no. Although I'm fairly sure we haven't departed the planet Earth. But, you know, I've seen pictures of the moon, and it looks a lot like this – so maybe we did." He couldn't help himself. His methodology of using humor and snarkiness to deal with tense or uncomfortable situations finally got the better of him.

Najila laughed, *he does have a decent sense of humor.* "No, we didn't leave the Earth, in fact, we've not left Kuwait. We are, geographically speaking, as close to the center of the country as it is possible to be," she then opened the door and exited the vehicle slamming the door behind her. Evan followed suit and joined her where she was now standing at the rear of the vehicle.

Najila raised her arm and pointed a finger out toward the horizon to her left, slowly she panned to the right, "All of that, is where my people have lived for thousands of years. Surviving the heat, surviving the windstorms, surviving invaders, and surviving the desert. In all that time, we've never allowed ourselves to be overrun, and have always been loyal to both our faith and the community of man we occupy."

Evan listened to her and held back his desire to point out they were overrun by Iraq for at least a short period.

Dropping her arm to her side, she continued, "Beyond the desert, we tamed the shore first, then the waters; providing for our families and our tribes as we built for the future, and relied on our faith in Allah to guide us forward."

Najila turned to look at Evan's face to make sure she was making the impact she desired on this man. *If I lay the foundation correctly, he'll provide us with the words that will bring the world to understand, as my uncle desires.*

"I brought you here because before you start to meet and know the people, you needed to see and understand the roots of civilization.

The *alsahra'* gave birth to the nation of Kuwait."

As Evan looked out over the horizon, he found himself flooded with a thousand questions and suddenly felt at ease with himself. He realized he was going to be given a chance to find the answers to many of them.

# Chapter 6



*Liquid Gold Cafe, Al Jafra*

As he sat in his car parked down the street from the café, Maksim pondered his progress as he waited for his prospect to arrive. Given that he was now almost two weeks into the first phase of his plan for terrorizing the country, he was about to proceed from killing professional TCNs to killing low-level Kuwaitis. Little to no notice was paid to his activities up to this point. While searching the web to gauge reaction, the only articles he found regarding his targets were listed on an underground news source.

This caught Maksim off guard. Even in the most callous Soviet society, a death, outside of normal circumstances, was worthy of at least a minimal mention. He could understand vehicular mishaps might be too mundane to garner any sort of notice by the larger media outlets. Lack of notice caused him to move quickly after the first two, and on to methods that could not be mistaken for unfortunate accidents: Slashing the throat of one victim, throwing another from a rooftop, and killing a third with a shotgun blast to the face. These would have led to screaming headlines at home, but here… nothing. The clue he blatantly left on all the bodies, was not mentioned either. *Such a deeply entrenched caste system sees so little value in those toward the bottom that their passing, no matter how violent, was ignored entirely. Ah, but soon. Soon it will change.*

Movement in the distance caught Maksim's attention. The shape of a young man coming into view as he plodded through a vacant lot just ahead. Maksim glanced at his watch and noted it was 8:42PM, the prospect was almost 20 minutes early. *Impressive.* As the figure drew closer, more details became visible, and it was apparent the person was wearing an off-white. The traditional Indian outfit of a long shirt with baggy trousers signaled it was likely this was the person for whom Maksim was waiting. He watched as Nassar entered the café while remaining motionless in the car. Rechecking his watch, it was now three minutes before the appointed time. Maksim withdrew his phone and began typing.

```
< Change - Go to Curry Barn on 6th Ave
```

A moment later came the response,

```
> OK
```

When Maksim raised his head from his phone, he saw Nassar come out of the door and head toward the destination he specified. Confirmation. He waited a few more minutes to see if Nassar was being followed. When nothing else stirred, Maksim started his car and drove the short distance to the Curry Barn.

Dressed as a westerner, Maksim walked past the restaurant's front window heading for the entrance. He looked into the establishment and saw Nassar sitting at one of the tables, nervously staring straight ahead.

"*As-salamu alaykum*," Maksim said, tingeing his Arabic with an American accent, as he took a seat directly in front of Nassar.

"*Wa `alaykum as-salâm*," Nassar replied, and as he did so, he began to rise as show respect to the man who just arrived.

Changing to English, Maksim told him, "Please, please sit down. We don't need to draw any attention to ourselves. Do we?" He looked over at the waiter who began to walk towards the table and waved him off.

"Oh, sorry."

"So, first tell me your name."

"Nassar"

When he failed to fully answer the question, Maksim prodded him, "and your surname?"

"Bhabra"

Maksim exhaled loudly as he leaned forward, "You know Nassar, even though our entire relationship will be secret, to each other we have to be honest, or else there can be no trust," Maksim let his eyes purposely grow cold as he stared into Nassar's eyes. He wanted Nassar to be scared of him, too scared to lie. While Maksim was not positive, *all these people look more or less alike*, something about the boy's physical features, accent, and attitude was wrong for a TCN. *Of course, when is a TCN examined closely?* "So, let's try this one more time – shall we?" Sitting back, he asked again, "What is your name?"

"Nassar," then looking down he added "*Al-Enezi.*"

The name hit Maksim like a lightning bolt. *The features are Arabic!* Up to this point, he was less than successful meeting an actual *Bedoon*, now one fell into his lap.

"You see. Things are much better when they're based on honesty. I'm Kevin Pauley," *Well, at least one of us will tell the truth,* "Tell me more about yourself, Nassar."

Maksim's training was primarily how to eliminate people quickly and quietly. However, to accomplish his primary mission, he often needed the ability to convince people to work for him, and at times not in their own best interest. This is why his Siberian Rime training included a condensed course in skills patterned after Dale Carnegie's methodologies.

The syllabus from which Maksim was taught skipped over the need to genuinely like other humans, in favor of ways to fake sincerity. As for the rest of the skills, they served him well. Maksim would repeat the person's name several times during a conversation and feign interest in what the person said. He would fill conversations with questions about the person, giving them long pauses to pad with talking about themselves. Additionally, he paid them well, to clinch their loyalty. Maksim would pass out bills freely while thinking, *Carnegie might have perfected his method if he hadn't failed to take advantage of greed as an influencer.*

Nassar was not typical of the others he hired thus far. He was smart, making him easier lure into the scheme. *Intelligent people are simple to fool because most think they are too bright to be taken advantage of.* Once the plan was in full swing, his ego would keep him loyal, and willing to convince himself what he is doing is for the best, regardless of the truth. The young man's veiled hatred of the establishment would also make him malleable, and easy to string along.

With a rapport established and his loyalty ready to flourish, the rest of their conversation differed little from any of the others Maksim held with people he hired to perform menial tasks in association with his projects. He provided Nassar with a cellphone to be used only between them and warned him against telling anyone else about their association, the same as he had Rajeesh.

"Now, to seal things between us and to ensure your availability when I may need you, take this as a standby fee," as he said this, Maksim slid a 20KD bill across the table toward Nassar, who immediately scooped it up and put it in his pocket.

"Yes, yes and thank you for giving me this opportunity. I won't disappoint."

"I am sure you would never intend to; I'll be in touch shortly. Enjoy your dinner."

*Dinner?*

On his way out of the restaurant, Maksim walked over to the waiter and handed the man a folded bill telling him to bring Nassar whatever he wanted. *Feed the ego then feed the stomach.*

Within moments, Maksim was back in his car, and after watching Nassar order his meal, he headed toward his next meeting of the evening. This meeting, however, would not end pleasantly for the other party, Rajeesh. But, at least the transgression led Maksim to a prized resource. *Out of gratitude, I'll make his death quick rather than drawing it out. Perhaps.*

He met Rajeesh at a bus stop bench, in front of a multistoried building still under construction. While they exchanged minor pleasantries, Maksim produced a bottle of water from the canvas shoulder bag he was carrying. After breaking the seal, he offered it to Rajeesh who took a small sip. He withdrew another bottle from the shoulder bag before putting it on the ground while the two sat in silence drinking the water.

"Rajeesh, you recall when you first started working for me I said you were never to say anything to anyone about me or our arrangement?"

The young man immediately knew what this was about and the unforgivable act he committed. *Why did I say anything to Nassar?* To give himself a moment to compose a response, he took a large drink from the water bottle and swallowed it, "I would never do anything to break your trust, Boss."

"Ah, but you did. You not only made someone else aware of my existence, you even provided him with my phone number. The private phone number I gave you in confidence," Maksim was keeping his voice composed. He knew calm to be far more psychologically unnerving than anger.

*He knows – I'm so stupid,* Rajeesh took another deep drink while trying to keep his hands from shaking, "I only told him you were looking for help, nothing else. By all which is Holy, I swear."

Maksim sat in the quiet for a moment to let the paranoia build within his victim. Giving him a side glance, he could see Rajeesh was beginning to have difficulty swallowing and was attempting to solve this by finishing the contents of the water bottle. *Go ahead, drink it all down.* Rajeesh started to lean to one side, then realizing something was wrong attempted to stand up to leave, but instead, his body crumpled onto the ground. As Maksim looked down at him, he sneered – *it's far too late for escape.*

As Rajeesh regained consciousness, he was too dizzy for a detailed look at his surroundings. He appeared to be in a barren room which was illuminated by a small lantern. Not seeing anyone else, he wrongly assumed he was alone. As his head cleared, he attempted to move first his hands then his legs realizing he could move neither. *I've been paralyzed? Drugged! I've been drugged.*

While Rajeesh was unconscious, Maksim dragged his body into an equipment storage room on an upper floor of the building across from the bus stop. Using some of the scaffolding material, Maksim created a makeshift rack and bound Rajeesh to it making use of lifting straps which were handy. Even though he secured the man's legs and arms, he did not blindfold or gag his victim, at least not at this point. Now, as Rajeesh began to regain his wits, he became *a delicious feast of fear ready to be served.*

Even though he could not see Maksim, Rajeesh began to verbally plead with him rather than attempting to resist or escape. This was precisely what Maksim expected. *He's offering himself up as a sacrifice to my will.*

"Please, I thought I was helping by telling my friend. You asked me if I knew anyone else, you did not say how to put them in touch with you," Rajeesh spoke to the emptiness hoping Maksim would somehow hear him and at the same time hoping he was alone. "You don't have to do this. You don't even have to pay me; I'll work for you for free. Please, you don't have to do this."

To Maksim, the pleading was part of the spiral down, which eventually led to permanent silence. He was surprised the volume and quantity of the boy's pleas increased so quickly, but then *he's still holding onto hope somewhere deep inside of him.*

Maksim grabbed a bit of torn t-shirt from the ground and stepped purposely towards the Rajeesh from the darkness. His sudden visible appearance caused Rajeesh to immediately go silent but slackjawed. As Maksim stuffed the rag into his victim's mouth, he saw the young man's eyes go wide realizing the only hope left, talking Maksim out of whatever was coming next, now vanished. The only hope left for Rajeesh was minimal pain.

Maksim stepped back for a moment and examined his handiwork. His breathing began to quicken as he physically started to react to the terror he was enjoying from his victim. Maksim reached into his shoulder bag and slowly withdrew a large sheathed knife. While he stared directly at his victim's eyes, he unsnapped the sheath and began to gradually remove the blade. *Could it be? Ah yes – his fear is growing.*

The anxiety caused by his situation overtook Rajeesh, and his mind, still clouded by drugs, was failing to provide him with any logical recourse. When he saw the knife's shimmering silver blade, any remaining control vanished as he began to flail and pull against his bindings in panic, and attempted to scream without result. He felt a sudden urge to vomit but realized if he did so he would likely drown because of the rag stuffed in his mouth. Rajeesh swallowed the acidic bile to suppress his urge to vomit.

Maksim walked back to Rajeesh and slowly began to cut away his clothes, leaving him totally naked, exposed, and vulnerable. He noticed tears were now streaming from the young man's eyes and his body was trembling. *Excellent.* Leaning forward towards his face, Maksim leaned in until Rajeesh could feel his breath on his skin, which caused him to quiver and tightly close his eyes.

"Shhhh," Maksim said as he extended his tongue and slowly licked the tears from Rajeesh's face before retreating. Maksim could feel the arousal rise within his body as his victim cringed and quivered with fear. "Why didn't you listen. You've made all this necessary."

Taking a step back, Maksim moved directly in front of Rajeesh and waited until he opened his eyes. Smiling, he lifted the knife directly in front of the man's face. Once Rajeesh reacted, Maksim quickly lowered the blade and pressed the edge against the man's chest, causing him to respond as if electrocuted. Then, Maksim tilted the blade's angle and shaved a section of hair from the man's body. Upon lifting the blade from his victim's flesh, Rajeesh began to wildly fight against his bindings and attempt to scream again.

Moving his lips to Rajeesh's ear, he whispered, "Don't worry my friend, this blade is so sharp you won't even feel the cut until the blade has long sliced through your flesh," Maksim then moved to the other side of the room and turned out the light pitching the room into sudden darkness. While it would take a few minutes for his eyes to adjust, he knew the darkness would cause a tenfold rise in the alarm his victim was feeling. After first kicking off his sandals to allow greater stealth, he used the shadows for camouflage. Maksim was able to creep back close to Rajeesh. He watched the man desperately turning his head from side to side looking for his tormentor.

While his face was turned in the opposite direction, Maksim lurched forward and sliced the man down the left side of his body from shoulder to waist. He watched as Rajeesh's body went stiff shaking uncontrollably-- surprisingly the man did not scream at all. The only sound was the initial splatter of blood as it hit the concrete floor, then the creaking of the bindings being pulled taught. The smell of the iron from the blood beginning to fill the air drove the arousal within Maksim to a higher intensity.

As he loosened and tightened his grip on the knife, Maksim could feel the stickiness of the blood which sprayed upon it. Then, tightening his grasp, he knelt and sliced the man again, this time from his outer thigh to his knee. Rajeesh's body went stiff as the sound of blood's splatter filled the room followed by the clicking of the bindings as he pulled against them. Using his free hand, Maksim reached forward and ran his hand across the open wound on the man's leg covering his hand with blood. Then he held his hand in front of his face and licked off the crimson wetness.

Maksim was skilled at the delicate art of slicing into another human while leaving them alive until they died from exsanguination. He was unsure how long he went at it, but he knew Rajeesh must have felt it was an eternity. Maksim lost count of the number of cuts he made into the man's body. When he realized the last few did not result in any additional blood flowing onto the floor, his bloodlust finally abated. At some point during the process, Maksim tore off his own clothes, wanting to feel the blood flow upon his bare skin. Once naked and covered in blood he experienced the first of at least two orgasms he remembered enjoying.

Now as he was regaining his composure, reality replaced his unbridled fetishism and the problems his lust created flooded his brain. The severely abused body needed to be dealt with, in such a way to cover its violent end, while preventing even trivial curiosity. *This kill cannot be attributed to Satan.* Equally urgent, was his need to exit the building without being seen in his current blood-soaked state. After turning the lantern on, he pondered these issues as he returned to the scaffolding, where Rajeesh's blood-drained body limply hung. He cut the bindings on the man's limbs and allowed the corpse to fall to the floor. As he observed the crumpled flesh, an epiphany flashed across his brain as to how he might wash the blood off.

Going to the roof, he discovered the building's water tank was already installed. Even though there were no residents, it appeared to have water inside of it. Still holding the knife in his hand, he flipped the emergency release lever on the water tank and was immediately blasted by the hard flow of extremely hot water. Lacking soap, he used his hands to rub his skin and work the congealed blood from his flesh. After several minutes, he felt he was sufficiently free of Rajeesh's blood.

Returning to the storeroom, he sheathed the knife and dropped it into the canvas bag. Since he kicked off his sandals before the cutting began, they were still clean. Looking around the room, he found a thin drop cloth he could fashion into a wrap that would at least let him depart the building without too much notoriety. With his exit taken care of, he set about dealing with the body.

Even though the primary construction material for the building was concrete, there was plenty of lumber lying around, which Maksim gathered and stacked atop Rajeesh's body. While he was collecting lumber, he discovered a can of turpentine, which he now poured over the wood, guaranteeing a quick, hot fire. All he needed now was a delayed heat source to give him time to leave before the building exploded in flame. There was a book of matches in his bag, so all he needed to find was a cigarette butt.

Exiting the building, he knew there would be a location where the workers would gather to smoke. It did not take long before he discovered the smoking area and a butt with quite a bit of smokable material left on it. Returning to the storeroom, he placed the cigarette in his mouth and lit it. Once the ember was glowing, he put the filter end of the cigarette into the book of matches, closed the cover, and placed the poor man's fuse near a spot where the turpentine pooled. With this taken care of, he stashed the lantern in his bag and exited the building. After driving a block or so away, he stopped to observe the result of his efforts.

As expected, the ember of the cigarette continued to burn until it got close enough to the matchheads for the heat to cause them to explode in flame. The flame provided a heat source to ignite the turpentine, which in turn lit the lumber, starting a fast, hot fire. Maksim knew the body would not be obliterated but felt the fire would be hot enough to disfigure it and mask any evidence of what happened earlier.

As he watched the building burn, he was surprised it took the Kuwaiti fire department almost half an hour to arrive. *I guess unoccupied buildings aren't a high priority.* This delay guaranteed there would be no evidence left to prompt an inquiry. After all, anyone who was inside a building still under construction, in the middle of the night, would not have been someone worth worrying about.

*Najila's Villa at Shamal Mazraea*

Najila sat at the table, still in her robe, enjoying a quiet cup of tea before the day began. After two weeks with the American writer, they developed a routine, which was becoming familiar and welcome. She came to appreciate his disciplined approach to her uncle's project, even if she had not begun to understand the man. No matter what they were working on, he found a way to slight her or make her wonder why she accepted this assignment.

For the past two weeks, she did precisely what Evan requested and showed him the entire country in broad strokes. Daily, he would join her in her SUV, and they would head off in a different direction. They were not taking time to explore the villages or settlements they passed through. Instead, it was a windshield tour of the diversity that existed within the 7,000 square miles which made up Kuwait. As they drove, they would talk about the cultures which lived within the country, the tribal nature of the citizens, and how they managed to avoid being a theocracy, while at the same time holding true to their Islamic roots.

"Were you aware there are several Catholic churches in Kuwait? In fact, there are other Christian churches located here as well."

"Really? I'm surprised to hear that. A lot of what we hear in the US about the region has more to do with the intolerance of the more restrictive regimes, rather than more permissive governments," as he said this, Evan withdrew a pen and notebook from one of the then zippered pockets on the side of his Go-bag.

"Possible idea for a story?"

"Maybe. I'm trying to capture things I find of interest as we make this tour so we can look into them with more depth later, in case I think readers might also be interested."

After their first week together, he suggested they establish a Sunday through Wednesday workweek. Evan wanted to keep Thursday set aside for himself as a dedicated writing day. From his past experience the Middle East, he was aware Fridays were the holy day of the week for Muslims, and Saturdays were used for shopping and doing other personal business. Najila was amenable to this arrangement. It gave her time to spend on horseback with her uncle on Thursdays, and Fridays for the family. Saturday, she claimed for herself.

As they began the first day of the third week, she was glad their wanderlust period was over, and they were going to start exploring the country and culture in earnest. Evan was not the only one who was making notes over the past two weeks, although Najila was doing so mentally. Traveling the country from border to border reminded her of so many things she appreciated about her homeland that she wanted to ensure he was aware of. *After all, my uncle didn't say I couldn't gently nudge him towards the best of who and what we are.*

*Penthouse, Hotel Sultana*

Evan's morning was much less relaxing. Over the last two weeks, he was unsuccessful at preventing the round-the-clock incursions into his room by the *valet elves*. Things were continually being done, straightened up, cleaned up, and delivered by these invisible helpers. *They might be well-intentioned, but I don't appreciate the stealth.* The last time he approached Roshan about the matter he was told flatly repeated complaints might lead the hotel to terminate the employees. Evan did not want to cause someone to get fired, he just didn't want them sneaking around. However, this morning took him to the edge.

After he finished showering, he walked from the bathroom naked to the closet to pick out his clothes for the day. After laying out the chosen shirt and pants, he went back into the bathroom to find his fingernail clippers. Upon walking in, he discovered all of his accouterments once again returned to their predesignated spaces. Until now, discoveries like this were a minor irritant, but for some reason this time it triggered a reaction within him which raised his anxiety level to the point where he began to hyperventilate.

Walking back into the bedroom, he sat down on the bed, closed his eyes, and immediately start his guided imagery technique. Mentally he grasped one of the pre-chosen scenarios from his past. His mind took him years into the past and thousands of miles away as he redirected the thought energy which allowed his anxiety to grow instead into recalling every detail of his chosen scene.

His mind took him to a spring day – he was enjoying the feel of sunbeams snaking through the leaves of the large tree he was lying under. The temperature was perfect, and the cloudless sky allowed the sun to cast a brilliant golden light on everything around him. Evan was lying on his back, his head resting in the palms of his hands. Beneath his hands, he could feel the cool blades of grass, which came in contact with his skin. As he stared up through the leaves of the tree, it was as if each leaf and the light peering through was part of a giant mosaic. A slight breeze caused the leaves to shiver, which shattered the static mosaic, turning it into a kaleidoscope thrown into motion. The accents of the twinkling sunlight seemed to turn off and on as the leaves moved.

Even as the visual was becoming more active, he found himself becoming more relaxed, as the muscles in his body began to let go of the tension they were holding. As the leaves settled, they parted, allowing a sunbeam through to dance across his face. He closed his eyes and let the sudden burst of sunlight to warm him. As the light began to move again, he tilted his head back to try to catch it or find a place where it was steadier. Then he felt a shadow deliberately moving across his face until it completely blocked the sun.

Evan's breathing began to slow. When he was finally in full control of his breathing, he allowed the scenario to fade before he opened his eyes. *This shit ends today.*

Upon rising, he quickly dressed and continued with his morning ritual for his regular departure. Gathering his Go-bag, he walked over to the elevator and pushed the button. When the elevator arrived, rather than entering, he leaned and triggered its return to the lobby. As the doors closed, he stepped back into the dark corner beside the elevator and waited in silence. Almost as soon as the door closed, a female figure entered the room and began to gather the coffee pot and cup from the conference table.

"Hello there," Evan said as he stepped out of the shadows scaring the woman so severely she dropped the cup shattering it. The look on her face was one of fear and she was visibly shaking. She was frightened of Evan and the situation she suddenly found herself in.

"Please, don't be afraid. Everything's okay. I think we just need to have a little talk. What is your name?" *Damn, I didn't mean to scare her to death.*

She did not look at him directly, but instead stared at the floor, finally saying "Jazlene."

"Well, Jazlene, my name is Evan. Please, have a seat and let's talk for a minute."

She waited until Evan set his Go-bag on the table and took a seat. Jazlene pulled out one of the chairs and sat down, smoothing her starched uniform once she was seated. He noticed she was not Arab, nor a TCN from somewhere on the Indian subcontinent. Her eyes and thin, small build told him she was probably a Pacific Islander. *Filipino?*

"Jazlene? Such a pretty name," Evan hoped distracting her might also calm her.

"My parents could not decide between Jazlyn and Jolene, so they took Jaz, from Jazlyn and lene, from Jolene." *Why am I telling him about this?*

"A great idea to combine them. I want to tell you how much I appreciate all of the things you have been doing for me every day since I arrived," As he said this, he watched her shoulders begin to relax; her eyes finally go from staring at the floor to meet his. *Nice start, now I need to find a way to tell her not to do what she was told to do by her boss?* "I know you've been told I am some sort of important man who needs to be taken care of in a particular way."

Jazlene nodded, *it is precisely what I was told.*

"Well, that's not really true. I'm just a regular person, and while I need some things taken care of, most of them can wait until after I've left or can be taken care of while I am here without you sneaking around."

A look of both concern and confusion crossed Jazlene's face. All of the training and instruction she received for this job stressed she was not to be seen, heard, or noticed. Things were to be taken care of as quickly as possible while she remained completely invisible. *Now, this man wants me to do things differently. But he's so important. What do I do?*

A question crossed Evan's mind as he watched her reaction to his last statement, "Tell me, Jazlene, how exactly are you getting in and out of the room without me seeing you?"

Aside from her instructions regarding stealth, she knew she was supposed to answer any questions from a guest completely. She stood and paused for a moment to let Evan know he was to follow her. Then she walked into the bedroom and over to the far wall where she pressed on the panel. When Jazlene moved her hand, the panel popped open revealing a small room behind it. Turning towards him, she pointed at the now open secret space.

Walking over to it and glancing inside, Evan saw the space behind the panel was just large enough for a person to sit on the folding chair which was secreted there. *Was she really always here? And in the dark?* The thought appalled him, *how could the management of the hotel treat her so shabbily* and also eerily aware *she's been watching me continuously.*

"Okay," he still wasn't sure what he was going to say to her, but he would have to gauge his words by how she reacted, "From now on, you don't hide in there anymore," pointing at the cubbyhole.

"But sir," she began to plead in thickly accented English.

"No, it's not what I want you to do. Aren't you supposed to do what the guest wants?"

Jazlene nodded slowly, still not sure how she was supposed to balance what he was asking for, with what she was told.

"From now on, while I'm in the room you can stay in the other bedroom unless I call you out for something. Of course, when I leave the room you can come out and do whatever needs to be done. Also, if I'm not in the room you can feel free to hang out anywhere you want to." At some point, she stopped nodding along with his instructions, so Evan paused for a minute and looked at her directly. *I need to make sure she understands*, "You don't need to hide from me. Do you understand?"

Jazlene heard from friends many things were demanded of valet maids like herself, to include orders for sex and performance of other illegal activity. *This man requires less than what my duties demand.* She nodded even though she was confused.

"Fine. Just make sure you understand. Starting now, you no longer have to stay in the niche, and you no longer have to hide from me. If I'm in the room and I'm getting dressed or doing something elsewhere it looks like I want privacy, you can stay in the other bedroom or ask me. Are we clear?"

Hearing it restated, did indeed make it clear to Jazlene and she nodded with less hesitation, "Yes, sir."

Evan smiled at her, trying to signal his own benevolence. Realizing Najila would be waiting for him downstairs, Evan walked back into the sitting room and picked up his Go-bag, as he headed toward the elevator. Jazlene followed him.

"I should be gone most of the day, but when I get back would it be possible for us to speak again?"

For the first time, she smiled at him, "As you wish."

Without saying another word, Evan pushed the button, stepping into the elevator when it arrived. Turning around as the door closed, he saw she was still standing at attention as he left. *Well, at least that's better than her hiding in a crypt in the dark.*

Jefzar Al Bourisli did not join law enforcement, like so many others, because he wanted a position of power. He wanted to be a detective. Growing up, he discovered Sherlock Holmes, Hercule Poirot, and Philip Marlowe, both on the page and on the screen. They taught him observing the smallest detail was how a good detective could eventually figure out exactly how something happened. Doing so might also lead you to the other goal of the detective: determining a perpetrator's motivation.

Jefzar was selected to attend the British Police Academy, and once he graduated, with honors, he went on to participate in several crime investigation seminars provided by other Middle Eastern nations, as well as the United States. As a result, his law enforcement education was among the best in Kuwait and led him to rise quickly within the ranks of the police force. However, the rise was so fast he went from being a patrolman directly into leadership; it skipped his original goal of being a detective. As time passed, he managed to arrange a transition plan which would place him in the ranks of detectives, but then the Gulf War happened. Once it was over, the decimation of police ranks due to fatalities and self-exile pushed him into an un-sought Sector Chief position.

Being a man of duty, he accepted the position and forever put his dreams of being a detective away. However, many of his officers knew he was always on the lookout for interesting crimes, which might call upon his skills of deduction and reasoning to solve. But not today, today he sat at his desk, doing the paperwork that kept the wheels turning. Jefzar was validating entries in the Big Book against the individual handwritten folders.

The Big Book measured 80cm long by 45cm wide and was 10cm thick. The leather-bound ledger was a tool left over from the protectorate days under the British, and it was presumed the almost 1,000 pages in the book would be sufficient to last a full year. Each page in the book possessed columns for date, time of day, crime committed, etcetera, but no horizontal lines, allowing for each crime's entry to be as long as necessary. This characteristic was a lasting similarity between it and the British ship's log, after which it was initially patterned. The Big Book was meant to be the single repository for all crimes, and due to its size and weight, over the years it gained its own human carrier, who shuffled it from office to office within the police headquarters as needed.

From the time Jefzar came into the department, he wanted to get rid of the Big Book and introduce a computerized database of information, but no one was willing to entertain the change. So, law enforcement was forced to continue with a single shared book with all the information for the sector inside. Because of the time and effort spent moving it from place to place, Jefzar decided early on he was only going to deal with the Big Book once a week, rather than daily.

As he started his workweek, he sat with a pile of files to his left, which he signed as he verified the information entered in the Big Book. An arduous task, which required no ability whatsoever, other than the ability to compare one to the other to ensure both were identical. As he went through the files, which were in time/date sequence, he noticed something unusual.

Within the past week, there were two deaths which were ruled suicide, one leaped from the top floor of a building while the other died from a self-inflicted shotgun wound. *Unusual to have multiple suicides in a single week.* Jefzar opened and reviewed both files and noticed the victims were both professional TCNs who worked as skilled technicians in government jobs. *Not the usual suicides.*

His curiosity was raised, and he wondered if he might be looking at some sort of trend, so he flipped the Big Book to the week before. *No suicides, but a pair of traffic fatalities and a victim whose throat was slashed.* The

Book listed the latter as a possible murder. *Possible? How exactly does one slash his own throat, or accidentally cut the throat of another?* All three victims were listed as being TCNs who held government jobs. Jefzar felt a sudden thrill at the possibility of discovering a pattern. *Five deaths in two weeks?*

He made a note of the file numbers for the three earlier incidents then completed his paperwork within the Big Book. After withdrawing the two suicide files from the current week's stack, Jefzar called out for the Book's handler to come to get the tome and the remaining files. As the handler was about to depart Jefzar's office, the Chief handed him the file numbers he had written down and told him to have his secretary retrieve the files. Sitting back in his chair, he reached out his hand and patted the two folders that remained on his desk. *Probably nothing, but it might be something.* Opening his center desk drawer, he withdrew a pack of cigarettes and lit one, pulling the smoke deep into his lungs. His wife was after him to quit, but today was not the day.

*Hotel Sultana*

After making a quick stop at the restaurant, Evan proceeded out the front door of the Hotel Sultana and found Najila parked there in her black SUV. Once he inside the vehicle, rather than placing his Go-bag between the two of them, he set it on the floor by his feet then slipped an insulated cup into the cup holder in the center console.

"Decided to take a coffee to go?"

"No, I noticed whenever we eat a meal at the hotel if you don't order tea, you would order pomegranate juice. I thought I would bring you some for the road."

"As you say, it is indeed my favorite. Thank you very much. This so thoughtful," *So, Evan was paying attention. Not only that, he is trying to be nice; an excellent start to the week.* Najila lifted the cup out of its holder and took a drink to show her immediate appreciation for Evan's effort. Upon placing the cup back in the holder, she dropped the SUV into gear and headed out from the hotel. Najila turned onto the highway and headed past the refinery.

"I looked over my maps and realized we have covered almost all of the public paved roads in the country, except for a few leading to restricted areas."

"Restricted areas?"

"Yes, both Kuwaiti and United States military bases are restricted from general public access."

"Oh. I guess I can understand the need."

"It wasn't always that way, before Saddam's invasion they were completely open to anyone. But ever since, many strategic areas, like the KOC refineries, and the Greater Burgan oil field, are now closed without proper identification."

"Yeah, it's not unusual. Probably a good idea for security. By the way, I delivered my first article to your uncle yesterday."

"Really? You didn't tell me you plan on doing so, I could've done it for you."

"No problem, it was just 1,500 words or so on some of the history of the country. It was good to see Hamad again, he's such a nice guy."

"As you say, he is well respected and truly tries to embody the concepts of being every man's brother." After a moment she added, "I love my uncle."

Evan nodded, recalling the events of the day before.

He called Hamad Friday evening to tell him he completed the first story and needed to deliver it to him before sending it on to Arlen.

"Wonderful news, were you going to email it to me?"

"Um, no. Actually, I wanted to deliver it to you in the morning so we could talk about a few things if you don't mind."

"Ah, I see. I will send Roshan to pick you up, I am currently at *Rihlat Alsahra'*."

"No need, I'd like to attempt to drive out there myself, if it would be okay. This way, I will know how to get there on my own for times when it proves necessary."

"Curious, but completely acceptable. Have you been provided directions?"

"Yes, and I have a GPS to help me get there."

"Wonderful, I'll see you in the morning."

The following morning, Evan obtained one of the hotel's luxury SUVs and drove to *Rihlat Alsahra'*. He was thankful the GPS continually assure him he was on the right path, even though he did not appear to be on any path.

Upon arrival, Hamad greeted him leading Evan into the *diwaniya* for refreshment and talk. After a brief discussion of family status, Evan handed Hamad the first of many articles he was required to produce over the next six months. As Evan watched, Hamad withdrew reading glasses from a pocket within his *dishdasha* before he glanced over the article without reading it in depth. He then looked up at Evan as if wanting his approval to read the article immediately.

"Please, go ahead. Let me know what you think," as Evan said this he leaned forward and took one of the dates from the omnipresent fruit platter gracing the center table.

The article was meant to lure readers in for the rest of the series, even though each column could be read separately. This one gave a brief history of Kuwait and the events leading to its present status in the world. Evan watched for changes in Hamad's expression as he read the words. As Evan watched Hamad, he noticed once again the man was fiddling with his worry beads while he read the document. Looking up, Hamad nodded at Evan as he flipped from the first to the second. After finishing the third page, Hamad removed his glasses and smiled broadly at Evan tightly holding the pages in his hand.

"Exactly! You've managed in just a few words to cover the country's birth, adolescence, and growth into maturity."

"Thank you, I was hoping by providing a little background it would make the rest of the articles more accessible."

"Indeed, you've done this. I think you've successfully whetted the reader's appetite for more."

"Thank you so much for saying so. I'm glad I'm on the right track."

"Yes, and I'm so pleased you decided to deliver this in person, even though email probably would've been easier for you."

"No problem, I wanted to get your reaction and feedback firsthand," *Well, now that he's happy with me, it's a good time to ask.* "I also wanted to ask a favor."

"Favor?"

"Your niece, Najila…"

Hamad stopped playing with his *tasbih* and slipped it into his pocket as he leaned forward toward Evan. "Now, now. Just like in America, an uncle may be a protector of his niece but only has so much influence over her. If this favor is about Najila, you'll need to speak with her directly."

"Uh no, it's not really about her. The first day we met, she brought me to *Rihlat Alsahra'* so we could go riding in the desert." *Interesting, he allows his niece to make her own decisions without his influence.*

Hamad shifted his position and leaned back against the pillows behind him, trying to stifle a laugh. Naveed told him of the American's attempt to ride and how he was thrown from the horse.

"Indeed, I was told about the misadventure. But was pleased to hear you attempted to get right back on the horse after being thrown."

"Yes, but I think it may have had more to do with my stubbornness than the desire to ride."

"Perhaps, and if it were just your stubbornness, it would explain why you didn't attempt to ride a third time." Noticing the curiosity crossing Evan's face, Hamad continued, "Did you know within Abrahamic faiths, Allah often requires three repetitions from the faithful?"

Evan shook his head.

"In Islam, *wudu* requires the washing of each body part three times, many prayers are repeated three times, and the word *talaq* is repeated three times to formalize a divorce." Hamad adjusted his position, leaning forward and assuming the role of teacher to Evan's role of student.

"Even Christianity many things are based on the number three: the cock crowed three times, Father Son and Holy Ghost, and even the three crosses on the hill during the crucifixion of Jesus, Peace be Upon Him."

Evan found himself considering Hamad's words, as he started to put together the significance of the number three throughout his own spiritual life.

"I understand Rabbis turn away converts three times before accepting their request for conversion. Three is such a vital part of our life, and it has been provided by Allah. We owe him at least as much effort in all we attempt."

"You're saying on my third attempt, Allah might've given me a different outcome?" Evan maintained a poker face while asking this, as replays of every "two try" event in his life ran through his mind.

"Can you say with certainty he wouldn't?"

*You can't fight basic logic. Every time I converse with this man, I see more and more why he is called the Wise One.*

"With that in mind, we'll try this once again, and we'll start with you communicating with the horse."

"I'm required to learn to speak horse?"

Hamad laughed in response, "No my friend, we need a horse which speaks English."

Evan was brought back to the present when, after almost two hours on the highway, Najila was taking an unmarked exit to a smaller side road. Over the past two weeks, he learned asking where they were going usually only led to more questions. Now, he just sat and watched the scenery pass by and waited for arrival at the destination.

Watching the pride Najila displayed while showing him her country was a bit awe-inspiring. She was knowledgeable, and even though not everything he was seeing was positive, she highlighted the positive about the direction the nation was taking. Her optimism was contagious. He also learned that, by withholding comment, she would sometimes reveal a bit more of herself while trying to fill the silence.

She told him how she came to live with her uncle and aunt after the Gulf War, which led to her brief career with him, and eventual education in the United States. He could only imagine how difficult losing your family in a warzone could be, but at least she was part of an extended family, which not only stepped up but also loved and supported her. In the worst of situations, it was not an adverse outcome.

After another hour on the side road, Najila slowed the SUV and pulled off. Evan looked through the windows and saw nothing except for a small stand of trees off to the side of the road. He looked over at her awaiting an explanation.

While keeping her hands on the steering wheel, she pointed in front of them by lifting a single finger.

"Just up ahead is a US military base, of course, we can't get in, so there's no need in going there."

"Okay." *So why did we stop here?*

"Kuwait has never been a standard tourist destination for Westerners, so when the base was first established, there were many things Kuwaitis take for granted which US troops found fascinating. Like camels."

As if on cue, an old man dressed in desert robes stepped from behind the small stand of trees where he was sitting in the shade. Moments later the camel on the other end of the rope he was pulling appeared. The old man heard the SUV approach and stop, so thinking it was a group of GIs, he came out to ply his trade. Even though the spot was unmarked, it was a well-known landmark among American soldiers as the place to go to have your picture taken while riding a camel.

"Have you ever seen one up close?"

"Uh, no. Is it true camels spit at you if you get too close?"

Najila giggled, "It is true of some of them. I told you most Arabian beasts tend to have a strong spirit."

"Wonderful."

They both exited the vehicle and walked toward the old man.

"Five-minute ride, five American dollars." The old man's voice was thickly accented and hoarse. As he spoke, he revealed a distinct lack of teeth. He held his open palm with spread fingers toward them to emphasis five.

Najila spoke to the man in Arabic, and after several exchanges, she turned to Evan motioning him toward the camel.

"I told him you were a close friend of *Al Hakim*, so he is going to let you ride *gratis*."

"You know, the last time I tried to ride something in this country, it didn't turn out well."

"As you say, but aren't you willing to take another chance?"

*But this is something new, so I may have to get thrown off three times.* Even though she was wearing sunglasses, Evan could imagine her eyes sparkling as she spoke the words.

"Fine"

As Evan walked toward the camel, the old man had the camel kneel so it could be boarded. Once Evan was in the saddle, the old man tapped the animal on its flanks causing it to rise to its feet. Najila was using her phone to take pictures of Evan on the camel as the old man led the animal around a well-worn path. As the trio rounded the track and was close to Najila, Evan spoke to her, "This is a very bumpy ride."

"Yes, as you say, the camel has a unique gait. It moves both legs on the same side and at the same time, as it moves forward. You are continually being tossed from side to side, unlike a horse."

"I'll say."

Najila laughed out loud, as she watched them go further down the path and out of earshot.

When the ride was done, the old man again directed the camel to kneel so Evan could get off. He took a moment to shake the man's hand.

"Do you think he would mind answering a few questions?"

Najila spoke to the old man in Arabic, and he replied shaking his head and pointing towards the horizon. She nodded turning to Evan.

"He says he has no time today; he needs to get back to his camp for lunch. Maybe tomorrow."

After Najila translated, the old man bowed his head toward Evan and turned to depart. As he led the camel away, Evan used one of the few Arabic phrases he knew *shukraan lakum*, which caused the old man to turn and wave before walking away.

As they walked back to the SUV, Najila asked Evan where he learned Arabic.

"In my travels, I've learned you should always enter a country with at least a few phrases in your pocket: Hello, thank you, please, etcetera. In fact, I know how to find a bathroom in at least six different languages."

"It never hurts to know where to find a bathroom." *Maybe there's more to this man that I first thought.*

When they were back inside the SUV, Najila made a U-turn and headed back to the main highway.

As they were riding into the city, Evan withdrew his notepad from his Go-bag to record a few thoughts. Since the old man did not have time for an interview, he thought Najila might be able to provide some details.

"Was the camel handler a *Bedouin?*"

"Quite likely. I told you before the *Bedouins* are quite resourceful. At some point, some American probably offered him some money to pose with his camel or for a quick ride. Realizing he could make a few dinars providing the service, the camel-herd positioned himself where the customers were."

"Simple, but ingenious."

"As you say."

Because the journey to the base and back was so time-consuming, Evan called it an early day and asked to be taken directly back to the hotel. As they were driving back, Najila turned on the radio and moved her lips as she silently sang along with the music. Evan found himself stealing side-glances at Najila as she did this. Up to this point, he considered his association with her functional. She was his guide and nothing more. But now, by the end of the drive, he decided there was a feminine side to her, which was mentally and physically attractive.

# Chapter 7



Amr paused for a moment and leaned on the broom he was using to sweep up the stable. He completed almost a third of the time he owed *Al Hakim* but, in those weeks, he found the spiritual satisfaction of labor. His parents wanted to provide for him a privileged life, where he was not weighed down by menial tasks. Unintentionally, this led Amr to a mindset where he was above both the labor, and the people who served him. It also robbed him of the joy that could be found in accomplishing a job yourself. In the end, his behavior was that of a spoiled brat who spent his time searching for fulfillment in the degradation of others.

Amr's parents immediately paid the monetary fine which *Al Hakim* imposed; therefore, it had little impact or effect on him directly. But the labor portion of his penance rested directly upon his shoulders and thus a direct impact on him and his personality going forward.

The labor penalty might have a multiplier effect on the wrong side of Amr's nature if the servitude was nothing more than busywork. But Hamad saw to it the chores given to the young man were those that allowed him personal pride in his accomplishments. Every job given and completed correctly also led to praise and a sense of fulfillment. As a result, Amr's attitude and viewpoint were slowly changing and becoming more positive.

In a society accustomed to the rich getting out of legal difficulties by paying victims blood money in exchange for their forgiveness, Hamad was reverting back to penalties being taken in sweat from the guilty. As the fine was being paid, other changes began to occur.

While he worked, Amr got to know his fellow laborers. It was the first time he ever held a conversation with a TCN, and he came to know them as fellow human beings. His attitude toward them changed, and even interactions with the laborers in his home shifted. The change was gradual and was being noticed by those around him, including his parents.

"Amr," Hamad said startling the young man from his daydream. "I hear from trainers you would like to move on to something more complicated than sweeping."

"If it would be allowable, *Al Hakim*. After spending time working around these beautiful animals, I would like the chance to be able to work with them more directly."

Hamad nodded thoughtfully as he considered Amr's proposal. Withdrawing his *tasbih* from his pocket, he began to work his way through the beads as he pondered the situation. It was not lost upon him the young man was asking to be allowed to work with animals when it was cruelty to an animal that brought him here in the first place. But as he watched Amr, Hamad realized the prior act was less one of cruelty and more one of boredom and power seeking.

"Allah teaches us a man is capable of significant internal change and growth. Therefore, we must be willing to forgive. I will speak to Naveed and see what he might need help with, for which you would be best suited."

"Thank you, *Al Hakim*, I appreciate your consideration of this, and I appreciate your faith in me."

Resting his hand on Amr's shoulder, Hamad looked directly into the young man's eyes and said, "Your sincere efforts have earned both my faith and consideration. Keep up the good work."

Amr was not sure what to say, so he just nodded and went back to work sweeping the stable floor. *Al Hakim believes in me. Truly something to be proud of.*

Hamad was leaving the stable when he turned at the door and watched Amr work. The scene made him recall the first day Khaled started to work in the stables the day after he graduated.

His son insisted upon transporting himself to work, but Hamad could not resist the urge to stop by the stable to see how he was getting on. As he stood in the doorway, he saw Khaled with a broom and shovel in hand beginning to clean one of the empty paddocks. As Hamad watched his son, he was proud he raised such an amazing young man. Even though he was born to a higher station, he chose to start his work life here and earn his way to his destiny.

Hamad turned and left the stable, walking back toward his *diwaniya* and a scheduled meeting, which was to take place in a few moments. Hearing a sound behind him, he turned to find his son standing there with a wrapped box in his outstretched hand.

"*Baba*, I meant to give you this last night as a thank you but could never find an appropriate time."

"A thank you?"

"For supporting me through my years of school and getting me started here."

Hamad took the small box and tearing into the wrapping paper opened it to reveal a *tasbih* nestled in tissue paper. As he withdrew the prayer beads and held them in his hand, he looked closely and found they were singularly unique. Rather than being made of a single material, each of the three sections of 11 beads was made of a different material. One section was blue amber, another black coral, and the third of natural pearls. Both of the dividing beads were made from mahogany. The handle piece was made of ornately carved ivory with the three beads hanging from the tail matching the material for each of the three sections.

Hamad was never one to carry a *tasbih*. While he would never speak against anyone who did, he felt the item was little more than a socially endorsed nervous habit. He saw hundreds of different styles of *tasbih* throughout his life, but never a set quite like these.

"I made this for you myself, picking the beads a few at a time as I earned money to buy them at the *souk*. These beads," Khaled said as he pointed to the mahogany divider beads, "I carved myself from small blocks of wood."

Khaled was apprehensive, his father was utterly silent as he stood looking at the *tasbih*. *He doesn't seem to like it, have I somehow insulted him by giving him such a personal item?*

Hamad dropped the box to the ground, while still holding onto the beads with his hand, then he reached out and grabbed his son by the shoulders pulling him close in a tight embrace. It was not unusual for Hamad to hug his son, but this time it was done to hide the tears welling in his eyes from being humbled that his son would honor him with such a wondrous gift.

"My son, my son. Such a wonderful gift. Thank you, I will carry them with me always."

Khaled placed his arms around his father, to return his embrace and they stood there together sharing the moment.

"Now, you do not want Naveed to scold you for wandering away on the first day. Get back to work." As he said this, Hamad broke the embrace and allowed his son to return to the stable. Watching him go, Hamad flipped the *tasbih* in his hand a few times before placing it into his pocket where it could be found from that day forward.

With his reminiscence fading, Hamad felt a tear running down his cheek as he patted the *tasbih*, which was ensconced his pocket. He then turned and left Amr to his duties.

*Meeting Tent in Al Jahra*

Talal rose from his chair and raised his hands in reaction to the cacophony of voices that burst out as the discussion turned to the Caliph Kinship. He was tired of continually fighting back the younger men within the group who saw the Kinship as salvation. Talal knew better; such an alliance would lead to nothing more than a change of masters, for as soon as the Kinship was in control they would immediately shift from friendship to dominance. He heard from friends elsewhere in the region about how the group operated in their countries, as the Kinship shifted to imposing a theocracy on the population.

"My friends, I know what it is like to have growing impatience while waiting for change which seems to never arrive. But we must guard against sacrificing our future to achieve a change today. We all hear the Caliph Kinship promises change, but at the same time are they offering us leadership opportunities within the organization? Are they accepting inputs from us on what the future will look like, or are they dictating it?" With the opposing voices settling down and listening, Talal pushed things further by calling out his primary concern, "Are they doing anything more than using our own faith against us, to demand our participation in a revolution of their design as opposed to our own?"

The room again exploded in a blur of voices each competing with each other for control of the conversation.

Talal fell back into his chair and buried his face in his palms. *We'll never be taken seriously until we stop fighting amongst ourselves long enough to speak with a single voice to demand our place in this society. As long as we are fighting amongst ourselves like this, we will never unite.* Even with their own population being killed indiscriminately, they could not stop the infighting long enough to come together. *No one seemed worried in the least about the deaths of TCNs or Bedoons.* Talal risked much being here, and he began to question the wisdom of what he was doing, with the risk so high.

The separation of social groups within Kuwait made it possible for him to assume this role within the realm of the *Bedoon* while continuing his covert role as a TCN which he had lived for decades. No one from one group would ever encounter the other daily, it was extremely rare the two even interacted. It always seemed to him remarkable a native-born Kuwaiti would hold a place lower in the caste strata than a TCN. *But such is the life I lead.*

In addition to the usual exchanges between arguing factions, Talal was also troubled by the fact his son Nassar did not return to the meetings. Weeks passed since he heard from his son, and he was not quite sure what to make of it.

Maksim was wearing a *dishdasha*, but instead of wearing a *gutra* he wore a crocheted *kufi* on his head. He found the *kufi* to be a better choice while driving because the crocheted beanie did not affect his peripheral vision. He took off his sunglasses and looked into the rearview mirror at his reflection. His eyes were clear, but due to the amount of dust in the air today he felt them burn and expected them to be bloodshot. Looking into his own eyes for a moment, he reflected on his soul.

The SVR created in him an ideal killing machine. Ideally suited for the *wetwork* the organization needed to have accomplished in a flawless manner and without question. Strangely, Maksim never had an issue with any assignment he was ever given. It was only when he saw the end to what he was accustomed, that Maksim began to look beyond the SVR, for something which would allow him to continue the work he enjoyed. His lips drew back in an involuntary snarl revealing his teeth before he refocused his eyes on the road ahead of him. Maksim put the sunglasses back on and peered through the windshield looking for his next victim.

Before leaving his apartment this morning, he packed a cache of sports equipment into his trunk. After being in Kuwait for a short period, he saw that a soccer ball could serve as a great icebreaker between strangers. Having such equipment readily available, allowed him to take advantage of such an opening, which might lead him to his next target.

It was not uncommon for sociopaths to have a particular victim type on which they concentrated. Some would pursue only women with specific hair color or people of a particular age group. Because there was usually a clandestine political agenda behind Maksim's killings, no such definable pattern would ever be found. As a result, throughout his life, his psychopathy led him to find sexual pleasure through the act of killing, rather than the victim. This assignment, however, was pointing him in a different direction, as each killing was designed to fit a particular pattern rather than avoiding one. *Now, I need an actual Kuwaiti.*

He turned off of Six Ring Road, and into one of the neighborhoods without noticing its name. After completing the exit, he turned onto the first available side street, into what appeared to be a residential area, with side-by-side houses. He slowed his speed not only to avoid the jostling from the ever-present speed bumps, but also so he could observe his new hunting ground.

It was late afternoon, and still devilishly hot, so there were few pedestrians on the sidewalks. As Maksim passed the few who were there, they were attentive to the sound of his automobile as it approached from behind. *Perhaps it is too early for hunting. Drawing attention means creating a memory.* Rather than risk discovery, Maksim exited the housing area and was working his way back to the highway. *When the sun goes down, I'll come back.* Then, his eye caught a figure walking across the vacant lot. He turned onto the worn path that crossed the lot and drove toward the person he saw walking there.

"*As-salamu alaykum,*" Maksim said through the open window once he pulled alongside the figure. The man appeared to be in his mid-20s and was dressed in a *dishdasha* and *gutra*.

"*Wa `alaykum as-salâm,*" Fehaid responded as he leaned down to look directly at Maksim. His body language told Maksim he was guarded and suspicious.

Maksim continued in Arabic, "My friend, I hope you can help me. I was looking for a coffee shop that is supposed to be in this neighborhood. I was supposed to meet a cousin there. Perhaps you know of it?"

Fehaid relaxed a bit before he responded, "I'm not sure, I'm not from here myself, I was just visiting with a friend, and I'm on my way home."

Maksim looked at his wristwatch, then toward his prospective victim, "I am so late now it does not matter anymore, I guess. Perhaps I could offer you a ride home, my friend?"

Fehaid took only a moment to decide. He could feel the cold air coming from inside the car and sitting in the air conditioning for a ride home was much better than walking. He walked to the opposite side of the car and got in. Once they were moving, Fehaid told Maksim his Hawalli address.

Maksim purposely took a circuitous route toward Fehaid's home. As they drove, he struck up a conversation with the young man attempting to reassure Fehaid he was an actual Kuwaiti and not a non-native. During the discussion, Maksim came to understand the young man worked in a customer service center for a local company, which was owned by another of his relatives. Not unusual for a society based on nepotism and *wasta*.

Maksim purposely took a turn through a neighborhood that was only partially occupied due to ongoing construction. He knew at the end of the block was a large open field which would serve his purpose nicely. As he drove, he shifted the conversation from Fehaid to sports, and discovered the young man's deep interest in cricket.

"I played while I was at university, I was quite good and almost became a professional player." As Fehaid said this, Maksim realized any remaining apprehension the young man might have felt was gone and he was relaxed and ready.

Maksim slowed and parked the car on the street in front of the open field.

"You know, I just happen to have wickets, a bat, and gloves in the trunk. Perhaps a quick demonstration of your skills? I've been looking for fellow cricket enthusiasts to form a league."

It struck Fehaid that such a proposal seemed a little odd, but then he would never pass up a chance to demonstrate his skills. Upon opening the trunk, Fehaid was delighted to see the variety of sports equipment revealed there. They gathered the needed items and headed toward the center of the field. Once there, both men dropped their loads, and Maksim told Fehaid to position the wickets so he could drive them into the ground.

As Fehaid held the wicket in his hand, he looked toward Maksim who was using the cricket bat to hammer the staves. For a split second, the expression on Maksim's face surprised Fehaid as it turned from friendly into a sneer as the bat came down. Instead of driving the wicket into the ground, it curved, and the bat's edge struck Fehaid square in the face breaking his nose and front teeth as it knocked him backward onto the ground unconscious.

As Maksim stood above Fehaid's body, he looked around to see if anyone was observing them. After he was sure they were alone and unobserved, he proceeded to make several quick strikes with the bat, breaking Fehaid's arms in two places before breaking both of his legs. He then made several more hits on the center mass of the young man's body, shattering his ribs and pulverizing his internal organs. Fehaid was probably already dead when Maksim drove the bat into the top of his skull several times turning it quickly to pulp.

Maksim stood above the corpse panting, sweat pouring down his body from the effort. He found himself wholly disappointed he did not feel his usual surge of sexual arousal during the killing. *Maybe the heat and the physical exertion kept me from it.* He knelt down and gently ran his hand over the side of Fehaid's face.

Maksim was careful not to damage the young man's face because he wanted him to be recognized easily. Except for the initial blow which broke Fehaid's nose and teeth, his face was untouched. Maksim allowed himself to run his hand down his victim's torso and by doing so he could feel the broken bones below the surface as the body began to bloat from internal bleeding. While he stroked the body, he also observed the odd angles of the broken legs and arms. As he admired his workmanship, he felt a stirring and arousal as his own body physically reacted to the carnage in front of him. *Ah, there it is…*

*Hotel Sultana*

As Najila sat in the SUV, she looked over at Evan who insisted on driving today. While she sat in the passenger seat, Najila found herself taking stock of this man she had been working with for the last month.

At first, she did not much care for him, as he seemed to possess much of the arrogance she despised in many Americans she encountered in the past. But after a while, she realized what she first took for arrogance was merely a lack of knowledge about her culture and country. Once things were explained to him, he quickly adapted to the new information and adjusted his viewpoints accordingly.

She also noticed he didn't ask questions just to provide his opinion but instead was earnestly interested in what he was asking about. Evan repeatedly insisted he was a writer and not a journalist, but based on her observation he possessed a natural talent for finding the true story underneath what could be immediately seen at first glance. He never accepted first impressions as the whole story, and wanted to know everything that surrounded what he was seeing. This type of behavior caused her to want to accept him, rather than finding his presence immediately objectionable.

As she looked at him today, she found herself not immediately averse to his presence. Then, without it even occurring to her, she found herself staring at him with a more primitive eye. *I know he's older, but still — he has kind eyes and the lines around them don't show age, they're the evidence of many smiles. His lips…*

"Najila? Where am I supposed to turn? You said you had something special in mind for today."

Najila immediately sat up straight in her seat and took a quick glance around to determine exactly where they were. Upon getting her bearings, she extended a finger toward the windshield.

"Just up ahead there, turn left and then immediately right when you get inside the neighborhood."

Evan was used to the way the streets were laid out within the city. There was a definite logic to the way the numbering sequences were done in Kuwait. It made it easy to find specific locations, as long as you possessed the full address of where you were headed. However, if you lacked any of the details, you could quickly find yourself hopelessly lost.

This was only the second time Evan drove with Najila as a passenger. On his days off, and in the evenings after their day ended,

Evan was exploring the country on his own using one of the Sultana's loaner vehicles. In addition to needing to get to *Rihlat Alsahra'* for horsemanship lessons, he was trying to become comfortable in his new surroundings. To Evan, it meant exploring the territory in and around where he lived, and gradually expanding the exploration to the points beyond. In doing this, he discovered much of Kuwait came alive at night, when the sun went down, and the heat began to abate. In some ways, it was two different worlds.

"You mentioned you were in the Air Force and took part in the Gulf War, even though you weren't in Kuwait. Tell me, what did you hear about Kuwaitis during the war?"

This was not going to be an easy conversation. Evan's memories of what he was told back then about her countrymen were not at all favorable. There was no way to sugarcoat the stories of cowardice and weakness when confronted by the Iraqis. The minute the invasion began, the Kuwaiti Air Force took off and rather than engaging the enemy — ran. The royal family, as well as the rich and powerful of Kuwait, escaped to Saudi Arabia. The entire country fell within hours. Now somewhat familiar with the locale, Evan realized how easy an invasion would be, and how a protracted war against overwhelming odds would've only served to destroy the country itself.

Evan's lack of response confirmed what Najila assumed about his perception of Kuwaitis during the war. So, rather than letting the uncomfortable silence persist she decided to let him off the hook.

"Let me guess, you heard as soon as the Iraqi's crossed into Kuwait the entire military retreated rather than fighting. Then, they allowed the Iraqi's to occupy the country without resistance for six months while the rest of the world flew in to mount an invasion," Najila paused to allow Evan to react.

"Pretty much that's what we heard in the West, but after being here, I wonder if there was not more to it."

"As you say, there was much more to it. Did you know there were Kuwaitis within the country who formed a resistance and fought the Iraqi's daily during the occupation?"

"No, I never heard about that."

"Yes, and also in the hours before the initial invasion for the liberation of Kuwait, a group of resistance fighters bravely stood for a last stand of sorts using rifles and hand grenades against Iraqi tanks during the *Battle of Al-Qurain*. The battle started as a result of an accidental discovery, but it quickly escalated when the Iraqis realized who they were fighting against. While pillaging from unarmed civilians in their homes, they accidentally happened upon the operations center for the *Al Messilah Group*. The group was responsible for blowing up vast quantities of Iraqi supplies and troop convoys."

"Sounds kind of like the French resistance during World War II."

"Exactly! With most of our country's leadership in exile, and only a smattering of people with military experience left behind, citizens began to form an internal resistance movement, which grew as news of an external liberation effort spread. Their mission was to ensure every day that Iraq held on to our nation would be costly. Turn left here."

She instructed him to turn into what seemed to be a now-familiar middle-class neighborhood filled with single-family homes, each separated by chest-high walls. Every so often, they would encounter overly tall speedbumps meant to prevent speeding through the residential area.

When it was apparent another turn was not imminent, Evan let his mind drift to thoughts of the almost sensual tone of Najila's voice. Having listened to her speech for the last few weeks, he was beginning to find a certain sexiness in her accent.

"Let me back up and explain the situation as it existed. You see, the Iraqi occupiers were cruel and barbaric. They were under strict orders to steal anything of value and return it to Iraq as seized spoils of war. Of particular interest were scientific and medical devices. Iraq did not have access to them due to the economic embargo they had been under."

"I remember seeing news reports about Kuwaiti babies being removed from incubators and left to die while Iraqi troops stole the devices to ship to their homeland."

"As you say, the entire period was heartless and cruel. Also, the troops were under orders to shoot anyone who displayed any kind of resistance, and houses which displayed any sort of defiance were destroyed. As time went on the situation deteriorated with Iraqi troops stealing whatever wealth they could carry with them as personal spoils. Legitimized robbery became the norm."

*She speaks so calmly about this, but I recall Hamad telling me she lost her entire family during the first week of the war.*

"Just up ahead there, turn right. Now, during this horrible situation, Kuwaitis began to form small battle groups to fight back against the Iraqi enemy. Over time, the groups started to obtain weapons – some were even purchased from Iraqi troops in exchange for food and water. Kuwaiti women were responsible for transporting the illegal weapons from place to place within the city, getting them to where they were needed. As time passed, the groups began to get more and more daring in their missions, which moved from simply causing disruption to actually confronting and killing Iraqi soldiers and disrupting Iraqi supply lines."

"Wow," Evan said, as he made the right turn, he noticed a small sign announcing the neighborhood as *Al-Qurain*, "These were not soldiers doing this but civilian activists who rose up because their country needed them?" He could see her nodding out of the corner of his eye, "We never heard about any of this in the West."

The street they were traveling on opened into a cul-de-sac with similar yellow brick houses surrounding a small parking lot in the center. All of the homes appeared to be well maintained, except for one, which showed large holes through the brick front walls. In front of the house, and behind its iron gates, were a rusted van and large American sedan both heavily damaged. There was a Kuwaiti flag flying on a pole in front.

"Park just over there," Najila said as she motioned to an open parking spot in front of the damaged house, directly in front of a lifeless Iraqi battle tank, "this is the last stand of the *Al Messilah Group*."

Evan pulled into the parking spot as instructed and put the car in park. He noticed Najila was in no hurry to exit the vehicle, so he left it running to provide air conditioning while she sat and talked.

"The *Al Messilah Group* was one of the larger ones, having 31 members. Much of what you will see inside talks only about the men in the group, but some women worked with them as well – as I mentioned they were used to move in and around the city because they were seen as non-threatening to the Iraqis. The members of the group strongly believed in Allah and their cause, taking an oath to sacrifice everything to uphold the pride and honor of their country."

"We mutually pledge to each other our Lives, our Fortunes, and our sacred Honor –," Evan said in a low voice.

"What?"

"The last line of the Declaration of Independence. An oath was taken by the document's signers. Most of them lost everything but gained their freedom."

"As you say; the same was true here. Most lost everything, including their lives. The lesson here isn't just nationalism, what made this group unique was its 31 members weren't from the same background, class, faith, or origin. The group included both Sunni and Shiite Muslims, and members from Iran. This was a group driven by a purely nationalistic cause. As a result of their varied backgrounds and origins, the group itself became a well-known example of unity to all Kuwaitis."

*The first time she is spoken about Sunni and Shiite. A divider we've yet to discuss but one we'll eventually have to cover.*

Najila opened the door of the vehicle and got out, Evan did the same. Then the two walked toward the iron fence, which surrounded the site of the final battle.

"Isn't *Al Messilah* a neighborhood with a beach up towards *Salmiya*? Or was he a leader of the group?"

"As you say, their location is where they got their name. When the group became more active and began sniping Iraqi soldiers and planting bombs on Iraqi munitions trucks, the Iraqis set up stronger control over the *Al Messilah* area to clamp down on subversion. That was when the group moved here, to the *Al-Qurain* district," Najila spread her arms so Evan would know she was speaking of the entire neighborhood they were standing in. "At the time, this was an area of new construction, and the Iraqis were unfamiliar with it. The Group relocated to *Beit Al-Qurain*, the house of Bader Nasser Al-Eedan," she now nodded to the house directly in front of them, "they based their operations out of this grouping of villas."

Evan was still not used to the heat, and even though it was early in the day, it felt like the sun was attacking him personally. So, when Najila walked through the gates and into the shade of the building in front of them he welcomed the abrupt change. The change was more to his liking when they entered what was labeled as the *Al-Qurain Martyr's Museum*.

The museum was constructed on the first floor of the house and featured many of the items from the occupation as well as displays of various relics from the battle. Unlike many museums, this one was designed in a more shotgun-like pattern where visitors entered on one end and walked straight through to the other. Off to each side were alcoves featuring display cases and enlarged photos of events that took place during the occupation.

Evan noticed what seemed to be a guide just ahead of them standing and talking to a couple. Even though the voices were faint, he could make out a British accent from the couple as they asked questions and sought additional information. The guide looked over toward them with a quizzical expression on his face and made eye contact with Najila. She shook her head as if to say she and Evan would be fine on their own and did not need his assistance. The guide then returned his attention to the British tourists in front of him.

Even though the entire facility was new construction and also possessed a fresh coat of paint, Evan could smell the familiar scent of a past fire, which probably consumed part of the original structure. This was a different viewpoint of what occurred during the lead up to the invasion. He was younger when the Air Force deployed him as part of the Gulf War. At the time he gave little thought as to what it felt like for those within the country who were trapped by an occupying force. For the first time, he was giving his attention to a different point of view.

As they walked past a series of enlarged photos, Evan found it difficult not to be moved by the heart-rending enlargements of the images of the *Al Messilah Group* members and the families they left behind. Most were young, and there was a certain innocence in their faces as they stared into the camera not knowing where their destiny would eventually take them. Shell casings, machine guns, and various documents lay in the display cases just in front of the photographs.

The documents, which were in Arabic with English translations below them, included orders given to Iraqi troops which were in effect during the occupation. The rules included things like "Burn and destroy all the homes on which there are slogans hostile to our leadership, the pictures of the defunct Al-Sabah dynasty, or the Kuwaiti flag." "Burn and destroy every district in which any military, security, or Popular Army individual is martyred." "Arrest any person who owns, or keeps at his home, a weapon." "Annihilate any hostile demonstration." Having this side of events thrust into his consciousness brought about realizations he never before considered. *This is what was going on inside the country the US and coalition had come to liberate.*

The more he walked and read, the more he understood the terror of the civilian population, and the bravery which it must've taken these resistance fighters to willingly march into a battle against such an overwhelming adversary.

Part of the display was a detailed chronology of the battle, beginning with the accidental discovery of the *Al Messilah Group* by an Iraqi soldier. The battle started on the morning of 24 February, four days after the start of the coalition air campaign and four days before the land invasion. The Group was in the house gathering their weapons and discussing plans and their role in the liberation. They were one of the two resistance groups given a significant role during the land invasion.

That morning, Iraqi forces began arresting Kuwaiti youth from their homes for use as human shields and to hold as prisoners of war in case they were needed for exchange later. A van carrying Iraqi troops, the same van that now sits in front of the house, came upon their villa during a random search of the neighborhood. The vehicle stopped in front of *Beit Al-Qurain*, and an Iraqi soldier got went toward the house. He rang the doorbell at the gate but got no answer. An Iraqi officer then ordered a soldier to jump over the fence and attempt to enter the home.

The soldier peered through the windows and could see resistance members inside wearing identical shirts with *Al Messilah Group* printed on the front. On the back, in English, were the words *Kuwait Force,* which was meant to help coalition forces more easily identify them. Realizing what he was looking at, the soldier ran back to his commander to report his observations.

The commander ordered his troops to spread out around the villa and demanded the occupant's immediate surrender. Sayed Hadi Al-Alawi, the resistance group's leader, climbed to the roof upon hearing the soldier's approach. He was keeping an eye on the situation from there, when the Iraqis gave the ultimatum. Al-Alawi was quick to respond, that the Kuwaiti resistance members chose to fight rather than surrender.

The chronology Evan was reading included quotes from surviving members of the Group.

"Al-Alawi shot the Iraqi soldier, the two sides exchanged shooting until 6:00 PM, when Iraqi Army forces requested tank support, as well as Republican Guard forces, who then surrounded the house from all sides," Saleh said.

As he read this, Evan reached out his hand and touched the plaque using the reality of physical touch to confirm what he was reading. Evan had been in enough battles himself to realize once the tank showed up, there is little more rifles alone could do. He lowered his head and slowly shook it as the reality of the situation took hold. Hearing a noise to his right, he raised his head and looked to see Najila standing patiently waiting for him.

Najila walked to the end of the display and stood before the door leading to the villa from the museum to allow Evan a chance to read the plaques without interference. *I didn't expect him to actually take the time to read all of the displays. This man is so much deeper than I first imagined. Is it empathy or admiration?* Evan ignored the rest of the chronology and walked toward Najila, who opened the door so they could enter the villa itself.

As they left the climate-controlled Martyr's Museum and entered the villa, the stark reality of the battle became as clearly evident as the heat that immediately surrounded them. The villa was left as it was at the end of the fight. Sections of walls were missing, floors completely gone, and twisted metal rebar was exposed throughout. There were huge holes in the exterior brick walls from tank fire, glassless windows, and fixtures torn from their foundations. When climbing the steps and walking through the battle site, Evan felt the familiar pangs of respect and awe he experienced while visiting other places of liberation against tyranny.

Throughout the villa, small plaques identified where the men lost their lives, were captured, or hid to evade arrest. Najila found herself translating these out loud in English for Evan, her goal to evoke a visceral emotional reaction from him. On the more damaged side of the building, Evan climbed as high as possible, finding himself looking down upon the Iraqi tank their car was parked in front of. Through a massive hole which was blown through a brick wall, he could clearly see the tank sitting where it was on the night of the battle, frozen in time.

Thoughts ran through his mind of the night in Afghanistan when he sat in a Humvee and glanced off to the side just in time to see an RPG for being fired. He knew what it was like to be under fire from an enemy with a superior weapon; then another thought crossed his mind.

"Do you remember seeing the image of Tiananmen Square where a sole student faced down a tank? It went worldwide," as Evan said this, he turned to face Najila, then pointed toward the Iraqi tank, "This was so different – without the world as a witness, this tank was firing without restriction or mercy against a poorly equipped group of civilians whose sole motivation was rescuing their nation." His mind reeled as thoughts of what took place here flooded it. *Such bravery, to continue the fight even when you know all is lost.* He then began to feel the precursors of panic rise within him, then without invoking his visualization technique, he grabbed the panic and willed it away returning to calm once again. *That was a first.*

"I know your uncle wants me to write about the good things going on in this country now, but sometimes great things happen in history shouldn't be overlooked. I think before I write any more about now, I need to document what happened here for the Western world."

Najila nodded in agreement. She realized this experience touched this man more deeply than anything else before. "As you say, there is a story here which should be told."

As they made their way down through the structure, Evan told Najila he wanted to return to the museum to pick up a copy of their brochure, so he could ensure the facts were correct when he wrote his piece about the battle. She nodded and at the bottom of the stairs led him back into the Martyr's Museum. Both were disappointed to learn the facility was out of the English version of the document. Instead, Evan selected a copy in German hoping he could remember enough of the language to translate it later.

As they walked back down the hall toward the exit, Evan stopped for a moment at a photograph of American General H. Norman Schwarzkopf. Next to it was a memo from the General expressing his regret they did not reach the house four days earlier – as it could have prevented the slaughter. He pondered it for a moment, *isn't that true in both peace and war, it's all about timing?*

The two walked back toward their vehicle, Evan told Najila he would like her to drive so we could make notes while things were still fresh in his mind. She agreed, and once the two were in the vehicle, she backed out and headed back toward the *Sultana.* Najila knew the emotion of the visit was draining enough for one day. Neither made note nor saw anything unusual about the black sedan with blackened windows parked on one of the side streets as they drove past making their way out of the neighborhood.

Talal ducked down just before their vehicle went by, rising in time to watch as it made the turn setting them upon the path to their next destination. It was unusual for him to assume the role of Talal while performing a duty he was assigned as Roshan. Hamad tasked him with random surveillance of Najila and Evan and doing so in a suit and tie might make him stand out too much in many places in Kuwait. His *dishdasha* and *kufi* allowed him to blend into the local populace as part of the usual scenery.

Talal sat behind the wheel of his vehicle motionless, realizing he should wait a few minutes to avoid the possibility he would catch up with Evan and Najila. As he sat there, he found himself staring at *Beit Al-Qurain* through the windshield. It was his first time here since before the liberation. Then, he was on a mission to deliver information to Al-Alawi of the *Al Messilah Group* about the upcoming coalition ground assault. The group was to meet up with coalition forces and help guide them to locations where the Iraqi troops were located.

However, when Talal arrived he knew immediately this day would end in sorrow. As he drove toward the villa, he saw from between the adjacent houses parked in front of *Beit Al-Qurain* were two Iraqi tanks. Since Talal was on a courier mission instead of a combat one, the only weapon he carried was a folding knife. Little help against the tank, but still he felt the need to stay and observe what was going on so he could report back what he witnessed.

The purpose of his cover was to allow Talal to be ignored as a TCN rather than being identified as a Kuwaiti. As such, he was able to observe the battle from a vantage point between two villas on the opposite side of the street. If anyone noticed him, they did not bother to challenge him assuming Talal was just a TCN who wanted to watch what was going on, and not someone who with a more sinister reason for being there.

As Talal watched, he saw Al-Alawi directing resistance members to various positions in different parts of the structure. He realized Al-Alawi was trying to confuse and disperse the Iraqi soldiers. The tactic was beginning to have an effect when the tank started firing artillery rounds at the building. The tank could've easily leveled the building within minutes, but for some reason, it was being utilized to surgically take out vantage points that were being used by the resistance to fire upon the troops.

Unknown to Talal at the time, the Group was running out of

ammo, and they knew there was no way to make it out of the villa alive. Al-Alawi gathered his fighters and told them to prepare to escape while he created a diversion.

Al-Alawi again made his way to the roof of the battered structure, carrying with him a Kuwaiti flag, what was left of their grenades and his weapon. As he looked over what remained of the wall surrounding the roof, he could see over a hundred Iraqi troops below firing at the villa along with the two battle tanks blasting their structure.

Talal watched as he saw Al-Alawi's figure upon the roof, pulling pins from grenades and dropping them into the gathered squads of troops below. When the frequent small arms fire ceased for a moment, Al-Alawi turned and raised the Kuwaiti flag in a final act of defiance. While the troops were running from the grenades, one of the tanks – seeing Al-Alawi– fired its main gun toward the roof, as Talal covered his eyes not wanting to witness the end of a brave leader.

The silence after the loss of Al-Alawi lasted but a moment, when small arms fire started up again from the structure until gunfire from the Iraqi troops below silenced it. The Iraqis then swarmed the house and took the *Al Messilah Group* members who remained in the house prisoner.

Talal witnessed the hours of the battle. He would not find out all the details until much later. The battle lasted 10 hours and, in the end, 19 mostly untrained Kuwaitis held off over 100 Iraqi troops including a contingent of elite Republican Guards and two tanks, with only small arms and a smattering of grenades. Talal was not surprised to learn the only reason any of the resistance fighters surrendered was there was no ammunition remaining.

Before Talal left, he saw the captured *Al Messilah Group* loaded onto a bus and taken away. He would later learn they were taken to their home neighborhood of *Al Messilah* and executed, without trial, at *Sabah Al-Salem* Police Station. Their bodies were returned to *Al-Qurain* and thrown into a vacant lot to serve as a warning to others. In the end, only the seven who escaped the villa survived.

As he stood here now, years later, he realized this was the first time he reflected on the events of that day. When he was here last, he immediately left to meet up with the West *Fintas* resistance group to prepare for a land invasion, which was to occur within days. He took no time to reflect on what he witnessed in *Al-Qurain*. Even after the war, after seeing so much, this was one of the events he was forced to suppress due to the sheer numbers of atrocities he witnessed during the occupation.

Now, even though faded through time, he realized the fighting spirit he saw from the members of the *Al Messilah Group* was something that would have given anyone pause. These fighters were united by a single sense of purpose, and by the ultimate goal of seeing Kuwait freed from its occupiers.

# Chapter 8



*Sector Constabulary*

It was now just over a month since he discovered the possible pattern in TCN deaths. Since then, Jefzar took it upon himself to review all reported deaths in the country. He was looking for some thread connecting them together. On the near left corner of his desk was a stack of folders for cases that drew his interest. Currently, there were nine of them, and it was now part of his daily routine to review at least one folder in-depth daily with his morning coffee. Now, having reviewed each file at least three times, he was wondering if he was trying to make something out of nothing.

All of the deaths took place at different locations. The victim's death resulted from a variety of causes, including a possible suicide, pedestrian accidents, drowning and the self-immolation of a possible arsonist. Jefzar demanded additional vigilance from his officers, which resulted in the discovery of a mostly scavenger and insect devoured body in the desert. However, the corpse failed to match any missing person report and did not show any signs of a questionable cause of death.

As he took another sip of his coffee, he reached into his desk drawer and withdrew a cigarette, which he held unlit between his fingers. He began to knuckle-roll the cigarette between his fingers as his mind went over all the details. He knew there was something there, but could not find a minor tear in the wrapper which would allow him to rip it open. Then he began to ponder what commonality wasn't remarkable about the cases. *They were all TCN's, the last few were professionals, but the first were just menial laborers. The body found in the desert doesn't fit at all.*

Dropping the still unlit cigarette onto his desk, he took a pile of folders and placed them directly in front of him. Taking the folders from the top, one at a time, he separated them into two piles – laborers versus professionals. When he reached the folder for the body found in the desert, he created a third pile – *wildcards*. Nine dead bodies. Five were laborers, three professionals, and one wildcard. He considered the three collections for a moment before he picked up the wildcard folder and stashed it in his bottom desk drawer. *The distractor is gone, but there is something in these eight. I'm missing something.*

Picking up his desk phone, he quickly keyed in the numbers for Evidence Storage. During a brief conversation, he directed the clerk to bring him any and all evidence, as well as personal property, connected to the folders on his desk. He then read the eight case numbers to the clerk demanding this be given top priority before hanging up. After placing the phone in the cradle, he leaned forward, putting his hands on his desk, then considered the folders as if somehow one would jump out and hand him a clue. *Nothing.*

Re-stacking the eight folders together into a single pile, he slid them again to the corner of his desk and placed the cigarette he had been playing with on top of it.

It was almost lunchtime when the clerk from the Evidence Storage room appeared before Jefzar's office open office door with six large and two small evidence boxes on a dolly. The Sector Police Chief had moved on to other business after making his request and was currently on the phone when the clerk arrived, so he left him standing in the doorway. After ten minutes, Jefzar realized the call was not going to end as quickly as he thought, and he cleared his throat to get the clerk's attention then pointed to the corner where he wanted the load left.

The boxes were still sitting there, unexamined, two hours later when one of the sector's officers, Mubarak, knocked on the open door and proceeded to walk into the office without being prompted.

"Sir, this came in overnight but is not in the Big Book yet. I thought you might want to see it as soon as possible."

Jefzar raised his eyes from the paperwork he was reading and looked at the uniformed police officer standing in front of him. At first, Jefzar was angered by Mubarak's interruption, but as he was about to tear into the officer for walking into his office without knocking, he noticed the folder in his hands.

Without saying a word, Jefzar extended an open hand to take the folder from the officer. Looking at the cover of the case file, he could see the code for a dead body. He immediately calmed down, then thanked Mubarak. Leaning back in his chair he opened the folder.

As he looked at the 8 x 10 black-and-white photo of Fehaid's brutally beaten body, Jefzar picked up the cigarette from on top of the stack of folders and began to twirl it between his fingers again. The young man's face was clearly visible, and Jefzar knew eventually someone was going to recognize this victim. *This victim is an Arab, likely a Kuwaiti.* He felt confident of his identification, even though the folder currently listed the victim as *unknown male/unknown origin.* As he flipped past the picture, he found the body was discovered in a vacant field near a neighborhood which was currently under construction. *Which means no witnesses and no one to interview.*

Behind the pages of the report, there was a small folded piece of paper inside a transparent plastic bag which was stapled to the folder. The evidence information was written on the bag in black marker. The writing stated this piece of evidence was found was in the pocket of the victim; an added note from the Crime Lab said no fingerprints were found.

Jefzar held the bag upside down and shook it, so the piece of paper fell on his desk. With one hand he carefully unfolded it. A single word in Arabic stared back at him: شيطان. He found his chest tightening as if he was unable to breathe. His trance was ended by the sound of the cigarette's crack as he snapped it in two between his fingers.

*There was nothing in the other reports about a finding like this, but maybe…* He kicked his desk chair backward and quickly rose, stepping over to the pile of boxes in the corner of his office. Ripping the top of the first one, he began to go through its contents looking for something similar to what he was just given. His diligence was rewarded as he pulled a similar plastic evidence bag containing another piece of folded paper. Dropping the bag on his desk, he set the box aside and proceeded to the next.

Shortly, six baggies were laying on his desk and inside of each one was a carefully folded piece of paper. Seated at his desk again, he began to open each baggie and carefully unfolded the piece of paper inside of it. As he did this, he placed each of the case files in a row across the top of his desk in chronological order, then laid the empty baggie on it with the unfolded note on top.

When he finished, he looked down at his handiwork. Only two of the boxes lacked the commonality of the folded note. In his mind, he considered the possibilities. *The arsonist and the traffic accident. Possibly just an oversight, doesn't mean there wasn't one. This alone doesn't tie the deaths together, but I know the killer for one was the killer for all. There's more here than the beat down of a young man gone awry. Something far more evil and sinister.*

"Mubarak!" Jefzar shouted as he continued to look at the evidence laid out in front of him.

Within seconds the panicked police officer stood in front of him at attention.

"I think I may have discovered a thread running between these cases. But first, we need to organize all of this evidence and validate everything I've found so far. Set up in the conference room next door, and lay all of this out," Jefzar motioned with his hands across the files on his desk and pointed to the now disheveled boxes sitting in the corner, "in there so it can all be properly examined."

As Mubarak turned to go, Jefzar added, "Send in my secretary on your way out."

Moments later a young woman timidly knocked on the door frame, having been summoned. Through the open door, she could see Jefzar standing over his desk.

"Zainab," Jefzar said as he picked up the two folders which remained without evidence on top of them. "I need you to find out who the detectives were for these cases and I need to see them immediately. Understood?"

"What if they are off-duty or on vacation?"

"Immediately means now. I don't care if they're off-duty or on vacation. I need to speak with these detectives as soon as possible. Am I clear?" He glared at her.

Zainab stood motionless for a moment then turned and left without saying another word. A few moments later, Mubarak, reappeared with another officer and they began to pick up the evidence boxes so they could be moved to the conference room. Jefzar was still standing behind his desk, staring at the folders which remained, and the small pieces of paper resting on top of each of them. His eyes moved from one folder to the next as he let thoughts connect and disconnect while they ran free in his mind.

He knew the notes were all from one person, written by the same hand. He knew the person who created them was either the killer or an accomplice. *More likely a single killer, adding his signature to each of these murders. Murders? There can be no doubt now.* Each note contained only a single word on an identical slip of paper. شيطان – *Satan.*

*Rihlat Alsahra'*

Before Evan exited the SUV, he saw Naveed heading toward him with a horse in tow. This was not the same horse he rode before; this one was jet black, whereas the other one was chestnut colored and smaller. It made him apprehensive since his mount was going to change as Evan was just starting to get used to it. Of course, he was still at a beginner level of riding, making circuits around the corral under the watchful eye of Naveed. Since starting his private riding lessons, he had not been thrown off again, which allowed him to at least claim temporary victory over gravity.

"This is the horse which will turn you into a horseman," Hamad said coming up from behind Evan.

"He looks a lot bigger than the other one."

"He is, a full two hands taller," Naveed interjected as he intersected with the two other men.

"Naveed, take the horse to the corral so Evan can meet his new mount and they can get acquainted. This horse is a stallion, not a gelding, so it will also have greater spirit."

Naveed walked past, leading the horse behind him. As Hamad and Evan watched, Hamad turned to Evan and said,

"If you recall, I told you that you needed a horse which spoke English. Well, we have been preparing this stallion for a buyer in America, and unlike most of the others we train, this one has been trained to understand English."

"You really think it is going to make a difference?"

"Indeed, it will make all the difference. A man and a horse need to be able to communicate on many levels, verbally is just one of them. Humans communicate primarily verbally, but also sometimes with body language. A horse will communicate with his performance. If there is a downfall in any method of communication, it can lead to calamity."

"I think I understand, hang on a second, I have something for you." Evan opened the door of his vehicle and retrieved a folder from inside.

"This article is a little different because it has multiple parts. The story was just too involved for me to tell in just a thousand words."

Hamad took the folder and opened it, glancing at the title at the top of the page, then looking at Evan with raised eyebrows he asked "The *Battle of Al-Qurain?*"

"Yes, Najila took me there last week, and I have been working on a good way to tell the tale for a Western audience ever since. In the end, it became a three-part story. This is the first two parts." Evan said as he pointed to the folder.

Hamad nodded, closing the folder, "I look forward to your telling of the story. It is one of great bravery and unity among our people."

"I agree, and stories about heroism should be shared far and wide, and never be forgotten."

"Indeed," Hamad then turned and seeing Naveed reached the corral with the horse, he turned back to Evan and said, "The time comes for you to meet the mount which will either make you a horseman or defeat you. The choice is yours. By the way, the stallion's name is

Cochise."

"Cochise?" Evan repeated, remembering the name, "Like the Apache Indian chief? That Cochise?"

"Indeed, he was named by the buyer. A rancher who lives in Nevada. He mentioned Cochise was known as a brave defender of his homeland and a man of great dignity," after considering his words for a moment, Hamad added, "after watching him for the past few months, I can tell you this horse is becoming the embodiment of the name."

Hamad then turned and hugged Evan, which was now a custom between the two.

As Evan walked toward the corral, Hamad walked toward the stable to take his own mount out for an evening ride in the desert.

It was unusual for Hamad not to bridle and saddle his own mount. Time did not allow him to perform those tasks this evening without cutting into his riding time. Within minutes, he was mounted and headed into the horizon at full gallop. As *Eadala* carried them deeper into the desert with each gait, Hamad left the concerns of the day behind them. Instead, he embraced memories of a happier time when Khaled was still part of his life. The steady rhythm of *Eadala's* gallop took Hamad's mind from the present to the past.

Once his son began working at *Rihlat Alsahra'*, it was not unusual for Hamad to encounter him in the stables when his routine brought him there. It was a peculiar dance, neither realized they created, to purposely avoid any appearance of familiarity between the two.

Whenever they encountered each other, neither would speak but whoever made eye contact first would give a slight nod to the other when they looked back. Today, it was Hamad who spotted Khaled first as his son was grooming one of the horses. After a moment Khaled looked up to see his father looking toward him. When their eyes met, Hamad gave a slight nod and the young man returned to grooming the horse without saying a word or responding nonverbally.

While the two were in proximity to each other, each would track the other movements loosely so as not to arise suspicion. Then, when either left, the other would follow nonchalantly so the two could speak as soon as they were safely out of view. Hamad appreciated these quick conversations as it allowed him insights into his son's daily life. Since graduating high school, Khaled was spending much of his time during the day at work. In the evenings, he would depart after quickly devouring supper and not return until almost dawn. The two enjoyed a distinct closeness, and this facilitated them in being able to maintain their relationship.

"I'm surprised to see you so energetic and happy this morning, I know you didn't come in until almost three," Hamad said as he turned to face his son just outside the stables. Khaled's smile was broad, and his father knew it was from some deep joy inside of him.

"Yes, it was a very late evening but entirely joyous."

"Out with your friends, I suppose?" as he began to dig for more information about his son's joy, Hamad retrieved his *tasbih* and began to unconsciously count the beads as each slipped between his fingers.

"To start with, but then the rest of the evening I spent with a girl I met a few weeks ago."

Hamad suppressed his smile and just nodded, hoping to hear more if he didn't interject at the moment.

"*Baba*, I know you don't know her or her family, but she is so special and so beautiful. She is smart and funny and every moment I am with her my heart feels so full of joy. Her smile is the embodiment of happiness and her eyes…" Khaled paused for a moment, wondering if he was saying too much, too quickly. The way he met her was not the way men were supposed to meet suitable women. Dating was a family affair in his culture. His apprehension was exacerbated when he realized his father was no longer fiddling with his *tasbih*.

After letting the silence exist for a few moments, Hamad broke it by merely saying, "I see," as he began to run his beads between his fingers once again.

Khaled looked into his father's eyes. The man said so much more there than he did with his words. What he saw today was not anger or judgment – it was acceptance and understanding.

"Was it like that way with *Umma*?"

"Yes," Hamad's response was immediate and honest, "from the first time I saw her. So, when will we get to meet this mystery woman who seems to have captured my son's heart?"

"I'm not ready just yet," Khaled knew his family name alone could be intimidating, let alone meeting the family in person. He had not approached her about meeting them and was not quite sure how he would even present the idea to her. But he knew she was probably already thinking about it as their relationship moved from acquaintance to friendship, to something which was becoming more physical.

"Well, when you are, you be sure to tell your mother well in advance. You know how she is about keeping things proper and socially correct. Don't deny her the pleasure of getting to show off a bit to this lady who might be the one who steals her son away."

He desperately wanted to hug his son, but both were trying to maintain a professional distance at work, and he did not want to affect the masquerade. Khaled agreed, but after taking a quick look around for observers, he reached out and grabbed his father giving him a firm hug. Hamad placed his arms around his son and hugged him in return. Seconds later Khaled turned and returned to the stables without another word.

As he watched his son walk away, Hamad stood thinking to himself. *I guess it is time for him. I was a year younger when his mother and I were paired by family. I can only hope this girl turns into as good a wife as Huda has been.*

The sting of sand granules hitting his face returned Hamad to present, and he pulled back on the reins to stop his horse. Looking at the haze in front of them he knew they were riding into the outer edges of a sandstorm. After removing the *agal* from his *gutra*, he quickly rewrapped the piece of cloth, so it now protected his face leaving only a slit for his eyes. Looking forward at the storm he considered his next action. *Eadala's* long eyelashes would serve to keep the sand from blinding the horse if he chose to ride on, but it would still be uncomfortable for the horse. *Riding through a sandstorm was its own extraordinary adventure* Hamad thought as the desert became an airborne cloak around him – surrounding and shrouding him from the outside world.

He made his decision and spun the horse around, heading back to the stables. *Eadala* was again striding at full gallop. The storm remained at their heels until they arrived at the stables and it overtook them. Rather than stopping outside and walking the horse in; he rode directly into the stable tent and dismounted once they were inside. Once back on the ground, Hamad handed the reins of his horse to Amr, unwrapping his face and using the cloth to wipe the sand off. He noticed in one of the paddocks Evan was brushing down Cochise, so he walked over.

"You know, I'm not going to pay you extra for working in the stables."

Evan stopped brushing the horse and moved to one side so he could see Hamad directly, "Well, Naveed said you set the custom for taking care of your own mount after a ride. I'm just following your example."

Hamad laughed, "Indeed. So, tell me, did you have a good first ride with your new mount? Was it easier on a horse who understands English?"

"You know, I almost felt what you were saying was more of a symbolic thing than an actuality. But you were absolutely on point. I began to talk to the horse, and Cochise began to calm down and do what I was asking. I had no idea that's how these things worked."

"Yes, it is exactly how these things work, at least for a properly trained horse. A sandstorm is upon us, so it is not a good time to head to the city. Care to meet me in the *diwaniya* for some tea and perhaps a bit of *sheesha*?"

"Sounds like it would be nice, but you may have to explain how the whole *sheesha* thing works. I have seen the pipes in cafés, but have never partaken of one."

"Indeed, I'll have it prepared, as well as some tea and a tray of fruit. Come over to the *diwaniya* when you get done here."

"Sounds great," Evan turned and returned to brushing the horse down.

A short time later, the two were sitting on the large pillows of the *diwaniya*. The table the center was graced with cups of tea as well as a sizeable ornate *sheesha* in the center. The bowl at the top of the *sheesha* released a constant curl of smoke which wafted upwards to the top of the tent.

The two men's time together started with the traditional conversation about goings-on within each of their family. Hamad showed great interest in Evan's description of recent events with his sons as well as his parents. Evan was enjoying this back-and-forth about personal matters, as his time with Najila was primarily business. Lacking any friendships in the country, there was no one to speak of such personal matters. Hamad provided Evan with an empathetic and interested listener he had been missing.

When it was his turn to speak, Hamad started off by talking about his niece. "You know, Najila has started to say some very nice things about you. In the beginning, I think she was a bit guarded, but she has come to respect you and is enjoying your time together."

"Really? Well, I'm glad. She seems to have loosened up over the past few weeks and is showing a more personable side. It's making my work much more enjoyable," Evan found himself choosing his words carefully. If you were in the United States, he might've said more or even complemented Najila's beauty, but it was not the way things were done here. Particularly when speaking to a woman's uncle.

"She told me you enjoyed your trip to *Al-Qurain* and found many similarities between it and other heroic battles in history. I always thought an easy parallel would be between the battle which occurred there and your Alamo."

Bright lights suddenly flashed in Evan's mind; *how did I completely miss that?*

"But then," Hamad continued, "such a comparison might actually take away from the Battle's importance in our history."

*That's true, maybe it's a good thing I missed the parallel,* "I fully agree. When I wrote the article, I wanted the battle to stand on his own rather than it being compared to anything else."

"Very good, very good. I look forward to reading it." Hamad flowed from the conversation directly into showing Evan how to smoke from the *sheesha*. He demonstrated the technique, placing the tip of the hose into his mouth before gently sucking the smoke in. Once he finished the draw, he slowly released the smoke through his pursed lips.

Evan picked up the hose nearest him and repeated what he had seen. The coals burning in the *sheesha* possessed an almost citrus taste mixed in with the tobacco. Hamad nodded approvingly, even though the ability to smoke was not a difficult task to learn or master.

For the next hour or so, the two men sat drinking tea and smoking. Each took turns telling tales about their childhood and parents. It was through this conversation Evan realized how universal the events of growing up were: the innocence of youth, and discovery of the world around them. The two men grew up in different worlds, but shared a sense of wonder, and the autonomy a person craves as they grow older.

With the wind calming, they bid each other farewell as Evan headed back to the Sultana. It was late, so he quickly stripped off his clothes and climbed between the sheets of his bed. While lying there, just before fading off, he found he was pleased with himself. *Najila is beginning to say nice things about me?* He smiled and faded off to sleep with the memory of her beautiful eyes fresh in his mind.

*Maksim's Apartment*

"Shit," Maksim exclaimed before jamming his burned finger into his mouth. He was tempted to throw the offending soldering iron across the room but knew it would do nothing to relieve the pain. But, he also knew putting the digit in his mouth provided no relief either. Removing his finger from his mouth, he examined it for a moment. The soldering iron burnt through the latex glove, exposing the flesh underneath, and an oblong shape on his finger was beginning to redden.

He rose from his chair and went to the kitchen to retrieve a piece of ice. After removing the ruined glove, he pressed the ice against the burn on his finger. Returning to his worktable, he again took a seat and looked at the device in the table in front of him. Lowering the arm lamp toward his handiwork, he began to mentally map its function.

Beginning with the power source, a disc-shaped three-volt lithium battery, the wiring progressed to an already paired Bluetooth receiver. Once the signal was received, the battery would send power through various bits of wire, capacitors, and circuitry eventually fulfilling the device's ultimate function – detonating a half kilo of C4. Composite 4 was not his first choice for an explosive charge; he would've preferred Israeli Semtex, but it had yet to arrive from his supplier in Dagestan. He obtained this locally from a Syrian supplier, now deceased, who made the mistake of delivering it to him alone just across the border with Saudi Arabia. It would be functional for this particular mission, but he needed the more moldable and stable Semtex for the final act.

Once he was satisfied with the triggering device he created, he flipped the device over with his still gloved hand and exposed the bottom of the circuit card it was all built upon. It was no bigger than a credit card. Picking up the silver Sharpie pen that lay on the desk, he held the circuit board between his gloved fingers and slowly drew his signature on the green fiberglass – شيطان. Maksim blew on the ink gently to dry it, and after a moment turned the device back over and placed it in a small black plastic box of equal dimensions which was about four centimeters tall.

Maksim slipped the two wires used to cause detonation through the hole in the flat piece that served as the cover for the box. The final step was to place and tighten the small Phillips screws in each corner of the lid to hold it in place. After he accomplished this, he removed the one glove he was still wearing. Leaning back in his chair, he looked at the nondescript black box now sitting in front of him.

What was inside the box in front of him was yet another enigma exclusive to this mission. He was trained to build each bomb he constructed with a unique signature, changing styles and methodologies. This prevented multiple devices from being threaded together to determine a pattern. This time, he created the bomb with specific techniques that would be repeated with every device he built during this job. To ensure there was no doubt as to the origin of the device, he included the signature which, to date, no one was detail-oriented enough to realize as such. *But soon, soon.*

Maksim reached across the table and retrieved a metal box. After putting on a new set of latex gloves, he opened the box and removed what an ordinary observer might think was a block of clay. Using a knife, he cut away a half kilo piece of the C4 placing the remainder back in the box, which he closed again.

Next, he slid a powerful rectangular neodymium magnet from the side of his workbench to a spot in front of him. This particular magnet would keep a payload of up to 20 pounds secured to whatever metal object the magnet was attached. After working the C4 with his hands for a few minutes, making it pliable, he began to form it around the magnet leaving one flat side of it exposed.

With this step complete, what sat in front of him was the size and shape of a small breakfast bun. He inserted the inch-long detonator into the C4, molding the material around it leaving only the two wires for the detonator exposed. The only steps lacking for completion of the bomb was attaching the wires from the trigger to the detonator, and molding the trigger into the top of the C4.

When complete, he would have a fist-sized explosive device, which the magnet would allow him to attach to any metal surface as he passed by. After he was a safe distance away, but still within range, he could use his cell phone to trigger the device via Bluetooth, causing a massive explosion.

*Well, ready for the morning.*

But tonight, there were things left to do. After covering the worktable with a bedsheet, Maksim left the apartment and headed to a pair of connected garage spaces in *Fahaheel.* When he arrived, Maksim sent a text to Nassar.

```
> Open the door
```

A moment later, the garage door began to roll upwards exposing an open bay into which Maksim pulled his car. As soon as the car was inside, Nassar closed the door again. Maksim exited the vehicle and was immediately slammed by the heat of the unvented garage bay. *It's over 50° centigrade in here. How does this man tolerate it?*

In the connected bay, was a familiar Nissan in silver. All of the doors of the vehicle were open, and Nassar was now standing near the open hood drinking from a bottle of water.

"You have been keeping both of these bay doors closed?"

"Yes, Boss. All the time, as you instructed me."

Maksim heard a whirring sound coming from his left, and he looked to see a small box fan sitting in the corner circulating the stale hot air. It was not accomplishing much if anything at all. Noticing the fan drew his boss' attention, Nassar quickly said,

"I brought it from home, Mr. Pauley. It is frightfully hot in here, especially during the day." When Nassar stopped speaking, he was suddenly frightened by Maksim's intense reaction to what he was saying.

"Open the door, so I can back my car out but get in after you close it," Maksim said as he turned to get back in his car.

Nassar did as he was told, and soon the two were driving down the highway toward the city. Neither spoke, Nassar out of fear for his job or possibly worse and Maksim saw no need to explain himself to this worker bee. Soon, he pulled off the highway and into the parking lot of a large appliance store. Still silent, he departed the vehicle and went into the store leaving Nassar to sit in the car. *At least he left it running*, Nassar thought as he enjoyed the cold air the SUV's climate system was putting out. After a half-hour or so, Maksim returned with two employees in tow. Each was pushing a flat cart stacked with large boxes.

Maksim knocked on the passenger window and motioned for Nassar to get out and assist with loading the boxes into the car. It was then Nassar noticed the boxes were labeled as containing portable air conditioning units. He was immediately calmed. On the drive over, Maksim convinced himself this was about the mission. If he began to kill off his laborers because they were dying of heatstroke, it would not be a good thing. This would prevent such a possibility, and also would guarantee the garage doors remain closed as he demanded.

Once they returned to the garage, Maksim directed Nassar to unload the cooling units and hook them up. Then, Maksim stepped over to the Nissan and began to observe Nassar's handiwork. Overall, Maksim was pleased. Nassar proceeded precisely as he was told. His instructions were simple: remove everything from the car which could possibly be removed to reduce its overall weight without destroying the aesthetics or functionality of the vehicle. The idea was to get rid of weight but at the same time leave the Nissan appearing normal and still operational.

The pile of metal parts, bits, and pieces sitting in the corner were evidence of how much was already removed from the car. Maksim noticed Nassar took the initiative to remove the metal frame from the back seats of the car and stuff the seat covers with straw. Of course, no one could sit there, but they would appear normal with the weight having been reduced by at least ten kilos.

Upon completing his inspection, Maksim said, "Nassar, you have done extremely well."

The young man beamed, "Thank you, Boss. Perhaps I could get a bit more weight out of the car if I removed some of the inner metal panels and perhaps the footboards as well."

Maksim stared at Nassar for a moment, *ingenious*. "Yes, it would be a good idea for the panels but leave the footboards on the passenger side. We will need them. Do you know have all the tools necessary?"

"Most definitely."

"Then have at it." Maksim then pulled a roll of bills from his pocket and peeled off two 20KD notes. He handed the bills to Nassar, "Your wages, and also a reward," peeling off two more 20KD notes, "for your good idea," *and for continuing to keep your mouth shut.*

Nassar was still thanking Maksim as he backed out of the garage to leave. His wages on this job were good, to begin with; this was even better. Perhaps he would go to see his father and waive the money in front of his face to show he was not only independent now, but thriving.

Maksim watched as Nassar faded into his rearview mirror. He was sure the man would remain silent and loyal. As he often did, he was gradually increasing his employee's wages to guarantee his silence. *Loyalty is best when it is bought and paid for.*

On his way back to his apartment, Maksim encountered several instances of standstill traffic and at one point was actually rerouted due to an accident. These inconveniences caused him to rethink his methodology of detonation for the bomb that sat in his apartment. *Suppose at the last minute I was routed away from my target, or out of range to trigger it via Bluetooth.*

Upon arriving at the apartment, he returned to his place at the worktable and pulled on a pair of latex gloves. He carefully unscrewed the cover of the trigger box and removed it. After removing the circuit board from the box, he used the soldering iron to melt the connectors which allowed the Bluetooth receiver to function. After removing the receiver, he replaced with a rudimentary countdown timer. Before soldering it into place, he used a system of DIP switches to set the timer for seven minutes.

Because of this change, he needed a way to start the timer without deconstructing the device again. To accomplish this, he inserted one end of a four-centimeter-long narrow strip of plastic between the battery and its terminal to prevent the two from connecting. There was no display showing time remaining as seconds ticked away; after all, this was not Hollywood, and no audience would be watching the timer, allowing their anxiety to build as the minutes ticked down.

He placed the lid back on the trigger. He allowed the free end of the plastic strip to hang out one end of the box. When he drove the screws back in, he purposely left the two on the side of the case nearest the exposed plastic strip untightened. This way, he could quickly pull the plastic piece out without having to deconstruct the trigger to do so. Before putting the box down, he shook it violently back and forth gently pulling on the plastic tab to make sure it was still firmly attached. *I don't want this sliding out and starting the timer before I'm ready.*

After placing the device back on the table next to the lump of C4, Maksim looked down at the pieces which, when combined, would create the bomb he would use to kill a Kuwaiti Parliament member in a few hours. He was satisfied but the moment of tranquility was short-lived as his phone began to ring. He pushed the button necessary to connect the call, before he pressed the phone against his ear without saying a word.

Huda hated the way this man answered a phone. Aside from a certain level of disrespect, she felt she was taking a risk in speaking first, even though her number was blocked and she was doing her best to disguise her voice. She was following the news and knew things were progressing as planned, but she knew she needed to make him aware of the latest developments.

"Things seem to be progressing," *a cautious statement, and one which could mean anything.* She felt reassured.

"But of course. The next phase will begin tomorrow."

"Splendid. You should know, someone has taken notice."

"I see."

"Yes, the trail of crumbs you have left have at last garnered interest and are being followed."

"Well, isn't that what we wanted?"

"As long as the trail is leading where we want it to go."

"But of course. Has the latest transfer taken place? I need to obtain more supplies, as we move to the next phase and beyond."

*It's always about the damn money. Well, what else can you expect when you hire a mercenary. No emotional connection – they don't understand the satisfaction obtained from revenge.* "Yes, as we agreed." As she said this, Huda could hear Hamad coming toward their room. "Carry on." she said curtly before disconnecting the call.

As Hamad entered the room, Huda turned toward him as she slipped her phone into the pocket of her *abaya*. "Did I hear you on the phone with Jefzar?" she asked the question knowing the answer. Moments ago, she stood outside of his office as the two carried on a conversation concerning Jefzar's excitement over having possibly discovered a serial killer. She felt unremorseful at having listened to the call. *Really, if the man wanted to keep anything confidential, he shouldn't be using a speakerphone.*

"Yes, it would seem he's discovered some sort of connection between several crimes, and he was quite excited about it."

"How interesting, but then Jefzar has always been quite the detective."

"Indeed," Hamad said having retrieved the item he came for but as he walked toward the door, he gave his wife a quick kiss on the cheek.

After his departure, Huda stood in the room alone, feeling the excitement coursing through her as she realized her plan was becoming a reality.

Maksim looked at the phone for a moment to ensure the call was ended. Sliding the back cover off the phone, he deftly removed the SIMM chip, and inserted another he retrieved from inside the cover of his wristwatch. Turning the phone on, he waited for it to connect, dialing a phone number manually. When the other party answered, he provided a 36-digit account number from memory, and requested the current balance. After a few moments, the employee of the First Caribbean International Bank provided the information to Maksim, and he disconnected the call without saying anything further. The deposit was complete.

Maksim then dialed another number into the cell phone. Once connected, he heard another dial tone. He then punched in the numbers for a burner phone belonging to his contact in Dagestan. When the call was answered, there was only silence. Neither party spoke for a few seconds, Maksim heard the other party say a single word before the phone went dead: *Polnyy* – Complete. *Well, 700 kilos of Semtex is on the way. Each brick specially disguised per my specifications. Good.*

As he nodded to himself, Maksim removed the back cover from the phone yet again and removed the SIMM chip, placing the original chip back in the phone. After replacing the cover, he returned the remaining SIMM chip to its holding place in the back of his watch. *It'll take three or four days for the shipment to get here-- then I will have everything I need.*

Turning the watch over, he noticed the time, and realized there were three or four hours yet before he needed to be in place for today's activities. A crooked smile crossed his lips as he thought about seeking out some hired entertainment for an hour or so. Going to his bedroom, he shuffled through the miscellaneous items that ended up on his dresser at the end of the day. He searched through the pile of receipts, scraps of paper, and coins, and withdrew a business card he was handed a few days ago. There was only a single name on the card, Jasmine, and then below the word *Private* and a phone number.

A call was placed, and a half-hour later Maksim opened his door to greet a tall, thin Chinese woman whose eyes were so glazed it was impossible to miss her intoxication. At first, a brief look of concern crossed her face as she visually evaluated the level of risk he presented. It was only momentary; his appearance was typical Westerner, not law enforcement. Then she reverted to the well-rehearsed aura of overt and available sexuality.

Maksim estimated her to be easily over 35 and as a result, she was wearing too much makeup in an attempt to hide it. *She was unsuccessful.* Upon seeing her in person, he was half tempted to turn her away at the door but realized he didn't have time to get a replacement before he needed to leave on his mission.

He allowed her to enter the foyer so he could examine her a little more closely, while blocking her from coming any further inside. She immediately wrapped her arms around his neck greeting him as if he was a long-lost love in an attempt to quickly move the situation from one of the strangers to one of the intimates.

Even though Maksim kept the lights in his apartment dim, he could clearly see the needle marks on the insides of her elbows. Since he did not plan on contracting a fatal STD during this mission, he quickly negotiated a price for oral gratification only and handed her the payment. She quickly folded the bills tucking them into the small purse she was carrying, then reached behind her and unzipped her dress. She let the garment drop to the floor dramatically and stepped out of it leaving her standing naked before him.

Jasmine slowly lowered herself to her knees while maintaining eye contact with Maksim even as she took him into her mouth. *My, she is very talented.* The physical side of him began to enjoy her attention, while he allowed his mind to review his recent killings and the predicted chaos, and death which would be wrought by the bomb he just finished constructing.

He let his mind flow back and recall the feel of the other prostitute's throat in his hands while enjoying the look of terror in her eyes as he slowly squeezed the life from her. *It was such a mix of fear and surprise, then terror and ultimately acceptance.* Maksim found himself beginning to involuntarily thrust his hips forward. Soon, he found it necessary to place a hand on the back of Jasmine's head to hold it still against his motions.

Maksim allowed his mind to easily drift onto the next memory, which ended with the dead eyes of the Nigerian staring back at him from just beneath the surface of the water. The smell of the ocean surrounded him, and he found himself thankful for the seawater which filled the lungs of his victim and prevented another breath from ever entering her body. The lifeless corpse layout before him, just beneath the surface of the warm seawater. Even if someone were on the shore, they would've never been aware of what was happening. The memory of sexually molesting the woman's body beneath the surface of the water caused him to grip Jasmine's head tighter as he began to hold it with both hands.

He recalled the smell of Rajeesh's blood; Maksim's entire world was suddenly reduced to one sensory input. Then the feel of the blood as he sliced the man open – hot, thick, and flowing over his own naked body. Covering him and taking him over the edge in an orgasm brought solely from those two sensations. His pace was quickening...

Every swing of the cricket bat – a release as it sailed through the air before crashing into its target. He found his mind reveling in the split-second, between the bat's impact and the feel of the bones beneath the skin fracturing under the force of the blow. Each strike its own release. Each impact a singular thrill. He knew he was close, and pulled Jasmine's head hard against him. He could hear her on the verge of choking but didn't care; he focused on the sound to take him over the edge. *In a few hours, in a very few hours — blood, mayhem — death.*

He stifled and swallowed the sound which was trying to burst forth from his lips then released her head allowing her to complete the act as she saw fit. Still panting, he looked down and saw her blank face looking up toward him *a smattering of confusion but not fear.* When Jasmine was sure she made eye contact with him, she slowly licked her lips trying to appear sensual. This caused Maksim to break eye contact with her and instead lift his eyes skyward. *What a piece of trash.*

His original intent was to take care of her, as he often did with slag of this ilk, but he was logical enough to know he didn't have time to do an adequate job of it. *Perhaps a session afterward would serve me better, let the tension build.* He lowered his hands to his sides, and Jasmine mistook the motion for being an offer of assistance. She took one of his hands, and he involuntarily helped her return to a standing position naked in front of him.

*Her eyes are so blank, it's almost unnerving.* Then, she slowly raised her face and leaned forward as if to kiss him. Maksim took a quick step backward; there was no desire to be intimate with her. She was there to provide a service, which was now complete.

"I would like to see you back, Jasmine, at say ten o'clock?" Jasmine nodded, retrieving her dress from the floor, pulling it up around her. She then turned her back to him in an unspoken request for him to zip it up. Maksim did so, then lowering his hands to the hem of her short dress, lifted it and felt her ass. She leaned into his hands, releasing a moan, which expressed more sensuality than anything done to this point. He began to slide his hands around her hips in front of her, but then thought better of it and removed them from her body allowing the dress to fall back in place.

Reaching behind her and opened the door, but before she walked through it, he produced a 10KD bill which he held in front of her as she walked out. Taking the bill from his hand, she then pulled his hand to her mouth, kissing his fingertips and taking his index finger into her mouth — swirling her tongue around it. When she released his finger, she turned and winked at him before disappearing down the hallway.

As Maksim close the door, he looked at his watch realizing there was enough time for a quick nap. *This day is shaping up.*

# Chapter 9



*Premier Office Tower 2, Kuwait City*

Sheikha swirled the bristled brush around the rim of the toilet while doing her best to ignore the smell of the disinfectant. The aroma was not entirely unpleasant, but when you are cleaning the last of eight toilets in a bathroom, it began to have an adverse reaction. Choosing to allow the chemicals to have a moment to achieve their effect, she left the bathroom for the corridor where the air was less dense. Once there, she leaned back against the wall and slowly slid down until she was seated on the floor. *I'm ahead; I can afford to take a break.* After permitting herself, she closed her eyes and leaned her head back on the wall while she let her mind wander to the past.

After weeks of exchanging text messages and glances across the room, the two were able to finally spend time together with the aid of friends covering their rendezvous. At first, they would sit across from each other so they could look into each other's eyes as they talked. It quickly progressed to them sitting side-by-side, holding hands and leaning against each other as they discussed their own world views and hopes for the future.

Then came their first kiss, which according to desert lore, was an intermingling of their souls as they shared a single breath. As their physical exploration became more intense, their need for more time alone increased. Soon, each was sneaking out of their homes at night and staying out until almost dawn together.

Sheikha never feared his touch or exploration of her body, welcoming his hands as she also reached out for his flesh beneath her fingertips. She knew where this was leading, even though she knew that to be a respectable married woman in the future, she would have to remain a virgin. Her faith would allow an intended husband to annul the marriage, if he found his wife was not a virgin when they were married, even if he was the one who was responsible. She began to mentally debate what this meant and why. *If I'm saving myself for one man, and I'm with the man now; what difference does it make, as long as he is the one I give my virginity to?*

The reflection of the argument with herself snapped her back to the present where she sat in the hallway of an empty office building. Looking back, she never regretted accepting self-serving logic as justification for indulging her physical desires. She never regretted anything about her time with him. *How could I regret knowing and loving my soulmate, and giving everything to him?* Sheikha was not ready to return to her duties just yet, so she shut her eyes again and indulged her remembrance.

The feel of his body upon hers was now familiar as was the smell of him and their sex. This was the third time they made love. Gone was the massive apprehension she felt previously and also the fear of pain her mother warned her would be inevitable the first time. She did not experience any pain at all, but she did not feel any physical pleasure the first time either. Overall, their first time together was driven by the passion of the moment; aside from an overwhelming fear of being caught, it was a mindless act driven by physical need.

Their second time was more memorable, but she still did not feel the physical pleasure and release she read about in Western magazines. Sheikha began to wonder if sex was going to be just another duty she was expected to perform as a woman, like her aunts described. Then came the third time.

This time the fear of being caught was not there as they were far out in the desert and could see anyone approaching for miles. Her virginity, something she was told to guard since she was a little girl, was long gone, so the anxiety was no longer present either. She knew the man she was with loved her, and she loved him. This time, it was something familiar and something welcome. The two of them moved as one and with deliberation, as if the evanescence of the moment could be abated if they injected their soul into the act.

Then, as Sheikha felt his body tense, she wrapped her legs around his and pulled him deep inside her. This motion led to her feeling something different through her entire body, it was as if her body began to involuntarily tighten like a spring. With each of his thrusts, she felt her body tense until she became aware of new sensation growing inside of her – an unknown pressure was building. Then she felt sudden waves of heat coming from his body, causing a dam burst within her. All of the built-up pressure was loosed at once in a pounding release that came in waves, pounding Sheikha's entire body and making her lose muscle control. It wasn't once or twice, but many times. Powerful surges of bliss enrapturing her body from head to toe surged upon her without warning.

As his thrusts slowed then stopped, Sheikha found herself floating away on a wave of tingles which seemed to dance across her naked flesh leaving her with a feeling of blissful fulfillment she never felt before. She then realized, at some point, she bit into the flesh between his shoulder and neck to silence her desire to scream. Sheikha released her bite searching for his mouth so she could kiss him. She felt wonderful, she felt complete.

In the following weeks, they continued to spend as much time as possible alone together. They were not only exploring each other physically but mentally as they became more enraptured with the other. Every time they met, Sheikha discovered something new about him, which only increased her feelings. It was in the memory of these times she found solace, when the hard reality of a *Bedoon's* life became hers.

Sheikha was pulled from the memory to the present, as she on the floor of the office building. Her body longing for his touch, she was filled with sadness knowing she would never feel his body against her again. She allowed herself to again drift back and recall the look on his face the night she told him she was pregnant. It was not one of shock, or rejection but one of welcoming the unexpected news as a thing of joy.

"I love you," he said after staring into her eyes for a moment after her announcement, then he took her in his arms and kissed her deeply.

"We must begin planning now for our child's arrival. First, you will have to meet my parents; I know you've been putting this off, but with this turn of events we can no longer delay it." He could see the fear across her face as soon as he said these words. Sheikha responded by only nodding as the reality of what would take place next hit her. *Now, is when his parents find out you, a Bedoon, will be the mother of their grandchild.*

"Nothing to worry about my love, my father and mother will love you as I do. Once we have taken care of the introductions, we will immediately start preparing for our wedding, and entering a life together. A life for the three of us."

She nodded again, speechless at how much distance he covered in just a few words, *how drastically our life is going to change – so quickly.*

Sheikha was fearful, but felt comforted while she was there with him. Looking back, she should have realized there was no way this optimism could ever be a reality. He stepped immediately through two of the most emotionally charged and challenging parts of life by brushing them aside, without giving consideration as to how stressful each was going to be. In the coming days, he would tell her of his father's acceptance and welcoming attitude toward her, while he remained silent about his mother's feelings until the day he announced his mother wanted to meet her.

"She wishes to meet with you before you meet my father," Her reaction was visible as her entire body tensed in reaction to his words. "Don't be concerned, she just wants to get to know you one-on-one before bringing my father into things."

"Have you told them about me? Have you told them I am pregnant?" Sheikha asked him wanting to know what kind of familial disaster she might be heading into.

"Relax, I have told them both how much I love you and how wonderful I think you are. I did not tell them about the baby, I didn't want to overwhelm them until they got to know you at least a little."

Sheikha felt a little reassured; she would only face one hurdle at a time with these people. Her culture placed importance on the man's family and not her own. She had not considered what her own parents might say or do, but if issues with his family were settled, they would have to approve. *For my Baba and Umma's acceptance, his family will have to accept me first. But will they?*

A sound in the stairwell at the end of the corridor snapped Sheikha out of her trance and back to the present. She quickly rose from the floor, and walked back toward the restroom she was cleaning.

*Of course, in the end, my family never met him or his family. The only thing they knew was I was unmarried and pregnant, and it was all they needed to banish me from their home. The shame was enough for them to break all ties with me from that day forward.*

Being *Bedoon* was to be at the lowest end of the caste, but being a single unwed mother, was to find yourself spit upon by even the lowest.

Maksim considered using a motorcycle for this part of the job, but in the end settled on using an automobile, as it would garner less attention. The problem with being in an automobile in the middle of the morning commute in Kuwait City was the traffic. The road infrastructure was not bad, and there was almost a logic to the way the streets were laid out. The problem was the attitude of the drivers behind the wheel.

Native Kuwaitis held the belief because they were Kuwaitis living in Kuwait, they alone possessed some sort of priority over everyone else. As a result, they drove as if everyone else needed to get out of their way. This naturally led to numerous minor fender benders, which resulted in streets being blocked while arguments of fault took place.

Unlike many who were on the road with him, Maksim needed to be at a specific place, at a specific time to intersect with his target. Sitting next to him, under a folded newspaper, was the completely assembled bomb he created the night before. All he would need to do is pull the plastic strip from the device and drive closely enough to affix the bomb to the target vehicle via the magnet. Seven minutes later, the bomb would explode, destroying the car, its driver, and anyone unlucky enough to be nearby.

In order to blend in with the majority of the people who would be out and about this morning, Maksim chose a *dishdasha* and *gutra*. The *gutra* blocked some of his peripheral vision, but he was willing to put up with it since it helped cover his face from the side. He was aware of where the traffic cameras were, and managed to map a route that would avoid any of them capturing a view of him straight on.

Progress was very slow; the car in front of him inched forward, then finally began to move at a slow pace. He followed the vehicle closely feeling anxious because he knew he needed enough time to get to his ready point. Maksim was relieved when he saw the sign for the street he needed and turned off of the main thoroughfare onto the side street. He quickly made a U-turn positioning himself so he could merge into traffic as soon as he saw his target pass by.

Moments later, the white Mercedes-Benz belonging to the targeted Parliamentarian, passed by on the street in front of him. Maksim quickly pulled forward and made a right turn onto the street. His target was in the far-left lane so he immediately began to jockey for position, moving from the far-right lane toward the white Mercedes. As he began to gain position on the vehicle, he looked into his review mirror and noticed the car behind him was occupied only by a driver was busy talking on his cellphone. *That will keep them preoccupied while I do this.*

While he was between two lights, Maksim gunned his vehicle and brought it to where his driver's side window was even with the rear of the Mercedes. He took a quick glance in the mirror and saw the man behind him was looking down at the screen of his phone, so Maksim reacted. While keeping his right hand on the wheel, he picked up the bomb from the seat beside him with his left. Holding in front of him, he took the end of the plastic strip between his teeth and held it while he pulled the bomb away, activating the bomb.

He was about to extend his arm out the window and attach it to the target vehicle, when a horn blasted to his right and the nose of a BMW cut in front of him forcing him to brake to avoid a collision. Now, the rear panel of the Mercedes was no longer beside him but several feet in front of him and he couldn't reach it. Worse yet, he activated the bomb and it was now seven minutes until the explosion.

He laid on his horn, hoping to force the car which cut him off to move faster or something, to allow him to make up those scant few feet so he could attach the bomb. Instead, the car in front of him flashed its brakes before it stopped even though there was space now in front of him to move forward. *The bastard is playing some kind of one-upmanship game. Fuck.*

Suddenly, there was a movement to the right of him and the lane was empty, he could move into it from the center lane without effort. Maksim did so, and remained toward the tail end of the BMW while he reached in the center console and pulled out a long folding knife. Opening the knife has he inched forward, he waited until the driver side window was even with the BMWs rear wheel, then he reached out with the knife and stabbed the back tire causing it to immediately start losing air. Within a few feet, enough air leaked out that the car was now sitting on its rim and making a grinding sound as it rolled forward.

The right lane continued to move and as he slowly inched past the now stopped BMW, Maksim watched as the driver got out to examine his completely flat rear tire. He kicked it then pulled the cellphone from his pocket to call for assistance. After clearing the stopped BMW, Maksim weaved back into the center lane and began to make his way toward the Mercedes again. With five minutes left, he was at last even with the rear panel on the car, and he extended the bomb out the window and gently placed it on the vehicle, letting go as soon as he felt the magnet attach. A quick look around and the only person who might have seen him was another driver who was looking down at his phone rather than paying attention to the road.

Maksim planned to take the first right turn available after planting the bomb then double back toward his point of origin on a parallel road. What he did not count on was the right lane being closed in front of him due to a fender bender and his escape route being blocked. There were less than four minutes to make his escape or risk being caught in the explosion or at least the traffic jam aftermath.

With the right lane closed, he was left with a choice between getting behind the white Mercedes to make a left or, speeding up to get ahead of this snarl of traffic. Once he was ahead, he could take the next right available no matter where it took him. He opted for getting into the left lane, and immediately changed lanes finding himself directly behind the Mercedes and his bomb. Being familiar with the area, Maksim knew as soon as he cleared the overpass they were on, he would be able to make a left turn and escape. The Mercedes abruptly changed lanes, moving to the center and Maksim came face-to-face with the stopped vehicle directly in front of him.

Maksim had no idea why the car stopped, all he knew was there were three minutes left to place as much distance as possible between himself and the Mercedes. He could see the intersection would allow him to make a left turn just ahead. *Can I make it there in time? Why is this dumbass stopped?* He exited his vehicle and stormed up to the driver side of the stopped vehicle asking the man in Arabic if he needed assistance. The man nodded, saying something about not being able to get his car started. Maksim told him to put the car in neutral and he would push the vehicle off of the road. Moving to the back of the vehicle, Maksim placed his hands on the trunk and began to push. Slowly it moved forward as he continued to lean into the vehicle.

Traffic in the next lane began to move, and as Maksim pushed the stalled vehicle forward. *At least the bomb is moving away from me if I can't move away from it.* As soon as the car he was pushing moved far enough forward that Maksim was sure there was space enough to navigate through, he stopped pushing and went back to his own vehicle. He had less than 90 seconds left.

Once inside his vehicle, he started the car and threw it into gear, pulling forward and immediately making a left turn. As he did so, he saw the bewildered face of the man sitting in the stalled car, which was now in the center of the intersection. A block later, Maksim made another left-hand turn while looking down at his watch as it counted the remaining ten seconds before the explosion.

He felt the rumble of the ground beneath his car before he heard the sound. Maksim allowed himself to smile, with the realization his bomb went off as planned. Then, seeing an available side street he made the turn and began to snake his way back to his apartment. In the distance behind him, he could hear a multitude of sirens wailing. Maksim found himself becoming aroused and felt a deep sense of satisfaction since he knew he already arranged for release to deliver itself to his door within an hour.

As soon as he entered his apartment, he stripped off his disguise and immediately entered a cool shower to wash away the sweat from both the heat and intensity of his just-completed errand. Almost as soon as he finished drying off, he could hear the knock at the door. Wrapping a towel around his waist, he strode through the apartment and opened the door a crack. After confirming it was Jasmine, he left the door open while turning and walking back into the apartment.

Jasmine entered and stood in the doorway, which led into the living room. Maksim retrieved his wallet taking a single bill from it, he walked back and handed her a 100KD bill. He saw her eyes go immediately wide, then narrow as she wondered what dastardly acts would be required of her to earn what amounted to a weekend's wages.

"The rest of the day?"

"Yes," she said as she folded the bill and put it into her small purse, "How you want me to start, Baby?" Not waiting for a response, she was already unzipping her dress and dropping it to the floor.

Maksim just stood still, the towel still wrapped around him. *Any effort at this point should be hers and not mine.* She glided over to him, pressing her body against his, wrapping her arms around his shoulders, and running her fingers down his back. She raised her face toward his and looked him in the eyes before closing them again and gently pressing her hips into him. Maksim noticed her eyes were both glassy and dilated. She probably used the first payment to obtain a fix of whatever she was shooting into her body. *Her problem, not mine.*

He could feel her hands playing with the towel and within seconds it fell to the floor. She then lowered herself to her knees and began to pleasure him. He let this go on for a moment, before he lowered his hand to her to pull her up.

"No, not this time. The bedroom is over there," Maksim released

Jasmine's hand using his eyes to indicate the direction where he wanted her to go. She complied. He followed her, but paused in the doorway as she climbed onto the bed and began to erotically grind her naked body against the bed.

Rolling onto her back, she looked up at him as she slowly spread her legs and said, "Come on Lover, I'm horny. I want you."

Maksim looked at her for a moment before he walked over to the bed. Rather than immediately climbing between her legs, he sat on one side of the bed, then lay on his back with his hands behind his head.

"You on top but first," he said to her pointing to the bedside table.

Jasmine rolled over to the side, and opening the drawer on the bedside table found a package of condoms. She opened it with her teeth popping the prophylactic into her mouth. She rearranged herself, her mouth even with his waist, then expertly unrolled the device on him using only her mouth and tongue. She shifted her position and slowly lowered herself onto him as he entered her.

Maksim knew for the amount he paid, it would almost be expected he would go bareback. At this point, he was so aroused he was tempted to do this in spite of possible STDs. But, since this act was going to create a detail, he was going to have to deal with, he did not want to increase the amount of evidence he was forced to deal with, to include DNA.

Looking up at her from below, Maksim watched as she arched her back and performed a myriad of bodily gyrations she knew he would enjoy. As he watched the light shimmering on her dark hair, he moved his hands from behind his head to under the pillow while she thrust her hips into him harder. Maksim could feel her using muscle control to grip him tighter, while she began changing the rhythm of strokes against him – first faster, then slower, then faster again.

While Jasmine was pleasuring him, Maksim found what he was looking for under the pillow; the cold handle of his sheath knife. This was the same one he used on Rajeesh and the thought made him throb. As he lay below her, watching her, he gripped the handle of the knife with his right hand but then moved his left hand from under the pillow up toward her face gently caressing the side of it. Jasmine's reaction was to tilt her head into the palm of his hand as she quickened her pace. Rather than slowing again, she continued building speed taking his index finger into her mouth. She sucked on the digit while she swirled her tongue around it, copying motions Maksim enjoyed earlier. He could feel his release rising.

Jasmine was a professional who knew how to read her client, and after releasing his finger from her mouth, she lowered his hand to her throat placing the web between his thumb and forefinger directly on her trachea before releasing his hands, and giving him the option of what to do next.

She was now sliding up and down on Maksim at a furious pace, and somehow managed to add a blend of muscle contractions and pulses, which made the entire feeling more intense for him. She then felt his hand begin to close around her throat and began to consciously prevent herself from panicking. After all, just because the man was hiring a whore did not mean he was a murderer.

As Maksim felt himself about to go over the edge, he gripped the knife handle more tightly. Without realizing it, he also began to tighten the hand resting on Jasmine's throat. She willed herself not to allow the anxiety of being choked to take hold and instead arched her back to push him into her further. As he reached his zenith, Maksim abandoned his plan to pull the knife from under the pillow to slash her throat and instead withdrew his empty hand and placed it on top of the one already on Jasmine's throat, and began to tighten his grip in earnest. Being a skilled killer, he knew just how far he could take this and still not kill her. As he continued to meet her downward thrusts, he could feel the strength and life leaving her body and this caused him to thrust against her that much harder.

Jasmine's moans, which had been filling the room, were silenced as the same hands which were preventing oxygen from reaching her lungs, preventing sound from exiting her throat. The rush of taking her to the edge of life and her not fighting against his doing it blended to extend his orgasm even longer. Jasmine's body began to crumple upon him, as her consciousness left. When he felt her body beginning to fall backward, he released her throat and pulled her toward him. As he did this, her limp body slammed down on him splashing the pools of sweat which now covered both of them.

As he lay there under the weight of her body, he waited for her to begin breathing again. One minute, then two; *I may have to use CPR to bring her back.* Her body shuddered as she coughed and began to gulp air into her lungs again. After Jasmine's breathing returned to normal, he felt her raise up and look down at him. He stared up at her, and saw minor elements of petechial hemorrhaging appearing in the whites of her eyes. She began to speak, but instead coughed when no sound came out. Trying again, in a hoarse raspy voice she was finally able to be heard, "You like? Good for you?"

Maksim saw no need to verbally acknowledge his preference, even though she allowed herself to basically become a sacrifice to his pleasure. So, he nodded slowly as he ran his hands down the sides of her naked body.

"Maybe come back for more days?" Even though she knew she would have some bruising on her throat, and didn't particularly care for the headache being choked out would give her, clients who paid her this well for a day's work were few and far between.

Maksim needed to give this some thought before he responded. *She was good, incomparably good – but was the pleasure worth the risk?* He moved his right hand from her flesh back to its prior position under the pillow and slowly wrapped his fingers around the knife's handle. *It's not too late to solve this situation.*

Jasmine sensed hesitation on his part. Rather than using words to sell herself to him, she chose her skills to bring him around. Even though her head was throbbing, she began to slowly slide down his body, kissing and licking his responding flesh as she went. As she began to take him into her mouth, she could feel his hands on both sides of her head before hearing him say, "Yes, I think a few more days would be a good idea."

When he was again sated, Maksim allowed himself to gently doze off floating blissfully. He knew when he woke up he was going to have to come up with a plan to deal with her, *but right now I'm satisfied.*

As Huda sat with a cup of tea in her hand, she gazed out the window feeling oddly satisfied; everything was now set to happen. It'd taken years, years to plan how she was going to make things happen, and to accumulate the money to pay for it. She heard revenge was best served cold, but her pain from the slight that led to this end were anything but cold in her memory. Memories she allowed herself to often recall.

Khaled had been working in the stables for a few weeks and it was almost that long since she saw him for any length of time other than his appearances at dinner. But today, he made it a point to come home early from work and after showering approached her as she sat reading a newspaper at the kitchen table. The staff was gone for the day, and his father was not home yet so he joined her at the table in a rare private moment.

"Your father tells me you are doing a great job at the stables."

"I really enjoy the work, it is hard and it is hot, but I am learning much from Naveed and the others."

"I see," Huda did not want to take charge of this conversation, Hamad told her their son was anxious to speak with her about a girl he met. So, she allowed lengthy silences to hang, rather than directing the conversation, which was her normal style.

"I suppose it is hot and difficult, which is why you must begin planning for your future beyond cleaning out paddocks and brushing down horses. You have fantastic opportunities waiting."

"I know, I know. The family business awaits, but can't you see it is important to me to know how it all works. From the bottom up – so I will know every nuance."

"I see." *I wish he would get to the point, I know he has one.*

"It looks like everyone's already left for the day."

"They have; I am just waiting for your father to get home to put dinner on the table. You and I are the only ones here right now." *I'm not sure how much clearer I can be this would be the time you need to speak.*

"That's a good thing, I wanted to talk to you about something. Someone."

"Oh?" *At last.*

"You see, I've met someone and I would like for you and father to meet her as well. I know you both will love her as much as I've come to love her."

"I see. Where did you meet her?"

Khaled quickly launched into a brief history of how he met Sheikha, and all the things about her he found endearing. He was so enraptured in his own words, he did not see the disappointment and anger rising in his mother's face.

*A girl he met in a café? A family we do not even know? No investigation of their history or lineage?* The questions flooded Huda's mind one after the other has she listened to Khaled speak. She was taking in his words, but ignoring the emotion or the subjectivity he was giving about how great he thought everything was. This is not good. *At least he hasn't mentioned her being pregnant, which would just add permanence to this disaster.*

When Khaled's excitement slowed and she felt she gave fair time for him to express himself, Huda took his hand in hers and smiled at her son.

"Well, she does sound like something – special. You say her family name is Al-Shammari?"

"Yes, but to be honest I have not met her family yet."

*Another plus, the fewer with knowledge of this entire madness the better. It will be easier to deny it ever happened later.*

"I see. Well, it is no matter. What might be a better idea is for me to meet her first. After all, this girl is pursuing my only son. Then it will be easier and less threatening for her to meet your father. At least then, she will feel she has someone on her side when she meets him."

Khaled's face was beaming. *The poor boy is so smitten. Doesn't he realize how beneath him this girl is? If she were not poorly brought up, she would never have considered becoming involved with him, without his family's approval. Not only that, her own family is unaware of this. She is probably nothing more than an opportunistic piece of trash.*

Khaled agreed to her offer of a one-on-one meeting with Sheikha, and they set a date for the meeting. Huda carefully selected the date and time when she was sure both Khaled and Hamad would be busy at *Rihlat Alsahra'*, and thus far away. It would be easy enough for her to send away the staff while the two spoke. Her goal for the conversation was simple, send this woman away from her son, and guarantee she would never return again.

Khaled rose from the table and walked over to his mother, then leaned forward to hug her from behind. Leaning her head to the side, she nuzzled him for a moment enjoying the closeness she missed since he started work. *Since he started wasting his time with this Sharmuta.*

Huda was magnificent at masking her disdain for Sheikha. In the days leading up to their eventual meeting, she projected the attitude of a woman welcoming an ideal wife for her son into her family. Underneath the façade, she was angry and hurt her son had done this without her. Because of the insult, she could feel nothing positive toward this woman who was trying to steal him away.

When the day arrived, when the two were supposed to meet, events unfolded as she hoped. Both her son and husband left for *Rihlat Alsahra'*, and she sent the staff away for the afternoon. She arranged for an employee to pick up Sheikha and bring her to *Shamal Mazraea*.

When Sheikha arrived, Huda noted she was wearing a *burqa* and *hijab*, but not a veil. Even though it'd been years since Huda wore a veil herself, she somehow saw insult in the girl not wearing one. As they exchanged initial pleasantries, while standing beside the car she arrived in, Huda noticed the young woman's beauty. *I can easily see the cause for the initial attraction my son felt.* She gave the girl a customary hug, then kissed her on both cheeks before turning to lead her toward the front door.

Welcoming her into the main house, Huda led her to the sitting room, where tea, and various pastries and fruit were laid out by the servants before they left. Sheikha's nervousness was easily visible, this was more than just meeting her betrothed's mother; she had never been in the house this beautiful and opulent. Khaled's mother was wearing rings with large diamonds and other precious stones. *There's no doubt Khaled is far richer and more important than he ever said. Why would he want a girl like me?*

Even with the shock and fear she was experiencing, Sheikha managed to keep her composure and maintain a polite conversation with Huda. In spite of her animosity, Huda guided the conversation in such a way it was less an interrogation and more the patronizing curiosity of a future family matriarch. Huda knew more about this girl than her son ever told her.

After Khaled told her about the new woman in his life, Huda called a security firm she used from time to time when screening new household personnel. Within hours a dossier was produced and delivered to her by Wilhelm Weber, the director of the security firm. Even though he was a German ex-pat, he spoke fluent Arabic, understood the customs of the region, and always provided her personalized service.

Recently, he even provided her with an electronic gadget to help her deal with a possible breach of confidentiality by one of her housemaids. All Huda needed to do was plug the device Wilhelm provided into the servant's phone, removing it a few seconds later. From then on, she could plug the device into her own phone and it would allow her to monitor all of the text messages being sent by the housemaid. When giving it to her, Wilhelm told her she could also send messages that would appear to come from the servant's phone. Huda was amazed at the capability of something so small.

Huda only spent a few moments skimming the dossier. She did not need it to make her decision regarding this woman who was now in her son's life. Huda's purpose in requesting the dossier was to present it to her husband, if needed, as evidence of Sheikha's questionable background and family. One thing in the folder did serve to raise her ire toward the woman: her family, the Al-Shammari, were not Kuwaiti — they were *Bedoon.*

Now, as Sheikha sat drinking tea and telling Huda about her family and siblings she was unaware of the woman sitting across from her had already decided Sheikha's fate. The only thing left was for Huda to determine the best way to dispose of her.

When the subject turned to how she and Khaled met, Sheikha told Huda about the cellphone he gave her. "I was a little confused by it at first, but then I got used to how it functioned and it turned into a wonderful tool for us to communicate."

"Yes, when I first got mine it took me a while to learn all the capabilities it possessed," then a possibility occurred to Huda. "You see," as she spoke, she withdrew her own cellphone from the pocket of her *burqa*, "my newest one lets me push on the screen with my finger for some things, and for other actions I have to use buttons."

This prompted Sheikha to take out her own cellphone from her purse. Sheikha held it out for Huda to see as she was describing how the phone worked. Huda took it from her hand and pretended to be examining it. It only took a moment for Huda to realize this phone was the same make and model as her housemaid's, *so I could use Wilhelm's device to eavesdrop on this girl.* Rather than returning the phone to Sheikha, she lay it down on the table in front of them.

As the conversation progressed, Sheikha found herself providing more information than she realized. Huda's relaxed manner caused her to feel comfortable, and as a result, she dropped her guard. Topics which normally would've been withheld from any but her closest friends were suddenly coming out of her mouth, as if she were speaking to someone she knew for years. Eventually, she made mention of the nights she and Khaled spent alone. While Sheikha omitted the fact they made love during these encounters, it did not take much imagination on Huda's part to realize what took place. *My son, my dear, dear son, tempted by the pleasures this Sharmuta offered. She's pregnant, no doubt. Pregnant and planning on using it to force my son into marrying her. Alkaliba! Conniving Bedoon. Using my son's honorable nature against him to work her way into our family to gain legitimacy and wealth.*

Sheikha stopped speaking midsentence, it was obvious something she said disturbed Huda, she was now staring off into the distance, but the hand holding her teacup was beginning to shake. *Ya lahwi! What have I done I've said far too much and now, now this woman I needed to impress is probably disgusted by me. Khaled, why'd I ever agree to this.*

"Mrs. Al-Bourisli? Is everything okay?"

Huda suddenly shook her head, bringing herself back to reality, then turned toward Sheikha and smiled.

"Sorry my dear, distant memory of the times I spent with Khaled's father before we were wed. Isn't it nice to be alone and enjoying the time with the man you love?"

Sheikha found only slight relief in these words, she knew she said too much and needed to be more guarded.

The sun began to descend and as it did the heat in the room began to build even though the house was fully climate controlled. The curtains on the windows were left open, as they usually were in the morning, but with the staff gone, there was no one to close them as the sun went down. Rather than taking it upon herself to close the curtains, Huda chose to use the situation to her advantage.

"Come, Sheikha, let's move to the sitting room on the other side the house where things are not so warm." As she said this, she picked up the tray of edibles and handed it to Sheikha. While doing this, she carefully slid the girl's cellphone under one of the napkins sitting on the table. Upon standing, Huda placed both of their teacups on the tray that was holding the teapot and picked it up, then turned to lead the way to another room in the house.

Upon arriving in the afternoon sitting room, Huda set the tray on the table was between two of the chairs. She then took the tray from Sheikha and set it down as well.

"Come, let me give you a quick tour of the house," Huda said as she immediately walked back out of the room they just entered. Sheikha followed her as Huda made a circuit of the large home. Several of the rooms were half as large as Sheikha's family apartment. There were multiple bathrooms, ablution rooms, sitting rooms, a very ornately decorated *diwaniya*, a home office, small rooms for the domestic staff, and the master bedroom. When Huda reached the master bedroom, she did not open the door as she had for all of the others but instead just identified what was behind the closed door.

Before taking the stairs to the second floor, Huda excused herself for a moment under the guise of going to the bathroom. Instead, she returned to the master bedroom and after closing the door behind her went directly to her dresser and searched through one of the drawers looking for Wilhelm's device. Finding it, she slipped it into her pocket and returned to find Sheikha still waiting at the base of the stairs.

The second and third floors were not as interesting as the first. Both floors were taken up by large bedrooms, each with their own bathrooms and sitting rooms. The third floor featured a home theater and balcony with several sets of tables and chairs.

"This house. It's just so amazing. I don't think I've ever seen anything like it," Sheikha said as they were heading back down the stairs to the sitting room where they originated.

"Yes. Our family has worked hard throughout a lifetime to achieve this. Hopefully, our good fortune will continue, *insha'Allah.*"

As they entered the afternoon sitting room, it occurred to Sheikha her phone was missing.

"I must've left it in the other room."

"Have a seat dear, I will go get it for you."

After ensuring Sheikha was sitting down and would not be following her to the other room, Huda returned to the sitting room where they began the day. She walked toward the table and threw back the napkin which concealed the cell phone, as she took the cloning device from her pocket. As soon as the phone was in her hands, she connected the device and waited for the green LED light to appear on it signaling the target phone was successfully compromised. Feeling satisfied as she completed this, Huda pulled the device from the phone and slipped it into her pocket before turning around and walking immediately without warning into Sheikha.

"Oh!" *Did she see what I was doing?*

"I'm so sorry, you seemed to be gone a long time I thought maybe you were having trouble finding my phone." *Does she suspect, I suspect she was reading the messages Khaled and I sent to each other?*

"No problem, dear, I found it," as Huda said this, she held the phone up and offered it to Sheikha who immediately took it and smiled back at her. *I don't think she saw me using the device on the phone, but she is nervous about me being alone with her phone.*

"Thank you so much. For something I'd never before possessed, this has come to be very important to me." *Well, if she did read something private, she is not acting as if she did.*

"It is how you and Khaled communicate. I can see why you'd be concerned if it went missing." *Now I will be able to read every word between the two of you.*

They returned to the afternoon sitting room without further discussion of the phone but Huda's inquisitive nature about Sheikha's family and other details seemed to have faded. The deep open-ended questions she had been asking gave way to those that only required single word answers. *Whatever magic was between us seems to have gone away, or maybe the woman is just tired.*

When the conversation ground to a halt, and the silence permeated the room for a few minutes, Huda suddenly rose to her feet.

"Well, my dear, I've enjoyed our time together but I must get busy and prepare dinner for Hamad and Khaled."

"Oh," Sheikha said, surprised at the sudden end to their first encounter, "Please, let me help you."

*An offer of help? If this girl was anything other than a Bedoon opportunist, she might be a possibility.* "No need, no need. I can take care of this easily. Besides, I'm sure you need to be helping your own *Umma* to prepare the meal for your house."

"If you are sure I can't be of help."

"Don't even concern yourself with things here," as Huda said this she started to walk toward the front door, leaving it to Sheikha to follow her. Once at the door, Huda opened it and saw the driver had returned. Now he was sitting under the shade of the trees waiting to be summoned. She nodded toward him, and he immediately understood it was time to return this person to where he picked her up.

The last few things Khaled's mother said concerned Sheikha as they seemed to indicate a chilling of their relationship and an effort by Huda to push her away using terms like *your house* and *things here. I'm not sure what I said or did wrong. I hope Khaled won't be angry I didn't make a suitable impression on his mother*

Even Huda's farewell embrace, lacked the warmth of the one she was welcomed with upon arrival. It even lacked the kisses on the cheek, which the welcome included. As soon as she was in the car, and headed for home, Sheikha withdrew her cell phone from her purse and typed out a quick text message to Khaled.

```
> All strted well but ended strngly
```

Almost immediately, she received a reply.

```
< Don't worry, sur you did fine. Wrkng.
```

The last word told her it would be a while before he could carry on a conversation with her. In the interim, she would torture herself going over every minute detail of the day's events. Part of her wanted to accept the fact everything went well and maybe it was just the rush to start supper that caused the change in Huda's temperament. Somewhere deep inside her though, she was sure the woman was masking a rejection of her in the way she sent her off.

As soon as Huda closed the door, withdrew her phone and plugged the cloning device into it. Everything connected just in time for her to see the brief exchange between Sheikha and her son. *My son, you couldn't be more wrong. She was nowhere close to fine.*

She removed the cloning device from her phone and quickly selected Wilhelm's number from her contact list. He greeted her by name when answering, she always found it a bit unnerving even though she was well aware her number was revealed to him when the call was placed.

"Wilhelm, I have a small favor to ask of you."

"My company and I are ready to serve."

"Wonderful. I would like you to retrieve the cellphone of the woman you researched for me earlier."

"No problem. I'm assuming you want this done as quickly as possible and without her knowledge."

"Yes."

"It shall be done this evening."

"Very nice – and Wilhelm, this favor is between you and me."

"No one will ever know. Your confidence in my confidentiality is well-placed."

"Thank you."

Huda hung up the phone and slipped it into her *burqa* pocket.

Sheikha and Khaled would probably have one last text discussion before the girl was relieved of her cellphone. Sometime tomorrow Khaled would receive a text message from her ending their relationship because she felt unworthy and telling him she was going to terminate her pregnancy. *I can't be sure she's pregnant, or she even told him. But even if she wasn't and hasn't, that added bit of surprise can only work in my favor.*

She knew to have his relationship terminated this way would devastate Khaled. It was a pain Huda wished she could have prevented, as she truly loved her son. Her concern over him making a mistake that would haunt him for the rest of his life, served as an adequate justification for her action. *He may feel a few weeks or months of pain, but soon enough it'll be gone. Better than decades of having a manaqib aldhahab as an anchor tied around his neck, ruining the rest of his days.*

Taking a sip of tea, Huda sighed heavily. The entire plan she launched that day ended badly. She had underestimated her son's attachment, and as a result, she was left with years of anger and resentment, and no way to rid herself of them. *Until now.*

Events she placed in motion now were going to grant her relief from the pain. She would have the final revenge against the people who were responsible for taking her son.

# Chapter 10



A week had passed since the explosion killed a member of the Kuwaiti Parliament, along with six others who were unlucky enough to be too close. Since then, information about Jefzar's effort to piece together clues regarding a possible serial killer spread like wildfire through the Kuwaiti law enforcement's informal grapevine. From there it jumped to the civilian populace, and it did not take long for the press to start hounding him at his office and home. Each wanted to be the first to report any goings-on within the investigation, and resorted to publishing any rumor regardless of how outlandish or unlikely.

"It's true, I saw the article online myself," Jefzar insisted as he leaned forward and took a slice of mango from the tray sitting on the table. "They reported Satan himself was eating a hamburger at the Johnny Rocket burger stand in *Al Jahra.*"

"How outlandish can you get. Everyone knows *Shaytan* much prefers the French fries from Smashburger."

"Well, that might be true," Jefzar said patting his stomach, "they're irresistible but do evil things to my waistline."

Both men laughed, and Hamad told one of the house staff standing by to bring out the *sheesha*. As they waited, an uneasy silence fell over them. While Jefzar was normally lighthearted when with his brother this entire situation was weighing heavily on upon him. When the water pipe was delivered, the servants departed, and Jefzar felt free to discuss the troublesome situation openly with his brother.

"You know, I spend several hours a day staring at the evidence we have and trying to gather more. Luck was the only reason I was able to connect a pedestrian fatality to the string. An ambulance driver found the killer's note stuffed in the victim's pants pocket. Sometimes I run into a dead-end; a body was found at a construction fire, we weren't able to identify it. The blaze was probably arson, but there was no note – or it was consumed in the fire.

The victims are just so scattered, the only thing in common is the handwritten note found on their bodies. The *nadhil* was bold enough to even sign the bomb," he paused and sucked on the mouthpiece of the pipe before he allowed the smoke to escape his lips as he continued to speak, "How often does a killer openly sign every bit of carnage while leaving no clues as to motive. Without which, I can neither find him nor prevent the next assassination. Perhaps it is *Shaytan* himself."

Hamad pondered Jefzar's words for a moment before he spoke, "You say you can find nothing connecting any of the victims. True?"

"Absolutely. There've been TCNs – both skilled and unskilled – Kuwaitis, and of course now a member of Parliament."

"So, what's lacking? Maybe what's missing will tell you who he will go for next."

"Well, no Western ex-pats."

"Perhaps the killer is from the West," as Hamad said this, he took a sip of his tea then withdrew his *tasbih* from his pocket and starting from the handle, subconsciously began to count each of the 33 beads.

"The thought occurred to me, but in addition to signing each crime with the Arabic word for Satan, I think they're just too many details for a Westerner to be able to handle by himself. You see, a certain level of insider knowledge comes into play with each of these crimes which are allowing our killer to remain anonymous to us."

"So you think the killer might be a Kuwaiti?"

"No, it just doesn't have the right feel for it to be a citizen."

"A disgruntled TCN perhaps?"

"A possibility, but it would take a good deal of income to be able to afford the setups for each of the crimes. Plus some of the victims were TCNs."

"Well, was there anything the politician was working on which might have served as a motive?"

"Nothing specifically. The only legislative matter the man was part of was legislation regarding the *Bedoon*."

"Such as?"

"Well, if you recall, there were many changes after the liberation removing specific rights and such from *Bedoons*. He was part of the coalition which created the legislation, but he always felt they should have gone further fulfilling the full 1985 policy proposal of the Minister of Interior. He was about to introduce a stricter set of rules and policies. From what I could gather, there was no opposition to what he planned. It was also so boring the press didn't consider covering it worthwhile, I found out about it one of his assistants."

"Hmm," Hamad took a deep draw of smoke letting it waft out of his mouth, "An equal opportunity killer, who also took out a politician who wasn't doing anything overtly political. Indeed."

"Yes, he seems to be killing a little of every group," then it struck Jefzar like a thunderbolt, "It isn't who he is killing, it's who he isn't."

Hamad was confused. He looked across at his brother, who had moved from a recumbent position to one setting straight up and facing him.

"He hasn't killed a *Bedoon*, because maybe he is a *Bedoon!*" As he said this, Jefzar became more excited – his mind throwing bits and pieces of each of the killings together to support this conclusion.

"A *Bedoon?*"

"Yes, think about it. Who moves around within our society without being noticed? What kind of person would know how to do things under the table and to obtain materials outside of normal channels, to go unnoticed?" Jefzar stood up and began to pace back and forth allowing his mind to race forward, "Who could hide in plain view, with their race blending them in with any other of our population. If you go by appearance alone how could you tell a *Bedoon* from a Kuwaiti? Not only that, a few changes of wardrobe, hairstyle, and at a glance, the killer could pass for a Pakistani, Indian, or Bangladeshi. It would take a closer examination or a citizenship ID card plus other documentation to absolutely tell the difference for sure," he paused for a moment and looked down at Hamad.

"Hmm. So obvious, I'd never have considered it. You would

seem to be on to something," Jefzar's brother replied as he returned to counting the *tasbih's* beads, "Indeed a fascinating theory – well worth pursuing."

Jefzar stood silently for a moment, contemplating the possibility he just verbalized to his brother. He wasn't seeking to confirm its truth but instead mentally reviewing his idea to ensure there were no logic holes before he began to pursue it as a likelihood. Hamad watched as his brother's expression turned from one of puzzlement to one of a man who just caught sight of his prey and was preparing to pursue.

"I'm guessing you suddenly have duties needing your immediate attention?" Hamad raised his eyebrows as he said this to his brother, not seeking an answer but an affirmation.

"Yes, if you'll forgive my rapid departure. It would seem I may have discovered a trail which needs to be followed."

Hamad rose from where he was sitting and walked to his brother, giving him a firm hug he held him by his shoulders and looked into his eyes, "What was it Sherlock would say? *The game is afoot?*"

The determination in Jefzar's eyes did not abate, but he could not help but smile at his brother's comment. As he nodded his head, "Yes. Or as my brother would say, *indeed.*"

The two men embraced again, before Jefzar turned to leave the *diwaniya*. Within moments, his police SUV was speeding across the sand so he could begin sifting through the evidence again, but this time with a possibility in mind. Hamad departed as well, but he was only headed to his residence tent at *Rihlat Alsahra'*, leaving his servants to clean up after bidding them goodnight.

Later, while lying in bed next to Huda, Hamad shared the topic of his and Jefzar's discussion. Given the public interest surrounding his task force and the rumors being spread daily, both in the press and through social media, he was not surprised she seemed to also have a keen interest. After asking many probing questions, Hamad also shared the theory Jefzar came to regarding the possibility of the murderer being a *Bedoon.*

If he could have seen her face in the darkness, he might have questioned her excited expression as it was neither logical nor understandable. But by morning, Hamad would remember nothing of their discussion anyway, the only thing he would recall from the night before was her unusual sexual aggressiveness. Given the length of their marriage, the occurrence was not one to be dwelled upon as a question, but just remembered fondly.

Hotel Sultana

As Najila slowed the black SUV to a stop in front of the hotel, she found herself smiling at Evan who was there awaiting her arrival. Over the weeks, the rancor she initially felt for him slowly faded – first into acceptance and understanding, now into something strangely like friendship. He gradually started chipping away at the wall she built around herself against Western men, and she began to understand him as a human being. Sure, there was still much he did not know about Kuwait or its culture, but unlike many of the Westerners she knew before, he sought to understand and learn, rather than cling to expectations based on preconceived notions.

As he entered the vehicle, he placed a cup filled with pomegranate juice into the center holder and his Go-bag on the floor. Once seated, he buckled his seatbelt and turned to Najila, "So, what adventure did you have in mind today?"

"Well, like any society, ours knows the benefit of a good education. I thought you might find in elementary school interesting."

"Sounds terrific," as he spoke, Evan reached forward and unzipped one of the side pockets on his Go-bag and withdrew a small bottle of Tylenol. He poured three into his hand before replacing the top and putting it back in its assigned compartment.

"Headache?"

"Yeah, sinuses. I'm guessing the weather is about to shift. Changes in atmospheric pressure can give me a killer headache." As he

**203**

said this, it occurred to him he had not paid attention to a single weather report since his arrival. *After all, the weather was always the same. Hot and dusty.* Occasionally, the wind would change direction or speed, which contributed to more dust. Aside from that, rain was scarce, and the temperature never seemed to differ more than a few degrees from one day to the next.

"Oh, I'm sorry to hear you're not feeling well. Perhaps the school should wait for another day?"

"No, not at all – I'll be fine. Are we going to a *madrassa?*" As he said this, Evan popped the three Tylenol into his mouth, and after taking a single bite to break them up, he swallowed them dry. He did not say anything, but his headache was getting gradually worse as time passed. Knowing his own history, he dreaded where this might go in the next few hours.

"Those are primarily for religious education; I will be taking you to a regular elementary school. I've actually picked two schools for you to see. The first one is taught in a mix of Arabic and English, with a student body is made up primarily of Kuwaitis. The other is a private school which is taught entirely in English. The students there are a mix of Kuwaiti children as well as those of foreign diplomats. Something you might find of interest; the school was named in honor of General Schwarzkopf."

"I'm guessing it was named after the liberation?"

"As you say. Immediately following the liberation, there was much gratitude toward him and Americans in general."

"It always helps if the people you've liberated are thankful afterward," his joke fell flat. *My head is starting to kill me, I wish the Tylenol would kick in.*

Najila nodded at the comment as she stopped at a traffic signal. She took the cup of pomegranate juice from its holder and took a sip of what had now become a daily ritual. When the light changed, she replaced the container and pressed on the accelerator as they continued down the road for several moments in silence.

After making several turns, she pulled the car into a parking lot in front of a gleaming white building with large tinted windows. As they got out of the vehicle, Evan saw the large sign in front of the building announcing it was *The General Norman Schwarzkopf English Elementary School.*

"The Brits run this?" Evan asked as he withdrew his phone and took a picture of the sign. He noticed the wind began to pick up, and there was now more sand and dirt in the air than earlier.

"No, it is about the language spoken at the school, not the nationality."

"Got it," Evan had more questions, but the wind was so dry it felt as if it was stealing the moisture from his body straight through his skin. So, he wanted to get inside as quickly as possible.

The two of them walked into the school. Evan removed his sunglasses but quickly found himself wishing he could leave them on to suppress the light which was causing his headache to grow. The two followed the signs in the hall which took them to the administration office suite. There, they met the Principal, an older Frenchwoman who had been in charge of the school since it opened. Without being asked, she explained she relocated to Kuwait as an expatriate when she was married to a German petroleum engineer who came to work for the oil company. After their divorce, she decided to stay, eventually taking this position with the school. Evan jotted a note to himself that he might want to interview her later since it was highly unusual to meet an ex-pat woman who was living on her own in Kuwait.

After sharing a cup of tea, the three of them began a tour of the facility. In many ways, it looked like an elementary school found anywhere in the world. The school was technologically advanced due to its recent creation and the clientele of students attending.

The principal shared that, "aside from the children of diplomats, many of the students came from well-to-do Kuwaiti families. Parents choose to send their children here to provide them with exposure to other cultures, and to gain a superior command of English. The populace is rounded out by the children of ex-pats and a smaller group of scholarship recipients who are *Bedoon*." Through the fog of his headache,

Evan recalled hearing the word before, during his conversation with Roshan upon arrival. He made a mental note to ask Najila for more details later.

Without warning, the principal turned toward one of the closed doors and opened it motioning for them to follow her. Najila and Evan entered behind the principal and stood next to her at the rear of the room. At the front of the class, was a middle-aged man wearing a sports coat who was teaching a class of about 25 children in desks that were facing him. After listening for a few moments, it became apparent he was teaching literature, as they were discussing the anatomical parts that made up a short story.

"What grade is this?" Evan whispered to the principal as he tilted his head towards her.

"I believe the equivalent in the United States would be sixth or seventh grade; all of these children are 11 or 12 years old. They are the most advanced in this school, next year they will attend a school which will take them all the way to graduation."

As they spoke, one of the boys in the back row turned toward them and stared. From his vantage point, there was more stimulus coming from the rear of the room than from the front. When the principal noticed an observer, she waved her index finger at him, and whispered, "Meteb, turn around and pay attention," the boy slowly turned back toward the front of the room, but as he did three other students turned around to see what was.

"I think we need to move on," the principal said as she crossed in front of Najila and Evan and led them out the door after giving the teacher a short nod on the way out.

"When I was in school, if the principal knew my name, it would've been seen as a *bad* thing," Evan said once they were in the hall.

"Not so in this case, the boy is one of our *Bedoon* scholarship students, which is why I'm familiar with him. He is a brilliant student and usually well behaved. At 12, most children are still working on developing their attention span skills," without another word, the principal turned and walked down the hall pointing out the various specialty rooms as they passed.

As the morning wore on, the principal provided a complete rundown of how the school operated and the specialty classes available for the students. At the end of the tour, the three of them sat in her office with her again behind the large glass desk, and Najila and Evan seated in front of her in hardback wooden chairs.

"In addition, we often take field trips to various places in the country, so the students have a more well-rounded experience. Just the other day, a group of our 12-year-olds went to the aquarium at the Kuwait Scientific Center in *Salmiya*."

The mention of the Center caused Evan to look towards Najila, who was quick to respond, "Already on our list."

"Well," the principal said as she consulted her watch, "it is almost lunchtime if you would care to join us. We have both Western and *halal* offerings." As she said this, she looked directly at Najila, even though she was wearing nothing which would have identified her as Muslim.

"Thank you for your most generous offer, and I don't want to seem rude, but I have a bit of a headache which I probably need to look after, since I have other appointments this afternoon," Evan said as he began to stand.

The three shook hands, and the principal provided Evan with one of her business cards, should he have any additional questions for his article. She also asked to be notified as to when it might be published so she could keep an eye out for it. As soon as the two of them were back in the car, Evan laid back against the seat rest and used his fingertips to massage his temples.

"The Tylenol didn't work. Anyway, we could reschedule this afternoon's tour to another day?" As he said this, he peered through the windows and noticed the air seemed almost foggy due to the amount of dust.

"As you say," Najila began driving back toward the *Sultana* and at the same time withdrew her cell phone, quickly dialing in the number for the school they were supposed to visit this afternoon. Speaking in

Arabic, she apologized for the short notice but canceled the appointment explaining to the person on the other end she would be back in touch as soon as Evan felt better. When she hung up, she glanced toward the passenger side and saw Evan leaning on the door with his eyes closed. She proceeded back to the hotel in silence, surprised she felt more for him than just passing pity.

Once at their destination, Evan stepped out of the SUV without saying a word, only offering a grunt in response to Najila's farewell. After watching him enter the hotel, Najila was struck by an epiphany and left the hotel to pick up a few of the required supplies to bring the idea to fruition. After stepping inside, Evan felt a sense of relief, because he knew if he could make it to the elevator, he would be able to lay down and perhaps sleep away the throbbing in his head.

As soon as he entered the elevator, he turned around and watched the doors close while leaning back against the wall of the small cubicle. Even though the ride was a short one, he let his Go-bag drop to the floor. Now, out of public sight, he could give in to the pain he was feeling and allow himself the luxury of appearing weak. Upon the door's opening, Evan scooped his bag from the floor and walked into his suite. He took a few steps and immediately dropped his Go-bag into one of the chairs that surrounded the conference table. It was then he took a moment and looked out his window and across the horizon.

*Damn, I don't think I've ever seen the air so full of dirt.* The harbinger of Evan's sinus headache was fulfilled as a massive sandstorm began to fill the horizon in front of him. What was once a clear view of the refinery from his window, was now painted in a sand-colored haze — almost looking like a thick tan fog. As he was turning from the window in search of a comfortable chair, something caught his eye. Lying in the center of the table was a legal-sized manila envelope, he noticed his first and last name printed on it in block letters. *Probably just something from the hotel.* Dismissing it, he continued toward his destination, a sizeable over-stuffed chair in the sitting area of his suite. Once in position, he allowed himself to collapse and closed his eyes letting his head to fall back against the headrest. *Whatever it is, it can wait until later.* Then, a soft, lilting voice interrupted the silence.

"Sir? Are you okay?" Jazlene said as she stepped cautiously into the sitting room.

Since their initial meeting several weeks ago it was rare Evan saw or spoke to her, but he recognized her voice instantly. Without opening his eyes, he said softly, "Yes, Jazlene, I'm fine. I know you still have several hours on your shift, but why don't you go ahead and leave for the day. I've got everything I need."

"Are you sure Sir?" Her voice carried genuine concern, which told Evan she was questioning the *I'm fine* and not the *leave for the day* part of the conversation.

"Truly, it is just a bad headache. The best medicine would be some silence and maybe a nap. Just come back tomorrow as scheduled."

"Yes sir," Jazlene said as she slowly backed into the spare bedroom. She gathered her purse and wrap then walked directly to the elevator telling him she hoped he would feel better as the doors closed.

"Jazlene, about the envelope..." *too late.*

*At last, silence. I am truly alone.* Things were much quieter, but the silence only allowed the sound of the sandstorm raging outside to become more pronounced. Instead of allowing himself to be distracted by the sound, Evan began subconsciously using the guided imagery technique to separate himself from the reality of the noise and the pain he felt. Soon, the tension left his body as he found himself immersed in a much more peaceful and sensual world.

He mentally took himself to the familiar park. It was the same beautiful European morning, and the sunlight held a cheery brightness rather than punishing heat. One of the side benefits of having learned guided imagery was that the technique seemed to make all the memories more vivid, even those not directly connected to suppressing anxiety. Now, rather than terminating his session at the memory of the shadow passing across his face as he lay in the grass, he allowed himself to revel in what happened next.

The sudden shadow caused him to open his eyes, and he found himself staring up at her as she moved into position straddling him. Her eyes were brilliant green, and as he looked into them, she involuntarily flashed her eyes at him, signaling the passion she was feeling. Taking a moment to admire the beauty of her face, he let his eyes dwell on her lips. He saw her pink tongue dart between them, leaving them wet and shiny before she lowered her mouth to his. The kiss was slow and sensual. The way she kissed him always reminded him of the way one might devour a juicy, ripe peach. Slowly moving her lips as she tried to keep up with the juice which was flowing from the fruit, while her tongue explored all the textures of the fruit's flesh, pulp, and wetness.

As they shared the kiss, her hands went to the side of his face – the fingertips gently caressing him while her mouth explored his. He allowed himself to dwell in the kiss' moment before the scene transitioned to the next part of the day, which found them sitting in a small café.

As he sat across from her, he began as he always did with taking stock of all of the details of her appearance. The way the light was reflecting in her hair, how it shimmered when she made even the slightest move. Her fingers wrapped around her coffee cup as she put it up to her lips. While he studied each finger, he remembered the way they felt as she caressed his face earlier. Her eyes were bright and penetrating. There was not a thought she did not allow to be exposed, but at the same time, each was wrapped in a shroud of mystery. As he let the memory play out, he recalled the taste of the pastries and German coffee they were enjoying.

In his vision, the two of them were alone in the café. Even if others were there, they would not have seen her hand under the table and cloaked by the tablecloth as it slowly began to slide from his knee to his inner thigh. *No. Where this is going will do nothing toward relaxing me. But still* –. His mental exploration of the remembrance was so all-encompassing he did not hear the elevator when its doors opened behind him.

Najila entered the room quietly, kicking off her heels after stepping out of the elevator. She could see Evan seated in the chair facing away from the large windows which no longer provided the spectacular view but only a dim tan-colored reflection of light due to the sand in the air. It was easy enough for her to convince the hotel manager to allow her entry into the penthouse elevator; she was not sure how she would handle the next part of her plan. *I'm still not sure why I'm doing this, but somehow deep down it just feels right to do something to help him.*

Earlier, as she watched Evan exit the vehicle, apparently in pain from his headache, a memory from her college days crossed her mind. A friend of hers at school in Texas was plagued by similar sinus headaches from the changes in the weather there. Wanting to relieve her friend of the pain, Najila offered to try something to provide relief. She was introduced to the art of massage by a roommate, and one of the methods she learned was facial massage, which her friend said also helped to relieve pressure and pain from headaches and migraines.

The first time she tried this for her friend, she did not have the appropriate massage oil the therapy required, so she created her own, using a combination of unscented baby oil, which was on hand, and the only scent in her purse, *Lamsat Hareer*. With those two, Najila was able to create a unique mixture, which provided a relaxing massage accompanied by a bit of sensual aromatherapy. In the end, whenever her friend was set upon by the pain of a sinus headache, usually in the spring and early summer, she was able to relieve the pain through healing touch. Over time, she refined her personalized massage oil but always including *Lamsat Hareer*.

When she dropped Evan off, Najila realized she did not have the appropriate ingredients to create the scented oil necessary for her therapeutic facial massage. After a quick stop at the local *souk*, she now possessed what was needed in a small plastic bag. She retrieved a short water glass from the sideboard, then withdrew each of the ingredients one at a time and set them on the table. Carefully, she poured various amounts from each of the bottles she brought with her into the glass to recreate her custom facial massage oil. Once the potion was complete, she held the glass to her nose and inhaled deeply, enjoying the sensual fragrance. The scent also caused a jarring memory to fill her mind. *That's right. It was after one of those massages I slept with him for the first time.* Anything she was feeling for Evan up to now abruptly vanished, and she immediately began to have second thoughts about this whole thing.

"Jazlene? Did you forget something?" came the voice from behind her.

"Uh-no. It's me," Najila said spinning around to face the source of the voice.

Evan stood up and turned toward her, but did so too quickly and suddenly felt dizzy because the headache was messing with his equilibrium.

"Najila? Why are you – how are you…"

"Sit, sit back down. Let me explain," Najila continued speaking as she walked toward the chair where Evan was once again seated. "When I saw you get out of the car, I recalled a friend from college who used to get the same kind of headache. I used to give them a facial massage with some aromatic oils. It seemed to help the headache go away more quickly."

"A boyfriend?" *Why the hell did I ask such a question?*

"A female friend." *Okay, I lied but have I misjudged him? And if I have misjudged him, why do I find it intriguing he seems to have a tinge of jealousy?*

"I am dying here, so I'm willing to try anything that might help."

"As you say, although I'm not sure I like being seen as a possibility only worth trying because nothing else has worked so far," *Damnit. Stop trying to build walls between you.*

"I'm sorry, I didn't mean that the way it sounded. I do appreciate the effort you've made, and your willingness to do this for me. Honestly." *At least she seems to have dropped her resentment of my boyfriend comment.*

"Fine, just sit there and relax the way you were sitting before – lean your head back as much as possible and give me a minute to finish preparing. Oh, and roll the collar of your shirt under so it doesn't get any of the massage oil on it, it would probably stain."

As Najila left the room, Evan began fumbling with the collar of his shirt to do as she requested. With the distraction of his headache, he gave up the effort in frustration and unbuttoned shirt instead.

Once in the bathroom, Najila retrieved a washcloth and ran it under hot water. After squeezing the excess moisture, she folded it in thirds and carried it back to Evan. Seeing his shirt unbuttoned, she realized there was a simpler solution. She assisted him with taking the shirt off then tossed it onto the couch. Once he was back in position, she gently laid the damp washcloth across his closed eyes.

"It's not too hot for you is it?"

"No, it's fine." *A little warning would've been nice.*

Najila then took the phone from her purse and after a brief search through her Pandora playlists, picked one she thought would be relaxing, even though she created it for more intimate activity. In moments, the sound of the approaching sandstorm was almost drowned out by the voice of Nina Simone.

"Nice," Evan said as he began to allow himself to relax.

"Glad you like it; Nina is one of my favorites."

Picking up the glass of massage oil, she walked back to the chair where Evan sat. Taking a position standing directly behind him, she poured a small amount of oil into her hand and rubbed her palms together. As the oil warmed, it released its scent into the room.

"Mmm smells nice."

"As you say. It is a wondrous fragrance, and the aroma will help you relax so your headache will go away." As she said this, she lowered her hands to a position just an inch or so above his face telling him to take several deep breaths.

Evan was immediately surrounded by the aroma of the oil. Being an American, the scent of *Lamsat Hareer* was unfamiliar to him, but somehow it seemed to first tease, then fuel, an unfamiliar arousal within him.

"The scent of the oil. What is it?"

"Shhhh, you are supposed to be relaxing not acting as a reporter. This is a special oil I created for just for this purpose. It is a combination of things, but the strongest fragrance is from a perfumed gel known as *Lamsat Hareer* -- a touch of silk. Of course, *Lamsat Hareer* is also a very customized scent, with thousands of variations. Women here put it in their hair and skin. I particularly like this version as it has a wonderful aroma. Now, be quiet and let me get to work."

Evan acknowledged Najila's words with a quiet grunt then inhaled deeply partaking of the scent, which was quickly becoming a favorite. *Jasmine and something else.* Najila waited for him to take one more breath, as she placed her thumbs on his forehead at the hairline and began applying light pressure as she slid them from the center to the edges of his face. She gradually worked her way down from the hairline to his eyebrows. *He does have the strong forehead of an intelligent man and a nice strong jawline.* Upon performing the last stroke just above his eyebrows, she lowered the rest of her fingers until they were in contact with the sides of his nose. She let her hands rest there for a moment gliding her fingers across his cheeks.

Evan lay perfectly still beneath Najila's hands as they worked on him. He knew enough basic anatomy to be aware she was targeting his sinus cavities with her finger's pressure. What was surprising was how quickly it was starting to work on his pain. In just a few caresses, the throbbing ache within his head began to abate. *The smell, it is so unusual, but at the same time so familiar. Earthy, but at the same time floral.* His mind took off on its own and began to recapture thoughts that were playing through his mind when Najila first arrived and he saw her beautiful eyes for the first time. *Nope, can't go there.* He could feel her fingers now sensually gliding across his face aided by the slickness of the massage oil she was applying. *Yeah, a vision which could quickly get out of hand.*

As she poured more oil into the palm of her hand, she looked down at Evan's face. The light in the room faded even more from when she started, as the storm began to overtake the city. Her eyes now added details her fingers discovered while massaging his face. There was the scar near one eyebrow, barely visible on a man who was almost continually wearing sunglasses but she could see it clearly now even in the dark. *The lines on his face were obviously from smiling not from frowning in anger.* Also, though it was late in the day, his growth of beard only provided a slight resistance to the gliding of her fingers instead of a rougher sandpaper texture, which was typical for men of the region.

When she completed touching each part of his face, she began again. This time she started with two fingers on his forehead, the next time three, and on the final repetition four. With each circuit, Najila increased the pressure of her fingers slightly, to relieve more of the pain. Each repetition was completed when she used a single finger to draw an Arabic symbol in the center of his forehead. She knew the symbols would be meaningless to him, but it was how she was taught to cleanse the negative energy from her subject. First, she drew the symbol for peace, next hope, then beauty, and finally love.

After she completed drawing the symbol for love, she removed the washcloth across his eyes. Najila could also tell his headache was beginning to abate, as his eyes were closed but relaxed and not clenched. *I guess I still have the touch.* She was careful as she ran her fingertips across this previously covered part of his face and could feel the caress of his eyelashes under her fingers when she ran them across his closed eyelids. *I wonder what his touch would feel like? His fingertips upon me?* Almost as soon as the thought crossed her mind, she recoiled from it shaking her head and removing her hands from his face.

With Evans face complete, Najila placed her hands on him again, but this time she pressed her hands against sides of his head from just below his ears and glided down his neck. As she did this, she allowed her fingers to spread out and move across both of his shoulders. *Except for some minor scars, he has very smooth skin.* She noticed he did not attempt to pull away or demonstrate reluctance at having her hands on his bare flesh. *He seems to be willing to open up to me in such a personal way. Perhaps he is having thoughts of me that are more than just professional as well.*

Until she removed the washcloth, Evan had let his mind go blank, purposely not allowing it to put two thoughts together. But when her hands moved down the sides of his neck to his shoulders, he found himself once again in a café but this time with Najila. *Strange I haven't thought about her this way since our first meeting, even though we're together daily.* He brushed the scene aside in favor of staring into her eyes in a way he would never have allowed himself to do in reality. *Is what I see now my fantasy of her, or just a reality I haven't noticed?* Her eyes, with perfectly applied makeup accenting their natural beauty, were drawing him in. *Mesmerizing.* He was allowing himself to be drawn into Najila in a whole new way.

After massaging his shoulders and the back of his neck, she placed her hands flat on his upper chest and began to apply pressure sliding them down from his collarbone. *His flesh feels so good under my hands. I can feel it welcoming my touch.* Evan found himself softly sighing at the feel of her hands on his body as in his mind he continued to enjoy the vision of her eyes. *Is this what I'm feeling for her or has it just been too long since Marci left?* Najila's face was close to his as she slid her hands forward – *her breath on my face?* While he was mulling this thought over, his body was suddenly struck by lightning as her fingertips caressed his chest. Just as he was jolted, Najila was also shocked by the reality of what just happened. *My God, what the hell am I doing?*

Her mind raced for a moment looking for a way to back out of the situation, but then she looked down at Evan's face and saw he was tilting more upward, his lips parted. *Is he expecting me to kiss him? Would it be so bad?* The decision was taken from her as he abruptly closed his lips, deeply inhaled, then spoke, "Wow, my headache is gone." The peak was in view but vanished into dust.

"Ah. That's great," as Najila said this she quickly withdrew her hands from Evan's body and reached for a hand towel to wipe off the excess oil, "It would seem my job here is done."

Evan didn't want her to leave. He wasn't sure where this was going, he was just sure he did not want it to end yet, "Well, Doc, I didn't give you my insurance card at the start of this, so why don't I call Room Service and have them send us up an early dinner?"

*He wants me to stay,* "As you say. It might be a good idea if I stick around for a little while to make sure there's not a relapse." *That's it, humor will make me look like I'm not so desperate.*

"Super, let me get you a menu for you to peruse while I take a quick shower."

Najila nodded, taking the menu he retrieved from the sideboard. True to his word, Evan took a quick shower and was back in the room by the time Najila decided what she wanted to eat. After providing him with her order, Evan picked up the phone and spoke with Room Service. He duplicated her order for himself asking for two glasses of pomegranate juice to be sent up immediately.

"I don't think I've ever seen anything quite like it," Evan said, taking a seat at the table, facing the windows. Rather than sitting across from him, and Najila took the chair next to his so they shared the view.

"You realize we sometimes get much worse storms, even the occasional *Haboob*."

"Ah yes, my friend called them the *wall of sand*."

As they were talking, a waiter showed up, placed the two glasses of pomegranate juice on the table and departed without saying a word. Their discussion of weather oddities continued until dinner was delivered. As they dined upon grilled lamb chops with a side of *tabbouleh*, Evan began to delve into Najila's experiences while she was in the United States. She usually kept anything about her personal life closely guarded. Now, Najila felt a strange need to share all she was with Evan. They had shared a profoundly intimate experience, which made her feel as if she was ready to answer almost any question he asked.

"Seriously, it happened many times. One look at the color of my skin color and people in Texas would assume I was Mexican. I'd have guys trying to hit on me in Spanish, and I'd have no idea what they were talking about. Of course, in a post-9/11 world, it was better to be assumed Mexican than to be immediately suspect because I was Arab." *Damn, how'd I get off on this tangent? We went from laughing together to talking about this.*

"Every country has people who are narrow-minded or prejudiced. I hope you'll accept my apology on behalf of any idiots you met while in Texas."

"Deal" *Whew!* "It looks as if the post office found you," she said as she nodded towards the envelope at the other end of the table, in an attempt to change the subject, "Hopefully it's not a bill."

"No idea what it is," Evan got out of his chair and walked to the end of the table, picking up the envelope and examining it. Sliding a finger under the flap, opened it and slid a small stack of stapled papers out. Glancing at the print on the first page, he read the title to himself: The *Bedoons* of Kuwait, Citizens without Citizenship, by Human Rights Watch. *Bedoons. I think I'll keep this to myself for a bit.* "Nope, not a bill. Just a report on my rental car usage at the hotel."

"Well, that's no fun," Najila said, dropping the subject.

Evan put the envelope back on the table and returned to his seat next to Najila. It was hard for either of them not to be transfixed at the view outside the window as the sandstorm swirled around them but as the day faded away, so did the ability to see what was going on in the blackness. As the conversation dwindled, Najila finally remarked it was time for her to go and Evan offered to walk her down to her car. *Or maybe instead of sending her home, should offer her the guest bedroom. Too forward?* After delivering her to her vehicle and bidding her goodnight, Evan found himself pausing for a moment wondering if he should try to recapture the missed opportunity from earlier, but the moment had passed. He returned to his room, with only a memory of a moment that was never fulfilled.

As soon as he walked into the room, he picked up the envelope, then stretched out on the couch and began to read the 50 plus page report.

Even though the coffee shop was in a primarily Filipino neighborhood, no one seemed to notice Roshan when he walked in the door. After taking a quick glance around the room, he walked directly to the table where Jazlene was sitting and took the seat across from her.

"Did he get it."

"I left it on the table for him, but he when he got in this afternoon, he was not feeling well and told me to leave. I don't know if he opened it."

"Fine, fine." Roshan said, as he drummed his fingers on the table while looking around the café, "I am sure he will probably get to it when he is feeling better. I will have other things for you to take to him later." As he said this, Roshan stood up while reaching into his pocket before placing his hand on the table in front of Jazlene.

She understood his action and slid her hand under his so she could take possession of the bills now covered by his hand. Once he was sure she had it, Roshan lifted his hand and walked quickly out of the café. Jazlene slowly tilted her hand so she could look at the bills underneath and upon seeing it was a 100KD note fought to keep herself from yelling out loud. *...and I didn't even have to do anything illegal.*

Fahaheel Garage

Nassar looked down at his handiwork, carefully scanning the automobile from one end to the other. As he reached each section of the car, in his mind, Nassar checked off any modifications he was instructed to make by his boss and those he came up with on his own. When he completed his mental inventory, Nassar looked at the pile of parts in the corner. *A fair amount of metal, even more so when you consider I've started disposing of it-- piece by piece.* There was no way to measure how much weight he removed from the car, but he knew it was substantial. He felt he might be at the tipping point where any more removal would start to affect the structural integrity of the vehicle.

Walking over to the corner of the garage, Nassar sat down on a well-worn kitchen chair he had found and brought into the garage. Removing a cigarette from his pocket, he lit it and took a deep drag, filling his lungs with its acrid smoke. He had run out of things to do. *Good thing the Boss will be here in a few with my money, I just hope it won't be the last time.*

Nassar remembered the look on his father's face when he told him about this job. He asked him some probing questions, but Nassar thought his father on some level was impressed with his son's industriousness. He was unaware Roshan immediately set about investigating his employer and seeking answers to the questions his son evaded.

Nassar's reminiscence was broken by the sound of his phone notifying him of an incoming text message.

```
< Will be there in five
> OK
```

He rose from his chair and walked to the overhead door lifted it up a few inches and placed a fan near the opening to suck the cigarette smoke from the garage. Given all the rules Mr. Pauley dictated, it was surprising he did not include a no-smoking rule in the garage among them. *Doing this might prevent the Boss from ever verbalizing the rule.* After a few minutes, he lowered the door and returned the fan to its usual position.

A short while later, Maksim arrived, pulling his SUV into the empty bay while instructing Nassar to close the door as soon as he was inside. The inspection of Nassar's work was perfunctory he had been inspecting things continually since the effort started. The primary purpose today was to drop off some material and instructions for the next phase.

"You can read mechanical drawings?" Maksim said, as he withdrew a cardboard tube from the inside of his car and handed it to Nassar.

"Yes, Boss, no problem," *So, there is a next phase which will keep me employed. Good.*

"Fine, these will tell you the next steps in modifying the car," as he said this Maksim stepped around to the back of his SUV and opened the door revealing several sheets of thick metal and other hardware Nassar guessed would be required to satisfy the drawing's requirements.

The two men work together to unload the materials, carefully stacking them off to the side so Maksim would be able to back his vehicle out when it was empty. Nassar's mind filled with questions with each item they withdrew from the back of the SUV. In particular, the metal sheets which were over three centimeters thick.

As soon as Maksim departed, Nassar shook the drawings out of the cardboard tube and unrolled them across the hood of the Nissan. He flipped from one page to the next, noting the changes they were making to the vehicle. When he got to the last page, he paused as he tried to figure out why this modification was being requested. The drawing showed a metal sheet being used underneath the engine compartment to create a floor. Next, a piece long enough to run the entire length of the engine compartment was to be slightly curved then mounted at a 65° angle to the new floor. Because of all of the modifications, Nassar made previously, once this was installed it created an empty walled space with the car's engine on the passenger side. *Perhaps the man is planning on smuggling something, and this will give them space to hide it. But why not use something lighter? Why add back the weight I just took out? This angle, why would you want to do something like that? It takes away from the space to smuggle things?*

# Chapter 11



Evan pulled back on Cochise's reins to slow the horse from full gallop to gentle trot. Even though sunset was just beginning, he could see the lights of *Rihlat Alsahra'* coming on in the distance. As he became more self-assured, he would now ride out into the desert alone enjoying the solitude. He never went very far, but just enough to feel like he was accomplishing something. Evan was unaware Naveed tasked one of his men follow him from a distance for safety sake since *Al Hakim* made him personally responsible for the writer's well-being.

There were many things Evan hated about being in the desert, but the transition from dusk to twilight and finally night was something he came to love. Nights like this, when the skies were clear, the blue slowly fade to black as the sun went down. The sun would first turn the horizon into a shiny orange ribbon which became a darker slightly green color before it faded out, joining the sky above as it grew into a solid sheet of absolute black. Once twilight passed, the deepness of night would cover everything followed by the emergence of stars. *More stars than I ever saw anywhere in the States.* Of course, the location of constellations was slightly different, but his interest in those faded long ago as he chose to enjoy the overwhelming miracle of thousands of points of light instead.

Evan developed a feel for his route, which allowed him to arrive back at the stables just after the stars started to appear. By the time he brushed Cochise and put him away for the night, the entire sky would be lit up with millions of lights to illuminate his drive home. Occasionally, when Evan came out to ride, he would deliver his articles to Hamad. He began to look forward to those instances because he would join Hamad in his *diwaniya*. They would share cups of tea or smoke *sheesha,* as his benefactor read the article so he could discuss it with him.

This immediate review of his work was something unfamiliar to Evan, but he began to enjoy getting immediate feedback. Hamad's critique was always positive, as the older man marveled at Evan's views about the Kuwait he loved. Their relationship was becoming a unique bond both men valued.

About a week passed since the night of the sandstorm – the night he came to think of as *The Missed Kiss*. His explorations with Najila took them to the Science Center, library, and to the public school that was previously scheduled. Not once did a situation arise where he felt an invitation to partake of a first kiss. Of course, there was not a situation during their entire partnership, other than the one night in his room, where the opportunity presented itself. What occurred with every encounter since, was an increasing desire. He saw no way to be sure it was mutual or intentional, but every encounter they shared was now surrounded by the fragrance of *Lamsat Hareer*. In her hair - on her skin, every time she passed close to him, his mind was filled with the scent and the pondering of what might have occurred on the night of *The Missed Kiss*.

After bedding down Cochise, he headed towards the *diwaniya* hoping to encounter Hamad. Tonight, was not about an enjoyable diversion but a serious conversation he hoped would bring enlightenment. Evan thoroughly reviewed the *Bedoon* document that was mysteriously left in his room. Many of the findings were quite damning. Knowing there was more than one side to every story, Evan felt the need to get the other side of the story from a natural Kuwaiti, and not some nongovernmental agency with an unknown agenda. Much of what he read was basic statistics, and as such were likely irrefutable. He just could not understand the why's of such an injustice, which was allowed to go on for so long.

"Good evening Mister Davis," came the familiar voice of Roshan from behind him as he walked toward the *diwaniya*.

"Roshan, I thought we settled this," he said feigning anger as he spun around to face him, "please, call me Evan."

"Absolutely – Evan. Were you looking for *Al Hakim*? Did I

perhaps overlook an appointment?"

"Uh, no. No appointment. I was taking a ride and thought I might be able to have a quick word with him," *I don't think I've had more than a single formal appointment with him since I arrived.*

"Ah, I see. Well, *Al Hakim* and his brother, Jefzar, are at a camel race this evening."

"Really? They race camels?"

"Absolutely, it is quite enjoyable; if you place your bets properly, it can be quite profitable as well. If you would like, I could take you to where they are."

"Hmm, no. No thank you. I don't think I need another vice."

"Perhaps I could help you with whatever you need to discuss with *Al Hakim*." Evan considered Roshan's offer. Recalling his history, he knew the man and his family were in the country for a long time. *Based on what I read, it makes his status just above Bedoon.*

"Maybe you can, but the topic seems to be one which is quite sensitive to most people. No problem? "

"Absolutely no problem and I can assure you, I hold all conversations in the strictest of confidence," *Am I being presented with the opportunity I hoped for?*

Evan looked into Roshan's face and considered the man for a moment. He was sure Roshan would hold his confidences from anyone in the outside world, *but what about Hamad?* Money aside, his concern was the loss of favor from a man he had come to respect and value.

"Of course, it goes without saying my confidence would be strictly with you as long as there would be no harm to the Al-Bourisli family."

"No, no, no. Nothing as dire as that, just a question about Kuwaiti history and culture."

Roshan gave a slight bow with his head, "Then I stand ready to offer any information or assistance you might need."

Evan again considered his options and realized maybe Roshan was the best of all worlds since he was not personally involved like Hamad or Najila.

"I'm not sure quite how to start this conversation, but I would like to know how the *Bedoon* came to be what they are. Not how they became noncitizens, I'm fairly sure of the mechanics which occurred when Kuwait became an independent nation. I'm just not sure how they went about selecting who wound up being a *Bedoon* and who didn't and why they seem to be so – disrespected." *Well, if I was ever going to offend somebody at the international incident level, I've done it now.*

Long ago, Roshan learned to hide his emotions. Happy or sad he tried to maintain the same expression as a way of preventing anyone from being able to use his feelings toward a situation against him. He perfected this during the time of the Iraqi invasion. So, even though he was ecstatic at Evan's query about *Bedoons*, he showed no emotion at all. As he was formulating his response, their attention was drawn toward a fast-approaching SUV in the distance.

"Something must be wrong, it's *Al Hakim*," when the vehicle was close enough to see there were two silhouettes inside, Roshan added, "It would appear his brother Jefzar is with him. We will have to complete this conversation another time."

The SUV quickly closed the remaining distance to *Rihlat Alsahra'*, and skidded to a stop next to Roshan and Evan. Evan was surprised to see Hamad driving and watched as Jefzar got out of the passenger side shouting something in Arabic as he ran toward the parking lot located on the far side of the stable tent. Hamad reeled off several Arabic instructions to Roshan, who nodded before turning to head toward his car. Within moments, Jefzar drove past in a police SUV, speeding down the access road, with Roshan following shortly behind him.

As the dust began to settle, Hamad walked over to Evan and placed his hand on the writer's shoulder, "A bit of urgency. It would seem a criminal Jefzar has been pursuing just sent a letter to the local press," Hamad sought to change the subject by adding, "So, did you have a good ride with Cochise this evening or were you here for a delivery?"

"Uh, an enjoyable ride, thank you. No articles this evening. What were you saying about a criminal's letter?" *Fine, that did sound like I'm a reporter of some sort.*

"Good, good," Hamad dropped his hand from Evan's shoulder and tried to again steer the topic away from the hot news of the evening, "Your horsemanship is improving I think soon you might be able to ride with Najila again. She will be very impressed."

After a moment of silence, Hamad felt the need to respond to Evan's question, "Yes, a 20-page document, apparently some sort of manifesto, sent by the criminal to all of the newspapers in Kuwait."

Evan was beginning to feel lost inside the dual conversation, but tried to maintain a semblance of order by first responding to his statement about Najila then the document, "I hope so – but why would a criminal create a manifesto?"

Hamad gave up trying to change the topic and this time provided a straight answer to Evan's question, "It would seem this killer is being motivated by some sort of political agenda."

*A killer?* "I thought your brother was just a local constable of some sort." *Come on, Hamad, you need to give me the details.*

"Well, he is a Chief of Police for this sector. Actually," Hamad shifted his position and again placed his hand on Evan's shoulder as if to guide him in a different direction, "He is a fascinating story. At one point in life, Jefzar wanted to be a detective, but events guided him down a different path. One of many journeys altered by the Iraqi invasion, but I think Kuwait is better off with him as chief than as just a simple detective. Perhaps you should pursue a story about him at some point."

*Dammit, stop trying to change the topic.* "I don't understand, if he's not a detective…"

"Another fork in the road, I guess. Recently Jefzar was placed in charge of a special task force given the responsibility to track down what at first was thought to be a serial killer. Now appears to be something else entirely."

Hamad looked at Evan and could see he was visibly confused. He dropped his hand from Evan's shoulder signaling a realization trying to divert him was futile. *Perhaps a straight explanation would be the simplest course of action.*

"Let me start again. Over the course of a few weeks, several corpses turned up with questionable causes of death. Jefzar realized these were murders and was able to tie them together by a diligent review of the evidence. When he took the information forward, the powers in charge decided to create a special task force to track down what seems to be a serial killer," Hamad looked into Evan's eyes and waited for him to display some level of understanding.

"Okay, I think I understand that part. But now the killer has created a manifesto? Why?"

"Indeed. Apparently, the killer is claiming a political motivation for all his murders. As for why he created this manifesto now, I have no idea."

"A political serial killer?"

"It would seem, but then such a description doesn't seem to be totally correct either. Only time will tell," Hamad felt a pang of guilt for trying to redirect Evan. *An apologetic explanation might help maintain our rapport*, "Forgive my obvious subterfuge, but given your current assignment, I didn't want to risk you being distracted by something which may be no more than tabloid fodder. As with most people, Kuwaitis like a good story with lots of intrigue and strange turns. Since reporters want to sell papers, they tend to feed the fury by providing the most outlandish of theories."

"I think I understand what you were trying to do," *But, you were the one who promised me free reign in my stories and promised not to suppress anything based on content.*

Both men were silent for a moment, Evan felt a little uneasy in the silence but with no idea what to say to break it. At last Hamad spoke, "To add something stranger still, the killer is identifying himself as *Shaytan*."

"Shay---"

"*Shaytan*. The English translation would be Satan."

Huda sat in front of the laptop at the small secretary desk, in the room she considered her home office. The room's primary usage was as a private drawing room for greeting special guests. The Philippine mahogany secretary desk provided space to write necessary correspondence after visits. While never formally telling Hamad she did so, she instructed the staff the room was to be considered her private space, and as such, they were not allowed to enter the room unless allowed explicitly by her. This gave her a private area to make phone calls, write letters, and to surf the internet, as she was doing now.

Huda was intently staring at the screen, quickly reading the websites for the local Kuwaiti newspapers. Each contained similar stories and printed the full content of what was now being commonly referred to as *Alshaytan Bayan Rasmiin* – Satan's Manifesto. She scanned the document, not for content but to make sure her words were correctly quoted without omission. It was in this room she originally created the declaration. It was the one part of her scheme she felt could not be left to her mercenary.

What she created, was designed to seem at once rambling, and rationally idealistic. She stole sentiments and calls to action from a variety of the world's revolutionary documents. Since Kuwait was one of the freest democracies in the Middle East, it took something more radical to seem revolutionary. If anyone were to thoroughly explore the document's text, they would find she lifted portions from Marx's Communist Manifesto, Che's subversive diatribes, a bit of Mao's Red Book, and American socialist Eugene V. Deb's ramblings as well.

The introduction spoke of the many injustices and discriminations, which were forced on the *Bedoon* since the establishment and formal independence of Kuwait. In a unique twist combining revolution with theology, the document rationalized that *Allah* gave Satan free rein to both punish those who were guilty, and also bring about an uprising which would create a more just society.

The document laid out a model for an Arab Socialist Republic, which would be created by first stripping and redistributing all wealth in Kuwait. The foundation of this transformation was the elevation of *Bedoons* to not only full citizenship, but a version of reparational citizenship, allowing them to take charge of the country, wresting it from the current ruling class. All royalty would be stripped of title and position, while ordinary citizens would be allowed to remain as they were, although they would be required to give up any generational wealth acquired since the country's founding. But the manifesto's call to action went beyond Kuwait's *Bedoons,* and included a role and reward for TCNs in the new regime.

Early on, as Huda developed her strategy for revenge, she knew it would take more than a threat of a *Bedoon* uprising to elicit the level of violent and permanent response she hoped to encourage. It was long known the population of TCNs in the country was near to the total population of Kuwaiti citizens. When coupled with the *Bedoon* population, the total number dwarfed the population of Kuwaiti citizens. To create the illusion TCNs might join a revolution, the document offered something no TCN could have ever hoped for – naturalized Kuwaiti citizenship.

Huda managed to write an outlandish document that included an element sure to cause the fevered reaction she hoped for. The coup d'état and seizure of wealth was not only believable but entirely possible.

After finishing with the legitimate printed press, she selected the shortcut on her browser for *Liljamie*; it was the only news outlet that did not have the entire text of the *Alshaytan Bayan Rasmiin* online. Instead, the paper was running a variety of articles from *Bedoon* sources providing details on a number of their requests to normalize their status within the country. *No fire, all smoke.* As she skimmed through several of the articles, she noticed a majority were written by someone named Talal Al-Enezi. It was a name she did not know but took no time to ponder further as she heard a servant approaching then knocking on her closed door.

Before she closed the lid of the laptop, Huda selected an icon

Wilhelm assured her would perform a wipe of her web browser history leaving no details. Upon the program's completion, she called out for the servant enter, and they did so, bringing in a tray with tea and several small sweet cakes meant to be enjoyed with it. After the refreshment was laid out on the table in front of the sitting suite, Huda moved from the desk chair to one of the large comfortable overstuffed chairs. She retrieved a cup of tea from the tray and placed a pair of cakes on the saucer, before sitting back in the chair. Holding the cup under her nose, she breathed in the fragrant aroma, and let her mind dwell back to the incident that necessitated the need for revenge at this level.

"I don't understand this," Khaled's voice was still shaking although his body was no longer trembling. The initial shock of being cast away by Sheikha was giving way to the reality of what it meant.

"How could she have done this in such a heartless way. Of course, I possessed minor, lingering suspicions about her, but I hoped I was wrong," as Huda said this she walked over to the couch where her son was sitting and gently patted his back with the palm of her hand.

"We were just so close, I shared all of my hopes and dreams with her. She was the first woman I ever…" He buried his face in his hands partially to hide his tears but also to prevent himself from saying too much to his mother.

Huda's hand went from patting his back, to slowly rubbing it. *So, the Sharmuta was using my son's innocence to trap him. I did just the right thing in getting rid of her now.*

After a long silence, her son's sobbing finally stopped, and he sat back on the couch, staring into space.

"Let me see what she sent you." Huda held her hand out and waited for him to give her his phone. She knew the words she sent, this was a bit of theater so he would not suspect she was the one who sent the text.

> Will nvr work 4 us. Need to end ths. We r frm 2 wrlds & my family will nvr accept yrs. Best this way & don't look 4 me.

> It wasn't yr fault.
> I'm Srry

Huda could see he wrote and sent a dozen or so texts after receiving this one, all begging for some sort of explanation. Of course, there was no response. If she looked at the calling log, she would have seen he also called her repeatedly.

"She is ignoring me, *Umma*. She just vanished. I even went by her place."

Huda knew there was a likelihood he would seek her out, and arranged for the Al-Shammari family to be evicted on short notice. At the same time, Wilhelm appeared on their doorstep offering the family a new residence on the opposite side of the city. Rather than questioning the coincidence, Sheikha's father gladly accepted it as a bit of fortune in a crisis, and the family immediately relocated.

She speculated Sheikha, being a good daughter, accepted her fate, and relocated with her family. Having misplaced her phone, she was left with no way to contact Khaled directly and could only hope he would track her down so they could resume their relationship. *But that manaqib aldhahab will never come near my son again.*

For the next two weeks or so, Khaled remained in his room at *'Shamal Mazraea*. He did not go to work or show any interest in any activity. Huda convinced Hamad to leave him alone and let him heal. Hamad was puzzled by the entire event; he could not understand how his son could have misjudged this woman so badly and how she could have treated his son so shabbily. Very late one evening, Khaled disappeared for an hour or so in his SUV but then returned and went straight to bed without saying a word. It was reported to Huda later he went to Sheikha's old residence but after not being able to locate her returned home.

Then, one morning Khaled appeared in the dining room for breakfast, smiling and seeming like himself. Huda was relieved, as recently guilt over her actions began to pull at her. He departed for work the day after giving her a quick kiss on the cheek; she had no way of knowing at the time, but in less than a week he would be gone.

Huda took a shallow breath, her body trembling as she did so. Thoughts of those days always caused her to have a physical reaction to what happened. When Jefzar came to the house that sad day and told her Khaled was found dead, she felt as if her life suddenly ended with all purpose gone. She loved her husband, but her son was her life. Jefzar was able to have the cause of death listed as a motor vehicle accident, but it was a well-known open secret Khaled deliberately drove his SUV directly into the highway abutment. He was traveling at almost 200 km/h at impact.

A few days after the funeral, a letter arrived in the mail, and upon opening it, Huda immediately recognized Khaled's handwriting. She spent a moment, not reading the words but just looking at the shapes of the letters her son printed on the page. There was a certain beauty and artistry to the handwriting she wanted to appreciate, before she found out what words Khaled wished to convey. Words so important, he wrote them down rather than spoke them.

The salutation was for both her and Hamad, but in all the years since it was received, she never shared the letter or its contents with him. She never told Hamad about the letter. Even though she was the only one who knew of the letter's existence, the only part of the message she ever read was the first sentence. Those few words were enough to not only stab at her heart daily but to cause her to spend all the years since reading them planning an act of revenge, not only against the girl who created all of the problems but her entire tribe. Huda saw her as being responsible and wanted them all destroyed.

Realizing revenge would take currency, the day she received the letter she rented her first security box at the Bank of the Gulf. Upon opening the box for the first time, she placed a manila folder containing Khaled's last letter inside the box, as its first guarded content. Since then, the folder always remained on top of the contents of the box currently being used. It was there as a constant reminder. It was there is a symbol of the last thing her son ever created on earth. In all the time since, she never read the words beyond the first sentence Khaled had written:

"Sheikha's departure has broken my heart and shattered my soul into shards forever. I know no other woman will ever bring me happiness, as life with her would."

Her thoughts were disturbed by the sound from another part of the house. Looking at her watch, she realized what she was hearing was Hamad's arrival from *Rihlat Alsahra'*. Setting her teacup down, she stood and prepared to leave her space to greet him. Deep inside she felt a sense of satisfaction her plan for revenge was starting to crescendo towards its climax. *At last, my son will be avenged. Those who do not even deserve to be called human will pay the price.*

*Highway 306*

Looking in the rearview mirror, Maksim ensured the *kufi* was straight on his head, then looked down at his *dishdasha*, verifying his costume was complete. He needed to look the part of a Kuwaiti today. As he drove south toward the *Bedoon* compound, he found himself pondering the unique role he was playing in the entire scheme. *First, I create the suspicion and hatred, then I retaliate against what I've created. Who cares; in the end, I'm paid.* His mind then flipped from business to pleasure.

It was becoming normal for him to reflect on his sessions with Jasmine. She was nothing like any woman he was ever with before, not only because he was with her more than once, but because something about those experiences prevented him from desiring to kill her as soon as it was over. It was an added risk to his current mission, but he accepted the risk in trade for something he never experienced before. *Something about her willingness to step into situations where at any moment I could kill her. More than just that, she doesn't flinch at her own possible death as I wrap my hands around her throat and take her to the edge. No resistance. She's battling her survival instincts, suppressing the urge to fight to allow me this.* It was a new kind of thrill he never experienced before.

A vehicle's movement ahead caught his attention, and he slowed as a small older model pickup came onto the highway. This allowed him to maintain position behind the car rather than being in front of it. The situation was a disadvantage with no control over when the vehicle might turn off the highway and his speed limited by the truck's to maintain position behind it. *No matter, sunset will be coming on shortly and the longer it takes me to get there the darker the night will be.* As he drove, he looked into the distance off the sides of the road. Maksim could see small clumps of tents gathered closely together and illuminated by electric light.

The tents were familiar to him from his time in Afghanistan; they were the style the US military called GP Medium. The soft-sided canvas tent was a good size for use in the field by military units, being about five meters by ten meters in length. *Apparently, these were sold off as surplus after Desert Storm.* In truth, the US State Department, at the urging of the CIA, gave truckloads of tents and other equipment to *Bedouin* tribes who provided assistance during Desert Storm. It was seen as a win-win, since the intelligence provided was being purchased for a bargain, and the goodwill earned by giving the tents away would serve possible future needs.

As the sun disappeared over the horizon and the dark night of a new moon began to overtake the landscape, the truck in front of Maksim turned on its headlights. He, however, did not. This allowed his vehicle to merely disappear behind the other. It was not unusual for people to drive down the highway in this manner in the Middle East to avoid being seen. The only danger would be a hazard entering the road after the truck and before his vehicle arrived at the same spot.

To avoid boredom during the journey, Maksim began to go over the details of the explosives that were in the canvas backpack hidden underneath the panel in the back of his SUV. He created four devices that could be detonated remotely. The bombs consisted of two-meter sections of det cord. Like most det cord, the type Maksim was using was a piece of a flexible tube filled with pentaerythritol tetranitrate. Usually, det cord like this was initiated by lighting a fuse at the end of it, with the heat eventually setting off the explosion. For these devices, he used a nine-volt battery to power a heating coil which served as an initiator, with the process being activated by a call to an attached cellular phone.

If this were a routine mission, Maksim would have provided a secondary explosion targeting the cell phone so the evidence would be destroyed and unusable. As with everything else this job entailed, the idea was to leave somewhat concealed evidence behind, so it could be discovered with only a slight amount of ingenuity. He purchased the phones he was using today from a tobacco shop in a middle-class Kuwaiti neighborhood the day after the legislator was killed.

Twenty minutes after it entered the highway, the vehicle in front of him turned off the highway into the desert. Looking at his map, Maksim saw no road for the vehicle to take *so the travelers were likely Bedouins heading back to their camp*. He considered following the vehicle to convert the situation into a target of opportunity but then thought better of it. *Not all Bedouin are Bedoon.* With no vehicle in front of him, he turned on his headlights and drove another ten minutes before turning into the desert. Maksim stopped the SUV and shut off the engine. He reached into a bag on the passenger seat and withdrew a set of night vision goggles. After putting the NVGs on and adjusting them, he restarted the vehicle and proceeded into the deep desert toward a lighted compound, which could now be seen in the distance.

Five kilometers from the compound, Maksim stopped his vehicle before spending the next twenty or so minutes observing the compound from a distance looking for activity. It was now midnight, and most of the residents should have turned in, but he did not want the entire mission to fail due to a night owl up wandering around. When he was satisfied no one was active, he got out of his car and began to change into the black night operations clothing he brought with him. He would leave no witnesses behind so there were zero risks of one of them seeing someone military-style clothing and reporting it. The only evidence of who did what here was the evidence intended to be found.

He slipped the backpack containing the explosives and other equipment on, and made the short walk to the perimeter of the compound. Everything within the perimeter was the same as he reconnoitered days before. Once there, Maksim prepared the portable short-range cellular transmitter, which would provide service to the mobile phones he carried. Next, he wrapped the det cord explosives around the base of each of the three lighting stands within the compound. When he finished preparing the last bomb, he stood for a moment and glanced around at the four tents which made up the site. Maksim did this not out of contemplation but making mental notes about the distance between each of the structures and other obstacles lying between them. He was preparing to operate in a lightless environment.

Once outside of the perimeter of the compound, Maksim withdrew a small switch panel from his backpack, and powered on the cellular transmitter he would use to set off the explosives. Looking at the screen of his own phone he waited for it to connect and once it did, he quickly dialed the number for the first explosive device. As soon as it connected, he hung up and repeated the process for each of the remaining devices. At the instant, the final number connected, the initiator in the first device reached the critical temperature causing the det cord to explode.

Maksim pushed the night vision goggles back on his head and watched as the explosion cut through the legs of the light stand causing it to crash to the ground. Moments later, the second light stand collapsed significantly dimming the artificial light, which was wholly extinguished when the third light stand was destroyed. The only light remaining in the compound now was from the small fires the explosives left behind. Maksim lowered his night vision goggles and reached in the bag to withdraw an Israeli Uzi, along with several ammunition magazines.

The level of noise and frightened screaming in the compound rose as Maksim reentered the compound. He stood in the shadows at one end, which gave him a clear field of fire as the occupants of the four tents began to empty searching for the cause of the noise and the light's interruption. Maksim allowed each target to get a few feet from the door before he fired at them to prevent a backup of bodies from blocking the exit of the next victim.

*12, 13,* Maksim mentally counted the bodies as they fell. The total occupants of the compound changed slightly from day-to-day, but his surveillance revealed 38 people were usually inside its area. Men, women, children… Specifics were irrelevant to him as he cut each down without contemplation or deference. He mimicked an inexperienced vigilante using a different style of shooting for each victim. Some he would take out with a single shot, others he would dispatch with a burst of bullets. When his mental count reached 39 victims, he stopped firing and stood still to listen.

In the desert darkness, he could hear muffled crackling, as parts of the aluminum stands that held the lights began to react to the metal's temperature change. There was also the sound of gurgling as a victim's body started to succumb to its wounds. When the gurgling stopped, Maksim moved from his position to the center of the compound and began to perform a visual search of all the area inside its perimeter. A faint sound caught his attention. *Crying?*

He walked in the direction of the sound and discerned it was coming from one of the tents. Throwing back the flap, quietly, he entered the tent and stood in the middle listening for the source of the sound, which went from crying, to the sound of someone attempting to catch their breath while maintaining silence. The search led him to a pile of blankets near one of the tent's corners.

As he stood in silence, he saw the blanket was quivering. "Hello? Are you okay? I am here to help you. Come out," as he said this, Maksim looped the sling of the Uzi over his shoulder and let it fall to his side so his hands were empty and would appear less threatening. Slowly, the blankets moved back to reveal what seemed to be a teenage girl with long dark hair.

Maksim was careful to use a more regional accent when speaking, "There you are. I'm glad to see you are okay. I'm with the Army. I'm here to help you. What is your name?"

He was doing his best to seem non-threatening and at the same time powerful enough to protect her from whatever threat she was imagining disturbed her night. Maksim kept his arms at his sides as he watched her crawl from underneath the blankets and slowly stand. Even though she was making no sound, he could see her body tremble as tears poured from her eyes. Once she was standing, she was motionless for a moment as if making a decision then she ran towards Maksim throwing her arms around the man as she began to weep uncontrollably. If her face was not buried his chest, she might've seen his satisfied smile in the dark.

After a time, the girl was able to choke out her name, "Asami."

"You are safe now, Asami, the bandits who attacked your family are all dead. I've seen to it," as Maksim spoke, he gently caressed her back with his hand as he contemplated the most enjoyable way to take care of this minor detail. *But I need to take care of a few other details first.*

Maksim reached in his pocket and retrieved a small flashlight, and after turning it on, gave it to her. He told her to remain in the tent and get dressed while he ensured the safety of her family. After performing a complete examination of the compound, he was satisfied she was the only detail remaining, and returned to the tent.

The girl was dressed and was standing in the center the tent shining the flashlight from object to object within it. The expression on her face was one of both fear and confusion. Her appearance now made her look younger than she seemed initially, and lack of a *hijab* confirmed it. Maksim decided against his original plan for debauchery. Instead, he smiled at her motioning for her to walk out of the tent in front of him. As soon as Asami cleared the tent flap, her flashlight fell upon the bloody bodies of her family lying around the compound. Asami screamed and turned towards Maksim. As she did, he slashed her throat from one side to the other almost decapitating her. Her scream was immediately replaced by the sound of blood gurgling as the girl attempted to understand what just happened while her life quickly drained away.

Maksim was careful to step back as he slashed her throat and therefore avoided being covered in her blood as it spewed forth and she fell to the ground. He now leaned forward and wiped the blade of his knife off on Asami's clothing. Upon standing upright, he looked around the compound again, reveling in his handiwork. Opening his breast pocket, he withdrew a small piece of cloth with the Satan symbol drawn upon it in Arabic. He glanced around for a suitable placement to jump out at him, but there was none. Looking down at the *Bedoon* girl who lay in front of him on the ground, a thought crossed his mind. He dipped his finger in the girl's blood and drew a circle around the symbol on the cloth, then added a slash going left to right through the circle. Holding the fabric out, he examined his addition, and was satisfied. *Anti-Satan.* Maksim then lay the cloth over the girl's chest crossing her arms to hold it in place.

As he turned his vehicle back onto the paved road and toward the city, he withdrew his cell phone. He watched as the bars displayed went from four to three to one then he entered the number for the fourth bomb he planted at the *Bedoon* compound. Maksim pressed send waiting for it to connect. When it did, he removed the battery from it then broke the phone into pieces with his gloved hands as he drove down the road. Once the phone was destroyed, he began throwing the pieces out the open passenger window and onto the side of the road leaving a trail of parts to soon be discovered. Looking into his rearview mirror, he saw the giant fireball rise as the final bomb caused the compound's fuel tanks to explode.

Even with the enormous satisfaction he felt after a job well done, he needed another level of satisfaction to feed his hunger. Withdrawing his own phone from the SUVs center console, he quickly entered the number for the burner phone he gave Jasmine and typed in a two-word text.

```
< 1 hour
```

Her response was almost instantaneous, which is what he demanded in exchange for the inflated amount he was paying for her service.

```
> Yes
```

Sheikha walked down the dirt aisle between the tightly packed stalls of individual shops at the *souk*. She was carrying a few small plastic bags containing fruit, vegetables, and a new wire whisk. She never understood the West's preference for a single store selling all manner of goods when a *souk* provided the same variety but let you bargain with each individual shop owner. Except for meat, she found the *souk* to be preferential to even a standard grocery store.

The *Fahaheel souk* was very dynamic, so every time she visited there would be some new shops while familiar ones would vanish without notice or leaving a trace. It was part of what she loved about going there to shop over an establishment grocery store. This was also a place where she would not experience a high level of discrimination because of the dirt and the general nature of the facility; even the rich would dress down to go shopping there. Therefore, a *Bedoon* would not stand out unless challenged to provide a civil ID.

Within the *souk* were a collection of her favorite stores, those she made it a point to window-shop when there. Among them was a jeweler, Anwar Al Taiyeb. The *souk's* proximity to the Hotel Sultana and the owner's fluency in English and willingness to bargain with Americans caused the shop to be highly favored by Westerners. The shop's reputation was passed among the community, and led to the shop's swift trade in custom pieces. Sheikha knew she would never be able to afford any of the jewelry from the shop, but because of the high quality and originality of its pieces, things on display in its window were unlike anything anywhere else in Kuwait.

As she was looking at an ornate Lion's-head ring that had red jewels for eyes, she glanced beyond the window into the shop and noticed a couple talking to the shop owner. They seemed to be debating over the purchase of a set of wedding rings. Even without being able to hear the conversation, Sheikha could imagine the ongoing discussion.

When she looked at the woman, she found her attention being drawn to the woman's eyes and the way she looked at her man. *Such desire and love.* The thought immediately faded replaced by a sense of sadness remembering her own history, and how her path was solidified shortly after her family relocated and she lost contact with Khaled.

An envelope addressed to Sheikha arrived at the family's new apartment shortly after they moved in. As was custom, her father would review all mail upon its arrival and occasionally open pieces of mail he found important or curious, even if it was addressed directly to his wife or one of the children. On this day, the envelope that caught his attention was one addressed to his daughter by only her first name. It also lacked a return address. This curious piece of correspondence demanded his attention, so he opened it and read the neatly handwritten letter inside.

Within minutes, Sheikha's father was greeted with the news of Khaled ending their relationship – a relationship he knew nothing about. The letter went on, accusing her of infidelity, which led to his suspicion the child Sheikha was carrying was not his. He loved his daughter deeply, but it was not within his heart to accept a pregnant teenage daughter with no prospects for marriage.

Also, as a non-virgin with a reputation of being unfaithful, she would probably remain single and be forced to live at home for the rest of her life. This added to the disgrace for the Al-Shammari family. As he was mulling over these new realities, Sheikha arrived home and greeted him. If she arrived later, he might have considered a different course of action. However, he was a man of action, and at the moment, he only saw one way forward.

In less than an hour, Sheikha found herself in the hallway in front of the family apartment with two bags of belongings, and 10KD given to her by her mother. Her father did not say a word as he looked at her for the last time handing her the letter signed Khaled. He then withdrew into the apartment and closed the door, leaving his daughter alone and cast out of the family.

Sheikha stood on the threshold for several minutes listening to her mother cry. She knew her father would never change his mind once it was set, so she picked up her bags and walked out of the building. After walking a few blocks, it occurred to her she should read the letter for herself rather than relying on the terse interpretation her father provided during their final conversation. Sheikha withdrew the letter from her pocket and slowly read it one word at a time, allowing each word to sear her heart and slice deeply into her soul. She never saw Khaled's handwriting before, so she lacked any reason to doubt that he created the letter.

As with many intersections of life, bad choices usually outweigh the good, and it is the good choices that are often the most difficult. Rather than allowing herself to spiral downward, and perhaps find herself dwelling in the immoral shadows of society, she willed herself to seek out something better than the existence she was handed for her son. After a frightening night on the street, she was approached by a scout for a nongovernment charity, whose purpose was to help the homeless reestablish themselves in society.

She was provided with a temporary place to stay while she obtained employment and saved up enough money for a home of her own. Without any specialized training and her high school education abruptly interrupted, the only employment possibilities were those involving manual labor. She was told the organization ran training programs, which might lead to better opportunities. Those opportunities vaporized, once they found she was *Bedoon*.

Eventually, she was matched with a position doing the cleaning at night in a corporate building. Her employer was paying her under the table, and therefore paid her less than he would if she were a legal employee. However, there was some friendliness between Sheikha and her employer.

The ringing of the bells on the shop door as the couple departed broke her trance. *It hasn't been easy, but it could be far worse. Best hurry home and fix dinner, maybe margoogah chicken.*

As Sheikha was weaving her way through the labyrinth of stalls and shops that made up the *souk*, she began to have an uneasy feeling. The more she tried to suppress it, the more strongly the sense was tingling. As she walked past a shop of mirrors, she caught the reflection of three teenage boys following behind her. *Why would they be pursuing me?*

She made a turn down an aisle lined with shops already closed for the day, she began to breathe more quickly allowing the anxiety of her situation to take over.

"Hey!" A voice called from behind her, "Don't ignore me *Bedoon*, I know you can hear me," the teenager's choice of English to taunt her was also meant to further degrade her. Without saying it in so many words, he was bragging he was multilingual and ready for the world. It never occurred to him the only way he would be understood was if she also spoke English. *Bedoons* frequently spoke several languages so they could survive in the various environments where employment was available.

Sheikha's mind was racing; *what do I do in this kind of situation?* She knew if she continued down this aisle, it would eventually turn and exit the *souk* into a vacant lot located on one side of it. *I don't want to be alone with these three boys in a secluded place.* However, her only other option was to turn around to proceed towards the center of the *souk*, but in doing so, she would have to directly confront and walk past them. It almost felt as if they were closing in on her as the noise from their jeers and catcalls rose in her ears. *What do I do now? May Allah protect me.*

While the majority of the shops on this aisle were closed, the tailor shop which specialized in custom *dishdashas* was open, and as Roshan was exiting the shop, he directly encountered the three teenagers.

"Oh look, we not only have a *Bedoon* to play with but also a Paki *khara"*

Roshan stood still and took a moment to consider the situation. There were three teenagers, who were now maneuvering to surround him and a woman a short distance away who was staring back at him with extreme fear in her eyes. One boy was taller than the other two, the one who spoke was dressed in a soccer jersey advertising Wolverhampton, and the shortest of the three was making a poor attempt at growing a mustache. Apparently, the boys were pursuing the woman and saw him as an opportune target while en route to her.

"Gentlemen, how may be of service to you this fine afternoon."

"*Ayreh feek*, old man. The only service you can provide is to give us your wallet. Then we can have some fun with the *Bedoon* we found wandering in our country," as Soccer Shirt said this, he motioned toward Sheikha without looking toward her.

Roshan heard Sheikha make a small whimper when soccer shirt indicated her. The silence was then broken by a sound from behind him as the tailor closed and locked his door to prevent this altercation from being carried into his shop. He knew his hand to hand training was unpracticed and years old, still, *I'm reasonably certain I can take soccer shirt and mustache, but tall boy makes the odds less than generous*. Roshan started to contemplate if the amount of money in his wallet would be sufficient to get them to let him and the terrified woman go.

"My family once employed one of you Paki *khara*," Tallboy spoke up, "my brother caught him stealing money so *Baba* took him out to the desert and beat him until he couldn't stand. Maybe I should keep all the money this *alkalb* as on him and take it back as reparations." As he said the last word, he thrust his face right into Roshan's fiercely staring at him.

"*Tozz feek!*" Mustache said, breaking his silence, "You get your share, no more. I got plans."

"What plans?" Tallboy shot back, breaking his stare and turning toward Mustache.

"*Kess ikhtak,*" as Mustache said this, he licked his lips smiling broadly, laughing. He knew he was playing with fire, you didn't make a reference to someone's sister's vagina without expecting a bad reaction.

"*Kol khara!*" Tallboy took steps toward the Moustache, and the altercation might have escalated if Soccer Shirt had not jumped between them.

Roshan felt he saw an opportunity, so he took it.

"Gentlemen, I think I can assist in the situation. My employer, *Al Hakim*, negotiates such disagreements. Perhaps we should take this to him, and he can decide who should get the money, how much, and what fun might be had with the *Bedoon*."

It never ceased to amaze Roshan how many people in the country knew of his employer and the level of respect, or fear, they possessed. This time, he was counting on fear. It only took a moment for his words to sink into the three teenagers and he immediately felt the air of violence around them begin to dissipate.

"You work for *Al Hakim*, Paki?"

"Indeed; also, my name is Roshan. Roshan Patel." *Not Paki*

The other two boys said nothing as their interest in their original prey, Roshan's possible riches, and their exchange of insults were all forgotten. Both of them realized that being brought home by the police for this type of altercation would be seen as nothing by their families. However, being involved in an argument which required *Al Hakim* to settle, would have long-lasting ramifications.

"Okay Roshan, tell you what, why don't you just take the *Bedoon* out of here and make sure she never comes back here again, ever. Then we'll just drop the whole thing."

"Absolutely. But only if you feel it might be the best settlement."

Soccer Shirt said nothing but nodded. He then looked at the other two boys and motioned with his head for them to follow. The three walked past Roshan and Sheikha before they disappeared around the corner and out of the *souk*.

Sheikha was not sure who this man was, but he obviously welded some power. *Who was this Al Hakim?*

"Miss, if you'd follow me, I'd gladly escort you back to the center of the *souk*, we can use one of the other exits. Then, I'll call you a cab to take you home."

"I don't need a cab," *I can't afford a cab.*

"Nonsense, today's visit to the souk has been trying for you. My paying for your ride home seems the least I could do."

Without saying a word, she nodded and followed him. He walked as if he knew the maze of the *souk* as well as she did and they were shortly standing in front of the cab stand with him motioning one forward. Leaning into the window, he spoke to the driver handing him a few bills.

"He will take you anywhere you wish to go." Opening the back car door, he allowed Sheikha to get in and bowed toward her waving as she drove away.

Upon contemplation, as she was riding away, Sheikha realized she was now more confused than afraid. She had never been accosted by Kuwaitis directly, but she also never saw a TCN who seemed to have such power over them. Looking at her watch she realized because she was taking a cab home, she would make it back in plenty of time before Meteb arrived. This afternoon was indeed blessed, she exhaled feeling satisfied all of this happened because *Masha'Allah*, God willed it.

# Chapter 12



Jefzar knelt and looked closely at the body of the preteen *Bedoon* Jane Doe. He knew many officers in his situation would merely look for the fastest way to close this case rather than giving it an appropriate investigation. After all, the *Bedoon* were simply not worth the time. Jefzar's attitude toward these people was more socially conscious as he saw them as fellow human beings rather than something less. But what was done here; *no one so young should ever experience this level of violence, not even a Bedoon.*

The compound around him was now filled with his officers, gathering evidence while trying to preserve the crime scene. The local Constable only sent two officers and a mortician to collect the bodies and report findings after receiving calls about the fuel tank's fireball, which led to the discovery of the bodies. However, an anonymous call was placed to Jefzar, and once he responded, he called in a full team of officers as well as crime scene investigators.

Jefzar was continuing to walk the entire compound, never stopping in one place for too long and using his flashlight to illuminate the path ahead of him. He was trying to figure out the sequence of what happened and get a feel for the crime scene. Usually, this was difficult as he tried to avoid disturbing hidden evidence. In this case, so much evidence was strewn around it was harder to avoid tripping over it, even when being examined in the dark with flashlights. *There must have been at least five or six attackers.* When he first saw Asami's body, he gave it little more than a cursory glance thinking she was just another shooting victim. But when he went back to examine it in more detail, he realized how mistaken his assumption was.

He called over two of his officers to hold flashlights on the body while he examined it. Instead of being shot from a distance like the rest, she was violently attacked up close. The fatal wound was obviously her throat, which was transected from one side to the other. As for what else may have befallen this poor child, those were harder questions a medical examiner would have to answer. Jefzar was relieved to see her clothing was not torn even though it was utterly blood-soaked, which probably meant she was not sexually assaulted. While not touching the body, he tried to gather some sense of the attack. There was no bruising on her arms and no resistance wounds showing she fought her attacker. *What the hell happened here? She knew and trusted her attacker?* The way her arms crossed her torso may or may not have been positioned by the attacker.

Jefzar reached forward to close the girl's eyes which were still partially open. As he did this, several large spotlights were being switched on to illuminate the compound for the crime team. It was as if the sun suddenly rose. This blast of light illuminated the corpse for the first time. As Jefzar looked down at the body for the first time from the closer vantage point, he saw underneath the girl's arms lay a square of cloth which was not part of her clothing. He called for one of the photographers to come over and record the scene before the two officers lifted the girl's arms out of the way so he could get a better view of the piece of cloth. *It could be nothing, it could be something.* The photographer continued to shoot pictures as her arms were lifted, and when they were away from the cloth, the graphic upon it was clearly visible. *Khara! This wasn't random, and it wasn't part of the serial killer's string. This was a new killer or killers. An anti-Satan, who kills Bedoons in response to Satan killing everybody else.*

"Bag it," he said to one of his officers as he rose from the body, "and tell the medical examiner I want the report on this one first."

Remaining any longer at the crime scene was not going to tell him any more. There'd been a marked increase in altercations between *Bedoons* and citizens since the start of these killings. Once the manifesto was published, those incidents expanded to include TCNs. This was possibly the first killing associated with the backlash against those on the bottom tier.

As he was walking back to his SUV, one of the CSI technicians stopped him and informed him there appeared to be only a single attacker. All of the shots were fired from one vantage point, and there was only one set of boot prints found thus far in the compound. *A single person? We have someone reacting for blind revenge. None of this is going to end well.*

When he departed the compound, his original intent was to go back to the Constabulary. Now, he realized he was going to need advice on how to calm a public that was used to overreacting to any random situation. *"Feek!"* He shouted as he made a sharp turn with his vehicle redirecting it toward *Rihlat Alsahra'. I need the consul of my older brother. I need to talk to Hamad.*

Najila noticed since the face massage, Evan seemed to be more eager to start their days together. His greetings were friendlier, and his sense of humor seemed to be more in tune with hers. She prevented herself from dwelling on what might have occurred if things had gone on a few minutes longer, or if she leaned a little more forward. But suppressing those thoughts was difficult, as she sat waiting for him to come out the door of the hotel, or as she lay in her bed at night trying to sleep.

"So what wild adventures do we have on the docket for today?" He said as he opened the door and climbed into the vehicle all in one motion. It took Evan a moment to place the drinks in the cup holders which gave her time to recover from the thoughts she should not have been having.

"Today we go to church."

"Huh? Didn't we just go to the Grand Mosque a couple of weeks ago?"

"As you say, but if we were going to a mosque I would've said we were going to a mosque. What I said was we were going to go to church."

"You actually mean a church, the kind with pews, an altar, and hymnals?"

She nodded before adding, "Yes, I told you before there were several in the country. This one is Catholic. Would it surprise you to learn the Kuwait Oil Company was responsible for bringing Catholic services to the country? They did it for their employees starting in about 1947. In 1956, the company also built the first chapel in *Ahmadi* as a gift."

"It is one thing to allow something to exist but another to actually help it along."

"The story goes further, it was Sheikh Abdullah Al Salim Al Sabah who provided the land in Kuwait City for the Cathedral we are going to go see today. He supplied the land four years before Kuwaiti independence."

"It's difficult to imagine, a Catholic church on the Arabian Peninsula, so close to Mecca and Medina."

"As you say; the Holy Family Cathedral has managed to exist and thrive because of the grace and tolerance of the Kuwaiti royal family, its government and people." *Well, that should keep me from having illicit thoughts about him. Nothing like a trip to church to quell your ishq.*

Evan stared idly out the window as he thought about another question of tolerance of which he was aware: *Bedoons.* His attempt to discuss the situation with Roshan almost yielded a result before it was interrupted. In the end, he was left no closer to resolution than he was before he dared bring the topic up with the man.

*What about Najila?* While it was true she lived in the West for several years, and seemed to be pushing his perception of Kuwait's tolerance towards others – *is this something she honestly felt and lived or something she said?* After a few moment's thought, it occurred to him how he might work his way toward a discussion on the topic with her.

"As the years passed, I would assume the church expanded its membership beyond KOC employees and families."

Nodding as she spoke, "As the need for manual labor grew beyond what was available in Pakistan and Bangladesh, employees from

Indonesia and the Philippines were recruited. A good portion of those were Catholics. There are several different Catholic churches in Kuwait, built to facilitate attendance from believers residing in the same neighborhood. Of course, there is also a small number of Kuwaitis who are Christian."

"What about *Bedoons?*"

His jumping from a question of belief systems to one of citizenship and race surprised Najila, but she planned ahead for this eventuality. *But first, let's see what he thinks regarding the Bedoon situation before we walk down this path.*

"As you say, what about them?"

"Well, my understanding was they did not often interact with citizens or expatriates because as stateless people it was not permitted. Are they also seen as stateless when it comes to religion?" *Just keep tying the two topics together. Eventually, she has to provide a straight answer.*

*Apparently, he's been doing some reading or talking to someone about this to gain this level of knowledge regarding the Bedoon situation. Since the door open, we'll have to proceed.* "A difficult question, most *Bedoons* choose to live separate from the rest of society, preferring their own company to outsiders."

"I was led to believe their separation from society was not a choice they made but one which was made for them," *a little more confrontational.*

*Not only does he have the knowledge, apparently he has an opinion as well. Let's throw this back and see if we can get him to abandon the topic.* "Well, the same could be said of the illegal aliens in the United States."

*Touché, but not the same thing at all,* "It's not a really a valid comparison. From what I understand, the *Bedoon* in Kuwait was created during the creation of the independent state when citizenship was assigned to various groups of people. It left people who were already here trapped, with no status and no way to change it. Regardless of what you think of US immigration laws, illegal aliens chose to cross the border into the country, and created the situation by their own actions; not actions taken against them by the government. Those people also have a country they came from originally, whereas the *Bedoon* do not."

Najila was quiet for a moment, she was considering what he said and how best to confront his words with something which explained why the *Bedoon* situation was justifiable. Her innermost feelings were closer to his, than to those she heard voiced often by her countrymen. *I know what it's like to be cut off. The sense of desperation — part of the situation you find yourself in with no way to control what happens to you. My uncle is a good man who did his best, but eventually, I was left with a family which ostracized me, and there was nowhere else to go. Not the same isolation as a Bedoon, but the feeling of hopelessness and not belonging is one with which I can identify.*

She decided the best way to defuse the situation was by being bold and shifting the topic rather than continuing to argue or capitulate. "The way any nation handles its people has to protect the citizens and also reflect their heart," she carefully timed her action so when she spoke the word 'heart' her right hand landed on top of his left. *Not like me to use my femininity this way, but this man in so many ways is becoming the exception.* "I agree there are better ways, and I only pray and hope they will be found." When she finished speaking, she left her hand on top of his for a moment before she shifted its position so she could intertwine her fingers with his.

At first, Evan felt slightly annoyed at her attempt to settle him down or to create a distraction by touching him. Then, he reflected on what she was saying, and the calming feel of her hand on his. He knew it was unlike a woman from this culture to use her caress for a favor. The sincerity of her words, accented by her touch, meant she felt they were familiar enough he would understand what was being left unsaid. He was about to respond when he realized they turned into the parking lot of the Cathedral. *Maybe later.*

As they got out of the SUV, they were greeted by a young Indian priest who was watching for their arrival. Najila contacted the church beforehand to arrange a formal tour for the two of them, which would include the history of Catholicism in Kuwait.

During the tour, Najila was mostly silent, with Evan asking all the questions and Father John politely addressing each one. Najila was grateful he did not try to approach the topic of the *Bedoon* with the priest.

Near the end of the tour, Father John showed them the statue of *Our Lady of Arabia* and explained how during the Gulf War it had been knocked over and broken by persons unknown.

"The priests assigned to the Cathedral did their best to protect its people and property from the invading Iraqis. While the statue being broken might be seen as a failure, it was also a triumph, when the parishioners were able to restore it to its original glory."

"There was no significant or permanent damage to the Cathedral itself? That would seem to be a miracle in its own right, especially when it was located so close to the center of the city."

"Yes, we are also grateful that when the bombs destroyed the priest's homes near here, no one was injured. God was indeed looking out for us as we served his flock."

*Did it include the Bedoon? No, this is the wrong man and the wrong place for the question.*

When the tour ended, the priest invited both of them to come back for Sunday mass and let them know what time the service would be in English. After bidding the priest goodbye, Najila decided on a late lunch at the Hard Rock Cafe might prevent any further discussion of citizenship issues in Kuwait.

Evan learned long ago the one thing you can count on in any country in the world, was the hamburgers at the Hard Rock Café, so he was grateful when she pulled into the parking lot. The restaurant was fortunate to have one of the better oceanfront views in the country, and they enjoyed a friendly meal while both ignored the emotional discussion before going to the church.

"I was wondering if you had plans for our day off this week?"

*What's this?* "Not really, maybe a bit of shopping but nothing set in stone, why do you ask?"

"I was invited out to your uncle's house for a celebration in honor of Naveed. When Hamad asked me about attending, I asked if you'd be there as well. He said he was going to invite you later, and I asked him not to, so I might have the opportunity."

"I see. You are using my uncle's party as an excuse to ask me out for a date?" *That should make him a bit nervous.*

"Yeah, I guess so."

He could see the warmth in her eyes growing when he said this. Evan just formalized what both of them felt below the surface since the afternoon we spent together during the sandstorm.

"Well, I would be delighted." While speaking, she reached out her hand and laid it on top of his once again. *This time, I will kiss you and perhaps a bit more.*

Then as quickly as Evan brought it up the topic was dropped. It was as if it was off-limits to dwell on their upcoming evening together as it might somehow spoil it if they did. When they left the Hard Rock Cafe, on the journey back to the hotel, Evan noticed several of the businesses now displayed sandwich boards with quickly painted messages in Arabic out in front of them, *an upcoming holiday sale perhaps?* When they stopped for a light, Evan realized not all of them were in Arabic, "*Bedoons* Go Home!" *and how exactly are they supposed to do that?*

Najila was doing her best to not let her eyes settle for too long on any of the signs and was hopeful Evan would not see the ones she also noticed were written in English. The lunch was wonderful, and now she was looking forward to spending time with him in a much different role. All she needed to do was to get him back to the hotel as quickly as possible without another discussion about *Bedoons.*

Once again Nassar found himself standing beside the Nissan inspecting his work. The metal sheets he mounted in the engine compartment following the drawings did indeed create a walled space on the passenger side of the engine compartment. He found himself pondering why anyone would do such a thing, and why he would choose to isolate the space with such thick metal. Nassar knew he would probably never receive a direct answer about the rationale for such a design. If his boss was involved with smuggling – drugs, weapons, or artifacts – asking questions was a sure way to get killed.

For a *Bedoon*, getting killed seemed to be getting easier. He was surprised *Liljamie* chose not to publish the *Alshaytan Bayan Rasmiin*, but it was readily available. The copy he read was provided by the Kaliph Kinship, who printed hundreds of copies and distributed them among the *Bedoon* and TCN populace. *Shaytan* was proving to be a tremendous recruiting tool, although to date he had not declared opposition or alliance to the group. The words in the manifesto were more direct than those of the Kinship, but as it is said: the enemy of my enemy is my friend. So, anyone against the existing system was also a friend of the Kinship.

*Liljamie* was publishing many articles regarding recent escalating acts of violence against *Bedoons* and TCNs. Of course, the native Kuwaiti media ignored those events entirely. At least until this morning.

The slaughter which took place at the *Bedoon* compound was sufficiently violent enough it could not be ignored, and because it would lead to sales of newspapers, it was being given broad and continuously updated coverage. Most Kuwaitis, even those who were silent regarding the *Bedoon* situation, suddenly possessed an intense interest in what appeared to be a force working against *Shaytan* and by extension for them.

Nassar had yet to experience direct physical violence but knew it was probably coming. Someone shouted at him from a passing car, and he was once told to leave a restaurant when ordering food. More than once over the last few weeks, he wondered if it might be worthwhile to attempt the trek across the desert and into Jordan or Syria. There he could obtain a fake passport and move out of the region altogether. *Leaving my family behind, but maybe at the end finding life without this khara attached. Is a fight for citizenship rights even worth it anymore?*

Amr pulled his car into a parking spot in front of the museum at the site of the *Battle of Al-Qurain*. The labor penalty given to him by *Al Hakim* was complete, and rather than being a begrudging participant, Amr excelled at the tasks assigned to him. *Al Hakim* told him it was the only time he could remember someone earned a promotion while working their mandated labor hours. In addition to moving from cleaning stalls to taking care of the animals, Naveed spent a good deal of time with him teaching him not only about caring for horses but about being respectful of the creature's temperament, along with a few life lessons as well.

On his last night at *Rihlat Alsahra'*, he went to see *Al Hakim* to let him know he completed his hours and would not be returning. During the conversation, the older man mentioned the *Battle of Al-Qurain* to Amr, and its significance to Kuwaiti people. Amr was too ashamed to admit he never heard of the battle and on his own researched it, discovering the museum.

In the three hours between his arrival and the museum's closing, Amr explored the museum and the battle site. As he stood atop the building, looking down at the motionless tank and other vehicles below, he could only imagine the fear the man must have felt being the last defender. Then taking action against the enemy below as his bravery came to the surface. As he stood there, he watched a black SUV pull around the circle and the parking spot next to his car. A man dressed in Western clothes and carrying a backpack exited the vehicle, and rather than immediately entering the museum, he slowly began walking the perimeter of the fence which ringed the site. *How could I, a Kuwaiti, not know about this place, even this tourist nadhil knows.*

As Amr was leaving, he walked past the new arrival, who was now at the gate and holding a conversation with one of the museum's caretakers in English. From what Amr overheard, the tourist was asking for admission even though it was closing time. The caretaker was older, and probably felt some gratitude toward the West for Kuwait's liberation; he knew it was likely the tourist was going to gain entrance. Looking in his rearview mirror as he backed out of the parking spot to leave, he saw the two men walking towards the front door of the museum. *Told you.*

Maksim fought the urge to turn around and capture the license plate of the car as it left the museum. His concern was the young man remembering him or at least some details about him. He chastised himself for not dressing appropriately in case a situation like this presented itself. The original plan was to kill anyone inside the museum before he left to remove any chance of witnesses. Now, he could not leave bodies behind as this might be viewed as a straightforward crime rather than part of *Shaytan's* spree. At this point, everything he did, needed to somehow contribute to the chaos he was attempting to foment.

Since the caretaker gave him admission, he could not just walk away without drawing attention and being remembered. Instead, he spent the next 30 minutes or so being led through a museum in which he had no interest. As he strolled from exhibit to exhibit, he could feel the backpack shifting against his back, reminding him of the four thermite charges it contained. *It would've been a glorious fire.* Maksim spent too much time and effort creating the thermite, to just allow it to be wasted; for now, it would have to wait.

Maksim shook hands with the caretaker after the tour ended, and thanked him for sharing this part of Kuwaiti history. As soon as he was back in his car, and pulling out of the *Al-Qurain* neighborhood he took his phone out and prepared to send a text to Jasmine. He realized she was becoming a habit, but one he was thoroughly enjoying. *She provides an immediate release when I want, without the need to hunt, and so far without the need to clean up a mess afterward.* It might have been easier still if he just allowed her to stay with him, but he could not afford for her to get nosy, *or accidentally come across something she shouldn't.*

When he got back to his apartment, he was surprised she was

not waiting by the locked door for his arrival. Once inside, he put the bag with the thermite charges in his freezer next to the four individually wrapped charges already stored there. After ensuring the front door was unlocked, he stripped off his clothes on the way to the bedroom. Lying down on the bed, he rolled onto his back and slid his hand under the pillow until he felt the handle of the knife. He kept it there now and feeling its presence while he was with Jasmine became part of his ritual with her. The option to end her life at his whim added to his excitement. Satisfied everything was ready, he stared at the ceiling for a moment before closing his eyes to ponder this woman.

She was nothing like any female he was ever with before, not only because he was with her more than once, but because something about those experiences prevented him from killing her when it was over. She was an added risk to his current mission, but he was accepting the risk in trade for something he never experienced before. *But what exactly was it about her? Something about her willingness to accept my total control over her life. She never flinched or pulled away from my touch as I wrap my hands around her throat.* The thought made him smile.

"Baby?"

The voice was soft and trying to be gentle, although it lacked sincerity. Maksim felt her slowly glide one leg over his as she used it to slowly spread his apart. Jasmine brought her hand to rest on his crotch and began to massage it to arousal.

"I sorry I was late baby. Oooh, I feel you forgive me. Let me do this. Maybe you spank me for being bad." As she said this, she repositioned her body so her mouth could replace her hand on him. Maksim began to enjoy her attention while pondering her lateness. *She was probably late because she was scoring drugs before coming here. I wonder what the heroin level in her bloodstream is right now? But she is doing this so well, maybe all she need do is rely on muscle memory to guide her through.*

Maksim allowed his concentration to fade from everything except how his body was reacting. Before allowing pleasure to entirely overcome him, he reached under the pillow and took the knife in his hand, imagining how it would feel if he were to slash her throat as he came. *When the time comes, that's just how I will do it.*

"You know it's never meant anything to me, people are people. So, I cannot stand by and allow tit-for-tat vigilantism to break out," Jefzar had been in Hamad's *diwaniya* for the last hour, and for most of the time, he paced back-and-forth. The extent of Hamad's support was nodding silently or agreeing in single syllables with Jefzar's assessment of the situation, and how it changed since this morning's murders.

"My brother, I feel it is as you say. But the only way to calm the masses is to capture *Shaytan* and put an end to his spree. His arrest will put a stop to the chaos while calming those who feel the need to lash out against *Bedoons,* and to a lesser degree TCNs. As for your concern about what is being said in the press and online, I don't know of anyone who could accuse you of somehow favoring the *Bedoon* by purposely allowing *Shaytan* to remain free. It was you who first put the pieces together and found there was a pattern."

"Baah! I need a cigarette." Throwing the flap back on the tent Jefzar quickly exited and sought solace in an unlit corner of *Rihlat Alsahra'*. As he took determined steps to get there, he immediately lit a cigarette and let his mind mull over what occurred since early this morning.

His plan after driving back from the *Bedoon* compound was to come immediately here to seek the counsel of his brother. However, as he approached the city, he was summoned by the Chief of Police for an immediate meeting in Jefzar's office at the Constabulary. Irritated by the change to his plan, Jefzar obediently drove directly to his own office and immediately faced a gauntlet of reporters, while trying to get from his SUV into the building.

The mangled cacophony of shouts coupled with the flash of cameras prevented him from concentrating on any of the questions long enough to hear what was being said. *It didn't matter as soon as I walked into my office the Chief pointed his finger at me and accused me of misdirecting the task force to allow Shaytan free reign to kill Kuwaitis.*

The Chief spent less than five minutes dressing down his subordinate before storming out of the room and slamming the door behind him. As the echo of the door slam rang in his ears, it occurred to Jefzar why he had not been fired. *It isn't faith in me or my capabilities. He needs to keep me on, so he has a scapegoat. Based on our experience thus far, Shaytan will attack again, and it will be more dramatic.*

As he considered his next move, one of his officers knocked on the door and entered upon being summoned.

"Sir, I know you were driving back from the crime scene, so you may not be aware. Have you seen the things which are being said online?"

Jefzar was not a Luddite, but he was not an active participant on any of the social media platforms; he just did not see a reason to spend his time there. If he had been, he would have seen the basis for the Chief's supposition. Dozens of conversations were taking place concerning the day's events, and the killings that took place over the past few weeks. A majority of those conversations blamed Jefzar personally for what was happening; as the leader of the task force charged to apprehend *Shaytan,* he was being accused of using his position to delay and redirect the investigation so the killer would not be caught. Theories as to why varied from monetary payoffs, to Jefzar having a preference for young *Bedoon* girls.

Jefzar looked down on the ground and spat. As he took another cigarette from the pack in his shirt pocket, his brother walked up behind him and placed his hand on Jefzar's shoulder.

"When things calm down, people will realize not only were you doing your job, you were doing it well."

"I hope so," the younger brother said as he exhaled a lungful of smoke.

"You know, I never said anything when those decisions were being made all those years ago. In my gut, I knew they might be the wrong way to proceed for our people. Perhaps I am the one who failed, not you."

They were interrupted as Naveed walked by with a horse in tow. As soon as he was out of earshot, Jefzar leaned towards his brother and in a low voice said, "You realize this might not be a good time to be having a celebration for a non-Kuwaiti."

"What was it you said, 'Baah'? Well, Baah! He is part of my family, and I'm a Kuwaiti, therefore so is he. Especially on his birthday."

"I need to get to the Constabulary, even if it is only to prove I'm not one of *Shaytan's* minions, and for the record, I'm not. If you've got any ideas on how to quell this situation and prevent any more blood of innocents being shed, please let me know. I am out of ideas."

"Indeed. Give me some time, and perhaps after a *sheesha* and some fruit, I might come up with something. If you don't finish up too late, come and join me." *I'm worried about him, he needs a mental break to allow for re-tuning his thought process.*

As Hamad spoke, they refocused their attention on headlights in the distance there was headed toward *Rihlat Alsahra'.*

"Expecting company?"

"No, not at all. Perhaps it is my American writer delivering his latest missive. Najila said she was going to take him to the Cathedral in Kuwait City."

"It should prove an interesting read."

Jefzar waited until the vehicle was close enough to determine the occupant was innocuous before he walked over to his SUV and got in to head back into town. He waved at the inbound vehicle as he passed it, and noticed it was Roshan, *Unusual for him to be out here this late.*

The incident at the *Fahaheel Souk* convinced Roshan it was necessary to inform *Al Hakim* of his true lineage immediately. The decision was one of the hardest of his life. Roshan knew the current chaos brought him to a precipice where his exposure as a *Bedoon* was more likely than ever before. *I know if Al Hakim finds out before I tell him, it will destroy all the trust and rapport we have. There is a chance if I explain it, he'll understand why this was done and not see it as a betrayal of his trust and our relationship*. With that resolution, he decided it best if he spoke to *Al Hakim* at *Rihlat Alsahra'* this very evening. In fact, the evening was preferable as there would be fewer people around if the conversation was not as cordial as he hoped.

After Roshan parked and got out of his vehicle, Hamad walked over to him and shook his hand greeting him warmly, then immediately turned around and told the man to follow him.

"I'm glad you decided to come out here this evening."

"Was it Jefzar leaving as I came in?" Roshan knew the answer but wanted Hamad to know he noticed.

"Yes, Jefzar came out to seek my counsel. He's concerned about the current situation and mood of the people due to several events. I want to discuss my thoughts on how best to handle this with you first to get your opinion," turning back toward Roshan, Hamad bowed his head slightly before adding, "Your valued opinion."

"Absolutely, *Al Hakim*," *alas, no better time for the conversation I wanted to have but then no worse time either.*

Hamad held the tent flap open for Roshan, then followed him into the *diwaniya*. Hamad took his usual place, and once he was seated, Roshan followed suit on the opposite side of the table. The half-eaten platter of fruit, pitchers of juice, and dirty dishes from Jefzar's visit was cleared away. Clean place settings, along with freshly cut fruit and chilled drinks were now in their place.

Hamad reached into the pocket of his *dishdasha* and withdrew the *tasbih*. His motions with the prayer beads were slow and deliberate. He took every single bead in between his finger and thumb, and deftly felt the entire surface of the bead before using his thumb to push it down the string and proceed to the next. As Roshan sat watching him, Hamad was totally silent.

Roshan was familiar with Hamad's moods and the various ways he pondered problems when they occurred. Between the way, he was handling his *tasbih* and the distant stare in his eyes Roshan knew his boss was deep in thought. Occasionally, he would see *Al Hakim's* eyes narrow as if he came to some sort of conclusion, but then they returned to their distant stare without his speaking a word.

Hamad saw the problem as having many levels, and he was mentally reviewing all known facts before searching for a solution which would thread each of those levels. The simpler and more unifying the resolution, the quicker the chaos his beloved country was experiencing would calm. Of course, he could think like this alone, but by having Roshan there, when he did come up with a solution, he would be able to immediately discuss it with his trusted advisor.

"The problem, in its entirety, can and must end with this *Shaytan* person. He is the one responsible for the slew of killings, and he is the author of Satan's Manifesto-- *Alshaytan Bayan Rasmiin*. By annihilating him, I believe everything else will calm down," he felt it necessary to repeat the conclusion he reached during his discussion with Jefzar for Roshan's benefit. As he spoke the words, Hamad sped up the manipulation of his prayer beads.

"Now, in the beginning, the victims were TCNs followed by Kuwaiti citizens. Once the pattern was identified by Jefzar, it thrust *Bedoons* into the role of villain. Later, even though the killer's early victims were TCNs, he included them as a beneficiary in his Manifesto causing a schism between Kuwaiti citizens and them as well," Hamad looked directly at Roshan and raised his eyebrows seeking a sign of confirmation he understood. As soon as Roshan nodded, Hamad continued. "As if all this was not enough, an outside group, the Caliph Kinship, is attempting to use this wedge as a way of uniting the opposition behind their flag – although I don't think they are directly involved or in control of the killer. Now, it would seem, Kuwaiti citizens are starting to lash out by attacking both TCNs and *Bedoons* in the city. The latest escalation was the slaughter at the *Bedoon* compound this morning." Hamad took a moment to examine the *tasbih* in his hand and made a mental note to say a prayer for those killed later. He tucked the beads into his pocket, then Roshan broke the silence.

"*Al Hakim*, you say Jefzar is not close to apprehending *Shaytan*, so what do we do in the interim?"

"*Shaytan* raised his visibility and caused the ire of the Kuwaiti people when he released *Alshaytan Bayan Rasmiin*. Have you read it?" Roshan nodded his head, so Hamad continued talking about it without further explanation. "Thanks to the generosity of the Kinship, so have most of those who would benefit from the document. It's nothing more than a gift list for the *Bedoon* and others. A basic economic shift, which would take away from one group and give to another group without any consideration as to the cataclysm brought about by such a wholesale realignment."

Roshan cleared his throat, beginning to speak for the first time during this exchange, "If this document took things beyond seeding simple hatred to the reactions we see now, I think we would be best served if we can in some way provide a palatable alternative to the document."

"So, if we cannot bring in *Shaytan* himself we will at least sheer his horns."

The room went quiet again as Hamad considered what Roshan said. He slipped his hand into his pocket and once again withdrew the *tasbih*. Hamad tilted his head back and looked towards the ceiling of the tent trying to grasp an idea. After giving the beads several flips, he stopped and merely held them then said.

"Al-Enezi"

"Yes?" As soon as the word came out of his mouth, Roshan realized what he is done. Hamad immediately turned and looked at him quizzically. For decades Roshan trained himself not to answer to his given name and was successful until now.

"That was the name. The name of the *Bedoon* writer. I read a few of his articles after the Liberation. He talked about the need to bring the *Bedoon* population into full Kuwaiti citizenship, making them a true part of the country."

"You propose to present this man's suggestion as an alternative to the manifesto?" Roshan was still reeling at having learned *Al Hakim* read his articles. *Is it too much to hope for he is considering implementing them?*

"No, not at all. But this fellow is a calming voice and would be a calming alternative to *Shaytan* and perhaps the Caliph Kinship as well.

Roshan suddenly felt cold. He felt as if he was almost at the precipice of a dialogue that might eventually lead to the improvement of the situation for his people. Now it would seem, the only thing desired is to quiet the rabble, versus dealing with the real issue at heart.

"Find me this man, and let him know I want to talk to him. I believe his first name was Talal."

"Absolutely," as he said this, he rose and headed out of the tent.

Roshan considered for a moment simply walking out of the tent, then walking back in and presenting himself using his true identity— Talal Al-Enezi but immediately thought better of it. He was glad he did not tell *Al Hakim* of his true identity, at least not yet. Somewhere inside his heart, he felt the path they were on now was going to lead them to his life's goal. *I have been patient thus far, perhaps soon.*

*Penthouse, Hotel Sultana*

Evan walked purposefully out of the elevator and placed his Go-bag on the long table before continuing on into the bedroom. He was traveling to *Rihlat Alsahra'* every evening to ride Cochise and talk with Hamad. Tonight, Evan just wanted to do some writing, and try to find more answers to his question about *Bedoons* online. He was once again greeted by an anonymously-left gift of printed material. This time, a book of pictures of *Bedoons*. He changed quickly into a pair of shorts and a T-shirt before returning to the conference table and having a seat. Evan had just opened his laptop when he heard soft footsteps approaching.

"Good evening Jazlene, how are you doing?"

"Hello, Mr. Boss. I'm well."

"I've told you before, just call me Evan," as he said this, he turned around in the chair to face Jazlene. He paused a moment and waited for her to respond with some sort of request or explanation as to why she was there, but she only remained silent.

"Is there something you need from me, Jazlene?"

She stared at the floor speaking very slowly and softly, "I wonder if you might allow me to sleep for a few nights in the room where I stay during the day?"

Evan pondered the request for a moment, trying to come up with a nice way of saying no because he didn't want anyone in the penthouse with him.

"Is there something wrong with your home?"

"No, not at all. The problem is this one, there have been many instances where people from my country are being attacked or having things thrown at them on the streets. If I stay here, I would not have to walk to my neighborhood or from there back here."

When she finished speaking, she stood staring directly at him with her dark eyes full of seriousness and a tinge of visible fear.

*Okay, Mr. I Want to Be Alone. You can't exactly send her out, can you? You saw tonight what it looked like.*

"I guess it would be okay, for a few days. Did you eat yet?"

She shook her head.

"Fine. Tell you what, I'm going to do some writing right now but in about an hour go down to the restaurant and pick us up some dinner. I'll have a turkey sandwich with fries and a glass of iced tea, you can have whatever you want. Once you get it, bring it on up, and we'll have dinner together."

He had never seen her smile before. Evan had no way of comprehending what he gave her. Not only a safe place to stay while the world around her turned upside down but also dinner when she had not eaten since the day before. At this moment, she saw him as her white knight.

When Jazlene returned later with the food, Evan stopped what he was doing long enough for them to eat together. During the meal, he quizzed her about her home and how she ended up in Kuwait instead of anywhere else in the world. He enjoyed hearing her laugh as she told him stories of what it was like to grow up in the Philippines with her nine brothers and sisters. It was surprising to hear at one point she almost became a nun. When they were done eating, she cleaned up the table and took care of the dishes while he returned to his writing.

When she came off the elevator, after delivering the dirty dishes back to the restaurant, she walked up behind him where he was working on his laptop. She stood silently for a moment waiting on him to acknowledge her.

"Is there something else Jazlene?" Evan said as he turned to face her.

After she departed with the dirty dishes, he turned the lights down in the room to avoid distraction. Now, even in the dim light, he could see tears running down her face.

"Are you okay?"

"Yes Boss, I just wanted to tell you how much I appreciate what you're doing for me," she then lunged forward and wrapped her arms around his neck, hugging him.

Evan patted her back as she hugged him. *I am not sure what to do about this. Too many cultural things are swirling here. Well if I was going to feel guilty for saying "no" I should feel good for saying "yes."*

Without saying another word, she released her grip on him then turned to head towards her room.

"Goodnight sir," she said as she closed the door behind her.

Call me Evan he thought sighing in resignation as he returned to his work.

# Chapter 13

*Roshan's Villa*

Roshan lay on his back, staring at the ceiling. Normally by this time of the day, he would be at *Al Hakim's* office going over the night's correspondence and preparing for the day ahead. Not today. Today, he would take his time and reflect on what happened in the last 18 hours or so. So many twists and turns in the path ahead, and if he takes the wrong one, he will be lost forever.

Race-based altercations were occurring all over the country, and growing in severity and scope. *Shaytan's* Manifesto may have been the gasoline on the fire, but before it was published, there were several extremely graphic murders in the country. The fear from those quickly turned to anger, and now the growing retaliation, which promptly went from yelling curse words to the slaughter of an entire compound full of people. *My people.*

*Al Hakim* acknowledged reading the articles of Talal Al-Enezi. In fact, he was so impressed with the writing and his persuasiveness he directed Roshan to hire Al-Enezi to produce documents to counter Satan's Manifesto. *In reality, Al Hakim could've struck a deal with me while I sat with him in his diwaniya. Above all, I must find some way to resolve the duality I've lived since Kuwaiti Liberation, and be honest with my friend and boss about it.*

*For now, those two forks in the road appear to be the most dire, and time-sensitive. But I forgot the issues with Nassar.*

His son came by the villa several times over the past few weeks and each time bragged of a steady job and the money he was making. *I know, as a Bedoon, there is no way he could make this kind of money legitimately.* His duty as a father meant he needed to find out exactly what his son was doing, and who was paying him so much money. *He is letting the money cloud his mind against the risks associated with it.*

The list of decisions to be considered, and the actions Roshan needed to take continued to grow as he lay there doing nothing. *What about this American writer? I provided him with reports on the Bedoon situation. Then the one time he wanted to talk to me about it, we were interrupted.* He needed to figure a way to bring himself and Evan together for some time alone so they could speak openly. Roshan knew if he could supply him with enough information, it would also fuel his curiosity enough to write about *my people. Maybe some of Talal's articles or a picture book to re-re-pique his interest.*

Not to forget the Caliph Kinship. While never saying so directly, they were leading his people to believe *Shaytan* was somehow part of their team...*and some people are so hopeless they will grasp at anything that appears to offer them some small bit of something better. Why can they not see the only thing being proposed is to go from serving one bad master to another?* He could not blame them; his own group made little to no advance in months, whereas *Shaytan* at least made the topic all tongues were wagging about.

He rolled to his side and looked at his bedside clock. *Another 10 minutes have passed, and I've accomplished nothing.* Closing his eyes, he tried to decide if he was going to force himself to sleep or drag himself into the other room for a cup of tea. His cell phone rang removing the decision from him, at least for the moment. Roshan reached out and picked up the phone, glancing at the screen he noticed the number was said the identity was blocked. After pushing the connect button, he held the phone against his ear and remained silent. There was nothing but silence from the other end for a few moments. He was about to hang up when a voice said quizzically "Talal?" Roshan recognized immediately as someone from his *Bedoon* committee.

"Talal speaking," he said breaking his silence while he slowly brought himself to a seated position.

The conversation was short and to the point, because there was always the possibility someone was listening. Specifics were alluded to, and details were omitted. When Roshan terminated the call by pushing the End button, he felt the only thing to be thankful for was the caller brought him an issue he already knew existed instead of a new one. *What has my son gotten himself into?*

It would seem Nassar's employer was the same man who employed a young TCN named Rajeesh. Rajeesh's cousin was asked to help locate him when he failed to return home for several days. After doing a little research, the cousin now believed an anonymous body found in a burned-out building to be Rajeesh. No further action was being taken with the body because it was ruled self-immolation and therefore not a crime. Also, in the greater scheme of things, TCN deaths really did not matter to the authorities.

Usually, this would've put an end to it. However, during his search for Rajeesh, the cousin discovered he was doing odd jobs for an American. This all connected back to Roshan, when last night, someone reportedly saw Nassar inside a rented garage in *Faheel* talking to an American. There was absolutely nothing that said the same American who employed Rajeesh had now hired Nassar. There was nothing to connect the fire that killed Rajeesh to the American. There was nothing to say the American was paying Nassar to do anything illegal. *Nothing at all, except for the bad luck of a Bedoon in Kuwait, which almost guaranteed these things would all be connected.*

This concern was already on Roshan's list, but now it moved to the top. He opened his phone and selected his Nassar's number from his list of contacts. It went directly to voicemail.

"Nassar, it's your father. I thought we might get together today and have lunch to catch up on a few things. Give me a call when you have a moment."

He closed the phone and stared at it for a moment before tossing it onto the bed. He headed towards the shower to start the day.

He was about to walk out the door when he saw a stack of envelopes ready to be sent on the entryway table. Roshan picked up the stack and began to go through it. It consisted primarily of monthly bill payments, to include utilities. *Another of the costs of being a Bedoon.* His family was fortunate, as *Al Hakim* paid for your utilities as part of his salary even though he was representing himself as a TCN. When Roshan first started working for him, *Al Hakim* would make the payment directly, so he never saw the bill. Eventually, he asked if his salary could just be raised to cover the utility bill and he would pay it directly.

Of course, *Al Hakim* was agreeable as the end cost was the same. When he queried Roshan as to why he would want things this way, he remembered telling him: "If you pay the bill, I'll never see the true cost. If I pay the bill, even though it is covered as part of my salary, I'll see exactly what it costs and can understand the true economics of my existence." At the time his boss just nodded and made the change.

*Al Hakim* didn't realize what Roshan was doing was keeping track of another of the costs of being a *Bedoon*. If he were a citizen, utilities along with gasoline and many other things would've been subsidized. Instead, a considerable payment was going to a utility company every month to keep his villa lit and air-conditioned.

Roshan picked up the stack of correspondence, having decided to drop it by the post office on his way to *Rihlat Alsahra'*.

As soon as Jefzar closed the door on his SUV, he began to walk quickly from the vehicle into the front door of the Constabulary. Somehow, he managed to hit the sweet spot between the press leaving the front of the building from the night before and reappearing this morning. *I guess I could've gone in through the back door, but then I would've immediately been accused of hiding something sinister, creating more rumors as to why I was hiding.*

He retrieved a cup of coffee and headed for his office. Upon entering, he closed the door and pulled down the shade, isolating himself inside. As he sat at his desk, he placed his elbows on the desk and held the mug of coffee with both hands so it was just below his nose and he could inhale its aromatic scent. *No 7% solution for me.* The reference was to Sherlock Holmes' cocaine usage. Jefzar took a sip of the coffee, and set the mug on his desk. With all of the folders from the murders in the workroom next door, he possessed no actual evidence to distract him.

What he did have was his mental method for figuring out *whodunit*. He closed his eyes and leaned back tilting his chair. *Let's start with the most basic things.*

The victims until now were dispatched one at a time. *Did it mean the killer would continue the same way? Probably not.* Most serial killers accelerated as time went on, but this was different; this was someone killing for political reasons. In his mind, he made a note on his mental whiteboard and moved it to the side.

Until recently, none of the victims was of the same race. At one point the killer shifted from TCNs to Kuwaitis. Then the Kuwaitis he was killing became higher-level people. Another note was written on his mind's whiteboard and again shoved to the side. He rose from his chair and began to slowly pace the width of his office.

In the beginning, the killings appeared to be random or opportune. But blowing up the legislator – *it would've taken much planning. Not only for the bomb itself but also the escape afterward.* Jefzar paused from pacing for a moment recalling the report he read just a day or so before. Forensics of the bomb showed it was triggered by a timer was set for seven minutes.

*What about the cricket player? Was the boy playing cricket when the killer arrived or did the killer convince the boy to play cricket, then kill him? Too many variables – it must've been planned.* In his mind, he went over the remaining cases, and there was enough doubt in everyone for him to consider each must have been planned *at least a few hours in advance.* Another note for the whiteboard.

The noise outside of his office was beginning to pick up. Eventually, someone would knock on the door and disturb this process. Jefzar ignored the thought for a moment, and moved on to the next item. Sitting back down in his chair, he closed his eyes and leaned back in his chair allowing his head to tilt back and relax against the headrest.

The methods of killing were all over the map. If the bomb is considered highly technical, is beating someone to death with a cricket bat considered Neanderthal? *Or was it?* He made a mental note to call the coroner to ask some questions. Based on what he remembered from the file the blows were controlled and fairly exacting, to make sure the face was not struck while at the same time breaking every major bone in the body. *Absolute control…So, we aren't dealing with the bomber who beat the khara out of someone. We're dealing with someone who is very good at killing. Good enough to control themselves in a difficult situation.* He wrote the word 'experience' on his mind's whiteboard before pushing it to the side.

*Who has this level and variety of experience? Soldiers, cops, maybe engineers, medical people? Why would those people suddenly turn into the demonic salvation of the Bedoon?* Then, Jefzar was struck by a bolt of reason and inspiration. *The Law of Parsimony. Of course. Don't think zebra when you hear the noise of hooves, think horses. Occam's Razor.*

Standing again, he ran through the evidence in his mind taking a step with each revelation. He needed to make sure it would all match his epiphany at least close enough to begin to examine it and place it against the evidence. *It wasn't some zealot killer with multiple skills doing this for the Bedoon; it is a hired high-level assassin.* In his mind, he already crossed off all the items on his whiteboard and was now proceeding to his memory of each case. Continuing to pace, he took a step as he went through each case to ensure they could be found to match his supposition before he moved on mentally to the next file. Until they were all done.

Jefzar moved back to his desk, and sat down, facing forward with his hands upon the desk. He slowly closed his eyes and remembered a lecture he attended at Federal Law Enforcement Training Center in Atlanta: When you can completely remove all spiritual or emotional motivation for a particular crime, it always comes down to one thing: Money. Once that's decided, follow the money and you will find all the criminals along the way.

Jefzar opened his desk drawer and removed the crushed pack of cigarettes along with the book of matches. Striking a match, he lit a cigarette he had taken from the pack and inhaled deeply. *Follow the money. Indeed, follow the money. If I'm going to follow the money, I need to speak with a few bankers.* He rose from his desk and went over to his door raising the shade and unlocking it. Jefzar then open the door and shouted down the hallway "Mubarak!" He paused for a moment realizing it might be too early for the officer to be in, he shouted "Zainab!" Closing the door, he returned to his desk to see which of the two would arrive first.

"Sir?"

*Zainab. Of course. Mubarak would be out goofing off while she was working. It's okay; we're in a changing world.*

"I need you to call each of the banks and inquire if they facilitate transactions to other countries," *It almost seems like a waste of time because you will be a rare exception of a bank did not perform transactions internationally. But it might help lower the number of bankers we are going to have to talk to,* "Next ask each of them if they've performed transfers in the last 30 to 60 days, for any single amount over," Jefzar paused for a moment taking a calculator out of his desk. He punched in a few numbers to convert €75,000 to Kuwaiti dinar. "28,000KD. Once you have a list of those banks, bring me the names."

Zainab spun around and departed the office without saying another word. She knew from experience Jefzar did not need her to acknowledge what he said but to act upon it. After she departed his office and he was again alone, Jefzar sat at his desk tried to remember where he came up with the €75,000 figure.

*It seems so arbitrary now, but I must've based it on something – a report something about what a mercenary cost. No. Not a report, a movie. A Bollywood movie Feek!* He debated getting up and redirecting Zainab's efforts, but after a moment of consideration, he realized he was not going to be able to come up with any amount that was not more or less arbitrary. His final decision on the matter, before being interrupted by a late-arriving Mubarak, was to wait to see how many bankers came up with matching transactions. After taking a long drag on his cigarette he dropped it into the coffee cup, handing it to Mubarak with instructions to wash it.

Sometime overnight, Evan received a text from Najila

> Not feeling well. Day off?
< Sure. Anything I can do?
> Nice of u to ask, but no.
> Feel Better

With his day free, rather than immediately getting in the shower Evan walked into the living area and called down for a pot of coffee. As he waited for the coffee to arrive, he looked down at the long conference table with its various piles of paper.

Last night, after he finished writing the article about the churches of Kuwait, he reread the report from Human Rights Watch, and some printouts which arrived in a folder. The articles were not so much a history, as they were suggestions on how to resolve the *Bedoon* issue in the least convoluted way. Most of them were written by someone named Talal Al-Enezi. Setting those aside for the moment, he picked up the HRW report, deciding to read it in depth first, so he knew the history.

When he completed reading each page, he added notes on the back of the paper, including questions he wanted to get more details about, then tore it out of the printed report. When he finished rereading the entire 50 pages, he categorized each page and divided those into various piles. As he looked down upon the collections, he was still in denial about his role as a journalist versus a writer. Evan saw this more as a student constructing a report, rather than editorial research.

Once the coffee arrived, he picked up the cup the waiter poured, along with one stack of papers, then found a comfortable seat facing the refinery.

There were many things about the citizenship division process that just did not sit right with Evan. The only consistency was the lack of it, as the rules and definitions continually shifted. Initially, if you were in the country before 1945 you were considered a citizen. Then the law was changed, so residency was required since 1920. In about 1959 or so, when committees were set up to determine citizenship, there was a concerted effort to exclude people who were from specific tribes. In the end, they came up with three groupings of applications: full citizens, partial citizens, and potential citizens. The last group was condemned to be *Bedoon*.

Granted, the tribesmen brought some of this on themselves by failing to apply for citizenship or by not having clear enough handwriting for a proper determination to be made. *Imagine, the inability to determine citizenship just because you didn't loop your letters properly in cursive. Or whatever the Arabic equivalent was.* But there were also other factors, some *Bedouins* who were eligible for citizenship, did not apply because they were fearful that being given citizenship would lead to an end to their nomadic lifestyle. *What a mess.*

As with anything involving power, money can always be used to grease the wheels the way you want them to roll. There was evidence of several Iraqis gaining citizenship by bribery, even though it was widely known they did not live in Kuwait until well after its independence.

Evan stood and walked back over the table dropping one pile of papers on it to pick up another. After pouring himself another cup of coffee, he returned to his station and before starting to read again, took a sip of his coffee as he watched a shift change at the oil refinery far below him. Busloads of TCN workers were showing up to report for work, while other ones were departing. From here, it looked like nothing short of mass confusion, but at street-level, it was a concerted process, which took place a couple times a day.

The crackdown and increased scrutiny and persecution of *Bedoons* began in 1985, a few years before the Iraqi invasion. Then, the government adopted the policy proposed by Shaikh Salem al-Sabah, Minister of Interior, in an attempt to drive the *Bedoon* out of the country. The details of the policy took place over months and years – all the while it was kept completely secret. Evan looked through the interview summaries included in the report, which revealed governmental denationalization actions. The effect was chilling, and was nothing less than a systematic and targeted degrading of those people previously thought of as potential citizens, to a caste below a TCN. *Hell, with all that going against them, it's a wonder they didn't leave as quickly as possible.*

Even though potential citizens could be considered stateless, they were not treated as such within Kuwait until after 1985. Their rights were stripped away one by one, to include the right to government employment, education, and health services. During this time many *Bedoons* were still hopeful they would be granted citizenship, even after dealing with the most fluid of all Kuwaiti regulations: The Citizenship Law.

Evan read accounts where *Bedoon* families spent decades continually upgrading and changing the paperwork to match the laws designed to prevent them from ever gaining citizenship. The changes then went so far as to declare citizenship an administrative versus a vested right. The Citizenship Law provided an ever-moving target of rules, regulations, document requirements, and deadlines, which were used to prevent an applicant from ever reaching the goal of citizenship. The law prevented thousands of people from becoming recognized as citizens, even though they would've been, based on the original 1959 law.

Then in 1988, the most externally visible change in Kuwait occurred when the government stopped reporting *Bedoons* in their population counts. *The governmental bastards stopped considering them people.*

Evan read these words before, but now they were sinking in and being understood more deeply. The man he was working for, who he both admired and liked, was part of a government which did its best to strip an innocent people of citizenship for nothing more than being in the wrong tribe or not being able to do paperwork. *There was no purpose served here except for one group of people to claim dominion over another, using the power they only imagined being given. It's all about money.*

Evan's thoughts were interrupted by the sound of his cell phone's ring tone.

"Sir, it is Roshan. I hope I am not disturbing you."

"Not at all Roshan, I didn't have an appointment with Hamad today, did I?"

"Not that I'm aware of. I thought I would contact you since we did not complete our conversation the other day at *Rihlat Alsahra'*. Did you still need to speak to me regarding the matter of your concern?"

"You know, the need to complete the conversation is on my to-do list." *Hell yes, we need to complete the conversation; I need a better understanding of what I've gotten myself into.*

"Absolutely, then I will make myself available to you when you desire so we can take care of that detail."

Evan stopped himself from saying 'Now's fine, come on up.' He also wanted to finish reading the documents on the table and get a shower to clear his head before meeting with Roshan.

"How about you come by The Sultana, and we can have a talk over lunch?"

"Absolutely; should I meet you at noon in the restaurant?"

"No, tell you what, come on up to the penthouse, and we'll order lunch from here so we can have a little privacy as we talk."

"I'll see you then."

Evan hung up his phone, and before getting into the shower, he returned to the conference table and stacked all the piles of paperback into one pile with the title, *The Bedoons of Kuwait,* clearly visible on top. *If he sees this, maybe it will spur the conversation along.*

A few hours later, Roshan stepped off the elevator, and presented Evan with a bottle of wine.

"Really? I thought such things were unavailable here?"

"It is a rather difficult topic. The law forbids the selling of alcohol, but nothing specifically restricts the possession or consumption of alcohol. Within certain limits."

"But aren't you a…"

"Muslim. Absolutely, but I brought this as a gift, not as something of which I would partake. But please feel free to enjoy it with your lunch if you desire."

"Um, I think I will pass. I usually don't have a drink before five or six in the afternoon. But thank you for the wonderful gift," Realizing such a gift should not be clearly visible to the hotel staff, Evan excused himself and hid the bottle in a dresser drawer in the bedroom. Upon returning, the two selected meals from the menu and Evan called it in.

Moments later they were feasting upon their choices and carrying on a light conversation about Roshan's experiences with Najila as a child.

As Evan listened to Roshan talk, he could imagine what she must have looked like as a small girl, with long dark hair and eyes. He also thought such a time in her life must have been sorrowful, having just lost her entire family and being thrust into the world of a war orphan. Then his mind wandered onto the way she looked today and the wonderful scent of *Lamsat Hareer*, which seemed to completely surround and embody her presence.

When they finished eating, Evan stacked the dishes onto the cart and placed it to the side leaving the table bare except for the *Bedoon* report.

"When we first started our conversation a few days ago, we just got to the topic when we were interrupted."

"Absolutely. You asked me how *Bedoons* came to be such," motioning towards the report on the table, "I see you've been doing some reading on your own."

"Uh, yes. These," motioning towards the report and other papers, "have been anonymously delivered to my room, one at a time, since my first days here. I've read some of them, of course, but none of it really started to sink in until the events of the past week or so."

"Indeed, it does seem to be a troubled time at the moment. Did you know of the 300,000 or so *Bedoons* believed to be in existence, only half reside in Kuwait?"

"After reading the report, I'm not surprised. Kuwait doesn't seem to be a very welcoming place if you're a *Bedoon*."

"Absolutely; from 1985 on, the government has been steadily chipping away at the rights and benefits of the *Bedoon*. The government started blocking their employment, then took away their ID cards, eventually driver's licenses, and stopped allowing them to attend school. Next, they forced them to live only in specific areas, which are heavily monitored for minor infractions, allowing them to be deported or jailed. If they leave the country for any reason, *Bedoons* are prohibited from reentering. Because of the official position of the government, *Bedoons* became easy prey for anyone wishing to attack them for any reason. Such attacks go on with impunity."

Evan rose from his chair, and went to the room service cart and returned with a pot of coffee and two fresh cups as well as cream and sugar.

"Coffee?"

"Absolutely. The hotel serves a superior blend here."

"I've noticed TCNs like you are treated better than *Bedoons,* even though *Bedoons* are from Kuwait."

"Yes, curious isn't it? You treat your own countrymen worse than you would a stranger. It is as if they are, what you Americans call, *the redheaded stepchild?*"

Evan chuckled and nodded.

"Things actually got worse during the occupation, when the Iraqi army demanded all *Bedoons* become part of a Popular Army they formed. If a *Bedoon* failed to register for this, they would be immediately jailed. Some *Bedoons* attempted to help the country by participating with the various resistance cells which were formed during the occupation."

"Najila took me to *Al-Quarin.*"

"I know, you wrote a very nice article about the battle. I was surprised you did not make a comparison to the fight for the Alamo in your own country. It would've been valid."

"Thank you. I was trying to avoid the comparison so people would concentrate on what happened here. Anyway, after the liberation things got much worse for the *Bedoon,* didn't they?"

Roshan nodded his head "Yes, absolutely. Because some were forced to join the Popular Army, it served to allow the labeling of all *Bedoons* as traitors."

Evan shook his head and again rose from his seat, walking over to the large windows and looked down on the refinery in silence.

"Of the total Kuwaitis killed by the Iraqis, *Bedoons* maintained the all-too-familiar statistic of one-third. In fact, many who were serving in the Armed Forces and as police are still missing to this day."

"Wait," Evan said as he turned around facing Roshan, "you

mean even after everything that happened to them there were still *Bedoon* serving in the military and as policemen?"

"Absolutely. Most served as rank and file within the organizations, but even so, *Bedoons* were blamed with the failure to stop the invasion."

"From what I've learned since being here, nothing Kuwait possessed could've stopped the Iraqi army from rolling in. They were simply outmanned, outgunned, and out commanded," Evan surprised himself; it was the first time he said something openly negative about Kuwaiti officials. But from all he read, even though the Kuwaitis were brave people fighting for their homeland, some officers were just not capable of handling the positions *wasta* placed them in.

Roshan paused for a moment and considered the conversation he was having with Evan. *Surely, he is picking up my personal feelings about all of this. Do I tell them the truth now? Do I wait and maybe let him ask or guess?*

"As people were fleeing from the occupying force, the Kuwaiti government in exile set up a control point at *al-Khafji* and was examining those trying to gain admission into Saudi Arabia as refugees. The only *Bedoon* allowed to cross the border were active-duty military. Also, there was a requirement for a passport to cross the border, a document most *Bedoons* were unable to obtain. It was widely known amongst the community; the only country they could take refuge in was Iraq. Until the air war started, very few took the option, instead choosing to remain in occupied Kuwait with all the risks associated with it."

"I guess the air war and impending ground war was a bit much for anyone with a family to risk. A war zone is never a good place for civilians."

Roshan, nodded then paused to take a sip of his coffee before continuing. "After the liberation in February 1991, most Kuwaitis returned home. *Bedoons,* however, were blocked from reentering the country, and still are. The war became another way to discriminate against this population. Did you know, from its creation, the Kuwaiti Army's backbone was *Bedoon* soldiers? After the liberation, the Kuwaitis dismissed all but a handful. Even those who were rehired were significantly reduced in rank and pay when allowed to rejoin."

"I guess another thing I don't understand is many citizens and *Bedoons* seem to be from the same tribes, have the same last name and lineage, and even look alike."

"Absolutely. It is among the many things I've never fully understood either. Maybe you have to be a citizen to gain that knowledge," Roshan smiled at his own dark joke, but Evan remained stoic.

The room went silent, and neither Roshan nor Evan wanted to break it as each man sat alone in their thoughts, trying to digest the conversation they just completed. Roshan realized he went too far, and said too many things too strongly to back away. It was a discussion he never could have with *Al Hakim,* but for the first time in his life, he felt free to speak about the wrongs he saw and witnessed. After taking another sip of his coffee, he cleared his throat, which caused Evan to turn toward him.

"During the war for liberation, many *Bedoons* chose to serve with various resistance cells within the country. It was very dangerous for them because of the Iraqi's insistence on membership in the Popular Army. As a result, *Bedoons* who served with the resistance, in positions which would expose them publicly, often chose to hide behind assumed identities as TCNs. Iraqi soldiers were too busy trying to loot and control Kuwait to bother looking very closely at people, and the physical appearance was close enough the deception was successful."

As Evan listened to Roshan speak, he began closely examining Roshan's features. Not being familiar enough with the subtle physical differences between the races in the region, he accepted whatever a person told him as their nationality. Now, he was wondering if what he was hearing matched what he was thinking.

"Once the war was over, there was great excitement within the *Bedoon* community, hoping their loyalty would be rewarded with citizenship. Instead, as I've told you, the situation actually worsened. So, brave *Bedoon* who served the country loyally went from being heroes one day to again rejoining the lowest rung on the caste ladder the next."

"A hell of a transition."

"Yes, but not all chose to make it. Some maintained their TCN identities and chose to live their lives from then on as something other than what they were, while still hopeful justice would eventually come."

Evan sat looking directly into Roshan's eyes. His words just confirmed the theory he had been percolating through his mind since the beginning of this discussion. He wasn't sure he should speak and if he did speak what he should say.

Roshan rose from his chair and held his hand toward Evan, "My name is Talal Al-Enezi, and even though the government here thinks that I am a *Bedoon*, I am not. I am a Kuwaiti."

Evan immediately stood and took the man's hand. *Holy shit, where do we go from here?*

*Faheel Garage*

Last night, Nassar was startled awake by a text from Maksim telling him to show up at the garage early the next morning. He also received a voicemail from his father wanting to meet for lunch. He was waiting until after his meeting with Pauley before responding to his father.

Up until now, most of his work and been done in the evenings, and the reason why it was becoming more evident as the temperature began rising in the garage. He just finished powering on the last of the cooling units when Maksim arrived and sent him a text to open the garage door. Nassar did so, and as he watched the SUV pull into the garage, he noticed something was in the back covered by a blanket.

"I'm guessing you'll be appreciative of the cooling units today, eh Nassar?"

"Yes Boss, it was very nice of you to buy them for the shop."

"Well, you've been a very loyal employee thus far. No need for you to suffer if I could do something to prevent it."

Nassar nodded, not sure where this whole conversation was going. Until now most of his conversations with his boss were very direct. He would give Nassar instructions, Nassar would ask questions specific to the task, then Mr. Pauley would leave. This bit of back and forth was new and placed him on edge.

"Nassar, you know I'm an American, but did you also know I'm a Muslim?"

Again, Nassar nodded. He knew there were American Muslims so it was not a great revelation.

"It's true, but also as a good Muslim I've chosen to help organizations which are true to the faith when I can." *As I turn this relationship, I need to make sure he stays with me through the conversation.* "Please, have a seat."

As Nassar sat down, Maksim reached into his SUV and pulled out two cold bottles of water then handed one to him. After both men opened them and took a drink, Maksim continued, "there're a great many organizations which seek to spread Allah's word and to serve his people. The one I have chosen is the Caliph Kinship." *He would have to be stupid not to have heard of the Kinship and of their activities here and elsewhere in the Middle East.*

Nassar swallowed hard, trying not to let his surprise show. Even though he could quickly accept an American Muslim, one who was supporting an organization going against the government of Kuwait was a shock.

*Well, he wasn't expecting that.* "Indeed, as *Quran* 3:28 says 'Muslims must not take the infidels as friends,' so I have chosen a friendship with a group who best follows the sacred words. Given the same choice as a good Muslim, you'd do the same – true?"

Again Nassar nodded while taking a long swallow from the bottle of water. He preferred the words coming from the Kinship to any other source he heard. Not only did they seem to more closely follow his beliefs but they also claimed to have a solution for his people's struggle.

"In 9:5 it instructs us 'When the opportunity arises, kill the infidels wherever you catch them.' As I believe it, I also believe sometimes you must make opportunity arise. So, have you wondered why I had you do all this work on the car?"

Nassar glanced over at the car then back in Maksim. His perception of this man until now was he did not want him thinking about why something was being done. *Now he wants me to tell him my thoughts, is this some sort of set up?*

"Only a fool wouldn't be wondering something, Nassar, this isn't the normal way you treat an automobile."

The younger man glanced at the car again before deciding to take a leap of faith and tell Maksim his thoughts, "Making a hiding place?"

"A hiding place? Yes, Nassar, one might call it a hiding place. I prefer to think of it as a delivery space. There're many things which could be transported within this car, but only one thing to serve the needs of the Kinship best. As with all organizations trying to move things forward, one of their continuing ongoing needs is money. This space will help us transport goods for sale, bringing the Caliph Kinship millions of dollars over time."

"But, what are you transporting?" *Ya ibn el Sharmouta! What am I doing? Speaking without being spoken to.*

*He's with me*, Maksim smiled, reaching out his right hand and placing it on Nassar's shoulder as a way of showing his approval for asking the question, "What is being transported, indeed."

Maksim stood up and walked over to the Nissan, he lowered his head and looked into the vehicle for a moment shifting his eyes back to Nassar then for dramatic effect whispered, "Poison, Nassar, we're transporting poison."

Nassar thought for a moment, *what kind of poison would take up so much room. A poison bomb?*

Maksim could see the wheels turning inside Nassar's head. He let them spin for a moment-- *let him create his own narrative, one he can accept. Then when I provide him with my truth, he will mentally match the two together and accept it*, "Nassar, you've created a vehicle capable of transporting thousands of kilos of heroin, secretly received from our brothers in Afghanistan. Of course, we won't be doing it all at once; we'll move about 700 kilos a trip. But at the end of each one of those trips, €20,000 will be earned for the Kinship."

*Drugs not a bomb, but in the end how is it different? In Kuwait, getting caught moving such an amount of drugs would be classified as narcotics trafficking, which has a mandatory death sentence.* Nassar was not really worried, after all, all he did was build the car. *But now the man is saying 'we.'*

"You'll have a vital role in running the transportation operation, Nassar. You see, this car is only the first in a fleet of many. We'll use this car to test our process for receiving drugs, and onward transportation. Eventually, many Nissan's just like this one will be driven through Saudi Arabia, to ports in Syria, so our cargo can be transported to the United States. As it says in *Quran* 9:123: 'Make war on the infidels by leaving your neighborhood.' In this way, our weapon will leave our neighborhood and arrive in theirs. Nassar, we'll make war on them without risk to ourselves, killing them slowly, bit by bit. Then we'll use the dollars they paid for their own destruction, to fund our organization, which will defeat all infidels around the world."

Maksim stopped talking, allowing for all of the new information to be received, digested, and accepted by his employee. *Slowly, I'll turn him from worker to zealot apostle.*

Just a few weeks ago, Nassar met this man who became his salvation by giving him a job to help earn him the respect of his father, and provide him with the means of survival. Now, the same man was allowing him to serve because he believed in him and ultimately the same organization he wanted to support. *What of the risk? He talks of me being vital but what exactly does it mean?*

Maksim felt his quarry opened his mind to accept the bait he was presenting. *But the hook isn't set. Why?* Rather than staring at Nassar and making him self-conscious, Maksim rose and began to pace around the car, peering through the open windows at what had been created. Occasionally, he would murmur a compliment or two while reaching in and physically touching the adjustments Nassar made.

*He does seem to admire and appreciate the work.* The hardest part for Nassar to accept was anyone could see value in him. As a *Bedoon,* he was continually told he had no place, no value, no desired skills. Now, this American comes and tells him that he is worthwhile, and offering him a way to help his people. Maksim completed his circuit around the car and was now standing in front of Nassar once again. *Perhaps I misjudged him, it would be easy enough to get someone to do the driving later, but there is still much physical work to be done in preparation. Also, I'd need someone to probe the security to ensure the weakness stayed one. The SUV has sufficient space for me to transport his body.* As the last thought crossed his mind, he flexed his calf muscle, and could feel the presence of the knife he carried with him in case of necessities like this. *I will kneel down one side of him as if to check my shoelaces. Then I will extract the knife and while rising plunge it into his chest and put an end to this.* Maksim started to lower himself as if to tie his shoe.

"Boss, I really appreciate the opportunity you're offering me. I'll do a good job for both you and the Kinship."

When Maksim was knelt down, he loosened then retied his laces. He allowed his hand to gently caress the knife hidden under his pants leg as he stood back up.

"Perfect. As I said before, Nassar, we'll need to finish our preparation and run some tests with this vehicle, before we get an entire fleet. You'll be the supervisor of the fleet, with several drivers working under you. For now, do you have a problem with being the driver for the test phase?"

*Supervisor? People working for me?* "No, not at all. Whatever I can do to help."

Maksim smiled and Nassar and again placed his hand on the young man's shoulder in approval. *So, the hook is set.*

Before he left, Maksim helped Nassar unload the SUV. Once the tarp was thrown back, it revealed a stack of plastic-wrapped bricks. Unlike bricks of clay which weighed about two kilos each, these bricks weighed almost three kilos. Nassar stacked the bricks in the corner of the garage while mentally counting how many he was unloading. *100 bricks. Enough to guarantee a death sentence as a narcotics trafficker. But if all went as planned, it'd provide €10,000 to the Caliph Kinship.* With that thought, Nassar's concern started to abate being replaced by pride in the fact he was doing something spiritually right.

While Nassar unloaded the bricks, Maksim was sending and receiving texts on his phone. The tease of killing his worker was playing overtime in his psyche, leaving him with an aroused sexual appetite. As soon as he was done here, Jasmine would meet him back at his apartment.

"All done, Mr. Pauley."

Maksim turned to see a neat stack of bricks five wide by four tall by five deep. He instructed Nassar to cover the bricks with the tarp from the back of the SUV to protect them from the elements.

"Each brick is sealed in triple wrapped plastic. But I want to ensure none of it is accidentally torn open. We don't need to lose precious cargo along the way."

"So what do I do now?"

Maksim walked over to the passenger side of the SUV and withdrew a roll of polyurethane sheeting. Walking back, he handed it to Nassar, "Use this to line the inside of the space within the car. It'll help make loading and unloading easier and protect the bricks from damage while in transport. Just line the car's space for right now, don't put the bricks in place until we're ready for the actual test. I'll bring you the rest of this load later this evening."

"How many total?"

*Good, he's interested in the particulars instead of risks,* "233 total. A total of 700 kilos."

"And €20,000 for our cause."

"Indeed," *the hook was in deep.*

"A final task, I want you to start taking familiarity trips several times a day to the *Hotel Sultana*, Nassar. Just pull in the traffic circle, clear security, then sit there for a while near the door. After five or so minutes, go ahead and leave."

"Just drive there and wait then leave? I don't need to pick anybody up?"

"No, eventually we'll be using the site for the test transaction, so I want the security people to get used to seeing you and the car. Over time, they'll get used to both and begin to completely ignore you. Even better, they may stop inspecting the car every time you pull in. Do this at different times during the day, see you get to encounter all of the different people who work there."

Once Maksim departed, Nassar used his phone to text his father.

```
> 1900 would be better?
< Perfect @ the Stone Grill
> OK
```

Putting the phone back in his pocket, his eyes wandered over to the corner and the covered pile of bricks. He had never seen heroin before, except in the movies. Walking over to the pile, he picked one off the top and scrutinized it. It was hard to see much through the plastic wrap except it appeared grainy and brownish. He placed the brick back in the pile, before he covered it over with the tarp as he was instructed. Nassar then went to work putting the plastic liner into the Nissan.

Kuwait International Airport

Mordechai Shalach spent a lifetime working with the Israeli Mossad. His career was a blend of both field and control center operations. This mission was different; this would be his final field mission before the self-imposed exile to Mossad headquarters and a position as an asset recruiter. It would allow him to continue traveling and working outside the building, but would no longer entail the risks of working as an asset in the field.

After clearing customs, rather than fighting headed directly to the *Hotel Sultana*, where a room awaited him. The room booking, as well as the rest of his cover story, was provided using a fictional corporation. After all, not many Orthodox Jews visited Kuwait, and any such visit other than a political one would stand out. As a salesman for a company producing machinery lubricants, no one would glance twice at him or his curiosity concerning things around him.

Mossad was keeping close tabs on the Kuwaiti political situation, especially recently. With the Caliph Kinship growing in strength, and the upheaval caused by a recent string of murders and terrorism in the country, it was decided it was time for one of their agents to go in and make an in-person assessment. Israel counted on the stability of Kuwait to help maintain the stability of the Persian Gulf. Now, with TCNs, *Bedoons*, and Kuwaiti citizens dividing into factions, there was concern over the country's security. The presence of the Kinship was a significant wildcard, which made things even more dire.

However, the only goal Morty's mind at the moment was to get to the hotel so he could get out of this suit, which was not friendly to this climate, and take a cool shower. He would follow the shower with a quick nap, and maybe a light meal, then an evening of familiarizing himself with the situation, before beginning operations tomorrow morning.

After the taxi ride to the hotel, he decided his superiors were right in sending him to Kuwait now. His driver, a TCN, barely spoke on the way to the hotel when he made inquiries about stories the news agencies publicly reported. The upside of the driver's silence was it gave Morty time to observe through the windows various anti-*Bedoon* and anti-TCN signs, which appeared to be posted almost everywhere. He knew, from time spent in other destabilizing countries, that this was just a precursor to an explosion if the situation was not defused.

When Nassar walked into the restaurant, the smell of cooking steak made him suddenly ravenous. Looking around the dining room, he saw his father wave to him from a table on the far side of the room. As Nassar approached, Roshan stood up and hugged his son before the two of them sat down and were almost immediately approached by a waiter. After ordering, the two engaged in small talk regarding the weather and current events around the country, while both managed to avoid the subject of violence against *Bedoons*.

The conversation was dwindling to silence when their waiter reappeared with their meal. After first placing a 200°C lava rock in front of each of them, the waiter handed them plates of raw meat, and the baked potato each ordered as a side dish. Nassar by now was almost having stomach pains from hunger, and immediately began cooking his meat by slicing it into smaller pieces and laying it on the heated lava rock. With both men cooking, the table was filled with the sound of sizzling steak and surrounded by a fog of smoke from their efforts.

Roshan watched his son greedily devour his dinner, and wondered if the boy was doing as well financially as he claimed. *Perhaps he was just too busy to have lunch, and as a result, is hungrier than usual.* Nassar was sure his father was staring at him. Every time he looked up from his food he could see Roshan's eyes suddenly dart in a different direction. Finally, he decided to break the silence.

"Why are you watching me this way?" *Damn, I didn't mean to come off so angry.*

Roshan took a moment to think of his answer and while doing so cleared his throat and motioned for the waiter to come over. After asking for a glass of water, he felt prepared to handle his son's inquiry.

"You seem to be eating as if you were a man who was starved. I like to see you enjoy your food, but I'm left to wonder how well you're doing if you have so ravenous an appetite."

Nassar placed his utensils on the table and finished chewing what was in his mouth. After swallowing, he said, "I am doing well, I just missed lunch and breakfast today because I'm so busy right now."

"What exactly are you doing?"

*To lie not to lie? Does it really matter, does my father really care, or is he just looking for another reason to convince me what I'm doing is wrong?* "I'm doing logistics," using a fancy word for transportation he picked up online.

"I see, and for whom are you doing logistics."

"I am working for an American who needed someone with local expertise."

"An American? What expertise could a *Bedoon* supply he wouldn't have found in a Kuwaiti?" Roshan leaned forward and whispered, "Are you sure what you're doing is legal?"

Nassar had resumed eating, but upon hearing, this dropped the silverware and sat back in his chair. Consider the situation for a moment, as well as his promise to Mr. Pauley not to give away any details of their operation.

"Father, nothing I'm doing is illegal. In fact, what I'm doing will help benefit our people in the long run."

*Oh my God, the boy is being used. Please tell me this is not…* Leaning forward, Roshan kept his voice very low as he said, "Is what you're doing connected to the Caliph Kinship?" Nassar's expression was frozen

"No," Nassar lied, "Absolutely not," Nassar lied again, "In no way is anything I'm doing connected to them," Nassar lied a third time; *am I trying to convince myself?*

*A final push*, "Do you know somebody name Rajeesh? Did you know his body was recently found in the aftermath of a fire? A fire which was found to be arson?" Nassar was completely silent, Roshan knew the conversation was over. He held his hands up as if to say he was surrendering to what Nassar was saying, even though he did not believe a single word. *Not even the first lie.* He sat back in his chair, no longer hungry but filled with concern for his son's safety.

"You're a man my son, but it does not mean I as a father, will ever stop worrying about your well-being. There are too many people out there who will take advantage of your being a *Bedoon* to convince you to do illegal or immoral things. I don't want to see you trapped by either."

It was a familiar point they reached in every one of these conversations. Each of them knew they were never going to convince the other of their point of view. The only words left to be spoken at this point was to confirm their love for the other person.

Nassar slowly exhaled, then looked into his father's eyes, "*Baba,*

I know you love me. I need you to trust me on this."

Roshan immediately thought of several instances where the same phrase was used before, and trust was misplaced. His son had never done anything wrong, but too often Nassar allowed himself to be led the wrong way while being convinced it is for the best of reasons.

"Promise me this," Roshan paused until he was sure he possessed his son's full attention, "While you're doing your logistics, you'll not do it with your eyes closed. You will look at what you're facilitating and know for sure you are doing nothing wrong. Please?"

"All right, father, I promise."

The two men completed their dinner each enjoying a tiramisu for dessert. After exiting the restaurant, Roshan hugged his son close enjoying the feel of once again having him in his arms. As Nassar turned to go, he heard his father say, "I love you." Nassar took a moment to turn around and look at his father directly before telling him "I love you too."

As Nassar was walking home, something his father said became a small irritating thought, which would remain bouncing around inside his head. Rajeesh's dead body was found at the scene of a fire caused by arson. He called his friend many times, wanting to take him to dinner as a thank you for the information about the job. *Now he's dead, in a fire. Rajeesh was not an arsonist. A bizarre accident, maybe. Was it?*

# Chapter 14



Huda was pacing in her private space, waiting for her husband to depart, before placing a call to Maksim. As soon as she saw his truck go by the front window and out the gate, she closed the door and dialed her phone. The phone rang three times, then silence. *Why does this bastard test my patience this way?*

"I've heard nothing about the museum."

"I was there and prepared, the situation didn't present itself for the mission to be executed properly."

"Why not? This was supposed to be an attack on heritage, an attack on patriotism."

"You hired a professional, you're getting a professional job. When things aren't right, I won't be pushed just to meet some arbitrary goal." *Worse than amateurs in the field were amateurs trying to command.*

"How do you plan to make this up?"

"I thought I might copy an example from the past and go after Kuwait's black blood."

Huda immediately realized he was talking about was attacking the oil fields. During Liberation, the Iraqi army set fire to the wells in the Greater Burgan oil field. The disaster was not only one of money but also ecology and possibly the health of people in the region for years. *No, I may want unfettered revenge upon the Bedoon, but I'm not going to injure the heart of my country doing it.*

"No, not that."

Maksim was surprised; she was willing to go along with everything he wanted to do up to this point, regardless of who died or what was destroyed. Now he discovered a line she would not cross. Maksim planned on using the thermite charges left over from the failed mission at Al-Quarin. *Perhaps if I just use one or two instead of all of them and only cause some minor fireworks.*

"How about just a few wells?"

"No; none." She could hear his grunt of objection through the phone. *Maybe there's no need to set the wells on fire, it'd be just as upsetting to discover there was a plan for their destruction.*

"I'm unsure what you would have me do at this point." Aside from a few additional killings to solidify the wanton destruction possible, the only element left in this contract was the destruction of the Sultana.

"I have an idea. Why not set whatever plan you have in motion for Greater Burgan, but then notify the authorities before it takes place. Let them discover what *Shaytan* was going to do but let them prevent it. Would this not have a similar effect?"

*I may have misjudged her perception of what was going on here.* "Yes, perhaps at this point it would be as effective without the actual destruction. On another topic, will you be sending the next payment today?"

*Mercenary bastard,* "It is what I agreed to. Have I not done everything I agreed to? Never mind. What about the date for the Sultana?"

"Once we see the reaction to the oilfield, I'll be able to set a date for the next event. I plan to have it occur just as evening prayers are letting out to maximize the number of people in the streets when it happens." *And maximize the terror.*

"I don't want those details, when the time comes, just call me the morning it'll occur but provide no other details. I need my reaction to be earnest."

"As you wish."

For the first time, Huda provided him with her private number. She had no way of knowing that Maksim knew the number within an hour of the first phone call at the start of all this.

Since they both knew their business was done, the phone call was terminated mutually.

Huda left as soon as the phone call was over and went to the Gulf Bank. After withdrawing the cash needed from multiple boxes, she looked again at the manila folder she had been dancing with for all these years. With the climax to her plan nearing, she decided it was time the letter was read. So, rather than closing the folder away inside a bank vault again, today she was going to take it with her. That decided, she summoned Mohammed into the vault where the bills she removed lay spread out on the table in piles.

"Mohammed, I need to avail myself of your transfer service once again."

"As you wish."

"I want this 74,000KD transferred to the same account as before with First Caribbean International Bank."

"I will be happy to take care of that for you, Mrs. Al Bourisli, but I'll need the account number again. For privacy reasons, I don't keep records of such things."

*Well, an absolutely correct answer*, "I understand, here I'll give it to you again. Also…"

"No need for concern, Mrs. Al Bourisli. It goes without saying that the transfer will be done as two separate transactions," *to avoid Kuwaiti banking regulations regarding the reporting of foreign currency transfers.*

Huda smiled and transferred the 36-digit account number from her phone to a piece of paper. Once complete, she handed him the paper, and he gave her a short nod before turning to leave the vault and proceed with the transfer.

"Mohammed, there is no need for me to wait here for confirmation. I am sure you will have it taken care of properly." *And I have no desire to waste my time sitting in this bank.*

"Understood, Mrs. Al Bourisli. I'll walk you out."

Mohammed walked Huda out of the bank into her car. As she pulled out of the parking lot, she looked in the rearview mirror and saw Mohammed still standing on the sidewalk waving goodbye. *What a fool.* She was no longer concerned about what he did and did not remember. The events of the next few days would be so transitional he would have no time to mull upon his memories. The final payment to Maksim would take at least four transfers to remain below the governmental radar.

It was rare that Jefzar took lunch outside the building, unless he was already out for some appointment or other business. Today, he just needed the escape. Now, as he prepared to reenter the building, he realized why he should have just stayed inside. Luckily, he spotted the crowd of reporters from the end of the block. He phoned ahead and instructed his officers to line the sidewalk so he could get from his car into the building with only minor molestation.

Once inside, he was immediately confronted by Zainab.

"Sir, I have the bankers you asked for in the break room."

Jefzar continued to walk towards his office, so she fell in step behind him almost running to keep up.

"Bankers I asked for?"

"Yes sir, yesterday you asked me to contact all the banks to see who might have transferred over 28,000KD within the last 60 days."

"Zainab, I appreciate your zeal, but I just wanted a list of names, not the actual bankers."

"I understand sir, but every one of the bankers I contacted volunteered to come in and provide whatever assistance possible. After five of them did so, I set up a time and reserved a room for them to sit in until you could speak to each one individually."

*Of course, they were willing to come in, they want to be able to brag about being part of this investigation. Zainab played into their hands because as a young officer she wanted to make sure she was doing the utmost. When you were a young officer, you would've done the same damn thing.* "Ah, well then, I guess I need to start speaking to these men," he then paused to look directly at Zainab, "Men?" She nodded. *Well, at least I'm not going to have to deal with the complications of interviewing a woman.* "Fine, give me 10 minutes to glance at my email for anything on fire, then bring in the first one.

Five hours later, Jefzar was still in his office talking to bankers. Thus far, he spoke to six, all of whom reported transactions of large enough amounts to meet his criteria but were from legitimate businesses going to legitimate payees in other countries. All of the bankers carried computerized ledgers on wide sheets of paper so they could show him the transactions he sought. After the first banker, Jefzar realized this part of the investigation could have been done by Mubarak, or even possibly Zainab. Now, he was trapped into speaking to each one of them, so no one felt slighted at being handed off to a lower-ranking officer. Any insult or slight of these businessmen would probably lead to a phone call later from his superiors, on behalf of an upset bank president. *So, I will trudge on.*

This type of review revealed one disturbing fact to Jefzar; a massive amount of money was being transferred out of Kuwait to banks and holding companies doing nothing to help support the country. In other words, money that could have been building the Kuwaiti economy, was instead sitting in tax havens like the Grand Caymans. When he questioned one of the bankers about this type of transfer specifically, the banker told him many people transferred wealth in smaller amounts, so the Department of Taxation would not notice what they were doing. *28,000KD is a smaller amount? I have officers who don't earn that much in a year.*

The seventh banker was from Bank of the Gulf. Jefzar instructed Mubarak to bring the remaining representative from the break room into his office, and he would return momentarily. He then made a brief escape out the back door to a small patio where he immediately withdrew a pack of cigarettes from his pocket, shook one out, and lit it. As he smoked the cigarette, he mentally went over the interviews he conducted this morning. *Before I can follow the money, I have to find out where it came from – if not, I have to know where it went to so I can work it backward.* He stubbed out the cigarette after several drags and went back to his office.

The banker opened his computerized ledger sheet and started to flip pages, arriving at the one he sought then he began to explain each line on the page. Jefzar considered the man for a moment and surmised he might be inexperienced enough for him to get away with a little shove in the direction he wanted the banker to go.

"Stop. I don't mean to be rude, but I don't want to waste your time, or mine either. Perhaps it would be quicker if I asked you some questions so you knew what I was looking for then maybe you can think about anything which might be of interest."

"Certainly sir, anything I can do to help," said Mohammed.

"Wonderful. What I'm looking for is a transfer of funds from Kuwait, to either a bank with questionable legitimacy or one in a country having strict confidentiality regulations to prevent, say law enforcement, from finding out who the money went to. Do you have anything like that?"

"Actually, we have several similar transactions. Although I don't think anyone is hiding from the police."

"Of course not, there are probably logical explanations for every one of the transfers. Perhaps you, as their banker, would know what those logical explanations might be."

"But of course."

"Fine, with that in mind, are there any transactions remaining which might seem suspicious."

Mohammed sat for several minutes rolling his eyes from the left to right as he thought his way through the transactions he knew was on the ledger. At one point he opened the ledger again and flipped to a page as if to confirm something then shook his head.

"No sir, I can't think of a single instance where there was a transfer of money at or over 28,000KD within the last 60 days."

Jefzar had dealt with lawyers most of his career; as a result, when someone became very exacting when answering a question, he knew it was usually because they were trying to hide something by specifically excluding it. *So, what does this man not want me to know?*

"How about the last 90 or 120 days?"

"None I can think of, no questionable transfers at or over 28,000KD."

Jefzar pursed his lips together tightly for a moment, there were many words he could say at this point, and he didn't want to say any of them as they might come back to haunt him. After a moment, he finally spoke, "How about a questionable transfer within the last year over 27,000KD." *This could take a while if I have to work my way down to 1KD.* Then, it happened.

There comes the point during an interview or interrogation when the person conducting it knows they have just cornered their subject in such a way whatever comes out of their mouth next will be a direct lie or the absolute truth. Mohammed nervously smiled and seemed to look around the room as if he wanted to call for assistance.

"Well sir, if you put it that way, I know of a few transactions which have taken place meeting your criteria."

"Fine, open your ledger and show me those transactions."

"Well, the ledger was based on your original requirement, so those transactions are not on this ledger."

*Of course not.* "Okay, do you know the details of the transactions?" Jefzar was now speaking through slightly clenched teeth. He hated it when he was forced to lead someone by the hand through a maze to reach the answer he sought.

"Of course, sir, I'm the branch manager" Mohammed was about to find out what his bit of pride cost.

Jefzar quickly rose out of his chair purposely flexing his knees upon rising, so the chair flew into the wall behind his desk. The reaction from Mohammed was first to go pale then to tightly grip the armrest of the chair he was sitting in as if he feared gravity no longer would hold him there.

"I am tired of you, *kalb*. Right now, I think you're guilty of hiding money from the government to benefit criminals. As of right now: *kess* your ledger, *kess* your belligerent attitude, and *kess ikhtak*. I swear I'll have you buried under the jail by sundown if you don't start giving me the information I want. Who? Who was sending money?"

Mohammed swallowed then opened his mouth, but no words would come out. This caused Jefzar to walk from around his desk to beside the man, lean over toward him and scream into his ear.

"Tell me, you *ya ibn el Sharmouta!*"

In a voice more squeak than human, Mohammed said "It was your brother's wife, Huda. It was Huda Al-Bourisli."

Jefzar was in shock. He remained bent over beside the man his face still close to Mohammed's. His ears were ringing. His mind was in overload because he was not sure what to do next. Slowly, the ringing started to subside, and the sounds of the building began to encroach. Then he heard Mohammed sobbing. *He wasn't lying, it would be too easy to verify.*

Jefzar walked from his position beside Mohammed's chair back to his chair and collapsed into it. The man was now weeping so hard his body was shaking. Jefzar ignored it for a moment and tried to think his way through the information he was just given. He knew of the cash payoffs his brother took from mediating disputes, he participated in the process himself. He also knew Huda handled the money received, independently. *There, there is the source of the funds and the means for her to handle this without her husband knowing. But why? Why?* Jefzar knew before he could make such an accusation, he needed to have a motive, and right now any such motive escaped him. *What of my brother? How can I tell him this?*

The Greater Burgan

Looking in the rearview mirror, Maksim ensured the *kufi* was straight on his head and looked down at his *dishdasha,* verifying his costume was complete. He was sitting in his SUV waiting to go through the checkpoint for the Greater Burgan oil field.

The movement ahead caught his attention, and he took his foot off the brake and allowed his vehicle to roll forward taking up the space left by the car in front of him. *This entire process is a complete waste of time. In a moment, I'll convince these guards to let me into this area even though I lack any badges or appropriate permissions. A simple matter of knowing the right words to say to convince them of my importance.* He could see the guard leaning over to speak through the window to the driver in the car ahead of him.

Another irritant was the insistence of his benefactor to be directly involved with the mission. Man or woman, he never experienced an issue working for either until now. This woman insisted on inserting herself in his overall objectives in a way no man ever would. Her first overstep, sending a manifesto to the press, leaving him to deal with the additional heat. As the level of attention being given to his past and current actions increased, so did the possibility of discovery. Even though he felt he performed each of the actions flawlessly, Maksim could not help but feel the pressure of additional attention to his actions.

Now, rather than a simple insertion mission with mass destruction as the goal, he was being required to create a scene of a failed destruction. *I don't fail.* With the final event in the near horizon, he wasn't surprised she didn't even want to know when it would happen.

"Papers," the man in uniform said as soon as came to a stop directly at the guard's station.

Maksim paused for a moment and looked the guard over. The clothing he was wearing was not one of the standard military uniforms for Kuwait, but something with additional patches and frivolous details identifying him as part of an elite unit. The fact the guard garnished the outfit with a pair of Western-style mirrored sunglasses, told him a lot about the man and his ego.

"I'm hoping you can help me, I am in a bit of a hurry, and I know it'll be faster if I go through the oilfield rather than all the way down to the highway to go around," *let's see where this goes.*

"Turn around. This entrance for official business only, go back the other way," as the guard spoke, he waved his hands pointing to the road leading back out to the highway.

*Not so fast Abdul,* "My friend, I'm sure you've found yourself late and needing to save a bit of time. Perhaps it was something with your family or your job. Maybe even this job. Just let me through the gate, I'll drive the speed limit all the way through to the other side exiting without event or problem. I promise you."

The guard lifted his mirrored sunglasses, and considered Maksim for a moment before speaking, "Are you stupid? You're not allowed here. The rules state without papers, you must go back," he replaced his sunglasses, spat on the ground, and again pointed to the road behind Maksim.

Maksim did his best to assume a contrite expression before speaking. "Officer, I know you're in charge of this checkpoint because you're so amazingly good at doing your job. Not only that, I can see by the way you wear your uniform you're proud of the magnificent job you do," Maksim observed, as two things happened; the man began to stand straighter out of a sense of pride, and at the same time Maksim sensed the man was feeling an increase in his own empowerment and self-worth. The second reaction was the one Maksim would use against him.

"Since you're the one in charge here, you're the one that can make decisions which are vital to the security of the oilfield. Surely a man of your experience can see I'm just a simple man needing a small favor and not a threat to anyone or anything."

The guard again lifted his mirrored glasses, and his eyes narrowed as he looked at Maksim. Standing upright, the guard scanned the horizon, as if he was looking for anyone who might be testing him this way. He heard of others who lost their jobs by letting people in without the proper authentications.

"Let me see your citizenship ID."

Maksim leaned over to one side, and retrieved the necessary document from the glove compartment and handed it to the guard. The guard, who possessed no way of verifying anything about the citizenship ID, quickly glanced at the picture, then at Maksim, while making a big deal of pretending to read both sides of the card.

"No stopping. You drive straight through and out the other end. You stay on this road only."

Maksim smiled as he took the fake ID back from the guard, and proceeded to praise the man's judgment and appropriate use of his hard-earned position and power. The guard waved his hand after pressing the button to lift the wooden guard arm extending across the road. He then stood very straight and placing his hands on his hips as he watched Maksim pull through the checkpoint and into the oilfield.

*And now, you've let the wolf have access to your sheep.*

The Greater Burgan oil field was the location of one of the worst ecological disasters in the Middle East. Even though the Iraqi army was quickly withdrawing, with coalition forces in close pursuit, they took time to ignite almost all the wellheads in the oilfield, and to cut through existing pipelines, allowing the oil in the system and tanks to flow out. This tactic not only destroyed a source of income for Kuwait, but the thick black smoke from the fires filled the sky and the horizon for months. It was a lasting slight from Saddam Hussein, as his troops left the country.

Kuwait hired the famous oil well firefighter Red Adair to take charge of extinguishing the fires and recapping each of the wells. With massive financial rewards on the line for quick completion, it was done in record time. Kuwait then spent millions cleaning up the oil which spilled out and leaked over the sands, and into the surrounding waters. The result of this effort was what Maksim looked upon as he drove through the oilfield.

Being aware of the history of the area, Maksim was impressed at how pristine the area looked. Equally surprising was the amount of vegetation that was thriving in what was a severely polluted area. As he drove through, he began to look for landmarks to guide him to an opportune target he had previously identified from satellite imagery. As Maksim prepared to move from being a state operative to a freelance one, he was impressed at the amount of military-level intelligence freely available on the Internet.

Even though several vehicles were backed up at the checkpoint when he arrived, he had not seen another car since entering the oilfield. Since he passed several turn off points, it is possible the other entrants already departed the main road. Another possibility was, since the police did not patrol any of the roads inside of the Greater Burgan area, the other drivers chose to speed down the unpatrolled road. Either way, Maksim continually scanned for others who might have to be dealt with to maintain his anonymity.

When he reached the first turn off, he previously identified,

Maksim scanned the horizon in all directions before leaving the main road. Satisfied he was not being observed, he turned onto the side road, and in a few moments found himself in front of a large wellhead, which was surrounded by a four-meter-tall chain-link fence. The fence displayed several large signs in Arabic and English warning trespassers, and identifying it has #645. *Now, for history to repeat itself.*

After putting the SUV in Park, he retrieved the cell phone from his pocket. Looking at the face of the device, he could see four bars of reception in this area. *This will work.* He exited the vehicle and walked to its rear hatch. After opening the hatch, he lifted a floor panel which would normally give access to the spare tire. Instead, the area was being used to transport three primacord explosive devices. The devices were incredibly simple, and consisted of three meters of det cord plus a cellular phone triggering device.

Maksim took one of the devices along with a small tool bag then walked over to the gate, which passed through the fence surrounding the wellhead. With so much money being spent on security he was surprised to see this hugely valuable asset protected by a simple hardened Schlage lock. It took him less than a minute to pick the lock and enter the secure area. What stood before him was something looking like a plumber's nightmare, with various pipes attached here and there coming directly out of the ground, connecting to a pipeline which passed through the fence and disappeared over the desert horizon.

How any of this worked, was not Maksim's concern. The refinery engineer, who conducted the course for Siberian Rime, told them to simply attach the explosives as close to the ground as possible. They were to ensure the spot they selected was before any of the valves that made up what was known as the Christmas tree. By doing it this way, the explosion would result in the immediate flow of huge amounts of oil. It would also make recapping the well more difficult, since the structure of the old wellhead and any surviving parts from the blowout preventers would have to be removed before anyone could attempt stopping the flow of oil. While Maksim remembered the lesson vividly, he had never performed this operation in the field.

He started by selecting one of the narrower pipes, then Maksim wrapped the detcord around the circumference of it almost going twice around the pipe. He first used duct tape to hold the detcord in place, then placed a layer of tape over the entire package to camouflage it. He opened the battery compartment of the phone, and using a silver Sharpie, signed the battery cover شيطان before replacing it. Finally, Maksim pressed the exposed end of the det cord into a connector he attached to the back of the cellular phone. After turning the phone on, and ensuring it was receiving a signal, he used duct tape to attach the phone to the back of the pipe.

Maksim took a step back; his work was perfect. From outside the fence, the entire explosive device would be overlooked as it blended with the mangle of pipes and other equipment. *Now to take the functional, and make it not functional.* There were many ways to take a working bomb and make it not work. Maksim's task was to find one of those ways that would render the device inert, without making it look like it was done on purpose.

After giving it several moments thought, Maksim began another circuit of duct tape from the left side of the pipe and when it came around to the back where the phone was rather than lifting the connection wire out of harm's way, he ran the tape over it. The pressure across the exposed wire pulled on it, disconnecting it from the cell phone. *A bit of carelessness while placing the bomb, and no trigger.*

With no idea of the well's function, Maksim was hard-pressed to figure out how to draw attention to the well and allow the discovery of the bomb. After examining a collection of gauges, he realized if he loosened the one monitoring pressure, it would cause a small leak. The small leak would cause the pressure to fall and eventually bring someone out to inspect what was going on. A few turns with a pair of channel locks sent a spray of oil out of one side of the gauge's connector. Maksim watched as the pressure gauge began to fall very slowly.

Maksim threw the channel locks and tape into his tool bag and headed back to his car after locking the gate behind him. A short while later, Maksim exited the Greater Burgan and began to make his way back to Kuwait City.

Morty often used The Spa at the hotel to meet with confidential informants. Because the hotel was mostly frequented by Westerners, and the entire labor staff consisted of TCNs, it greatly reduced the chance of a CI being spotted coming and going. He would also spend a few KD to bribe the steam bath attendant to ensure no one was inside the facility, other than those Morty wanted there.

As Morty sat in the steam bath, wrapped in a towel, he leaned back against the tile wall and let the heat wash over him. Of course, the heat outside was always present but what was missing there was moisture. Here, the steam was so thick he could barely see anything more than the outline of the individual who just walked in.

"Mr. Henri? Are you in here?"

"Yes, Mubarak, come in. Have a seat. Enjoy a bit of air so thick you can bite it."

Mubarak walked further into the bath, and took a seat on the wall opposite Morty.

"So, once again I'm in Kuwait, and once again I look forward to you telling me about what's happening here." Thus, he began another in a series of situational reports from a Kuwaiti police officer who thought he was sharing information with a Belgian diamond and gold dealer.

Recruiting Mubarak was very easy, as police are severely underpaid in this country. But unlike many locations, where Morty could tell the CI he was working for the Mossad, here he needed to be a bit craftier. Mubarak was one of several CIs who Morty cultivated over the years, using the identity of a Belgian.

As Mubarak droned on, Morty let his mind wander and began to think about what he would be doing this time next week back in Israel. Then he caught a few words that interested him.

"… not quite sure why all these bankers were in the building, but somehow the Chief thinks it will help solve a murder case."

"Wait, what is your Chief's name again?"

"Al-Bourisli. Jefzar Al-Bourisli."

"And this Al-Bourisli fellow seems to think talking to bankers will help them solve a murder? Was the person who was killed late on their loan payments."

Mubarak laughed nervously; he only knew peripheral information because Jefzar was calling upon Zainab to assist with the case. *I need to do something about that woman.* "Not just one murder, many of them."

*Ah, follow the money.* "Please, go on."

Mubarak then told Morty about the shouting and banging things that occurred during the last interview. Then, how Jefzar and the banker from Gulf Bank left together.

"Hmm, sounds like your Chief found a clue."

Mubarak continued the next half hour supplying Morty with more minutia than information. If Morty was not retiring from the field, he would probably have to get rid of Mubarak, as his information often lacked depth.

As Mubarak was departing, Morty handed him two 100KD bills, which were tucked in a towel beside him. Morty remained in the steam bath for a half-hour longer while he contemplated his next move. In the end, he decided rather than trying to speak to the manager at Gulf Bank himself, he would have some technicians at home do a little remote auditing. *Obviously, following the money led to something.*

*Faheel Garage*

After completing three days worth of familiarity trips to the hotel, Nassar found Mr. Pauley was correct, once the guards encountered him two or three times, they began to abbreviate the inspection of his vehicle. Soon, the abbreviated inspection gave way to a quick look, only for appearance sake. With the guard walking to the back of the vehicle, opening the trunk then closing it without even looking inside. Nassar was learning not to doubt the wisdom of Mr. Pauley.

He looked inside the Nissan at his handiwork. The plastic lining on the passenger side of the engine compartment was perfect and completely sealed. He left enough overlap on the edges to be able to fold in and seal the contents in once the bricks were loaded.

The last few days were quite boring. Nassar's task of installing the sheeting was complete, and Mr. Pauley did not want him to start loading the bricks until the day of the test. Aside from performing the occasional familiarity run, he sat idle listening to the radio and trying to avoid reflecting on what his father said. He did spend some of his time reading about the fire in the discovery of Rajeesh's body on *Liljamie*. Nassar found comfort in the online comments, which seemed to blame *Shaytan* for the fire and death. *At least one of them blamed a nondescript American.*

His phone vibrated with the arrival of the text.

```
> Runs going ok?
< Yes, no problems
> Wait an hour before next run
< OK
> When complete, load up
> We test tomorrow
```

Nassar could not swallow. He begged for things to happen, he begged for a way to contribute to the cause. Now, within 24 hours things would begin to happen, and he would begin his contribution.

Maksim laid his phone back on the bedside table. He stretched out his arms and legs and looked at the lifeless body beside him. Jasmine's face was slightly pale, her lips a shade of blue. Looking at his watch, he decided to give her 30 more seconds. If she did not start breathing on her own by then, he would bring her back with CPR.

This was the first time he took things this far. He was on top, looking down at Jasmine as he tightened his hands around her throat. She looked directly into his eyes without a shred of fear. *If it was the fear exciting me so much before, how can the lack of it excite me even more?* In a few days, he knew he would need to dispose of her. *I know she doesn't fear my hands on her throat, but as the blade passes from one side of her throat to the other, I wonder if she will show fear then.*

Naveed Al Adwani was the only employee who had been with Hamad longer than Roshan. He had been around longer by exactly one day. When the war was drawing to a close, Hamad knew he would need the best expert horse handler he could find. Rather than putting out an open call for applicants, Hamad began a search based on the qualities he felt a world-class stable would need. One name kept appearing: Naveed Al Adwani.

Hamad found Naveed, working in the horse stables of a member of the royal family. After obtaining the approval from the man's current boss, Hamad offered Naveed the job as head of his yet to be established stables. The position was a huge step up for a *Bedoon* who was recently reclassified as a stable hand, even though he was the one running the stables. Hamad's reputation was known to Naveed, and when coupled with a promotion in position as well as a substantial increase in salary, he became the first employee in Hamad's new venture.

The celebration this evening was equivalent to what one might expect an employer to throw for an upper-level Kuwaiti employee. Whereas Naveed's position was certainly important to Hamad's organization, having such a celebration for a *Bedoon*, regardless of position, was unheard of. However, Hamad considered Naveed a member of his family, and as such, a fellow Kuwaiti.

The banquet accompanying the celebration was a showcase of

Kuwaiti cuisine. The main course featured both fish and fire-roasted lamb served with *biryani*, a rice dish. There were several different styles of rice, including *marabya* with shrimp, *machboos* with mutton, and *mashkhool* with potatoes and eggplant. Each dish featured its own unique spice palette and aromas. Dozens of other side dishes filled out the long tables on display.

All of Hamad's employees were invited to the celebration, as well as numerous family friends and professional associates. It was the type of event for which he and Huda were well known. Rather than being in attendance, Huda begged off claiming to have some ailment. He knew his wife well enough to tell she was faking to perhaps hide disdain for Naveed, which was surprising as Hamad thought she liked him.

Evan decided it would be a good time to premiere his riding talents to Najila, given the gaiety of the party. His plan was also for the party to be a first non-work event between them, and he formally invited her, even insisting he drive from the hotel to *'Shamal Mazraea*. Originally, he planned on picking her up at her villa, but she demurred, insisting her aunt might object because it might look too much like a date.

When she entered the penthouse, he saw her differently than before. She was always very careful with the way she made up her eyes and put on her makeup, but tonight was different. Her skin seemed to glow, and her eyes captured him at first glance. Once he was under their spell, he could not look away. She was wearing a black *abaya*, but instead of covering her hair she wore an almost transparent black net, which added more shimmer to her hair. The lipstick she was wearing was a lighter color, but it accented the fullness of her lips, *making them look so kissable.*

"Are we going to have a silent evening together?" As she asked this, she smiled to herself realizing her preparation for the evening was greeted with a perfect reaction.

"Uh, sorry. The way you look took away my words, you're stunning."

"Now, now. We're going to a public event; you'll not be allowed to stare at me this way without speaking all evening. People will talk."

"Pity there will be other people around." Evan motioned toward the elevator while putting on a light sports coat. As she turned to walk towards it, he noticed she was wearing her usual very high heels. *Every abaya I have seen makes the wearer look totally shapeless. Somehow you manage to make one look formfitting. Or maybe I've just been admiring your shape without realizing it.*

Evan decided to put his discussion with Roshan, aside this evening. Before she arrived, he had gathered all of his reading material and stashed it in one of the drawers of the credenza. Tonight, he would not think or talk or read anything about *Bedoons*. Tonight, was to be about him and Najila exclusively. *Well, with maybe a little Hamad and other family thrown in.*

Their drive out to the compound was pleasant, the conversation light and flowing between them. Evan occasionally would turn to catch a glimpse of her as he memorized this new image of Najila. She saw what he was doing, but chose not to mention it preferring to just enjoy the nonverbal compliment. When they arrived at *Rihlat Alsahra'*, she directed them towards a different path than he normally took to the parking area.

"This lot is used only by the family. It'll be easier to get in and out, given the size of the crowd."

It was true; there was a large crowd. Evan estimated if there were only one or two passengers per vehicle there were easily over 200 here for the event.

After parking the SUV, Evan walked over to the passenger side to open the door for Najila. He was hoping little acts like this would let her know he was considering tonight differently than their work relationship. As he held the door open, Najila deftly exited the vehicle and once on the ground turned to face Evan. Without warning, she placed a hand on his shoulder, and while caressing his face with her fingertips, began to kiss him.

The kiss was warm and wet. Evan felt the softness of her tongue against his as her lips pressed tighter. As he began to explore her mouth, he could feel her hips moving forward against him. His arm wrapped around her waist as she continued to caress his cheek while moving her face back so she could use her tongue to trace his lips.

Suddenly, she pulled back and after looking him in the eyes for a moment, shifted her gaze to the side and down.

"I wasn't going to allow another evening to end without at least one kiss."

Evan cleared his throat and began to remove his arm from around her, "I'm glad I didn't have to wait all night."

She looked at him and smiled, then purposely thrust her hips forward grinding into him, "Now behave yourself; we have a public evening to attend."

Evan saw motion over the top of the car and noticed Hamad was walking toward them. He took a step back, allowing Najila to walk past him and greet her uncle.

After Najila greeted Hamad with a hug, Evan shook his hand and accepted Hamad's customary embrace. The three of them walked from the parking lot, back to the main area where the party was being held. The evening was warm, but Hamad allowed several wind machines to be brought in to keep the air circulating, so it was not oppressive.

There was no formal rule separating the sexes at the party. However, Evan noticed the more traditionally dressed women were grouped together in one corner while the traditionally dressed men were in another. In the middle those who seemed to be less traditional, younger or maybe just more westernized, mingled together, male and female.

They were at a party surrounded by well over 200 guests, yet Evan found himself enthralled by the woman he brought this evening. As the two of them walked on opposite sides of the buffet table, she explained to him each of the dishes and what the main ingredients and flavors were for each. When they got to the dessert table, his plate completely full, she insisted he take a few *ghoriba*, brittle cardamom and butter cookies. With his plate full, he slipped a few into the pocket of his jacket.

"The flavor of a good Arabic coffee will bring out the flavor of the cookies," she explained.

Sitting on opposite sides of a long table, the two sat and ate their meal while talking to the folks on either side of them. The older gentleman seated next to Evan did not speak English, so Najila acted as translator.

"Apparently he doesn't believe anyone would get paid for writing words."

"Me too," Evan laughed as he said this, and the old man joined him.

As the evening wore on, and the sun's disappearance led to a star-filled sky. Najila was explaining the history of the music playing in the background when Naveed walked up. Both of them wished him a happy birthday. After thanking them, Naveed leaned towards Evan, "Your horses are ready."

After he walked away, a curious Najila looked up at Evan and asked, "What was that about?"

"I think it's time to prove to you I do have a little riding talent. Why don't you change into your riding clothes and I'll meet you at the stable? I've arranged for a pair of horses."

Najila was surprised, but also pleased, "As you say."

Evan watched her walk away to get changed before he headed to the stables. *Indeed.*

When Najila walked into the stable, she saw Evan standing next to Cochise, petting the horse, and feeding him an apple. It took a minute to sink in, but she realized what happened.

"Ah, so I'm being sandbagged. You've been practicing behind my back and have a new friend."

"Me? Nah, I've always been friendly toward Arabian stallions."

Najila looked behind Cochise and saw her favorite mount, *Almasafir*, saddled and ready to go. She looked around the stable, which was empty since everyone was at the party. Walking up behind Evan, she slipped her hands around his waist and placed her mouth next to his ear, and whispered into it, "If you catch up with me, you might get more than another kiss." Releasing him, she ran to *Almasafir*, and after slipping one foot into the stirrup, she told the horse, *"Tashghil kama riah alsahra'!"* She rose up and threw her leg over the horse, who was already running towards the open stable door.

The whole scene caught Evan by surprise, and he quickly climbed onto his own mount while muttering, "I guess that means 'gitty up go.'" By the time he cleared the stable and turned on to the trail leading toward the deep desert she was already nine lengths ahead of him. Evan knew he was already disadvantaged because, with Najila in the lead, she would get to pick which trails they rode. To someone unfamiliar, a span of loose sand might look like a packed desert trail. Making a wrong turn not only because you lose the race, but might also result in your horse breaking a leg.

Once Evan regained his composure, he leaned forward and began to speak to Cochise trying to convince the animal of the need to go faster explaining the girl on the horse up ahead was the goal Evan desired most. The words worked, and Cochise started to close the distance between him and *Almasafir*.

Najila rose in the stirrups, leaned her body forward becoming one with the horse. At no time did she ever turn to see if Evan was closing in on her or if he was even there. *What's behind me doesn't matter.* Aside from fiercely paying attention to her mount, and the trail ahead, Najila realized the bold step Evan had taken. *Not only did he do this for me, but he started weeks ago – before the storm and the face massage.* She fought to keep from smiling too widely and getting sand in her mouth, but the joy of the situation was there.

Evan saw her horse cut off to the left ahead of him, and followed. He was able to short the corner and gain almost two lengths while doing so. The advantage of being a follower was you knew exactly where you were going and therefore didn't need to slow down, but simply prepare. Before he made the turn, Evan was treated to a vision of her and *Almasafir's* silhouette on a background of millions of stars. *Liquid motion.*

Most horses can gallop about five kilometers before growing tired, but Hamad prided himself on conditioning his horses for eight. Najila realized she was quickly approaching eight and did not want to push either horse further. Looking up ahead, she spotted a flat area which might be a good spot for them to stop. *He hasn't caught me yet, but it doesn't mean he won't win.*

This was the furthest Evan ever rode at this pace. He was only half a length from *Almasafir,* and he was beginning to think he could smell the scent of *Lamsat Hareer* on Najila's hair and skin. He leaned forward, and said into Cochise's ear "If you have anything left, give it to me now." Evan felt the animal's stride change, then noticed he was inching up on Najila. Shortly, he found himself just behind her as Cochise continued to gain on *Almasafir.*

The first time Najila forced herself to look anywhere but in front of her, she turned her head to the side and found herself looking at Evan smiling back at her. *Damn — the man can ride.* She nodded toward the area where she chose to stop just in front of them. He nodded back indicating he understood and both of them slowed their horses. As they pulled off the trail and into this flat area, neither of them said a word.

Time was taken to supply the animals with water before Evan pulled two *agals* from his saddlebag and used them to fashion a makeshift horse hitch around the front legs of the horse as Naveed had taught him. After taking a drink themselves, they stood next to each other looking at the stars that surrounded them. Evan went back to his saddlebags and retrieved a blanket he slipped in there while he was waiting on Najila.

Evan opened the blanket and spread it on the sand in front of him so they would have a place to sit and relax before heading back. Najila, taking advantage of the situation, pushed him onto his back proceeding to straddle him. She looked down at Evan, then lunged forward kissing him hard while running her fingers through his hair. Unlike the kiss in the parking lot, which was exploratory, this kiss was driven. Driven by passion, and desire to devour.

Evan gave himself over to her, and followed her lead. As she began to explore her his body with her hands, he did likewise with his. *Her flesh is so smooth and soft.* He could feel her touch his skin, stroking it, then attacking him as if she wanted to crawl inside his body, instead of being left outside. Evan unbuttoned her shirt and slid his hands inside, but as he started to run his fingertips across her flesh, he thought better of it and helped her take the shirt off completely. She unbuttoned his shirt as well, before leaning forward to lie on him, their flesh in unrestricted contact.

Najila wrapped her legs under him, then using her body's weight rolled to one side, so he was on top of her. Evan raised himself up on his elbows and looked down at her, her face surrounded by her hair shimmering even under starlight, her eyes beckoned him on, and her mouth was waiting to be explored. He closed his eyes and leaned forward kissing her on the mouth, while his hands ran down the sides of her body, feeling the curves he memorized while in her presence for weeks. Her mouth attacked his neck biting into his flesh as he worked in between them to open her belt then her jeans.

There comes a certain freedom from being miles away from civilization in the deep desert. You know anyone approaching for miles would be visible, and you have found a spot, not behind closed doors, but an open space in the world. It was with this thought in mind, the Najila stood up and began to remove the rest of her clothing. Evan remained on the ground, not fearing being seen, but wanting to watch her and her silhouette blocking out individual stars as she statuesquely stood in front of him. *She looks like a statue carved from obsidian. Perhaps obsidian sent to cleanse the fuzziness from my psyche.*

When Najila laid back down, rather than straddling or laying on top of Evan, she laid beside him and curled her body into his. She placed one of her legs over one of his and an arm across his chest. It was a moment of nearness the two never experienced before and rather than speeding off from it, she wanted a chance to dwell within it. Evan's arm slid around her as he glided his fingertips across her shoulders and side. None of the passion left the moment, but the two of them paused to appreciate the moment before proceeding.

Najila began to explore his mouth again, just as Evan imagined. Devouring him like a juicy peach, using her lips to keep up with the juice which was flowing from the fruit, while her tongue explored all the textures of the fruit's flesh, pulp, and wetness. As she kissed him, she allowed her hands to begin exploring him again. Touching new places, enjoying new sensations, and knowing there was a symmetry to each caress, as both of them enjoyed the feeling.

It was Evan's turn, to use his weight to roll them over, so he was on top of her. He could feel her hands on him, gently guiding him until the two were one. Another pause, as they enjoyed the sensation of the moment – the first time. Then their movements began to quicken until they were both on the precipice of orgasm. Without warning, she arched her back entwining her legs around his. Her nails dug into his flesh urging him on. A moan began from deep within her and slowly found escape as she cried out into the desert night, and the two collapsed.

The two of them lay there entwined as they each caressed the other. Occasionally one or the other would start a kiss, which always ended with another exploration of each other's bodies.

"As much as I would like, we can't spend the night here. My uncle would send somebody to find out what happened to us."

"Yeah, I don't think we want anyone to find us like this."

"I agree, but I'm not ready to go back to a public demanding our separation."

"Tell your uncle, you're going to spend the night at the Sultana. Check in then you can come up to the penthouse, and we can enjoy the rest of our night."

"As you say; I like this plan, Evan Davis."

Najila kissed him one more time before getting up to look for her clothes and get dressed. Evan did the same and was pleased to see the trick Naveed taught him with *agals* prevented the horses from wandering off. Rather than galloping their way back to *'Shamal Mazraea*, they took their time returning it a moderate trot arriving back shortly after one.

Najila found her uncle and told him she was going to get a room and stay at the Sultana this evening. She explained she was going to work with Evan during the day tomorrow. While riding back in the SUV toward the lights of the city, Najila sat sideways in the passenger seat, with her back against the door. She pulled her legs up into the seat after removing her heels and was holding Evan's right hand with both of hers. She was using her fingers to gently caress each one of his while she stared at him from the passenger seat.

Rather than pulling her riding boots back on when they parked at the Sultana, Najila decided to go barefoot. Evan grabbed her boots and followed her into the lobby of the hotel. After handing her his elevator key, he guided her toward the check-in desk. The check-in process was almost painful, taking entirely too long but, after getting her key, Najila pretended to go up to her room. Looking back, and confirming that the desk clerk to be occupied by Evan she quickly headed for the penthouse elevator. Evan kept the desk clerk occupied by having him manufacture a new penthouse key card, claiming he lost his. When the new card was produced, he headed for the elevator.

When the elevator door opened at the top, he was delighted to see a string of clothes strewn across the floor. At first, he thought Najila would be waiting for him in the bedroom, but then realized he heard the sound of breathing and saw her sitting naked in the overstuffed chair with her legs hanging over the chair's arms. He immediately dropped her boots and went to her. *What was it she said? Many Arab things have a wild spirit.*

# Chapter 15



*Diwaniya, Rihlat Alsahra'*

It was far past midnight when Roshan through the flap back on the *diwaniya* and walked in. He knew he would find Naveed and Hamad together inside the tent enjoying a *sheesha* and bit a conversation. Hamad traditionally finished all birthday celebrations this way, a one-on-one meeting so he could properly recognize the person's special day while presenting them with their gift. Hamad felt this added to the sincerity of both the celebration and the gift.

When Roshan unexpectedly walked in, the two men sitting at the table turned and greeted him warmly. Though the meeting was intended to be private, neither man considered Roshan to be an interloper. He was quickly invited to join them and before he was even seated at the table a servant and brought out an additional hose and mouthpiece for his use.

"I was just telling Naveed about the time you and I were meeting with the Americans just before the liberation., Because Naveed was in a suit and I was dressed in robes, they assumed he was the negotiator, and I was just some desert *Bedouin*," As Hamad said this, he was slowly the flipping the *tasbih* back-and-forth in his hand.

Roshan turned toward Naveed, "Absolutely. I recall the incident, because even after we explained who we were, all of them still tried to converse with me rather than *Al Hakim* even though every time they did, I would turn to you and simply repeat everything."

All three men chuckled, then Hamad reached under the pillow he was sitting on and pulled out an envelope. "Naveed, you've been with me a long time, and I hope you'll continue to be here in the future," Hamad leaned forward and handed Naveed the envelope across the table. "This is a small token of my appreciation, not just for your service over the past year, but also in celebration for the many years to come."

As Naveed took the envelope, he quickly stood up and walked around the table to Hamad who was standing by the time he got there. The two men hugged, and Hamad kissed Naveed on both cheeks. Naveed returned to his seat and put the envelope into his pocket. Unlike some presents that are opened in public, Hamad preferred for his gifts to be opened later in private by the receiver. Later, Naveed would get into his truck to head home. While driving through the desert, he would open the envelope to find Hamad had given him 40 100KD bills.

The three men sat smoking and telling stories for another half hour or so before Naveed announced he needed to leave as his wife would be waiting up for him. Both Hamad and Roshan rose and accompanied Naveed to the tent flap where he exited.

While the two men were standing near the flap, Hamad turned and looked at Roshan, his expression not a happy one, "I take it some emergency kept you from attending this evening's festivities?"

"Absolutely," Roshan knew he took a risk by not attending the party, but he considered it worthwhile in hope *Al Hakim* would as well.

Hamad did not wait for Roshan to respond further but turned and headed back to the far side of the table where he took a seat and again took out his *tasbih*. Instead of flipping it back and forth this time he was twisting individual beads between his fingers, a sign he was agitated.

"I understand you're not happy about my missing the party, but I do have good news."

Hamad stopped playing with his *tasbih* giving Roshan his full attention.

"I was able to get in touch with Talal Al-Enezi," *Why did I word it that way? Why not just go ahead and tell him?*

Hamad held his breath for a moment waiting for Roshan to go on. When he said nothing, Hamad motioned with his hand for the man to continue. Instead of speaking, Roshan reached into his coat and took out a folded document, then handed it to him. Hamad eagerly he took the document, and first flipped through it counting the pages – *three* – then looked at the title on the first page, "Uniting Kuwait by Bringing in the *Bedoon*." Hamad cast the document onto the table, "This is not what I was seeking, this is probably nothing more than a rewording of the *Alshaytan Bayan Rasmiin*."

"No, *Al Hakim*, it is so much more. It defines a way to unite all the people of Kuwait and to correct the injustice of the past."

"What injustice? In the beginning, the *Bedoon* were given all the rights of citizenship without the title. They were allowed to work, receive allowances, go to school. How was it repaid?" Hamad stared angrily at Roshan who sat silently while the familiar rant went on, "They were ungrateful and insisted on additional rights to which they possessed no claim," Hamad's distress was increased by his exhaustion at the late hour. "Then, at the darkest hour of our country after we were invaded by thieves and cutthroats from Iraq many of them colluded with our enemy supplying them with the information they could've gotten no other way once they occupied our great nation."

Hamad stared at Roshan. His eyes shifting as he tried to regain his composure. A few moments passed before the silence was broken by the sound of the beads of his *tasbih* clicking against each other as he again began to slowly manipulate them.

Roshan was completely calm, he was prepared for this reaction, and now it was time for him to convince Al Hakim some of what the man knew about the past was wrong and most of what he knew about Roshan's past was a lie.

"*Al Hakim*, I fully understand your feelings. We have discussed this several times since I've been in your employ. At no time during those years have I ever given you my thoughts about your words or other facts you might not have known."

Roshan waited a moment for his words to sink in, if *Al Hakim* was going to blow up again there was no need in him continuing at this point. Instead, after decades of working with him, he knew Hamad's body language meant he was ready to listen. Roshan took a moment to remove the suit coat he was wearing and roll up the sleeves of his shirt before changing his position on the pillow, so he was more comfortable.

"You know how we met, but are you aware of what I was doing

during the occupation?"

"I assume like most ex-pat's you continued whatever job you held before the invasion if it was possible. If not, you stayed home hidden waiting for the liberation," *Al Hakim, always polite enough to never refer to me using the demeaning term TCN but always an ex-pat.*

"And *Bedoons?*"

"Probably pretty much the same, although many worked with our enemies and led the Iraqis to our supply depots and other spots of military interest."

"First, I will remind you after liberation, an extensive investigation was conducted with 20 or so *Bedoons* being arrested and held for trial on charges of collaboration. All of it was widely publicized. The investigations and trials ended with every *Bedoon* being found innocent. Those results were not published at all, aside from some official records documents in the government archives."

Hamad tilted his head and nodded slowly, "Is this true? How could I not know?"

"Absolutely. You, like most, were busy trying to rebuild the country torn apart by the invasion. You remember the arrests because they were widely publicized, while forgetting each arrest is meaningless without a conviction at trial – and there were none. Many of the suspects were beaten, starved, and mistreated while in custody. Several ended up leaving the country because they couldn't even find the most menial of employment after their arrest, even though they were cleared." Roshan shifted his position again, so he was leaning more forward toward Hamad. He was about to shock the man and wanted to make the situation more intense.

"As for me, during the occupation, I gathered with others who wanted to see Kuwait free once again. Our way of doing it was to become a resistance force. We disrupted their operations using any method possible. The longer we were at it, the better we became and the more militant our actions. We went from simply blocking streets with flipped over dumpsters and broken furniture to placing IED's in their path."

Roshan was watching for *Al Hakim's* reaction to his words. He noticed while he was speaking, Hamad's eyes widened, and rather than continuing to play with his *tasbih* he dropped it onto a pillow next to them. *I have his attention.*

"My good friend and associate served as a commando?"

"Absolutely, and proudly so. I performed hundreds of missions. I was at *Al-Quarin* when it fell; on the day the Allied troops marched into the city, I led British forces to locations where Iraqi troops were hiding in cowardice."

"Such dedication and bravery. I am surprised an ex-pat would involve themselves so deeply in a situation and a country not their own."

The time came for confession. Every word spoken from this point forward could possibly lead to the destruction of the two men's entire relationship. Up to this point, everything said, even though it disagreed with *Al Hakim's* beliefs and thoughts, was nothing compared to what was coming.

"Absolutely. Such actions would only be taken by a true son of the land being defended," Roshan continued to speak as he watched *Al Hakim's* eyes widen with realization. "Only a resident defending their home would participate in something so perilous and violent," *The truth may end everything I've learned in my life up until now.* "Only countrymen would risk their lives without question and without remorse as they fought to free the land they loved." Roshan could see the question in *Al Hakim's* expression, a question he was probably too scared to ask because of the answer.

"Roshan Patel was the identity I assumed as a commando, serving with the Kuwaiti resistance during the occupation. However, you've probably realized I am what you refer to as a *Bedoon*. I've never thought of myself as stateless, especially when I was fighting for this country's liberation. My country's liberation. I am a Kuwaiti. My real name is Talal Al-Enezi."

In the silence, Roshan watched as *Al Hakim's* facial expressions and body language went through many changes. It was as if he was fighting the truth he just heard inside his own mind. Every time he settled on a reality, something else would pop in and disrupt his mind before he could fully accept and embrace it. Hamad leaned forward and picked up the document he dropped on the table, holding it up in the air he said, "This? This is you?"

"Absolutely."

Hamad again receded into the silence of his own thoughts. At this point, Roshan had spoken all the words he could possibly say, except to possibly answer questions. The room remained in silence. Roshan tried to distract himself by watching the curls of smoke rising up from the bowl of the *sheesha*. After what seemed to be an eternity, Hamad nodded his head as if he came to some conclusion.

"I've just discovered my dearest most trusted associate has been lying to me for decades. While there may be very good reasons for it, at the moment, I am too tired to grapple with what those might be and why I should accept them and proceed on as if nothing happened. The hour's too late, and I am too exhausted to play those mental games," Hamad shifted his position but then decided to stand instead.

"Right now, I want you to leave. As of now, your employment is suspended. I want you to leave and not come back until or if I summon you. I need time, and I need distance from this to properly think through it all. Above all, I'm disappointed you didn't tell me in the very beginning or at some point shortly thereafter. You kept this up day after day after day. I'm angry, and I'm hurt. Now leave." As he said this, he pointed towards the flap of the tent.

Roshan grabbed his jacket as he stood up. Without saying a word, he turned and exited the tent going straight to his vehicle and departing *Rihlat Alsahra'* for what might be the last time.

"Hello," as she spoke Huda realized she missed looking at the caller ID leaving her with no idea who she was talking to. Ever since her last conversation with Maksim, when they set the plan for the Greater Burgan, Huda anxiously answered her phone whenever it rang. Even now, before sunrise.

"Today."

"What? Hello?" She pulled back the phone from her ear and saw the call already disconnected. *Today, at last, my son's death will be avenged.*

She was surprised to find Hamad already gone for the day. Because of last night's celebration of Naveed's birthday, he arrived home after three in the morning. When Hamad arrived home rather than being in high spirits, he seemed troubled and introspective, but she did not pry. Huda herself was anxious and withdrawn. *At some point today, I'll find great joy. Alas, if all goes according to plan Naveed will be leaving with the other Bedoons, and my husband will have to find a new employee. A minor cost for our country to be finally rid of these people.*

Huda and Maksim agreed previously to have the destruction of the Sultana coincide with the end of prayers. Since the dawn prayer period, *Fajr* already passed without consequence the next possibility would be *Dhuhr* at noon.

Rather than being surrounded by people who might observe her behavior a little too closely, she announced to the staff they would be given the rest the day off. "Please leave immediately and enjoy the rest of your day as a reward for your efforts last night at Naveed's party." *No menial laborer will ever question or refuse time off.* Within 10 minutes she was alone in the house.

She walked into Khaled's bedroom and sat down. Huda let her mind wander through warm thoughts of her and her son's time together. As usual, she dropped uncomfortable encounters from her reminiscing preferring to think of good times. One memory she never allowed herself to recall was the last time the two of them were together before the accident. Khaled was stilted and would not answer her questions as to why. He was cold and even refused to embrace her before he left. Khaled would never return. Of course, Huda never knew what occurred earlier that day which brought on his behavior.

Khaled answered the door and found himself facing a TCN in a khaki uniform lacking any identification patches for a company or personal name. The man's accent was thick, which made him difficult to understand. After a few attempts, it was decided the conversation would be held in English, as his command of the language was better than his Arabic.

"I'm sorry, you're here to pick up what?"

"Selling clown piece" the TCN spoke very slowly trying to enunciate every word. Finally, Khaled gave up and held his hand out for the clipboard in the TCN's hand.

The form attached to the clipboard and was in both Arabic and English at the top of the page was the company name, Wilhelm Weber Associates, along with the address for *'Shamal Mazraea*. His mother was listed as the customer point of contact with the service being a replacement upgrade for something called a 'Cell Clone Device.' In capital letters in the center of the page was the message in English "CONTACT HUDA AL-BOURISLI ONLY." *Like most TCNs, he spoke passable English but obviously couldn't read it at all.*

Since his mother was not at home, he decided to take care of this himself. Asking the TCN to standby for a moment, he went to the desk his mother used and tried to locate the item the TCN was supposed to upgrade. He looked through all of the drawers for anything appearing to be technical but came back to the door empty-handed. The TCN then withdrew the replacement device from his pocket and showed it to Khaled. Armed with additional information, he went back to his mother's desk and quickly found the cloning device.

After he handed it to the TCN, the technician plugged it into a brick-sized upgrade device. He then plugged the replacement he had shown Khaled into another port before he pushed a series of buttons. An abrupt beep sounded a few seconds later, and the TCN handed the new device to Khaled.

"Complete. Thanking you."

Khaled looked at the device in his hand as the TCN returned to his vehicle and departed. Unlike the device he found in his mother's desk drawer, this one showed the name of the manufacturer on the side in white writing, Clonemaster. Khaled was familiar with the concept of cloning a cell phone, as he upgraded his own several times. *Why would Umma need such a device?* He took the device with him as he headed to his bedroom where he pulled out his laptop and searched for the name printed on the side of the device.

He quickly learned the device possessed the capability to compromise and duplicate any cell phone it was plugged into. Once this was done and the device was plugged into a monitoring cell phone, software on the device would allow the user to monitor any traffic to and from the compromised phone. Once connected the monitoring cell phone could also disguise itself as the compromised phone. *She is almost tech-illiterate, would she even know how to use this?*

Out of curiosity, he pulled out his own cell phone and plugged the device in. Within moments, a message appeared on the screen.

```
Target Device Not Found On Network
PgDn For Options
```

He tapped the key specified and was shocked when it displayed the number for the phone he gave to Sheikha. For a moment he stopped breathing as the skin over his entire body began to tingle and his heart rate increased. *What the feek?*

A few more keypresses and the phone began to display the history of messages sent to and from Sheikha's phone once it was compromised. It also showed the messages sent to him from his mother's phone pretending to be Sheikha's. The messages which broke his heart and ripped the love of his life away from him. *How could she? Does Baba know?*

It is difficult for a son to think badly of his mother, but the shock of Huda's actions now gripped his entire physical being. His emotions went quickly from shock, to surprise, then to perception. Once in full grasp of everything his mother had done, his emotion turned quickly to anger against her. *Knowing the pain I felt, I can only imagine what happened to Sheikha.*

What happened indeed, when Khaled sought her out the entire family was missing. *Did Umma kill her?* He quickly convinced himself it was a step too far even with what he now knew, but the doubt was in his mind. All of the emptiness, pain, and heartbreak he felt when Sheikha was first torn from him returned with a vengeance. He realized none of it was true and somewhere out there, maybe, still existed the woman who loved him. *But did she? If she thought I cast her aside would she still care for me? What about the baby? Sheikha knew where I lived, but she never came here; perhaps Umma did...*

The scream escaping his lips was one of the final disappointment and resolution. *There is no further reason for me to continue. I've failed Sheikha and my child by accepting a truth which is now proven a lie. A lie forced on me by my own Umma. The hole within me will never be filled.*

Khaled returned the Clonemaster to the location in his mother's desk where he found the old device. He searched through the other drawers in the desk until he located some stationery and envelopes. After locating a pen, he began to write

*Dear Umma and Baba,*

*Sheikha's departure broke my heart and shattered my soul into shards forever. I know no other woman will ever bring me happiness as life with her would.*

Huda was completely unaware her deviousness was exposed, and her son knowing all reacted in a very self-destructive way. As she sat on his bed now, reminiscing about only the happy times. She never knew the responsibility for Khaled's suicide was not driven by a *Bedoon,* but was solely the fault of her own actions.

*Faheel Garage*

Nassar arrived at the garage just before sunrise. He considered performing one last familiarity check but thought better of it. He didn't want to risk the test occurring today. He pulled the tarp back from the 233 bricks stacked in the corner of the garage and cast the covering aside. After opening the hood of the car, and once again ensuring the plastic liner was completely sealed, he pulled on a pair of rubber gloves and began loading.

Because of the curvature of the metal plates he installed, it was sometimes difficult to get the bricks to lay flat, so they would all fit inside. As he finessed each brick into place, he began thinking about what his father said about being taken advantage of by outsiders. *But I'm not. What I'm doing will help our people and our country.* Even though he was trying to suppress his doubts, with every brick he picked up and put into place, he began wondering if transporting drugs was a good way for him to be spending his time.

After the last brick was in place, he changed gloves before beginning to spray it with a rather pungent fluid provided to him by his boss. According to the label on the bottle, it was synthetic deer urine. Once a light covering of this was sprayed across the entire pile of bricks, he pulled the excess sheeting over the stack and sealed it using a heating tool. Nassar noticed once he sealed the plastic, the odor from the deer urine seemed to dissipate. Each brick was now sealed four times, with a masking agent in the mix as well, in a process designed to keep drug dogs from alerting on the shipment.

Before closing the hood of the car, he removed the gloves he was wearing and put on another pair. His boss explained how the scent from various steps of the process could be carried from one layer to the next. Once it was closed, he went to the front of the Nissan and knelt down to take a look at the pitch of the vehicle. He was pleased to see even with 700 kilos of extra weight concentrated on one side, the vehicle was still level due to the modifications he made.

With the job complete, Nassar walked around to the driver's side door and got inside. Placing his hands on the steering wheel, he sat there for a moment with his eyes closed. Running through the details of the trip he would make later in the day. A thought occurred to him, which led him to lean over and open the glove box.

He removed the box previously, leaving only a small shelf which held an envelope with the car's registration information. Now, examining the loaded car, he could see the plastic-encased bricks stacked directly against the shelf. *Khara!* Getting out of the car he looked around and found a dirty rag which he stuffed into the back of the open glove box to prevent anyone who might look inside when the glove box was open, from seeing his cargo.

Because the day started so early, Nassar arranged some scrap cardboard on the floor to lay down to take a nap, it was several hours before *Asr. Today's the beginning of many great things for me, insha'Allah. I can feel it.*

*'Shamal Mazraea*

Hamad began speaking as soon as Huda answered the phone. "Did you sleep well? I tried not to wake you when I left this morning."

"I did, thank you for being so thoughtful, my husband."

"If you think you have enough time, Najila has asked us to join her at the Hotel Sultana for tea this afternoon. Say around 1500."

Huda went ice cold. There was a one in three chance the hotel would be destroyed while her niece and husband were inside of it. She swallowed hard trying to get her mouth wet enough to speak.

"I suppose it'd be okay, but why there?"

"Our niece spent the night there last night rather than trying to drive all the way home after the party. She was planning on spending today there working with Evan Davis anyway. I'm guessing he's working on his current article, and Najila is providing cultural insight," Hamad smiled to himself at the budding attraction he witnessed between the two, "Well, at least that's what she's telling her uncle. Personally, I think they're finding an attraction to each other."

*My niece's in the hotel now, at least it's not both of them. But is this cost worth it? Should I try to get her out of there? After all, she is my niece and not my daughter. Khaled was my son.*

"Well then, we can't ignore the invitation, can we. But I'll need to get moving now if I hope to be ready in time."

"Huda, you've got several hours, and I've never seen you not look lovely."

"Silly man, I'll call you when I leave for the hotel."

After she disconnected the call with her husband, Huda immediately placed a call to Najila. While the phone was ringing, she was thinking of some reason for the girl to leave where she was, and go somewhere else. Anywhere else. Instead of being answered the phone went to voicemail. Huda disconnected the call and immediately began to get dressed. She would have to go there in person to find her niece and get her out of danger.

Najila's phone would display the missed call; if she opened the phone, she would see her aunt called, and perhaps Najila would choose to call her back. However, until she went to the parking lot and looked under the seat of the SUV she and Evan arrived in last night, Najila would not see the message. Instead, she would remain sleeping, with her head lying on Evan's chest and her arm draped across his torso. The two of them, sleeping undisturbed, the morning after their night before.

As Huda threw on clothes, she tried to gather her thoughts about what was going on and how she could stop it, looking at her watch only an hour remained before *Dhuhr*. Even the best traffic, she would need at least 90 minutes just to get to the hotel from here, and she still wasn't ready. In desperation, she dialed Maksim's number. Maybe she could get him to stop what was started. The phone rang numerous times but never connected either to voicemail or to Maksim. In anger, she threw the phone across the room. After retrieving the phone, she walked out and got into her car. Moments later she was on the road heading towards the Hotel Sultana.

Najila awoke slowly but did not move. She was laying on her side, with Evan's body pressed against her backside, lying like two spoons in a drawer. His arm was over her with his fingers neatly tucked between her hip and the bed. Even though Najila partook of several lovers in her life, in the past 24 hours she had made love more with this man, than any other. While she felt soreness in some parts of her body, even now Najila still felt the thrill of his touch upon her skin. The touch of his fingertips – and of his tongue. As the thought crossed her mind, she found her thrusting her hips back into him.

She parted her eyes and immediately realized it must be later than it felt. The light in the bedroom pouring in from the large window in the sitting room told her it must be about noon. Feeling Evan's naked body behind her, she momentarily considered gently gyrating her hips to wake him and enjoy his touch again. However, the pang from her stomach was not going to allow her to wait.

Najila slowly extricated herself from under his arm and gently moved toward the side of the bed so she could make her exit. Grabbing his shirt off the floor, she slipped it on buttoning two of the buttons. While combing her hair with her fingers, she looked around the room trying to figure out where she might find a room service menu. Recalling Evan retrieved it from a drawer in the credenza near the conference table, she began to open the drawers looking through each for the menu.

When she opened the large bottom drawer, instead of a menu she found a stack of papers, books, and folders. As she was closing the drawer, the title of the top paper caught her eye… "Sad *Bedoon* Plight in Wealthy Kuwait." *What the feek?* She flung the drawer back open which resulted in a loud bang when it hit the stop at the back. Najila stood perfectly still but looked into the bedroom to see if she'd awaken Evan. After waiting a few minutes, she lowered her hands into the drawer and picked up the entire stack, taking it with her to the conference table where she sat down and began to go through it.

She had seen most of these books before, they would come out from time to time, hit the international news then spin out of the news cycle. Inside the folder were a bunch of articles authored by Talal Al-Enezi which appeared to be printed from a website. Najila would read the first few words of each article before flipping to the next page. *Why was he gathering this information? Why was he doing it secretly? A plan to hurt my country? My uncle? Me?*

Evan was awakened by the noise from the drawer, and after realizing Najila was not in bed went to find her. He was now standing in the doorway, watching her thumb through the pile of materials, the culmination of everything he anonymously received since arriving. *Well, not really anonymously anymore. Roshan arranged for them to appear in my room.*

Since last night, he gave little thought to anything beyond her. Even now, he found it difficult to not close his eyes and immerse himself completely in the scent of their lovemaking still lingering in the room. Instead, he stood very still waiting to see what she was going to do next.

At last, Najila reached the bottom of the pile and with two handfuls of materials was not sure what to do next. Giving in to her anger she threw them down the length of the table, scattering them with several falling on the floor. *I knew better than to get involved with this American, and I did it anyway.* He was not making any noise, but she realized someone else was there with her and turned looking directly at him. Her eyes were intense and angry; even though they seem to be wet she was not crying – she was beyond tears.

"This is really why you took the job, to do a bit of undercover work?"

"Undercover? All of this stuff mysteriously appeared on my table. Somebody wanted me to be curious about the *Bedoon*," as he said this he walked into the room, but rather than going to her he stood at the end of the table.

"Fine, as you say, but you never asked me? Don't you think you should have? I was supposed to be your guide to the culture here?"

"I wasn't sure how to even approach this with you."

"Approach it? Why because you didn't want to accuse me of personally abusing these people?"

"Most of this happened before you were born, and the things which occurred later was when you were a child. How could you be guilty?"

"Does it matter? You were just looking for a story. A way to condemn my people. Accusing them of atrocities."

Evan found himself taking a defensive posture as he spoke, his hand motions becoming more direct and excited, "I haven't accused anybody of anything. I'm not even sure how I feel about all this. I have grown to respect and trust your uncle, but how could he be okay with all of this?" He ended the sentence with a sweeping gesture indicating the papers scattered over the table. Then he went on the offensive, "Perhaps I should be worried you were sent here to spy on me? Why are you going through my drawers anyway?"

Najila stood up, she was so angry she could no longer control the volume of her voice and found herself screaming at Evan, "I was trying to order us breakfast. I was looking for a menu. Then I discovered your research materials."

Evan walked towards her, enunciating his words with each step, "I didn't want this, I didn't ask for this, it was dumped on me."

Her logic gave way to emotion, "You see me like some terrible person."

"No, no I don't. I see you as I've always seen you. A beautiful, strong, and intelligent woman. One who knows many, many things and shares her knowledge freely, while only opening herself and her true inner beauty to a select few," Evan began to calm down but knew this disagreement was far from over.

"I need time to figure this out, the sensuality and closeness of last night, this discovery. It's all so much. I'm going home." As she said this, she walked around the room, gathering up her clothes then marched past him into the bedroom slamming the door.

Evan dropped into one of the chairs. Looking at the scattered papers on the table and on the floor. *Thanks, Roshan.*

When Najila opened the bedroom door 15 minutes later, she was fully dressed and heading forcefully toward the elevator. Evan stood up hoping she would at least pause to say a word or two, but she skirted around him and continued walking. After pushing the elevator door, she turned around to face him.

"You know, your own country has problems with racial groups." Without realizing it, she insulted Evan in such a way he was going to feel obliged to defend it and himself.

"I never said it didn't, but in my country, we at least talk about it and don't try to hide it with secret programs designed to ruin people's lives by sweeping them to the curb."

"What about those who want to migrate to your country?"

"No comparison; your *Bedoons* were here when this place became a country. Also, before you talk to anyone about immigration, you need to make sure the person you're talking to wasn't an immigrant. I was, and I became a naturalized citizen because my country has a facility to do it."

While Evan was speaking, the elevator door opened behind Najila allowing her to turn and storm out without responding to his last statement. Unknown to Evan, Najila didn't leave the hotel directly but instead went to the room she rented the night before. Once there, she took a long shower and climbed into the bed to give herself to process what transpired in the last day.

Evan spent some time gathering up the papers Najila scattered around the room. He then organized the stack once again, but now saw no need to put it back in the drawer. His study of the *Bedoon* people was out in the open. Evan was drinking a cup of coffee while idly staring out the window when Jazlene stepped off the elevator.

Evan told her the night before not to come in until at least 1400 since he planned on a very late evening at Naveed's party. He mumbled a greeting and was not surprised by her puzzled look as she walked into the room with his clothes scattered all over the floor. She quickly picked them up and took them into the bedroom while he went back to stood staring out the window. Upon hearing a gasp, he turned around and saw her pull what he assumed were Najila's silk emerald green panties from between the cushions of the chair. He avoided eye contact as he walked directly into his bedroom to take a shower.

Jazlene had taken the time to throw his clothes on the bed and not put them away properly. When Evan walked in he picked up his shirt, the shirt Najila wore, and held it against his face breathing deeply the smell of her still on it. *There has to be a way to fix this.*

Mr. Pauley's instructions were very clear, Nassar was to enter the traffic ellipse no earlier than 1510. Once at the front of the hotel, he was supposed to stay there as long as possible until he received a call from his boss. According to what he was told, the call would take place no later than 1520. When he got the call, he was supposed to exit the vehicle, leaving the keys inside of it, and walk over to the *souk* where Mr. Pauley would pick him up and bring him back to the garage. It was a simple test, someone else would arrive to pick up the vehicle and take it across the desert to the coast for export.

Nassar was familiar with traffic at various times of the day in and around the Sultana. As a result, he entered the traffic ellipse at exactly 1510. Because of all the familiarity runs, clearing security at the front of the hotel was a non-event. Even though the guard lifted the hood of the car, he did not waste the effort lifting it far enough to see inside the engine compartment. Likewise, the trunk was opened and slammed in one motion. Nassar then pulled forward to the first spot in line and put his car in park, waiting for time to pass.

As he sat there, Nassar noticed three men in military uniform with automatic weapons, accompanied by a dog, standing next to the guards. The site of the animal troubled him, he reminded himself there was a death penalty in Kuwait for trafficking in narcotics, regardless of the benficiary. After a few minutes, the soldier walked the dog past the

Nissan, but the animal did not react or seem interested. Nassar rolled down the passenger window and leaned over to talk to one of the hotel security people when he walked by.

"What's with the drug dog?"

The guard looked over to where the dog was now sleeping, then back at Nassar "Oh, he's not a drug dog. In fact, his handler told me the only thing the dog reacts to is bombs. I told him if I saw the dog reacting, I'd react as well by running away."

Both men laughed, and the guard left to take care of the newly arriving vehicle. *Well, I guess I was stupid to think there might be a bomb in this car. It's just drugs.*

At this time of day, many people were arriving and departing the hotel, so the flow of traffic was steady at best, or stopped at worst. When Huda arrived at the hotel and entered the traffic pattern to drive up to the front door for valet service, it was stopped. The frustration the woman felt was almost palpable, and after a few minutes, she began to honk her horn in the hope somebody would move out of her way to let her through.

Evan hung up the phone from ordering room service when Najila appeared on the elevator and stormed into the room. She did not seem to be concerned about him as she walked directly into the bedroom mumbling something about car keys. After a few minutes, she came out with keys in hand and while walking by the overstuffed chair, noticed her panties, now folded and sitting on the back of it.

She gave Evan an icy stare as she picked them up and stuck them into her purse. Without saying anything more or looking at him further, she walked to the elevator and boarded it as soon as the door opened.

*Well, la di frigging da.* As soon as he thought it, Evan wished he had not. The discovery from this morning obviously hurt her especially after the events of last night. He was not sure what could be done to salvage their relationship but felt he needed to try. He walked over the elevator and pushed the button realizing it would be a moment before the machine returned for him. While he was standing there, Jazlene cracked the door to the bedroom and peeked out at him. Upon seeing her, she waved closing the door. A few moments later the elevator arrived, and Evan boarded it.

As soon as Najila stepped off the elevator, she walked over to the main desk to check out of the room she was supposed to have stayed in. In Kuwait, you are expected to let the management know you were leaving so they can make a fuss over you and ensure you will stay at the hotel again in the future. It was another of those personal service customs you get used to, and one which did make for a better stay.

As the manager was speaking Najila glanced over toward the windows at the front of the hotel and noticed the traffic was backed up. *Well, it'll take a little while to get out of here anyway.*

Sheikha had not been back to the souk since she was confronted by the three Kuwaiti teens. *I would not be here now if it weren't for Meteb's forgetfulness.* A school assignment required some fairly specific supplies they did not have at the house. *So here I am, risking life and limb for my son's education.*

While she was never much of a disciplinarian, she could not see rewarding the boy by letting him roam the shelves of the store as she retrieved the required items. She told Meteb to sit outside the store to wait for her. This was not as strong a punishment as she thought since he was sitting on the side of the *souk* which faced the Hotel Sultana. There was much activity to keep a boy occupied while he waited on his mother

Nassar stepped out of the car and lit a cigarette. Time was inching passed slowly, and he just wanted to be done with this. Only minutes remained before Mr. Pauley would call and he could depart. As he was standing there, he turned toward the row of shops and fast food places which made up the *souk*. Then he saw him, Mr. Pauley sitting drinking a cup of coffee and one of the restaurants. *Why would you be there? He should be in a car coming to pick me up.*

Thoughts raced through Nassar's mind, he remembered news stories he heard about bomb-laden cars detonated from a distance by cell phone. The remote detonation was called for because the driver was unaware he was about to die or because the driver did not have the guts to become a martyr. *I am no martyr.*

"You. You, back in your car."

As Nassar turned, he saw it was one of the soldiers with the dog a car length behind him motioning for him to get back in his vehicle. He threw the cigarette on the pavement and climbed back into the car. His curiosity turned to concern, and he opened the glove compartment and removed the rag he put in place to hide the bricks in the engine compartment. Taking out a pocket knife, he cut into the outside plastic wrap pulling it open until he could slide one of the bricks out.

It smelled horrible, but he turned it over in his hands several times before cutting into the plastic wrap covering the brick. He had never seen heroin in person but had seen pictures. *This looks like heroin.* In his excitement to gain access to the brick itself, the cut he made exposed the difference in the material of the outer and inner layers of the brick. Nassar looked into the cut through the outer heroin coating and into the Semtex explosive underneath. *Modeling clay? Oh my God, no! It's a bomb.*

After honking her horn continually for several minutes, Huda realized it was doing no good at all. Rather than continuing to wait, she exited her vehicle and began to walk across the parking lot to the entrance of the hotel.

As the realization he brought a bomb to the entrance of the hotel flooded Nassar's mind, the soldier who instructed him to get back in the car was dealing with a dog reacting to a whiff of the Semtex which Nassar exposed. It only took a moment for the soldier to realize which car the dog alerted on, and after summoning the two other soldiers, he lowered his weapon into firing position and pulled back the charging handle.

"You, out of the car!"

Nassar panicked not sure what to do. Somewhere in his mind, he felt escape was the best option, and he started the car.

Najila was just a few feet from the front door of the hotel when Evan got off the elevator and began to approach her. She did not notice him coming toward her, but instead saw a familiar face through the window in the parking lot, "Why is Huda here?"

As she was crossing from the parking lot into the traffic ellipse, Huda looked both left and right to ensure she was not going to be struck by an oncoming vehicle. Then she saw him leaning up against one of the buildings of the *souk* watching people pass by. *Khaled? My son, Khaled?* Huda immediately changed directions and turned toward the *souk* instead of going into the hotel. *My son has come back to me, I must get to him.*

Nassar tried to get the car to go into gear but instead was greeted by a loud grinding as one of the rods which would have allowed the gears to change was bent during the metal removal process. This delay allowed all three of the soldiers to get into firing position after charging their weapons. All three directed their weapons at Nassar.

Evan was almost to Najila when he looked out the window and saw the soldiers getting into a shooting position, a quick glance forward to where they were aiming led him to correctly assume the Nissan they were pointed at was a bomb.

*Where's Huda going now?* Najila thought as she began to step towards the door. Because she was focusing on her aunt, Najila did not notice Evan was running toward her. When he was directly behind her, he grabbed her around the waist knocking the wind out of her. Evan picked her up while spinning around and made the decision to head directly for the elevator he just rode down. Once inside, he began to repeatedly press the button to get the elevator doors to close.

Nassar's eyes shifted from mirror to mirror with each reflecting the image of an armed soldier targeting him. He kept shifting the lever up and down trying to force the car into gear and was at last successful. Flooring the car, he turned so he could exit the hotel as the soldiers behind him began to fire.

Across the street, Maksim's attention was suddenly drawn to the hotel and the gunfire. Realizing somehow Nassar must have been discovered, he pulled the cell phone from his pocket and dialed the number for the trigger he placed in the car last night while Nassar was gone. It was taking a moment for the connection to go through.

At the end of *Asr* prayers, crowds of people were pouring into the streets from the mosques. Most were headed home, so they quickly moved down the street almost giving the image of flooding water.

From where Huda was standing across the street from the *souk*, she could still clearly see Khaled standing there, and began to call to him to get his attention. Instead, she caught the attention of Sheikha who was exiting the store and immediately recognized her. *Oh my God, it's that woman.* Grabbing her son, she turned and headed down the aisles into the *souk* itself.

Huda was shocked, *the woman is kidnapping my son!* Then without looking, began to cross the street.

Bullets were riddling the Nissan, because of the amount of structural metal removed from the car, the bullets were piercing directly into the passenger compartment and hitting Nassar as he attempted to turn onto the street in front of the hotel. He only succeeded in angling the car in such a way the passenger side was now facing the *souk*.

Huda jumped back to avoid being hit by the Nissan, but immediately continued on her route toward the *souk* and was directly alongside the car when the blast was triggered.

The metal plates inside the car which were to direct the force of the explosion upwards at the hotel instead redirected the blast over the top of the *souk*. As a result, the massive force of the explosion went over the top of the market rather than into it.

The concussion from the blast still radiated out from the car and shattered the first three floors of *Kuat Zurqa'*. Once the bottom glass destroyed, an additional five floors of panes immediately fell because the supporting structure was gone. With only the top floors remaining, *Kuat Zurqa'* was gone.

# Chapter 16



Because the vehicle was not in the proper position, the metal plates inside the car intended to direct the force of the explosion upwards at *Kuat Zurqa'* instead directed the blast over the rooftops of the *souk*. As a result, the massive force of the explosion went almost harmlessly over top of the market rather than into it. The destruction did result in a berm of broken glass in front of the hotel which gave the appearance of a flowing stream.

The sound of breaking glass still filled the air when Sheikha's better nature took hold. Once she was sure her son was okay, she left the store where they were sheltered to provide assistance to those who needed it. The street was filled with smoke and dust which obscured her vision from all except the body of Huda which was thrown onto the sidewalk in front of the *souk*. Huda was covered in scratches and cuts but overall appeared to be okay. Sheikha possessed no medical training and therefore did not know Huda's internal organs had been pulverized by the overpressure from the explosion. As the woman lay on the ground bleeding to death internally her eyes were open and searching.

"Where is Khaled? Is he okay?" Sheikha heard the questions but was not sure how to answer them. The woman's eyes were darting around, searching for what she believed was her son.

Because Huda seemed to be getting more agitated, Sheikha knelt down beside her and told her Khaled was okay, and she needed to be lie still until help arrived. Like any mother who felt their child was in danger, the reassurance only served to make her more determined to verify her child's safety. When Huda attempted to get up from where she was lying, it resulted in her falling back onto the concrete then coughing until blood was flowing from her mouth.

Sheikha hated this woman. Although she lacked any irrefutable proof, she knew this woman was somehow directly responsible for Khaled choosing not to stay with her. By the time she composed herself after being thrown out of her home, it was too late to attempt contacting Khaled to straighten the mess out. He was gone.

As Huda lay on the ground looking up at the dust-filled sky, she thought the woman staring down at her looked familiar, but couldn't place her. Her only concern was for Khaled.

Through some freak occurrence physics, Nassar was thrown clear of the car during the explosion. His crumpled and dying body was lying underneath a date tree halfway across the Hotel Sultana parking lot. Because of his distance from the car, no one made the connection he was the one behind the wheel.

The windows of the restaurant where Maksim was observing Nassar, were completely blown out by the explosion. He suffered several cuts but was otherwise unharmed. As he walked out of the restaurant, he allowed the anger to grow within him. For all the planning and effort, as well as the money spent, the hotel suffered only superficial damage. *I still have several thermite bombs and some det cord left. Perhaps.* In his mind, he began to go over alternatives, perhaps even a second attempt. *Without guidance from an employer, perhaps the next move is my choice.* Sneering he turned and departed, heading back to his apartment.

Sheikha managed to keep Huda calm and lying still when the woman gathered the strength to suddenly sit up and demand her purse. Huda could only maintain a position for a moment before she fell back onto the concrete leaving Sheikha flabbergasted as to why her purse was suddenly so important. Meteb, being a 12-year-old boy, let curiosity get the better of him and left the store to find mother. He stood behind her with his hand on her shoulder while looking down at the strange woman on the ground.

"Khaled! Khaled, it's you Come to *Umma!*" Huda was excited and trying to move to reach out to her son.

For the first time, Sheikha looked at her son, not his hers alone but also as Khaled's son. She always felt the boy's eyes, and some mannerisms favored his father, but now she saw he looked exactly like a younger Khaled.

"What's wrong with her? Who is Khaled?" The boy asked as he backed away.

"Don't worry about it. She's confused. Look, over there that's her purse go get it."

Meteb did as he was told and after bringing it back and handed it to his mother. Sheikha showed it to Huda to calm her. The woman attempted to grab the purse but could not force her hands to function the way she wanted.

"Open it. Inside – there's a letter. There is a letter from you," her eyes were locked in a very confused Meteb.

Sheikha opened the purse and tried to find the letter the woman was talking about.

The elevator door closed before the explosion, but luckily it did not move from the ground floor. Now, with the power out, Najila and Evan found themselves trapped inside the small cubicle which was illuminated by emergency lights. Both were knocked to the floor when the compartment shifted as the blast wave pushed through the ground floor of the building.

"Are you okay?" He was trying to stand and lift her up at the same time. Still dazed, Najila was attempting to get her feet under her. At the same time, she found herself overcome by the emotion of the moment, and as soon as she was on her feet, she wrapped her arms around Evan's shoulders pressing her body into his.

"Wha..What was that?" She tightened her grip as her mind was trying to understand what happened and what to do about it.

In the panic of the moment, rather than being gripped with fear Evan found himself focusing on what you need to do next to protect Najila. *I guess my Satori kicked in, a good thing.* Because they were trapped, he was concerned fire might be coming toward them or, the building might be about to collapse onto them. *Either way, I need to get us out of this and away from this building.* He placed his hands on her hips and was preparing to push her back away from him so he could attempt open the door when she lifted her face and kissed him.

He found himself returning her kiss while he ran his hands down her back and pulled her into his body. Evan's reaction was completely understandable. The two of them were arguing moments before, but now, after something catastrophic, both were still alive and filled with the need to be closer. As Najila pulled back from their kiss, she looked into his eyes with a puzzled expression, as if she did not understand what she doing or why.

"I need to get the door open in case there's a fire or something else. We don't need to be trapped in here."

She nodded and took a step back from him while touching her mouth with her fingertips. *Why did I do that? I was so angry.*

Evan worked his fingers into the split between the elevator doors so he could apply some pressure against them and force them open. The design of the elevator included backup batteries in case of a power failure. These batteries powered emergency lighting as well as a small motor to open the doors if someone was attempting to open the doors manually.

The doors slowly slid open, and as the dust spun its way into the elevator, they could see the destruction across the lobby. Everything was extremely bright because with *Kuat Zurqa'* blown apart on the lower floors there was no filter for the sun's light entering the building. Evan blinked several times in a futile attempt to clear the dust, taking Sheikha by the arm he struggled to guide them toward what had been the entrance. The way was blocked by broken glass. Noticing a hotel employee in uniform walking disoriented through the lobby he went over and asked about an alternative exit.

They started moving in the direction the employee pointed to, while Evan's mind began to clear and he realized Jazlene was still in the penthouse.

"I have to go back after Jazlene, can you make it the rest of the way on your own?"

Najila nodded without knowing who Jazlene was and turned to kiss Evan once again. *Why am I doing this?* As the kiss broke, Evan found himself looking into Najila's eyes before he turned and went back to the front of the building. When he was checking in, the manager mentioned in the emergency stairway which was located behind the elevator. The stairs zigzagged from the ground floor all the way to the penthouse. *Time to see if I can find them.*

Jefzar was the first law enforcement official to arrive at the hotel. He was on his way from the Gulf Bank to his Sector Constabulary after picking up all of the ledgers and information regarding transfers to the First Caribbean International Bank made by Huda.

The documents Mohammed gave him proved without a doubt Huda was transferring large amounts of money out of the country, most likely used to hire and pay for the mercenary. What was lacking at this point was a motive. *Totally irrelevant at this point, even without one, the documents are sufficient to destroy her as well as my brother, and quite possibly the entire family.* As his mind was spinning on those facts, a call came in about a bombing at the Hotel Sultana. Upon hearing it, Jefzar quickly changed his destination turning on his lights and siren.

Jefzar had seen the aftermath of a large-scale bombing before. It was a few years after the Liberation when he was first appointed as Sector Chief. He was attending a training conference in Saudi Arabia and while there the Khobar Towers were bombed. Jefzar went, with a few associates, to the site of the bombing only to be blocked from entering, by US military personnel. It did not stop them from seeing the kind of devastation and mayhem that was possible. As he turned onto the street for the Hotel Sultana, he saw for the first time an attack on his own country.

Coming in from the outside into the scene of the explosion, it was quite obvious the wreckage of the Nissan was the origin point of the blast. Jefzar was amazed the car was not completely obliterated, it wasn't until after it was examined that it was discovered the metal blast direction plates protected the car from annihilation. He wove his SUV through the debris and crowds of walking people, to get as close to the Nissan as he could, before stopping his car and going the rest of the way on foot.

When he arrived at the car, he saw there was no driver behind the wheel. He scanned the area, *there is no way the nadhil could've walked away, so where's the body?* Finally, he saw the outline of a body lying in the street several meters away. After visually tracing the body's path back to the car to ensure it was the driver, Jefzar ran over and looked down on the lump of broken bones, blood, and torn flesh. *This is Shaytan? Or maybe just one of his minions.* Jefzar knelt down and began patting the man's pockets looking for identification. Upon finding nothing, he stood up and scanned the people who were milling about on the street.

Jefzar looked closely at the face of the man lying in front of him. *His features are Arab, more than likely Bedoon. Maybe I was mistaken. Maybe it is a Bedoon who has been doing all of this.* Even though he hated being wrong, it relieved him knowing his sister-in-law was not connected to a mercenary. *Besides, the entire scenario lacked a motive. A Bedoon doing this at least provides one.*

After several minutes of searching, Sheikha removed the only envelope she found inside the purse and attempted to hand it to Huda. The woman's condition was getting worse. She could barely manage to lift her hand and certainly wasn't going to be able to open the envelope.

"Open it, read about the *Bedoon sharmuta* who killed my beautiful son Khaled. The *alkaliba* Sheikha."

The words knocked Sheikha flat. *How dare this grizzled old woman insult me, especially when I'm trying to help her?* She looked toward her son to see Meteb staring back completely confused. She shook her head at him and held her finger to her lips telling him to be quiet.

After opening the envelope, she took the letter out and opened it. When she saw it was signed by Khaled, she could not help but run her finger over the letters feeling some connection to the father of her child, the man she still loved. Looking at the top, she saw it was addressed to his mother and father. *I wonder if there's another letter hidden somewhere addressed to me?*

The letter began by talking about his love for Sheikha. She felt her face grow hot and flush while reading the words from this beautiful man. He then quickly moved on, telling how his mother manipulated both Sheikha and him to create a schism forcing them apart. The final paragraph was heart-rendering as he talked about the emptiness he felt.

> *Baba, I've often heard you speak of how you felt about Umma, and how she made your days bright and warm. Every day was worth living, you told me, because you knew she would be part of it. Of all the people I met during my life on Earth, only one made me feel as if they were part of my soul which was removed at birth, then brought back to me later, making me whole again. There is only one woman I will always want to make love to, only one woman I want to have children with. Even though I may be young, there is only one woman I will love for the rest of my existence. Without her, there is no need for me to live on, and it would be best if I moved on to see if she is waiting for me there now.*

Sheikha could no longer control her own emotions and openly sobbed into her hands as they still held the letter. Upon hearing a gurgling sound from Huda, Sheikha dropped her hands and looked down at the woman. Her eyes were slits with her skin pale and looking as if it were made of crêpe. Sheikha shook her head before looking away, in doing so must have presented her profile in such a way Huda finally recognized her. She spoke softly but in a raspy voice, "It's you."

Any charity Sheikha felt toward Huda because of their shared humanity vanished. She looked directly into the woman's eyes staring at her coldly, "Yes, I'm the one your son loved. I'm the one your son chose to bear his child. Even though you did what you could to tear us apart, our love continues," she shook the crumpled up paper in front of Huda's face, "He knew what you did and when you prevented him from having me; he chose to end himself rather than having to face you day after day knowing what you did."

Huda's eyes closed, exhaling for the last time.

Roshan felt dread stab him in the chest as soon as he heard about the explosion at the hotel and he immediately jumped in his car and headed towards it. Now, as he walked up behind Jefzar, he knew the body on the ground was his son. Standing directly behind Jefzar he glanced over his shoulder into the face of Nassar, lifeless and staring upward into the sky. Roshan immediately spun away, the wail of a mourning father escaping his lips.

Jefzar stood up and turned towards Roshan.

"You know who this is? You realize this may be the killer who was calling himself *Shaytan*. If you know anything, Roshan, please tell me."

Roshan turned towards Jefzar, tears running down his cheeks.

"No, this man is no killer. He was being used by an American. An American who somehow convinced him taking this car to the hotel was something he needed to do to help his people. This man was a victim who possessed no idea as to what was going on, how he was being used. He was just trying to help and survive."

"So, you knew him?"

"Absolutely. He was my son, his name was Nassar. Nassar Al-

Enezi"

Jefzar was quiet for a moment, as he realized what it meant if Roshan was this *Bedoon's* father. *It also means, if Roshan is right, I'm still looking for a mercenary.* Jefzar turned back towards the car, and for the first time noticed a woman was lying on the sidewalk in front of the *souk.* It took him a moment to realize it was Huda. *This day is making no sense at all.* He turned and left Roshan kneeling over his son Nassar to walk over to the spot where Huda had just died.

"What happened here?"

Sheikha looked up at Jefzar and realized she might be somehow was held responsible for what happened.

"I don't know, I heard the explosion while I was in the store. I came out of the door, and this woman was lying on the ground. I was trying to help."

"You don't know her?"

"I've never seen her before," Sheikha lied, "I think she passed away just a few minutes ago. Perhaps she was too close to the explosion."

"Perhaps," Jefzar knelt down and felt for a pulse in the side of Huda's neck to verify her death. He felt nothing. As he prepared to stand, Meteb came back and placed his arms around his mother's waist. *The boy looks familiar. Maybe one of Al Hakim's cases. Just something about him.*

"Can I leave now? I was only trying to keep her company and comfort her."

"Yes, yes. Can I have your name?"

Look of surprise crossed Sheikha's face, she didn't need any trouble from this and talking to the police always ended badly for a *Bedoon.*

"It is just for me, I'm making a few notes. There is nothing wrong," Jefzar was in law enforcement long enough to realize why a *Bedoon* would not want to give him her name. He was about to drop the entire matter when she said,

"Sheikha Al-Shammari."

"Thank you, it may help."

She turned then she and Meteb walked away.

By the time Evan reached the fifth floor, he was panting hard. He sat down on one of the landings staring over the edge toward the top. *A long damn way yet to go.* Then he looked down, there appeared to be a small cloud at about the second story preventing him from seeing all the way to the bottom. He continued to look at it for several minutes trying to discern if it was smoke or just dust. *No way to tell.* It occurred to him if it was smoke, by the time he got to the 15th floor he might be trapped up there with Jazlene. *Not a good thing.*

The longer he sat, the steadier his breathing became but at the same time, his anxiety was starting to build. Evan was no longer focused on the emergency of the moment; he was now starting to dwell on all the possibilities, to include secondary or tertiary explosions within the building. *I can't tell if I'm starting to breathe faster or if I'm beginning to hyperventilate.*

He forced himself to begin has directed visualization. At the same time, he stood up and began to climb again. *I don't have time to sit here and calm myself down. I'm going to have to do it on the move.* Slowly, he began to take one step at a time, which would eventually take him to the top.

In his mind he returned to the magic of a spring day – he was enjoying the feel of sunbeams snaking through the leaves of the large tree he was lying under. The temperature was perfect, and the cloudless sky allowed the sun to cast a brilliant golden light on everything around him. Evan was pulled out of the vision when he felt his sweaty fingers slip on the handrail and was suddenly tripping down two or three stairs before he could stop himself. *I don't know, maybe this won't work, but at least I'm another flight of stairs toward the top.*

He changed his gait; walking up the stairs, he would step up with one foot, then bring both feet onto the same stair before proceeding on to the next. This change served him well until he got the 11th floor when soaked with sweat and trying to gulp in any semblance of oxygen; he collapsed onto the stairs and leaned against the wall. *Four more flights.* He was not allowing himself to think it, he knew once he got to the top it was 15 flights back down before he reached the ground level and safety. He slowly let his eyes close for a moment and tried to regain his directed vision.

He could feel himself lying on his back, his head resting in the palms of his hands. Beneath his hands, he could feel the cool blades of grass, which came in contact with his skin. As he stared up through the leaves of the tree, it was as if each leaf and the light peering through was part of a giant mosaic. A slight breeze caused the leaves to shudder, which shattered the static mosaic, turning it into a kaleidoscope thrown into motion. The accents of the twinkling of sunlight seemed to turn off and on as the leaves moved. It was almost like it was hypnotizing, allowing him to slowly enter another world, where he could allow himself to sleep.

Evan could not be sure if he were awakened by a noise or something internal. What he did know was there were four more flights before he got to the top, and he needed to do this in a hurry. A quick glance over the railing and he could see the cloud was which obscuring the view to the bottom seemed to be just a few floors below him. Rather than trying to think while he climbed, he just forced himself to move ahead as quickly as possible. By the 13$^{th}$ floor, he was barely catching his breath, but he knew he needed to continue. *Only two more floors.*

When Evan finally reached the penthouse at the top of the stairs, he could barely breathe. Soaked in sweat, he fell through the door as he opened it. The temperature in the stairwell had risen to 115°F, due to the power being off. Jazlene jumped back as he fell through the door. She had been leaning against the window, trying to look down to see what was happening.

"Sir, something has gone very wrong with this one."

Evan nodded, still trying to catch his breath. He walked over to grab a bottle of water off the table and consumed its contents in one drink.

"A bomb, in front of the hotel. I'm here to help you escape."

Jazlene's eyes grew very wide as she nodded at him.

"Can I get my things?"

"Yes, we probably won't be able to get back in for a while."

While Jazlene was in the bedroom packing her things, Evan placed his laptop into his Go-bag adding several of the documents regarding *Bedoons,* which were still lying on the table. He was fairly sure he could get anything missing from the Internet. When Jazlene returned, Evan pointed to the door, and the two of them began the trek down. *It seems to be a lot easier going down than it was coming up.*

Hamad was already on his way to the Hotel Sultana to meet with his niece Najila when he felt the explosion's shockwave rock his truck. He continued toward the hotel, and when he found the road blocked, he got out of his car and began walking. As he got nearer the hotel, he could see Jefzar's SUV in the middle of the road with its emergency flashers still on. Looking further ahead, he could see his brother knelt down on the ground.

"Jefzar! Hello?" Hamad cried out as he continued to walk towards his brother.

Jefzar heard his name being called, stood and turned toward the source. Upon seeing it was his brother, he looked down at Huda's body for a moment before quickly walking toward Hamad.

"Stop. Hamad, stop!"

Jefzar quickened his pace and closed the gap between himself and Hamad.

"Don't go any further brother, there is much blood and gore up there."

"*Shaytan?*"

"Exactly." *Truer words than you'll ever know my brother.*

He stood looking at his brother for a moment trying to figure out what he should say or perhaps if he should say anything at all. *I could just wait for the ambulance crew show up; they would have to inform the next of kin. You coward nadhil.*

"That's not all."

Hamad looked at his brother, he was confused by the way the man was acting.

"Is it Najila? Was Najila hurt? Or maybe Evan?"

Jefzar couldn't bring himself to speak but simply shook his head. He was looking into Hamad's eyes when he saw the flash of insight.

"Huda? She was going to meet me here. How did she… Is she okay?"

Jefzar slowly shook his head, placing his hand on his brother's shoulder.

"I must see her," as he said this Hamad tried to push past Jefzar.

"Stop. There is nothing you can do. You don't need to see Huda like this."

Hamad stopped pushing against his brother and fell into his open arms sobbing.

*Penthouse Stairwell, Hotel Sultana*

The cloud Evan saw on his way up was nothing more than dust, and only lasted a few floors. The trip down was arduous but they made it in one piece. By the time Evan and Jazlene reached the lobby, an organized evacuation was underway. They were immediately directed toward a rear exit in the hotel. The manager, upon seeing Evan, walked over to him and presented him with a set of keys to an SUV for his immediate use and a key card for a room at the Millennium Resort. The manager informed him his baggage would be sent over promptly.

After insuring Jazlene made it out of the hotel, Evan gave her his phone number in case she needed anything she felt he could help with.

She gave him a hug of gratitude before following the crowd of other employees moving toward a bus arranged by the hotel. Evan then began a search for Najila. After making a sweep through the crowd of people standing at the back of the hotel, he walked to where she parked the night before. Her SUV was gone.

Maksim's Apartment

It took almost an hour and a half for Maksim to make it back to his apartment from the Hotel Sultana. During the entire drive, he continuously kicked himself for relying on *a stupid son of a bitch local* for such an important part of his plan. He knew nothing for sure but surmised the soldiers somehow became aware of what Nassar was doing and began to fire on him. Rather than leaving the car, and therefore the bomb, behind he chose to try and use it to escape. *Idiot.*

He was not sure of what to expect from his employer, but he was certain he was not going to receive any further payments. Once that reality popped into his head, he mulled over his exodus for the remainder of the drive.

Upon arriving at his apartment, he walked in to find Jasmine lying naked on his couch covered by a small throw blanket. She was lying on her back asleep when he walked in. *Shit, I forgot about her.* Maksim expected today to be a day for celebration and a much needed time for release. His own impatience drove him to arrange for Jasmine to be available immediately upon his arrival. *Now it won't be celebratory, but perhaps a session with her will clear my head so I can plan better.*

Maksim left Jasmine sleeping and walked into the bedroom where he stripped out of his clothes and climbed onto the bed lying on his back. He didn't summon her immediately but gave himself some time to contemplate what successes he could find in today's events. The *Bedoon* Nassar was dead, and therefore, posed no further risk, while keeping the focus on racial disharmony as the cause of the bombing.

Also, even though there was not as much destruction as he wanted at the hotel, it was fairly significant and witnessed by a huge crowd. Video and pictures of the site will lead the news for weeks. He did see several bloodied bodies lying about after the explosion, *there was even one near the Nissan itself.* The reminiscence resulted in him becoming physically aroused.

"Jasmine!"

He waited a moment or two and was about to call her again when he heard her trundling in the other room. He raised his head so he could watch her entrance. She appeared in the doorway, holding the blanket around herself as she looked toward him giving him a glassy-eyed smile. *Unusual, he's excited before I even touch him. Well, it'll make things easier.*

Jasmine dropped the blanket as she crawled across the bed toward Maksim. She began by first teasing him with her mouth, while her hands ran across his body. As she became more familiar with him, the foreplay was less about exploration and more about the intensity of pleasure. This is not to say it was abbreviated; it was just more direct and effective. Her time with Maksim was not about how quickly it would be over, so she could be paid and move on, but how well she performed each session with him, so their alliance continued unabated.

Jasmine knew he preferred her on top, so when she was sure he was adequately aroused, she straddled him while arching her back as he entered her.

Unlike many of their sessions, this one seemed to go on forever before Maksim peaked out. Jasmine was grateful it did not end with her being choked out or otherwise rendered unconscious. It was nice not to have a massive headache at the end of what usually was an extremely physical workout. It was also unusual for them to fall asleep after. Of course, him giving her a key and telling her to arrive before him was also unusual. *Many new things.* Looking around the room, she realized it must be after sunset because it was so dark.

She gently slid off the bed, being quiet so as not to disturb him. She glanced at the laundry on the floor before picking up one of his T-shirts and slipping it on. Jasmine would've preferred to nap, but she needed to go to the bathroom and needed something to drink. After tending to the first need, she walked into the kitchen and looked for a glass in the cabinets. On her third try, she found a glass then opened the refrigerator hoping to find some chilled water. *Nothing.* She did notice a case of drinking water sitting on the floor in the corner. *Now I just need ice.*

She opened the freezer and saw several curious square items inside, each wrapped in freezer paper and taped shut. Forgetting her original quest, she took one of the square objects and began to examine it. *Maybe frozen meat?* After pausing for a moment to listen for any sound Maksim might be making, she began to peel back the tape on one corner of the cube. She lifted the paper off one end so she could see what was inside. The thermite was packed in an opaque container, and therefore not visible, but the wires and initiator were in the open. She stuck her finger in and was lifting the wires out of the way so she could see what was underneath when Maksim suddenly grabbed the bomb out of her hands and spun her around pushing her against the refrigerator.

"I look for ice," she insisted, realizing for the first time she was afraid of him.

Maksim dropped the cube back in the freezer and pulled out a tray of ice, which he held up in front of her.

"Ice"

Taking the tray, she slid out from underneath his grasp and went to the sink to extract the cubes and put them in her glass. Maksim stuck his hand in the freezer and rearranged the cube she opened, pushing the open side against the back of the freezer. He quickly examined the remaining items to ensure they were undisturbed. Jasmine handed the tray back to Maksim after taking the ice she needed. He threw it into the freezer and slammed it shut, causing her to jump. He then handed her one of the bottles of water from the case on the floor.

Jasmine poured it into the glass and without waiting for it to cool quickly drained the glass to abate her thirst. Wiping her mouth with the back of her hand, she noticed Maksim was staring at her. *What is wrong with him?* Without saying a word, he took two steps forward before sliding his hand between her legs then used his fingers to explore her. He lowered his face to hers and for the first time kissed her deeply. She sat the glass on the counter placing her hand on his shoulder before jumping up on Maksim wrapping her legs around him.

Breaking the kiss, she moved her head to the side, biting into the flesh of his neck hard. He enjoyed it. In fact, he wanted her to bite him again, and feel her nails dig into his flesh. Punish him for the failure and prepare him for the next phase. He turned and carried her back into the bedroom.

Jasmine was acting enthusiastic, but in her mind, she was fearful of what was going to happen at the end of the session. He was encouraging her to bite into his flesh so hard she was leaving teeth marks on him. Her nails scratched him so deeply his back was bleeding and yet he wanted more. They rolled all over the bed, devouring each other as if they were starved. She then pushed him onto his back, while gliding him fully into her as she straddled him.

Maksim looked up at Jasmine as he momentarily allowed his hands to explore her breasts before bringing them to rest on her hips as she rode him. Her half-closed eyes, looked down through him as he stared up trying to see if anything was connecting them other than their bodies. She increased the speed as she rode him. He allowed his right hand to fall off her hip, slowly working its way under the pillow until his fingers curled around the handle of his knife.

He slid his left hand up the curvature of her body until her thumb and forefinger rest across the front of her throat. She arched her back and rolled her head upwards to give him full access to the part of this act, which seemed to take him over the edge time after time. They never spoke as they coupled like this; instead, they seemed to feed off of each other's sexual energy and lust. With his single hand still upon her throat, he spoke.

"Jasmine."

She slowly rolled her head to the side and began to tilt forward trying to maintain a level of sensuality to the moment. When his eyes met hers, she could see from his eyes, he was about to orgasm. He closed his eyes as his breath quickened and face flushed. *He's close.* Then his eyes snapped open, and she felt such coldness she knew her body temperature must have fallen. Without speaking a word, he gripped her chin with his hand and pushed it directly upward.

She thought this was some signal she was supposed to return to her previous position with her back arched causing him to be pushed into her further making the moment more intense. But as she felt him throb inside her, he pulled the knife from under the pillow and slashed her throat from left to right as he held her head. The blade was so sharp, the move so swift, she never reacted all.

The splash of hot blood from her throat burst forth and covered Maksim as he lay beneath her. Jasmine's moans, which had been filling the room instantly turned to the sound of gurgling as the blood flowed through the gaping wound. The sudden rush of killing her and the smell of blood blended to extend his orgasm. Jasmine's body began to collapse upon him since there was no longer a functioning consciousness within it. When he felt her body beginning to fall backward, he dropped the knife and pulled her toward him slamming it down on him, splashing the pools of blood that now covered his naked body.

As he lay there under the weight of her body, covered in her blood and after feeling such an intense release Maksim knew he was going to have to deal with all of this, *but right now I'm sated.*

# Chapter 17

*Millennium Resort*

Evan tried to call Najila several times, but she never answered, he was unaware she did not have her phone. *I guess we're back to where we were, and she's ignoring me.* After arriving at the Millennium, he went straight to his suite where he threw his Go-bag onto the dining table and headed straight to the shower. After a lengthy shower to rid himself of the dust and sweat, he pulled on the hotel bathrobe and set up his laptop to check email. Arlen seemed to be the most persistent with 10 emails in the past six hours. Since it was midday on the East Coast, he decided rather than writing him back, he would simply call.

"Are you okay? We're seeing the news over here, and I know the Sultana is where you were staying."

"I'm fine, but a lot is going on here, and it still needs to be sorted out."

"Really? According to CNN, the entire thing was caused by some 24-year-old *Baudin*."

"*Bedoon*. But as usual, CNN is jumping the gun, and the initial impression probably isn't what really happened. Like I said, it's a bit confusing here, and some things need to be sorted out before it'll be ready for public consumption. It's after midnight now, so nothing more will probably be released until the morning."

"You know, if you write a couple articles on the side about what happened, I could probably market those to the *New York Times*, maybe the *Washington Post*."

"No thanks, I have enough going on with the job that brought me here. Bottom line, I'm doing okay. I will be in touch in the next few days to let you know who the bad guy actually was."

"Well, keep your head down. Getting tired of sending you on gigs only to have to worry about you getting blown up."

"You heard me tell you I'm still in one piece, right?"

"So far. Glad you're okay, keep in touch."

"No problem Arlen, I will."

While Evan was talking to Arlen, he was busily pulling all the documents he was given about the *Bedoon* from his Go- bag. He knew he was missing some of them, he simply didn't have enough room. He was hoping they would show up when his other property was brought his luggage over from the Sultana. A knock at the door made him hopeful his baggage arrived. Instead, standing at the door was a very dirty and sweat-soaked Talal.

"Are you okay?" *You look like shit.* Evan opened the door wider so Talal could come in.

"Mister Davis. I must speak with you. The bomb. It was not caused by a *Bedoon.* I think it may be someone who hired an American to do these things."

"An American? Are you sure Roshan – err sorry, Talal?" Evan motioned for Talal to have a seat at the table and the two men sat.

Talal nodded, "Absolutely. Or someone pretending to be an American. I don't know."

"Can I get you a bottle of water or something? You really look like you've been put through the wringer."

"My son. My beautiful son Nassar. He's dead."

"From the blast?

"Yes, he was driving the car with the bomb in it."

"I'm sorry. What?"

"Yes, this evil person convinced him somehow it was the right thing to do. My son would never do these kinds of things."

Evan's mind quickly went through the many TV reports he had seen, where the press was interviewing people after their children were responsible for some heinous act. All of them used words similar to Talal's. Rather than argue the point with the obviously heartbroken man, Evan just nodded.

Talal put his elbows on the table and let his face fall into his open palms. His body was trembling both from the situation he found himself in and dehydration. Evan stood up and searched his room refrigerator bringing back two bottles of water. He opened both, setting one in front of Talal. *I just have no idea what to say to this.* They both remained quiet until Talal calmed down enough to take a drink from his bottle. Then, as if he took the death of his son and put it into a box up on a high shelf, Talal again began to speak.

"*Al Hakim* suspended me. I told him my true identity, and he suspended me. I can't blame him; I lied to the man about what I was since before liberation. Do you know he tried to argue with me that the *Bedoon* were traitors during the occupation? Telling me such garbage; a man who fought with the resistance."

"Well, he placed absolute trust in you, and now he's found out another version of who you are. He'll get over it. You notice he said you were suspended and not fired?"

The thought did not occur to Talal before.

"What're you going to do now?" Talal finally asked.

"Well, I've still got a few months left on my contract, and I've one hell got of a story I need to tell."

"About what? The *Bedoons*? You may find doing so is not a good idea right now. There's enough circumstantial proof about the bad things that have happened. You may be here to witness the mass extradition of an entire race."

"You really think so? Without a lot of direct evidence to back everything up I can't see a government taking such drastic action."

"You forget my friend, there's a lot of difference between what you see in your government and what happens here. Here, they jail people for sending an insulting Tweet."

"Perhaps you're right. I don't know what to do. Hamad seemed to be such a wise and just man. I can't believe he is part of a system that allowed this to happen."

"You have to remember *Al Hakim* was never part of the government. He never knew the extent of what is happened here, to include the secret plan for the expulsion of all *Bedoon*. *Al Hakim* served the government by being a calm, levelheaded intermediary, who could see all angles of a situation and help guide everybody to the same vision and understanding.”

“A peacemaker.”

Talal took another drink of his water and nodded at the term Evan used.

“Yes, he is a peacemaker.”

Again, silence fell over the two men. Evan was okay with silence, it was better than all of the difficult subjects that were rambling around in his brain.

“I must go,” Talal stood up, and made an attempt to straighten his clothes, “I will be in touch tomorrow maybe things will be better.”

“No place to go but up.”

After Talal left, Evan sat in front of his laptop and started writing. He possessed so much information, and now even more from Talal. Just like when he wrote about *Al-Quarin*, he knew it was going to take more than one article to cover the topic. *Hell, it could probably take a dozen or more.* Rather than trying to limit himself, he let the words flow and created an article which discussed the history of the *Bedoons* from just before statehood through the policies developed in 1985.

When Evan was done splitting the story into multiple articles, meeting the word count requirements he was given, it became a series of four articles. Based on the split, he knew it would probably take another four to complete the *Bedoons* current status and cover suggestions for the future. With the writing done, Evan tried Najila’s phone one more time before finally turning out the lights at 2 AM.

Jefzar had been working on paperwork all evening, but it was not the only reason he remained in his office. He didn’t want to have to face his brother, he didn’t want to have to face the press, he didn’t want to have to face his own thoughts. By staying in his office, he could put his brain to sleep by working on paperwork and not think about the things he knew and the things he wishes he did not know.

At just after 0230, he walked out the back door of the building to have a smoke. He looked off in all directions as he smoked a cigarette and could see the lights of the city. He was often surprised by the number of lights remaining on, even when most people were sleeping. With his craving satisfied, he dropped the cigarette butt onto the ground and stepped on it before going back into the building.

After walking into his office, he closed the door and took a seat at his desk. It was then he noticed he was not alone. A portly man in a tan suit was sitting in a chair, which was pushed back into the shadows, against the far wall.

"Who the hell are you?" As Jefzar said as he thought about grabbing his phone to call for backup before he realized he was the only one in this part of the building.

"Let's just say I'm a friend who can help you out of a bad situation."

"A friend?" The man didn't appear to be armed and had yet to threaten him, so Jefzar sat down until he could figure out what he might do given the situation, "Friends usually have names."

"Call me Morty. My real name doesn't matter; in fact, it would complicate things if you knew it. You see, I work for Mossad."

*Could this be Shaytan?*

"Sure, and I'm CIA."

"No, I know the station chief and all of the agents assigned here, you are not one of them. You are Jefzar Al-Bourisli, sector police chief and brother to Hamad."

"How do you…"

"I told you before, I'm with Mossad, and before you ask – we were no part of what happened here."

Jefzar leaned back in his chair and stared at the man guardedly.

"I know many things about you Jefzar, you're what we call 'a good guy.' Someone not about politics, but about doing the right thing for good people. You are one who might put differences aside long enough to do something right for everybody."

"Is this where you offer me money to turn against my own country?"

"No, we don't want anything from you. Like I said, I'm here to help you out of a bad situation. Among the things I know, are the contents of the box in your trunk."

Jefzar's eyes went wide, *was this man watching me?*

"You see, my training was like yours. Follow the money. I know it led from the Gulf Bank to the First Caribbean International Bank. I also know from there it went to the account of a mercenary."

"So, you know who this *Shaytan* is? Tell me."

"Yes, I know exactly who he is and even where he is right now. But, you see, I also found out the source of the money. A bigger problem for you right now, isn't it?"

"Obviously" *where is this man going with this?*

"I'd like to propose an arrangement."

"Go on."

"My agency has certain specialists who can alter bank records all the way to the source. They can make the money which originally came from one place, look like it came from somewhere else entirely."

*If this is true, it'll hide the fact Huda was the one sponsoring everything. It would save my brother the embarrassment. It'd save the family.*

Morty could see the wheels turning inside Jefzar's mind. He realized exactly what could be done for him and the benefit, "I think you like the idea, no?"

"Perhaps. What would you want in exchange?" *There is always a quid pro quo in a khara deal like this.*

Morty smiled, removing a leather cigar holder from the inside pocket of his suit. He offered one to Jefzar, who turned it down, then pulled one from the case using his teeth. After returning the case to its origin, he took a cigar cutter from his pant's pocket and began expertly clipping the end of the cigar.

"As I said, I know who caused your problems here and where he is right now. I would like to take him with me when I go."

"No. Do you know how many deaths the man is responsible for? How many people were injured just yesterday by this *nadhil*?"

"My friend, believe me, I do understand how you feel. My people are serious about justice as well. This man is not only a mercenary, but he is also part of an organization the KGB created, called the *Siberian Rime*. I mean no disrespect or insult, but a man of this level will not be captured or killed by anyone under your command. It will take someone as ruthless and skilled as he is to bring them down."

"You plan to kill him?"

"I plan to remove him from your country and prevent him from ever returning. My plans beyond – are mine."

Jefzar stroked his chin, this was not an easy decision. *If the truth came out about Huda, it'd kill Hamad. He would no longer be able to function, which would wipe out the family business. The family itself would be in disgrace for generations. There is no way I could escape from this; I've already been accused of assisting the man as he went about his business.*

"If my people are not able to take him down, how exactly do you plan on capturing him?"

"This is the second part of what I would need from you. The easy part. I need you to clear your men away so I can bring in a few of mine to handle it."

"Mossad agents operating inside of Kuwait?"

Morty looked directly into Jefzar's eyes and said without emotion, "You truly believe my agents have never been here before? You do recall during your liberation, you were accepting help from anyone willing to give it. How do you think the allies knew exactly where to bomb, and exactly where the units were located in the city?" It was at times like this Morty prided himself on being a good liar with a vivid imagination. He was certain intelligence was probably shared, but aside from himself, he knew of no agent to ever step foot into the country.

Jefzar was aghast, but what the man said was both likely and could never be proven or denied.

"Fine. Fine…"

"Ah, good we have an agreement. I will text you shortly and tell you where I don't want your officers, so mine has a clear path to dispatch this problem. As for the bank records, if you were to burn the box of documents in your trunk," Morty stood and took a step towards the desk, then set his cigar lighter directly in front of Jefzar, "the only records remaining would be those in another country. Those records will show a group tied to the Caliph Kinship sponsored *Shaytan's* operation in your country."

Jefzar absorbed the words and smiled, "A nice twist."

"Well, the Kinship has been an organization of concern for others as well."

Jefzar nodded. Morty took a shallow bow as he walked out of Jefzar's office. Jefzar sat there a moment tapping his fingers on the desk, considering what he just gained and what he agreed to. *Damn, I should've asked him about the computer records and Mohammed. Maybe the next time we talk.*

Jefzar shook the last cigarette out of the pack in his pocket. He looked to the cigarette for a moment before smashing it between his fingers. He stood up, taking the cigar lighter, and sliding it into his pocket. *I have some trash to burn.*

Jefzar would later see an entry in the Actions Log, regarding a fire that occurred at the Gulf Bank Data Center. The fire was suspected of being caused by faulty wiring with one bank employee, Mohammed Al-Hajri, dead of smoke inhalation. It was unknown why a branch manager was in the data facility. The bank was retrieving backup data records from its off-site storage facility in Switzerland.

*Rihlat Alsahra'*


Evan arrived shortly after *Fajr*, the dawn prayer, and walked directly to the stable. Hamad was in one of the paddocks brushing down *Eadala*.

"You can't have gone for a ride this early," he said as he walked up and leaned against the wood rail of the paddocks gate.

"No, in fact, it may be some time before I feel like riding. It doesn't mean I don't owe my friend *Eadala* some care and an explanation for my absence.

"I heard about Huda, I'm sorry."

"Thank you. And thank you for rescuing Najila. She told me what you did. If your reaction were not so quick, she would've ended up like Huda."

"No problem, I think a lot of Najila."

"She also told me you have developed some opinions about the *Bedoon*."

"Well, actually someone was providing me information. I didn't go seeking it."

"Ah, yes. It may have been Roshan – or should I be calling him Talal. So many changes."

"Yeah, people should wear name tags."

"Why didn't you ever ask me?" Hamad stopped brushing the horse for a moment and looked at Evan, "About the *Bedoon*. Did you think I would lie to you?"

"I did a lot of thinking about what I read and had a hard time reconciling the person I've come to know and respect with the people who did this to so many *Bedoon*. I simply couldn't see you as part of it."

Hamad stopped brushing again, and looked directly at Evan with a cold stare, "You don't seem to understand. Regardless of the person I am, I'm also a Kuwaiti and therefore have to support the laws of my nation, regardless."

"I can't bring myself to believe you really see things that way," Evan raised his hand so Hamad could see the folder in it, "I brought you this. It's some very good writing."

Hamad stopped brushing the horse and walked over to the gate of the paddock where he took the folder Evan was offering to him.

Hamad opened the folder to the title page, "Ah, as expected about the *Bedoon*. A four-part series no less."

"Well, it's a big story. It took me a while to tell it fairly."

"Fairly to whom?" Hamad paused for a moment, closing the

folder, "You realize I will be exercising the termination clause of your contract."

"I fully understand, but I also know based on everything you ever told me you would not have wanted me to duck from writing this," Evan tapped the closed folder in Hamad's hand.

"*Allah yadhhab maeak wayubqik amnana fi rihlatik*," Hamad saw the puzzled look on Evan's face, smiled and added, "May God go with you and keep you safe on your journey."

Evan smiled weakly, still confused; he absent-mindedly nodded before turning to walk out.

Hamad finished brushing down *Eadala*. He knew the next few weeks he would have to stay at *'Shamal Mazraea* taking care of funeral details and mourning the wife he loved for his entire life.

'Shamal Mazraea

Hamad walked into his city home and realized how empty it felt without Huda there. The feeling of emptiness also struck him when Khaled was no longer there. He took out the *tasbih* and began to fiddle with it as he walked through the entire house. He told the servants all to leave, but having done so regretted it as the house felt empty. Upon reaching the kitchen, he took a seat at the table where he and Huda often ate breakfast alone together before he left for *Rihlat Alsahra'*, or whatever his business of the day was. Sitting down in his usual chair, he reached into the pocket of his *dishdasha* and pulled out the papers Evan gave him.

As he began reading, he reminded himself he knew everything in those documents; it's just the version he knew was government-supplied propaganda. *Bedoons were often dishonest and trying to cling to citizenship using fraudulent documents and made up stories. They didn't deserve citizenship, during the occupation – no wait; Roshan fought for Kuwait with the resistance. What else did I think I knew was actually false?*

He was on the last page of the document when the doorbell rang.

371

Hamad sat motionless thinking one of the servants would get it. When it rang again, he recalled he was alone so he rose and went to the front door. Hamad was greeted by a young woman on the porch holding a piece of paper in her hand. Behind her was the taxi which brought her here, Hamad could see a silhouette in the backseat along with the driver in front.

"Can I help you?"

"No, not really. I just have something for you."

"Something for me?"

"Yes, I was at the *souk* yesterday when the bomb went off. Well, my son and I were there," as she spoke, she motioned over her shoulder to the passenger who remained in the cab.

"I'm sorry I don't know how this…"

"Your wife, Huda. I was there trying to help her after she was injured."

"Ah well, thank you," *Why is she here? She appears to be a Bedoon. Looking for a reward?*

"Well, she asked me to get a letter from her purse and read it to her, but the police came and took her purse before I put this letter back in it," she waved the letter in her hand toward Hamad.

Meteb a grown bored with sitting in the taxi, so he got out and went to stand next to his mother. He put his arm around his mother's waist and looked at the man his mother was talking to.

Hamad looked down; the resemblance was striking. *This boy looks just like Khaled when he was young.*

Sheikha saw the recognition in Hamad's eyes. She wasn't sure what to say at this point. She did not want to have any more contact with this man than required. She held the letter out, hoping he would take it but he didn't he just kept staring at Meteb."

"I'm not Khaled," Meteb announced feeling uncomfortable with the man staring at him.

"How do you know the name?"

"The woman at the souk, she kept calling me Khaled."

Hamad looked up at his mother, *could it be?* "If I may be so bold, what is your name, Miss?”

“Sheikha. Sheikha Al-Sha…”

“Al-Shammari. Yes, I remember the name. The *sharmuta* who broke my son’s heart by leaving him.”

Sheikha was stunned. She tried to do the right thing by returning the letter, now she dropped it, grabbed Meteb by the hand, and headed for the cab.

Hamad stood there, surprised at himself for confronting the woman in such a fashion. But his emotions were very fragile. Before he turned to go back in the house, he scooped up the letter which she dropped on the porch. Opening it, he was surprised to find it was in Khaled’s handwriting.

*Millennium Resort*

Evan’s cell phone started ringing almost as soon as he got in the door to his room.

“Evan, tell me what you did. I’ve never seen someone fired this way.”

“Well, that was quick. It only happened a couple of hours ago. You already know?”

“I am the great and powerful agent. Kind of like the Wizard of Oz but with less smoke and no curtain. Seriously though, I’ve never seen somebody get fired and get a bonus.”

“Huh?”

“True; it was how I found out what happened. I got confirmation of a wire transfer. It’s three times the remaining salary under the contract. I thought it was gold he agreed to give you the balance of the contract even if he fired you, this, this I didn’t plan on.”

“Hamad was a pretty honorable guy. Maybe he just felt bad.”

“Okay, I get it. Anyway, I’ll have my secretary arrange for a flight out. It may take a day or so.”

"No problem, do you think you could market some freelance articles about Kuwait?"

"Maybe, whatcha got?"

"I found out about a race of people who live here but have been treated rather poorly since Kuwait became a country. It's what caused the rift between Hamad and me."

"Is it something you would write going forward? Everything you wrote up to this point actually belongs to him."

"Yeah, this would all be brand-new."

"Sure, sounds kind of socially conscious human interest."

"Okay, I'll send them on when I get them completed. I look forward to seeing you again."

"Yeah, be glad to have you back in the USA."

"Oh, wire me some money. Being unemployed has certain consequences like having to pay your hotel bill and restaurant tabs."

"It'll be there in a few hours."

Evan began to search through the boxes containing his things brought over from the Sultana. Eventually, he came across what he was looking for: the bottle of wine Talal had given him. Unzipping the side compartment on his Go-bag, Evan fished out a folding corkscrew, and after opening the bottle, he poured a bit into a coffee cup. Now, with the appropriate libation, he took a seat in front of his laptop and began to write.

*Maksim's Apartment*

Maksim awoke just as the sun was going down but rather than immediately getting up, he remained in bed lying next to the cold body of Jasmine. While lying there, remembering their last time together and how it ended, he would occasionally stretch out a finger and trace it through her congealing blood before sticking it in his mouth to savor her taste. *Maybe, I should've waited… just once more.*

Mentally he was dancing between fantasy and reality, toying with the idea of enjoying her once again when he was startled by the sound of knocking on the door. Maksim, rolled off the bed while retrieving the 9mm Beretta he had taped under the nightstand. Silently, he crawled from the bedroom into the dining area, once there he reached up and retrieved his laptop from the worktable and turned it on.

After the computer recognized his thumbprint, two keystrokes brought up a video stream being broadcast from a camera outside the apartment door. Standing in front of his door, was an older, portly man dressed in a cheap suit. *Might be a cop, but at least he's alone.* As he toyed with this idea, the man on the screen, turned and left without fanfare. *I need to get the hell out of here.*

Maksim remained where he was, absolutely motionless for another ten minutes before he got up and returned to the bedroom. He no longer had time to enjoy memories of Jasmine or contemplate making another, so he threw a sheet over her bloody corpse. Rather than getting dressed immediately, he chose to prepare for his exit in the nude, which would allow him to wash off any last-minute evidence before he headed to the airport.

After making a flight reservation for his departure, he began gathering anything which might link him to the apartment or to any of the crimes he committed. All of the items he collected were placed in a canvas bag next to the door. Next, he began to retrieve the various explosives from the freezer and positioned them around Jasmine's body on the bed. As he was doing this, somewhere in his mind, Maksim found himself imaging he was constructing a funeral pyre to honor Jasmine. A reverent sendoff for one who had departed.

As Maksim was cleaning up inside Morty was on the phone to his team outside. Morty instructed them to remain vigilant but not to enter until he gave them the go-ahead. He was hoping to be able to reason with *Shaytan* by providing him with an easy escape route and follow on employment. Unlike many of his colleagues, Morty always preferred talking his way to a solution rather than fighting or shooting. With his team en route, Morty departed the area.

Maksim's wiring together of the remaining explosives was artistic. Each item required different triggering mechanisms, each required different initiators and catalysts. If not properly implemented, one bomb could accidentally disarm another. His training with Siberian Rime left him a master of quickly working such things out. Shortly after he started, he was standing at the open doorway staring at the bed and mentally running through the sequence of events that would take place when the door was reopened. He predicted the explosion would cause enough structural damage to this floor that the floors above might collapse, and the ensuing fire would surely devastate anything or anyone who escaped the blast.

Satisfied with his creation, closed the bedroom door arming his creation. Maksim then took a shower washing the blood and sweat from his body as he prepared to leave for the last time. He picked up the canvas bag that was sitting next to the door and was shortly dumping items into a dozen or so dumpsters in a nearby TCN neighborhood. Only one item went into each dumpster. Individually, the pieces would raise no interest and would likely be gone before anyone came looking.

On the return trip, as Maksim got closer to his apartment, he began to feel on edge. Somehow the vibe was not right, and he became more cautious. Having been in place for several weeks, he was familiar with his neighborhood and surrounding streets. Maksim found himself forcing a return to an appropriate level of watchfulness. As he turned the corner onto the road in front of his building, he began scanning the people milling around on the sidewalk and street in front of it. His concern was people who did not belong there.

Maksim immediately ignored anyone over or under military age. Next, he excluded anyone female. *In this country, they're not commandos.* When he looked at what was left, there were three people worthy of suspicion. His sense of alert for these three was extremely high because of his own gut feeling; they just did not belong there. Then he noticed their haircuts -- bad, cheap haircuts. *Anyone with income enough to reside in this neighborhood would've spent the money for a precision haircut that suited them.*

Upon closer inspection all three of the men possessed muscular builds but rather than narcissistically showing them off, they were hiding them. *Is it something Kuwaiti, or Interpol?* Either way, he had attracted unwanted attention. Right now, in his apartment, there was the decaying body of an Asian prostitute. Probably trace elements of all of the explosives he used and specialty tools. None of which he could not live without or replace. Rather than turning into the parking lot, he depressed the accelerator and continued straight to the airport.

The three Mossad agents waited an hour for Maksim's return before being approved to breach his apartment to gather any remaining evidence. Their level of vigilance upon entering the apartment prevented Maksim's final strike from being triggered. The agents used a camera to peer into the bedroom from under the door. After determining that opening the door would trigger the explosives, the room was entered through an outside window which allowed them to disarm the bombs Maksim had left. Once he received the report from Bloch, Morty directed them to dispose of the body and clean up the apartment, so no evidence was left behind.

With their job done, the three agents headed to the airport, and as they departed the taxi that delivered them there, the aircraft above them was taking Maksim to Syria and on to his next mission.

Even though he was not successful in capturing Maksim, Morty felt confident he would never return to Kuwait. As his last field mission ended, Morty felt good about the overall outcome. The killer was stopped, the chaos the country experienced was starting to abate, and the Caliph Kinship was disgraced and deported. *To me, it's a perfect day.*

Once he boarded the Lufthansa flight, which would take him to Jordan and a connecting flight to Tel Aviv, he took out his phone and sent a final text to Jefzar.

```
< All complete. Farewell, Thanks, & Shalom
```

As Jefzar read the text, he smirked to himself, *Shalom?*

# Chapter 18



Hamad reread the letter a dozen times with little understanding of what exactly Huda had done. Whatever it was, it led to the death of their son. He realized he could either wallow in these thoughts or put them away somewhere in the back of his mind and remember her for the woman he loved and not the one who did these things. While waiting for his brother to show up, he walked out in the backyard and lit fire to the letter, destroying it. *Now, I shall consider it no more.*

Rather than simply honking his horn, Jefzar flipped the siren off and on several times causing it to chirp loudly and informing Hamad he was waiting for him. On the way to their destination, neither man spoke preferring to be alone with their thoughts as they watched the scenery pass by the window. Hamad took out his *tasbih,* and the beads clacking against each other provided the only sound for the two-hour trip.

As they got closer, Jefzar slowed the vehicle and finally pulled over to the side of the road.

"Are you sure you want to do this? There is no reason why you should accept this obligation now."

Hamad stared at his brother for a moment and considered his words, "No, it was just an obligation I was choosing to ignore."

Jefzar nodded and pulled the car back onto the road proceeding to their destination without saying another word. When he pulled into the lot and parked, the two men exited the vehicle and Hamad slipped his *tasbih* into his pocket before they climbed the stairs to the fifth floor.

"No elevator?" Jefzar asked, on the verge of panting.

"I guess not, maybe you should give up smoking."

"Bah!"

Jefzar double-checked the slip of paper in his hand, "This is it. Not too late to turn back."

Hamad scowled at him playfully and then knocked on the door. Shortly, Meteb opened it and stared the two men.

"Is your *Umma* here?"

Meteb shook his head but didn't say a word. Jefzar and Hamad looked at each other. Jefzar then stuck his head in the apartment and quickly looked around.

"Is she, maybe, sleeping?"

Meteb nodded. Jefzar turned to his brother and whispered, "I was able to find out she was working nights cleaning a building downtown. I guess we arrived during her sleep time."

"Would you be so kind, to wake your *Umma* and tell her we are here to speak to her."

Meteb shrugged his shoulders, "Who should I tell her is here?"

Hamad and Jefzar looked at each other, before Jefzar told the boy, "Let her know it is Hamad Jaber Al-Bourisli, also known as *Al Hakim*. Oh, and his brother."

"Hamed Jaber…" the boy slowly repeated.

Hamad interrupted, "Tell her it is your *Jeddi*, your Grandfather."

Meteb closed the door, leaving the two men standing in the hallway. Several minutes passed before the door was opened and standing there was a very sleepy looking Sheikha.

"You. What, you tracked me down so you could insult me in my own home?"

"No, please. I apologize for what was said the other day. You have to remember Khaled was my son. I didn't know the full story; I do now thanks to the letter you brought."

Sheikha invited the two men into her home, and they all sat at the table where she and Meteb ate breakfast.

Looking at her son, Hamad asked, "He's a bright boy like his father, isn't he?"

"Yes; I see so much of Khaled in him every day."

"I could show you pictures of Khaled when he was the same age, they look identical. You have done a magnificent job of raising the boy. Especially given the challenges you've experienced."

"Challenges? You mean the challenge of being a single mother? Or the challenge of being a *Bedoon*? Or maybe the challenge of being an unwed mother in a culture which demands virgins?" As soon as she said it, she regretted it. "I'm sorry, I didn't mean..."

Hamad took her hand in his, shaking his head, "Dear, don't concern yourself with those things. We're family and family must speak frankly to each other."

*Family?* Sheikha was surprised he used the word. Although everything Khaled ever said about him, proved he was a kind and just man.

"If I had known about the boy, and about the situation, you were left in when Khaled died, I would've done something right then. I didn't know."

Jefzar stood and went over to Meteb asking the boy if you would like to go out and play some soccer with the ball he kept in the trunk of his car. Meteb eagerly agreed, and the two of them left.

Once they were alone, they relaxed and Sheikha offered to fix him a cup of tea, which he accepted.

"What I'm about to offer you, do not feel obligated to accept. But whether you do or not, I would like to treat you as my daughter and get to know Meteb as my grandson."

"I think such a relationship would be good. Khaled always spoke about you with much affection."

Hamad used his hand to wipe away a tear, "He was an amazing son."

"You said you were going to offer something? Not to rush," Sheikha let out a forced giggle, "but I'm not very good at waiting."

"I'll remember that. With Huda and Khaled both gone, I have a very large house with no one living there but myself. I would like to offer you what would have been yours if you and Khaled were able to marry. Home and the support of your family."

Sheikha was dumbstruck.

"I'm not trying to turn you into a servant or anything, in fact, the house has several servants you would be handling... as it is your home."

*Servants?* "I'm not quite sure what to say."

"Please, take your time and consider it. It is an offer without expiration."

"What about Meteb's school?"

"He is about the right age for the same high school Khaled attended."

Sheikha's expression went from joyful to troubled, "But you see, he cannot. He is a *Bedoon* just like me. *Bedoons* are not allowed to attend Kuwaiti schools."

"I am a Kuwaiti, and you both are my family. Therefore, you are Kuwaiti."

"But the law…"

"Is wrong." it was the first time Sheikha heard a man raise his voice since leaving her family home. The fear that crossed her face shocked Hamad.

"I'm sorry, I wasn't yelling at you. I have an American friend who told me I'm a better person than accepting the way things are, when I know they are not right," he paused for a minute to consider what he just said, "I guess I should say I had an American friend."

"He is a writer, you see, and he has taught me many things about my own country, not the least of which is the entire *Bedoon* situation needs to be corrected, so the end result is they are welcomed home."

Sheikha was feeling many emotions, but when she heard these words, she knew where Khaled got his sense of fairness. She hugged Hamad and then kissed him on the cheek.

"Meteb and I would be more than happy to accept your invitation and become family."

"You know, I told Khaled there were many paths in life, and the ones you take are the ones which determine where you ultimately end up. I think you have chosen a very good path today; I will do my best to ensure the journey is a happy one filled with love."

After Jefzar and Meteb returned to the apartment, Sheikha told her son they would be moving as they were going to live with his Grandfather. The boy seemed excited at the news, but a bit cautious toward these new people in his life. Jefzar presented Sheikha with a new cell phone he purchased for her. Hamad let her know he would be in touch tomorrow to arrange for all of their belongings to be moved and taken to their new home.

When the two men get back in Jefzar's SUV, Hamad told them they needed to make a stop on the way back to *Shamal Mazraea.*

When Talal opened the door, he hit with a blast of light from the desert sun, after a moment his eyes focused on the dark silhouette standing between him and the source of the sunlight, Hamad. Hamad visited Talal's home only once in all the years he lived there. When he first moved in, Hamad came by personally to make sure everything was okay with the house he supplied. Since then, however, he never returned.

"Good day Rosh—Talal. Forgive me, it will take me some time to get used to the change."

"Absolutely, I understand. Would you like to come in?"

"Please." Hamad turned around and waved to Jefzar who was still sitting in his SUV parked in the driveway. He felt bad he was leaving his brother waiting for him outside, but this conversation was perhaps best if it were only the two men.

They walked into the home, and then into the living room, which featured Western-style furniture. Talal directed Hamad to an overstuffed chair, and then offered him a beverage, which Hamad declined. He then sat down in a chair opposite Hamad, and waited for the man to speak.

Rather than speaking, Hamad was looking nervously around the room. His eyes spent no more than a few moments on anything that caught his attention.

"I apologize, my home does not have a formal *diwaniya,*" Talal actually felt no need to apologize, but was hoping to prompt Hamad to move on with whatever it was he wanted.

Hamad sat back in the chair while withdrawing the *tasbih* from his pocket, he then began subconsciously counting the beads. Before he got to the third bead, Hamad looked down at the beads in his hands and smiled.

"Talal, have I ever told you where I got this *tasbih*?"

"Um, no, not that I can ever recall."

"It was a gift from my son Khaled. He selected each bead individually. Well, most of the beads he selected individually, the rest he carved himself. Until he gave it to me, I didn't realize what I was missing by not having one. Now, I can't imagine not having it in my pocket or in my hands."

"Absolutely, it is a very wonderful reminder of your son, and one you keep with you at all times, as a reminder of him."

"The past few days have been difficult for me. There has been so much loss. There are those things I thought I could trust and count on, which are no longer stabilizing forces in my life."

Talal shifted uncomfortably in his chair, he didn't like being thought of as anything less than trusted by Hamad. But he knew he earned the current scorn. Hamad looked up at Talal, and after a moment smiled, shaking his head.

"No, my friend, I was not talking about you at all. I was referring to Huda. I discovered some things she kept from me, which happened years ago. Things that should never have happened. An action she took, which eventually brought me such sadness."

Talal was confused, having no point of reference for what Hamad was speaking of and lacking a proper way to react. So, he silently nodded.

"Did you know, I'm a *Jeddi*?"

"What? When did this happen?"

"Based on Meteb's age, 12 years ago."

"Well, congratulations *Al Hakim*, albeit belated."

"Yes, I've much time to make up. More than that, I have things to make up to you as well."

Again, Talal found himself confused. He had not been part of

Hamad's process of sorting out what it happened, so again he lacked a point of reference on what to say or how to react.

"First, you are no longer suspended. When I reacted that way, it was pure emotion. I am a better person, at least I'm trying to be… you deserve better."

"Thank you, *Al Hakim*.

"In some ways, it's like my *tasbih*. Until I lacked your counsel and assistance, I did not realize how much I valued and needed it. As a result, the days ahead may be difficult."

"I'm sorry, *Al Hakim*, you lost me. If I'm no longer suspended, I'll be there as your most trusted advisor." As soon as he said the words, Talal grimaced knowing the reason they were at this point was he violated Hamad's trust.

"Indeed. Perhaps I should explain. You are no longer suspended because I'm firing you."

These were the words he expected when *Al Hakim* first suspended him, but everything in the conversation today was positive. *How have we reached a point where he needs me so much, he's firing me.* Lacking any other appropriate response, Talal finally said, "I see."

Hamad smiled. In all the years he worked with Talal, it was exceedingly rare he could ever surprise or shock him. *Indeed, he knows me so well he usually knows my decisions before I make them. I will miss him.*

"Indeed. During the time of the occupation, why did you join the resistance?"

"Because I was needed. My country needed me."

"Yes, and in the time since Liberation, you've spent many hours writing articles about what actions our nation should take regarding the *Bedoon* population. You did so because…?"

"Likewise, I was needed. I provided a clear, logical voice for a highly emotionally charged issue. A voice, by the way, I learned from you, *Al Hakim*."

"Indeed. Even though I knew nothing of those articles when you were in my employ, I've read a great many of them now. You were very logical and prolific."

"Absolutely; the only way to bring about change is to constantly remind those who have the power to create change."

Hamad nodded, "Yes, and Jefzar told me after doing a bit of research, you're a participant in several councils, which are working to make things better in our nation. I am to assume you did these things because it was needed as well. Yes?"

"Absolutely."

"In the past few days, I was approached by the Gulf Bank who informed me my late wife possessed several safety deposit boxes and upon opening them, I found they were filled with a substantial amount of money. Rather than trying to make up for charitable contributions, which should've been made over the years, I've decided to create a new foundation, to work on a root problem our nation has found itself dealing with since it became independent. My lawyers, later today, will formally create the *Nassar Al-Enezi Bedoon Reconciliation Foundation*," while he was saying this, Hamad was watching Talal for his reaction when he got to the end of the sentence. He was not disappointed.

Talal was first nodding along with what *Al Hakim* was saying, while in the back of his mind he was worried about how he was going to survive, being a suddenly unemployed *Bedoon*. Then the man came up with a solution; *not only a solution but a solution to honor my son.*

"The foundation will have a mission of bringing the *Bedoon* back into full citizenship in this nation. It won't be fast, it will not be easy, but it must be done. We're one people, and we need to begin to act like it. Oh, the reason I fired you was I didn't want your loyalties split. As the new managing director of the foundation, you'll be quite busy. I hope I can still count on you to be a close advisor and counsel when I need one."

"Absolutely."

Hamad stood and was preparing to leave, but Talal rose suddenly and took the man in his arms and hugged him. Such familiarity never happened in their old roles, but now the men were meeting on new terms as friends, and as equals.

"By the way, to be fair to you, the salary will include this house and a substantial raise. After all, you have much work to do, and you should no longer worry about things like utility bills."

Evan was looking at the words on his laptop screen, having just completed his third article for the New York Times regarding the *Bedoon* situation in Kuwait. He cloistered himself in his room while he waited for his upcoming flight back to the United States. He gave up trying to contact Najila, figuring if she wanted to resolve things, she would find him, and since his visit from Talal, no one else came by except for room service to deliver his meals. Just as he was finishing, his cell phone rang – it was his agent.

"Hey Arlen, I think I've got everything I need to get out of Dodge. I am sending you the last of the articles for the NYT in the next few minutes."

"Great, they seem to be eating them up. We've entered an environment where everybody is looking for something to be upset about, and you're telling the public about an injustice which actually exists. Something people should be upset about."

"Well, I'm just glad we're keeping the public informed I guess."

"And you keep saying you're not a journalist."

"I'm not, I'm a novelist."

"Fine, fine. Then I won't even tell you about this contract proposal I got in today."

Evan paused for a minute. Conversations with Arlen started out this way usually led to him being shot at or blown up. He exhaled, "Tell me about the offer."

"It's from something called *The Nassar Al-Enezi Bedoon Reconciliation Foundation*, but it actually came from Hamad's lawyers. Somehow, he's involved, I guess."

"What do they want?"

"Similar to your last contract, you spend six months there, but this time your sole focus is the *Bedoon* population."

"Let them know I'm flattered, but I think I'm done."

"I already told him."

"You what?"

"You keep telling me you're not a reporter, I'm not going to put you in this kind of situation again. At least not for the moment."

"Why are you even telling me about it?"

"When I said 'no,' they asked if we knew somebody who might be good. I figured you might be willing to put somebody else in the fire."

Evan thought for a moment, and reminisced for a moment on the look of her eyes, "I think I know someone who might be perfect. But I don't know if she would do such a thing."

"Opposed to the Middle East?"

"From the Middle East but opposed to the *Bedoon*. It'd be good if she learned a different viewpoint on them."

"I'll pass on a name, it's up to them to convince her to do it. Who is she?"

"Najila Al-Bourisli"

"Al-Bourisli? She related to Hamad?"

"Niece, she served as my translator and guide while I was here. She knows the country and the people. Just not all the people."

"I'll pass it on."

"Super, see you soon Arlen."

"Fly safely."

*Kuwait City International Airport*

As Evan made his way aboard the aircraft, he noticed the configuration of this Etihad Airbus was slightly different than the one he arrived on. Rather than each person having an individual cocoon, one person's area seemed to fit against another's. While standing, it gave the overall effect of each pair of pods appearing to be a Yen & Yang symbol.

The attendant helped him find his assigned pod, and before taking his seat, he began going through his Go-bag pulling out a few things he thought he might need in flight. His trip home would be different than when he flew into Kuwait months ago. Then, he was trying to learn about his new employer, and the country where he would be spending his time writing. Overall, he considered his experience to be very positive, even if it ended in his termination and Najila casting him aside without so much as saying goodbye.

Before he left, he heard rumors of the foundation Hamad set up to help the *Bedoon* obtain a better deal with the government. *It was the only way those people could ever hope to move forward; they needed somebody with the wasta to present more than the one negative viewpoint, which was continually broadcast to the public.* The choice of Talal to lead the group could not have been better.

Talal stopped by the room yesterday afternoon after *Maghrib* to say goodbye, and to tell Evan what impact he made in moving things forward. He was excited and energetic about where the future was headed. His only regret was the loss of life at the Hotel Sultana bombing, especially his son. Talal saw the loss as a possible necessity to move forward, "What was it your President Jefferson said? 'The tree of liberty must be refreshed from time to time with the blood of patriots and tyrants'?"

"I earnestly hope there will be no more blood loss from anyone."

"Absolutely; I will do my best to prevent it."

It was unusual to see Talal dressed in traditional Kuwaiti clothes instead of his Western suit and tie. *But I suppose it will help as he has to be seen as a Kuwaiti from this point forward to be effective.*

After digging out his book, and iPod, Evan stashed his Go-bag under the seat and began to make himself comfortable for the trip ahead by first throwing a pillow on his seat before lowering himself onto it gingerly. His posterior and lower back was still sore from the long ride he took last night. Just after Talal left, he received a call from inviting him out to *Rihlat Alsahra'* for a final ride on Cochise.

"Are you sure? Hamad might have a problem with that, our last meeting didn't end on good terms."

"He's not here tonight; he is moving his daughter-in-law and grandson into *'Shamal Mazraea*. To make sure he'll never find out about this, I've sent the other staff home, it'll just be you and I."

When he arrived at *Rihlat Alsahra'*, Naveed greeted him as if he were a long-lost relative. Since Talal moved on to bigger and better things, Naveed received a promotion as well, taking over Talal's position as Hamad's personal assistant.

"I miss being with the horses every day, but as I grow older, I realize running a stable is a younger man's game. Since I moved up, everyone else did as well, and we brought in a new trainee, a young man named Amr. He is learning the fine art of training Arabian stallions."

"Well, I'm glad it all turned out positively for you. I really appreciate you letting me take this final ride. It was one of my favorite times of day, to be alone on Cochise out in the desert. There is a certain spectacular beauty to it."

"Indeed."

Evan climbed aboard Cochise and turned the horse out into the desert, far away from civilization and onto trails used by thousands of *Bedouins* over the centuries. He could not keep himself from taking a path he rode once before when he wasn't alone, and pausing on a bit of level ground where he shared a night of intimacy. He put his knee over the horn of the saddle and lay back onto the horse and stared at the stars above him reveling in a memory, which will remain with him forever.

His final experience with Cochise was to ride at full gallop onto a path unknown to him but one he was experienced enough now to see in the desert darkness. Evan had no idea where the path was going to lead him, but he was secure enough in the knowledge he possessed sufficient experience now to take that path without regret or fear. He knew no matter where it took him, he would always be able to find his way back if necessary.

"Drink sir?" The attendant interrupted his thoughts.

"Sure, I'll take a Maker's Mark and Coke."

"I'm sorry sir, but alcohol will not be available until after we are out of Saudi Arabian airspace."

*Not quite back into the Western world yet,* "I understand, nothing for now."

"As soon as I am able, I will bring you the drink you ordered."

Evan closed his eyes for a moment, allowing himself to relax and prepare for the long journey ahead, he could hear the person on the other side of his pod, settling into their seat. Once the shuffling about settled down, he heard voices talking but could not make out the words.

"Sir?"

Evan opened his eyes and was greeted by a flight attendant holding a tray with the glass of what appeared to be pomegranate juice on it.

"Sorry, but I didn't order this."

"I know sir, it was ordered by the passenger in the adjoining pod."

"Adjoining pod?"

The stewardess motioned to the wall to Evan's right which separated his pod from the other, she then lifted the glass of her tray and deposited it on the tray table in front of Evan. *Must be some kind of Middle Eastern custom maybe?*

As he took a drink of the juice, the divider between his part in the adjoining one was opened revealing a familiar smile.

"You might want to drink several of those before we get to our destination, I know from experience it is difficult to find in the United States."

Evan almost choked on his drink but managed to contain himself. Before speaking, he took a moment to look at her, the beauty of her eyes, fullness of her lips, and the shimmering of her hair in the light. Then just as he decided what to say, the aroma of *Lamsat Hareer* struck him – *the scent of her.*

"Well, this is a bit of kismet," *but not one I mind.*

"As you say; it took me almost half an hour working with the airline's agent to get people moved around so I could have this seat," *I probably shouldn't have told him that part.*

"Why are you onboard? I know -- you want to make sure I'm actually leaving." *As usual, I cover-up tense situations by trying to be funny.*

"Really? I thought it was you following me."

He waved his finger at her, "you know, that might be possible."

Najila reached out and took his hand in hers, and then looked at him soulfully.

"I'm sorry for the way things spun between us. I was raised having very strong beliefs, and unfortunately, part of its strength is refusing to listen to any other opinion."

Her soft hand on his, *it just feels so wonderful,* "Be honest, you're not on this plane just to say that."

"As you say, it is not the only reason. It appears I was recommended for a position with a newly formed foundation in Kuwait. After being given a very strong incentive by the foundation's new director, I am to be its public communications person. So, I need to go to the United States to close out a bit of business because it'll extend my stay there longer than expected."

"Sounds great, but is it what you want?"

"It is time for me to re-examine a few things and deal with my own history. I think this may be a better way to do it, than trying to find only the positive as a guide."

"But weren't you living in Texas? This plane is on its way to Detroit."

"I know. When I negotiated my employment with my new boss, I explained I needed a short vacation, before I closed out things in Texas and returned to start my job." She gripped his hand tighter, and then began to gently stroke his fingers with hers as she looked deep into his eyes, "I owe you an in-depth apology, I owe you thanks for saving my life, and I owe you for guiding me to this new path, which I'm about to take."

"Maybe I'm just dense, but I don't understand."

"As you say, wasn't it you who told me the night chill in Western Michigan allowed you to have a wonderful campfire while you sat outside and enjoyed the view of the stars?"

"Yes, I seem to remember telling you that."

"I wonder if making love under those stars will also be as pleasurable."

Months had passed since Hamad was able to take a ride with *Eadala*. Now, as he listened to the horse's hooves hitting the hard sand, and the sound of a loose bit of fabric from his *gutra* flapping in the wind Hamad allowed himself to indulge in the freedom he missed. Things were changing, but he knew one thing was constant for him and his lineage: horses and the desert. He leaned forward and pressed the side of his face to *Eadala's* as he looked at the shadow up ahead. *A few more lengths.*

Hamad spoke to *Eadala* the way he had for years. Tonight though, the horse felt the urgency of the man to catch up with the pair riding in front of them and did not want to disappoint. *Eadala* lengthened his stride and lowered his body to become more aerodynamic as he managed to increase his speed even though he was already at full gallop.

Hamad smiled when he looked to the side and saw he was even with the flanks of *Fajar Jadid*. Within moments, he found himself even with the horse's rider. The situation was not lost on the other rider who looked back and saw Hamad preparing to overtake him. He immediately leaned forward to speak to his own mount, then he looked ahead at a fork in the path and knew as the rider in front he would get to decide which direction they would take. At the last moment, he veered toward the right forcing Hamad and *Eadala* to slow to make the same maneuver.

Hamad was taking it easy on his competitor, *but no more. It's time Meteb learns the next level of being a true horseman.* Within minutes, Hamad and his mount caught up and then passed his grandson and *Fajar Jadid.*

Hamad immediately pulled back on the reins of his horse, which served as a signal for Meteb to do the same. As they sat side-by-side on their horses, looking out over the desert, Meteb broke the silence,

"Am I as good a rider as my father?"

"Eventually, you will be better. It is the destiny of all sons to improve upon the accomplishments of those that came before them."

"*Jeddi!* That's not an answer."

Hamad spun his horse around, and then called over his shoulder as he urged *Eadala* to take off, "I will tell you if you beat me back to *Rihlat Alsahra*.'"

Meteb quickly turned his horse around and pursued his Grandfather.

Hamad could have easily left the boy far behind but chose to slow down so the two of them could ride side-by-side across the desert. The hot desert air blew across his face, and the occasional bit of sand stung as it struck his skin— – he felt alive and free. Sensing something, Hamad looked to his left and saw the spirit of Khaled as a wisp on the desert wind, riding with them.

# Glossary

This glossary is meant to be a simple translation of the words used in this book. There may be other possible unintended meanings based on regional or tribal uses.

شيطان—Satan

abaya– A simple, loose over-garment, essentially a robe-like dress, worn by some women in parts of the Muslim world on the Arabian Peninsula.

agal– The headband or rope that is worn on the exterior of a gutra.

Al Hakim– Complimentary. The wise one.

almasafir-- Traveler

ahlan wa sahlan-- Welcome

alkalb— Dog, but when used against a person it also means disgusting or filthy.

alkaliba—Bitch

Allah yadhhab maeak wayubqik amnana fi rihlatik-- May God go with you and keep you safe on your journey.

alsahra'– The desert

Alshaytan Bayan Rasmiin—Satan's Manifesto

As-salamu alaykum– Arabic greeting meaning Peace be unto you.

Asr—Midafternoon prayers

ayreh feek—Slang, fuck you

baba – Father

Bedoon– Slang term for the people left stateless as a result of Kuwait's Nationality Law of 1959. Originally derived from the Arabic phrase "bedoon jinsiyya," meaning either "without nationality" or "without citizenship." Variations: Bidun, Bidoon, or Bedun.

Bedouin– An Arab who primarily lives in the desert and works as a herder.

bidun jinsiya– Without nationality, the formal term for Bedoon.

burqa– A long, loose garment covering the whole body from head to feet, worn in public by many Muslim women.

der'mo–– Shit (Russian)

dhow– Arabic sailing ship

Dhuhr––Noon prayers

dishdasha– A long, usually light-colored, robe with long sleeves traditionally worn by men in the Middle East.

diwaniya– A reception area where a man received his business associates and friends.

eadala––Justice

Fajr––Dawn prayers

fajar jadid––New dawn

tozz feek––Slang, screw you

gutra– A headdress worn by men in the Middle East made up of a single piece of cloth and sometimes accented by an external band around the head, usually aka keffiyeh or Shemagh.

haboob – An intense dust storm carried on an atmospheric gravity current producing what visually looks like a wall of dust.

hajib– A headdress made of a single piece of cloth which covers the hair. Worn by women in the Middle East.

halāl – Foods that Muslims are allowed to eat. According to the Quran, the only foods explicitly forbidden (haram) are meat from animals that die of themselves, blood, the meat of pigs, and any food dedicated to other than God.

haram– Forbidden

Hathar–Arabs who worked skills and trades which led them to live within the city walls.

Iblīs– Satan's personal name.

'iinaha 'iiradat alshaytan– It is Satan's will.

Imam– An Islamic religious leader.

inaba– An Islamic act of penitence.

insha'Allah– If it be God's will.

Isha'a—Evening prayers

ishq-- Slang, horny. A passionate and irresistible level of love.

jaddi-- Grandfather

kalb-- Dog

kess-- Slang, vagina

kess ikhtak—Slang, literally "your sister's vagina", also "fuck your sister".

khara—Slang, feces, shit

kol khara—Slang, eat shit

Kuat Zurqa'—Blue Oculus, the name of the blue glass front of the Hotel Sultana.

kufi- A small round, crocheted head covering similar to a beanie.

La afham—I don't understand.

Lamsat Hareer - A perfume gel, the literal translation is a touch of silk.

Liljamie– *For All*, fictional underground electronic newspaper.

madrassa-- A Muslim school, college, or university that is often part of a mosque.

Maghrib—Late afternoon/sunset prayers

manaqib aldhahab—Gold digger. Someone who engages in romantic relationships for money or status rather than love.

Masha'Allah—God has willed it.

mazraea– A ranch

mudak—Asshole (Russian)

nadhil-- Bastard

PBUH- English abbreviation for "Peace Be Upon Him". A conventionally complimentary phrase attached to the names of the prophets in Islam.

Paki-- Derogatory term referring to anyone from Pakistan, India, or Bangladesh.

polnyy –Complete (Russian)

Qur'an– The Islamic sacred book.

rihlat– A journey or trip.

saluki– A Persian greyhound or tazi.

Salat al-'isha– Muslim prayer time between sunset and midnight.

Satori— Japanese, a state in Zen Buddhism where the person feels sudden enlightenment, full awareness, and focus on all details surrounding them.

shukraan lakum– Thank you

shalwar kameez– A traditional outfit on the Indian continent. The shalwar (baggy trousers) and the kameez (long shirt) are two separate garments.

Shamal– A northwesterly wind that blows across the Persian Gulf.

sharmuta—Slang, whore, prostitute, or slut. A woman of ill repute.

Shaytan– Satan

sheesha– A Hookah or waterpipe

souk-- Middle Eastern open-air market or bizarre

tabbouleh – A Middle Eastern vegetarian salad made mostly of finely chopped parsley, with tomatoes, mint, onion, bulgur, and seasoned with olive oil, lemon juice, salt and pepper.

talaq– Divorce affected by the husband's threefold repetition of the word, formally repudiating his wife.

tasbih – A set of Muslim prayer beads consisting of 33 individual beads.

telhas teeze—Slang, kiss my ass.

tozz feek—Slang, screw you.

umma—Mother

wa `alaykum as-salâm– And unto you peace, the usual response to As-salamu alaykum.

wasta– Perceived influence or power brought about by position, family or money.

Wudu– Islamic process for washing parts of the body, a type of ritual purification.

ya lahwi–Expression of surprise, similar to Oh my God.

ya ibn el sharmouta- Slang, son of a bitch.

# Notes

While this book is a work of fiction, the hardships and discrimination the *Bedoon* face daily talked about within these pages is very real and, unfortunately, little-known. *The Bedoons of Kuwait*, mentioned in this book, is a non-fiction report created and published by Human Rights Watch. You can read the full report here:

https://www.hrw.org/report/1995/08/01/bedoons-kuwait-citizens-without-citizenship

The Battle of Al-Qurain was a factual event that occurred in Kuwait just before liberation at the end of the Iraqi invasion and occupation. The story of the resistance fighters and how they face down overwhelming power and odds is impressive and awe-inspiring. Unfortunately, I am unaware of any English books documenting the battle, but there are several versions of the story available on the Internet.

# About the Author

Sheldon Charles is a decorated Air Force veteran, whose career has taken him around the globe, and given his writing a unique international flair. He is the author of *Three Paperclips & a Grey Scarf*, and *From Within the Firebird's Nest*. His last book (*From Within the Firebird's Nest*, the third book in the Evan  Davis Trilogy) held the Number One Bestseller spot for Russian Historical Fiction, and was in the Top Ten for War Fiction, for 2018. Sheldon currently resides in Michigan where he is a member of Michigan Writers.

# From the Author

I hope you have enjoyed reading this book. You can always find an up-to-date list of my Evan Davis tales and all of my other books, at my website: **www.valkyriespirit.com** Also…

**Sign up** -- Be the first to know when there is a new release by signing up for the Email Newsletter. I will only send emails when there is book news and will never release your email to others, ever. To sign up drop a line to newsletter@valkyriespirit.com

**Review it** --- Consider posting a short review with the vendor where you found this book. Reader reviews help others decide whether they'll enjoy a book.

**Connect with me** -- I'd love to hear from you, please stop by my Facebook page for updates on new titles, cover previews, and general discussion: www.facebook.com/TheRealSheldonCharles/

shel@valkyriespirit.com

**Evan Davis is back in his most daring tale yet.**

For decades, the United States and the Soviet Union trained thousands of nuclear weapons on each other—and those were just the weapons we knew about. Behind the military parades and bluster was a shadow war, and some of the deadliest weapons were kept far from the public eye.

*From within the Firebird's Nest* is a thrilling story about the resurgence of acrimony from the past. Years after the end of the Cold War, a former KGB agent plans to exact revenge on the United States by reactivating a horrifying bioweapon called the Crimson Firebird.

Our only hope of survival is an unlikely team of international spies and civilians, including a repentant former deputy of the Crimson Firebird Initiative, a former Stasi agent, and an American writer. Can these would-be heroes put aside their own complex feelings of the past long enough to avert an unthinkable catastrophe?

**At your favorite Bookstore, in eBook, Paperback & Audiobook.**